Amy Girl

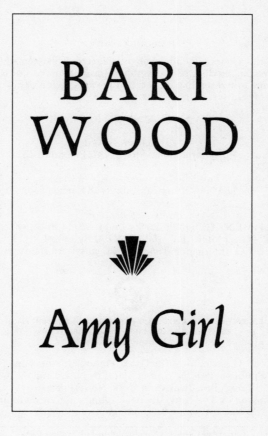

BARI WOOD

Amy Girl

NAL BOOKS

NEW AMERICAN LIBRARY

NEW YORK AND SCARBOROUGH, ONTARIO

Published simultaneously in Canada
by The New American Library of Canada Limited

Acknowledgment
SENTIMENTAL JOURNEY by Bud Green, Les Brown & Ben Homer. © 1944 MORLEY MUSIC CO. © Renewed 1972 MORLEY MUSIC CO. International copyright secured. All rights reserved. Used by permission.

NAL BOOKS TRADEMARK REG. U.S. PAT. OFF. AND FOREIGN COUNTRIES
REGISTERED TRADEMARK—MARCA REGISTRADA
HECHO EN HARRISONBURG, VA., U.S.A.

SIGNET, SIGNET CLASSIC, MENTOR, ONYX, PLUME, MERIDIAN and NAL BOOKS
are published *in the United States* by NAL Penguin Inc.,
1633 Broadway, New York, New York 10019,
in Canada by The New American Library of Canada Limited,
81 Mack Avenue, Scarborough, Ontario M1L 1M8

Library of Congress Cataloging-in-Publication Data

Wood, Bari, 1936-
Amy girl.
I. Title.
PS3573.O588A8   1987   813'.54   86-28558
ISBN 0-452-00534-9

Designed by Fritz Metsch

First Printing, April, 1986

1 2 3 4 5 6 7 8 9

PRINTED IN THE UNITED STATES OF AMERICA

To the memory of my aunt,
Faye Dorfman

PART I

FATHERS

ONE

THE DOOR BELL rang at ten on Saturday morning and Amy's mother thought it was the men from Sears coming to repossess the refrigerator. She wouldn't answer the door.

"You get it," she whispered hoarsely to Amy. "Look pitiful and tell them I'm out looking for a job and you can't let anyone in. They'll go away."

Amy left her mother sitting at the kitchen table and went down the long, dark hall to the front door. She was eight, small for her age, and everyone said she was pretty. Maybe the men would feel sorry for her and go away for a day or two.

Without the refrigerator they'd have to keep food on the porch. It was October, the leaves were turning red and gold, the air was dry and warm, and the food would spoil.

Last summer they took the dishwasher. Amy's mother tried to get some money out of Amy's father to pay the installment on it, but he was drunk and he lost his temper. He broke the front window and knocked her mother's front teeth out. Then he hit Amy with a glass and split the side of her forehead open. Her mother had huddled against the wall while her father pulled dishes out of the cabinets and smashed them on the kitchen floor. Amy had wiped blood

3

out of her eyes and watched him dancing through the broken glass in the harsh overhead light; he had looked graceful and happy. The breaking glass sounded like bells and the bits of china crunched under his feet like tightly packed snow. Amy had shut her eyes and imagined that it *was* snow, and she and Daddy were taking a winter walk in the woods.

He had gotten tired and stopped. He'd looked almost sad for a second, then he'd yelled, "Bloodsucking cunts," and left the house.

Then Amy's mother called the police and they took them to Danbury Hospital. A young blond doctor who smelled of tobacco and soap stitched Amy's forehead. He told her that he'd done a neat job, but there would be scar. It would fade in time, but she'd notice it when she got a tan. Amy examined it every morning. It was a thin white line that ran down her forehead and bisected her eyebrow. After he finished the stitching the doctor had asked her if she'd blacked out or gotten dizzy. She told him that she hadn't, but she did have an odd feeling inside her head.

"What kind of feeling?" the doctor had asked.

"A cold feeling, like a wind blew into my ear and went into my head."

The doctor looked surprised, then suspicious. He asked her to describe the cold feeling.

"It's like someone with icy breath blew in my ear and it went in and around, then got from my ear to inside my head," she told him.

But that wasn't right exactly. Because by the time the chill was well inside her head and behind her eyes, it wasn't a wind anymore but a thin stream of cool fluid, and she was sure that if she could see it, it would be thick and silver, like the mercury in a thermometer.

"Did this cold feeling make you dizzy?"

She shook her head.

"Blur your vision?"

"No."

"And you feel fine now?"

She stared at him. She was scarred for life, her mother had lost her front teeth, the dishwasher was doomed, and her father had run away. She didn't feel fine, but she could tell that the doctor didn't care. After a minute he had patted her and told her that her mother was waiting.

They took the dishwasher away and her mother got new teeth. The angels took her grandmother who lived in a farmhouse up near Newton, and her father didn't come back. Amy was sorry about Nana but glad about her father. She never wanted to see him again. He was big, loud, and smelly. The time before he had knocked her mother's teeth out, he'd kicked her mother in the middle, and she couldn't straighten up for a week; then he'd picked Amy up over his head like a basketball and threw her across the kitchen . . . or maybe it was the parlor . . . she couldn't be sure. She'd sailed through the air for an instant, forgetting the wall or cabinet or whatever it was coming in at her, and she had been exhilarated. Then she hit something and fell. Her mother said that she'd broken her collarbone. Amy was only six at the time, a real baby, and she couldn't remember whether she had gotten the cold feeling then or not.

The bell rang again and the weight of losing the refrigerator closed in on her.

"Please," she whispered, and she opened the door.

A woman about her mother's age was at the door. Amy looked past her. A shiny red car was parked at the curb, not a Sears truck with men waiting to carry the refrigerator away. The woman smiled down at Amy, "Avon calling," she said.

She was the prettiest woman Amy had ever seen. Her hair was pale gold, combed back from her face and fastened in a smooth bun at the nape of her neck; her eyes were bright blue, and as she leaned down toward Amy, Amy smelled gardenias.

"Is your mother home?" the woman asked.

Amy couldn't lie to her. "Yes."

"Tell her the Avon lady's here. I know she's busy, but I promise not to take much of her time."

Amy was conscious of the dingy hall and drab, dirty house. She didn't ask the woman to come inside. The woman belonged on the step, framed by the red-gold leaves of the maple across the road. Amy asked the woman to wait, left the door open, and went down the hall to the kitchen. Her mother was still at the table. It was only a little after ten, but the bottle of clear liquor was on the table and her mother was sipping from a coffee cup. Amy knew she was fortifying herself to see the Sears men stomp across the kitchen to the precious refrigerator.

"It wasn't Sears," Amy said.

Her mother looked up, and Amy ached when she saw the relief in her mother's eyes. "Fank God."

"It's Miss Avon. The Avon lady, she said to tell you."

Amy's mother laughed wildly, and Amy was afraid that Miss Avon would hear the hysterical sound her mother was making.

"Vi Avon lady," her mother croaked. Her mother hadn't put her teeth in yet. "Vash too fucking wonderful," her mother cried. Amy wanted to faint because her grandmother had told her that f-u-c-k was the worst word that anyone could say, except for taking the Lord's name in vain, and Amy knew that Miss Avon must have heard her mother.

"Okay," her mother cried, "bring 'er in." She fished in the pocket of her old pink robe for her teeth.

Amy glanced around the kitchen. One fluorescent tube was burned out, and the room was dim and green. The windows were dirty and the sink was full of dishes soaking in cold, milky water. Unscraped food had floated to the surface and it rotted and stank. The floor was sticky under Amy's shoes. Her mother saw her look.

"Bad?" her mother asked softly.

Amy nodded.

"Okay, we'll refieve ve Avon lady in ve parlor."

The parlor was bad too. Her father had kicked off one leg of the coffee table—her mother had propped it back up, but it listed—and things slid off it onto the floor. Burn holes pockmarked the furniture and rug; the air was full of dust. It sparkled on sunny days, moved in mysterious drafts, and settled on everything. But Amy's mother was right. It was better than the kitchen.

Her mother got her teeth in place and contracted her lips to settle them. Her mouth lost the shriveled look.

"Lead on, Chicken," her mother said gaily. Amy loved when her mother called her that.

They led Miss Avon into the parlor and settled her in the only wooden chair. It was scarred but still solid, and both Amy and her mother figured the lady would be happier sitting on wood than on stained upholstery. Miss Avon had a black leather case with her, and she eyed the leaning coffee table uncertainly and smiled. "Better not chance it," she said. Which made it all right about the table instead of the hot point of embarrassment it would have been if she'd pretended not to notice. Miss Avon slid her case flat on the floor, popped the catch, then paused. Amy thought of a magician she'd seen at school assembly before Thanksgiving last year. He'd stop just before a trick to build suspense and until the kids were breathless to see the trick; like Amy was breathless to see the contents of the case.

Then, with a flourish, like the magician, Miss Avon flipped the case open and Amy saw Spanish treasure. Chains and coins of solid gold filled the case. Emeralds and diamonds glittered in the dusty light coming through the smeared parlor windows. It turned out to be bottles and jars full of colored creams and liquids. Some of the bottles had crystal birds for stoppers, others were topped with shining brass, and the glass and their contents sparkled like jewels. Amy's mother gasped with pleasure, and Miss Avon looked proud.

She uncapped jars, unstoppered bottles. Sweet smells came out of the case, overcame the odor of musty upholstery. She selected several jars and sat next to Amy's mother on the couch.

"Let's try this. The color should be right." She started

smoothing creamy stuff from the jar onto Amy's mother's
face. The red veins in her cheeks and the chapped spots on
her nostrils disappeared, and right before Amy's eyes her
mother's skin turned smooth and glossy. Miss Avon opened
a long, silver tube and brushed black stuff on her mother's
eyelashes, smeared blue cream on her mother's eyelids.
Then came rouge powder and shiny lipstick applied with a
brush. Miss Avon combed Amy's mother's thick black hair
back from her face and said, "You're a beautiful woman."

Miss Avon took a silver-backed hand mirror out of her
case and held it up so Amy's mother could see herself. Miss
Avon wasn't lying to sell her products. Amy's mother *was*
beautiful. She was more beautiful than the ladies in the old
Vogue and *Glamour* magazines that Amy leafed through in
the dentist's office. More beautiful than the women in the
few movies that Amy had seen. Her mother was even prettier
than Miss Avon, and Amy was proud, and way back in her
mind sad, because she knew it wouldn't last. The teeth
would come out when Miss Avon left, the makeup would
wear off, and by tomorrow her mother would be shriveled
again; wearing her waiting-for-Sears-to-come-and-take-the-
refrigerator look.

"I'd forgotten," her mother said slowly, looking in the
mirror.

"We all forget sometimes."

The Avon lady listed the products she'd just used on
Amy's mother's face, ticking them off on her fingers. "Moisture-balanced under-makeup cream, moisture-balanced
foundation, creamy beige, silver gloss eye shadow—"

"Please," Amy's mother cried, "please don't waste any
more of your time. I don't have any money."

"None?" Miss Avon asked.

"None," answered Amy's mother. "I'm sorry. I shouldn't
have let you go through all of this, but I . . . I couldn't help
it."

Amy knew this was the moment when Miss Avon would
assume the look that everybody got when they knew you

didn't have money. It was an expression of cold, vague disgust that made Amy feel as if she'd filled her pants, even at her age, and people were too polite to say anything, but of course they noticed the smell.

Only Miss Avon didn't get that look; she looked interested. "Is your husband out of work?" she asked Amy's mother.

"My husband's gone."

"I'm sorry," Miss Avon said.

Amy's mother laughed shortly. "I'm not. He beat us up. See this?" She lifted her upper lip and showed her front teeth. "All false," she said. "He hit me in the mouth with a hammer . . . and this . . ." She pulled Amy over and pointed to the scar on Amy's forehead; Amy writhed, but her mother didn't notice. "He smashed her in the head with a beer glass. I hope he's in Afghanistan."

"How do you live?"

"My mother died this summer. She left me a farm up in the hills near Newton. It's run-down, but it's worth *something*. We're waiting to sell it, and when we do, we'll have enough to live for a few years. In the meantime there's welfare. It's not much, but it pays the rent on the house and buys us milk and cheese. I tried to find a job after he left. I really did try," Amy's mother insisted. Miss Avon nodded. "But I don't do nothing. Never learned to type, never even got through high school. See, I met Amy's dad when I was eighteen." Amy's mother knew it was an old story, but she told it, anyway. Most of it. He was a U Conn student, pre-law, working for the summer on the new shopping mall construction. She was a waitress at a diner off I 84; she'd quit school the year before so she could help the folks.

It was a long, dry summer; even the nights were warm, and there were a million places in those hills where two hot, pretty kids like Michael Kaslov and Evvie Montgomery could be alone together. He was handsome (like a dark version of Errol Flynn) and sexy. She couldn't get enough of him, and they made love in the woods, on the grainy beach of Lake Lillinonah, behind the Grange hall on a blazing August afternoon while the church ladies were setting up for the fair in front of the building.

By August she was pregnant, and she told Michael. He wasn't angry or much of anything, except a little annoyed. He said that she had to get an abortion. She expected him to say that. He was going to be a lawyer and it wasn't like the bullshit plans she'd heard from boys who'd gone to Limestone High. He was a junior at U Conn. He'd told her he'd scored high in LSATs (some kind of law exam) and he could get into a good school. Maybe Penn or the University of Virginia or even Harvard. His father owned a dry-cleaning store down in Meriden, and while he wasn't rich and had to pay to keep Michael's brother in some kind of home, he could manage most of the tuition. Besides, there'd be scholarships for a bright student like Michael, and government loans. He had big plans that didn't include an ignorant hill girl and her brat.

Evvie had agreed. She was sorry about the morsel of life that was growing in her, but she didn't think she wanted to marry Michael Kaslov, anyway. There was a tight meanness about him that she'd noticed during the summer. He borrowed small sums of money from her that he never paid back, never even mentioned it again, as if he had a right to it. He got her to wash his clothes in her mother's machine, iron his shirts, and give him free food from the diner. He never thanked her, he never did anything for her in return. They'd been lovers since June, and here it was the end of August and he'd never offered to buy her a meal or take her to the movies.

Most of all, he drank too much. She knew he wasn't drowning some secret sorrow or trying to get up the courage to face the challenge of law school. He drank to indulge himself, because he was spoiled. She understood how it could happen. He was a beautiful man, his father had a little money, his mother was dead, his brother was sick in some way that Michael kept secret, so Michael was all his father had, and the old man spoiled him. Michael would be a lousy husband and worse father, and Evvie didn't love him.

But in the end she couldn't go through with the abortion, and she told her father.

"My dad was a decent man," she told Miss Avon, "and he drove all the way down to Meriden to see Michael's father. I guess Michael's father was heartbroken because he had such wonderful plans for his son. But he was decent, too, and he said that Michael had to do the right thing. A man was nothing if he didn't do the right thing. They didn't mean to hurt us but the two men were talking about their first grandchild, and I guess they didn't want to see it born a bastard or, worse, turned into a bloody lump of nothing to be flushed down the toilet. . . ."

So Michael and Evvie got married. It wasn't so bad at first. Michael's father went on paying tuition, and the baby was healthy and beautiful. (Here Amy's mother smiled at her, and Amy smiled back.) Evvie had worked until her eighth month, and then she quit. She didn't go back after the baby was born, and it was harder and harder for Michael to study with the baby crying and the house in such a mess. Then his father died, and it turned out that there were already three mortgages on the dry-cleaning store.

Michael sold the store for just enough to pay off the banks, his brother went on full-time state assistance, and Michael quit school. He grew a beard and bought a used pickup. But Evvie was sure he didn't do anything all day except drive around to different bars. She thought he wanted people to pay him for just looking like a worker. Evvie tried to go back to the diner, but times were tough by then.

"Besides," she told the Avon lady, "we don't have much energy, Michael and I." She waved her hand around the shabby, dusty room. "It looks like this 'cause I'm lazy. All the way through to the bone, I guess. Mike, too, but he'd never say it. He got a few odd jobs here and there, but I think he made most of his dough screwing housewives. My mother couldn't help; all she had was a hundred and sixty acres of

Connecticut rocks. We had to scrimp to pay the rent here, to
buy food for us and the baby, and, of course, to pay for Michael's booze.

"The drinking got worse. Friends of his graduated and
went on to careers and to law and medical school. He turned
really mean and started beating up on me. I thought he'd do
it couple of times and get it out of his system, because he'd
never hit me before. It wasn't like him. But he must have
enjoyed it in some way, 'cause it got worse. He started beating her. . . ." She nodded at Amy, and Miss Avon threw Amy
a look of such compassion that Amy thought she would take
the beatings again if she had to. It was even worth the scar to
have this lovely woman look at her like that.

Amy's mother said, "I was afraid he'd kill us. But I was
afraid he'd really kill us if I called the cops. Then he left
finally. Thank God." Amy's mother stopped talking and the
women were quiet. Amy didn't know what to expect. The
Avon lady had been here a while; surely she would gather
up her beautiful bottles and leave soon. The noon whistle
rose, screamed for a second, then faded.

"My goodness," Miss Avon said, "I didn't know how late
it was . . ."

Amy's heart sank. The woman would leave now; she'd
go down to the inn for lunch, then go to another customer.
She'd pick her customers more carefully next time. She
would never come back to this street, and Amy would never
see her again. But the Avon lady said, "I'm not hungry for
lunch yet. I wonder if I could trouble you for a cup of tea."

Amy's mother beamed, and Amy leaped through the parlor door and ran down the hall to the kitchen, feeling as if the
soles of her feet barely skimmed the ground. She put the
kettle on, then raced back to the living room. The kettle
would boil in five minutes. It would take her three or four
minutes to find the tea bags, fill the cups. There would be
another fifteen minutes while Miss Avon drank the tea. Amy
remembered that there were cookies; cookies would add
more time, and she might be able to keep Miss Avon here for

half an hour or forty-five minutes. But the cookies were old and dried out, and the last one Amy had, tasted like cardboard.

The women drank the tea and talked quietly. Miss Avon turned out to be Mrs. Scott. Her husband was gone too. Mrs. Scott—she told Amy's mother to call her Betty—went to her husband's office late on the afternoon of his birthday. She was going to surprise him and take him to dinner to the Sail, a fine seafood restaurant on the Sound. The surprise was on her, it turned out. She'd walked into the private office and found her husband and his secretary doing it on the floor behind his desk. (Amy only knew vaguely what *it* was, but she could see that Mrs. Scott was heartbroken.) She had divorced Mr. Scott, took the house, the kids, alimony, and child support. So she had money. Not like when he was still around but enough to get by. She took this job for a little extra, and because she was sick of drinking all afternoon with other divorcees and waiting for the kids to come home from school. Now the kids were fourteen and sixteen, and most afternoons they went around with friends or stayed at school for ball practice or the drama club. She was going crazy until she'd found this job. . . .

She paused significantly and put the teacup down on the coffee table. Amy eyed it in terror, but Mrs. Scott had a magic touch, and the cup and saucer didn't slide off to the floor.

Mrs. Scott looked intently at Amy's mother.

"You could do the same, you know. You'd make a little at first, more later. You won't get rich, but it's something."

"I couldn't." Amy's mother gasped, putting her palms to her cheeks.

"You could. You're lovely. The women'll think that they'll look like you if they buy what you sell. I don't mean to make them sound like fools. They're not. But I've always thought that most women believe in magic. Makeup is like magic," she said softly.

"No . . ." Amy's mother gaped down at the dirty, ragged robe she wore.

"No clothes?" Mrs. Scott asked.

"No."

"I have some that'll fit you, I think. I'll talk to my rep this afternoon, and if you like, I'll come back on Wednesday with the clothes and give you some lessons in how to use and sell the stuff. What do you say? It's better than sitting here waiting for the day to end."

How wise Mrs. Scott was, Amy thought. That's exactly what her mother did, but Amy didn't know it until Mrs. Scott made her little speech. Anything was better than sitting toothless and half drunk in the filthy kitchen waiting for the sun to go down so she could have another drink, waiting for the next show on TV, finally waiting for the late news to end so she could go to sleep.

Please, Mommy, Amy prayed, *please say yes.*

Amy knew what her mother was thinking. She would put this wonderful lady to a lot of trouble, and then she wouldn't be able to get out the front door and down the path to the sidewalk, much less up and down the streets of the neighborhood ringing people's bells, singing out, "Avon calling." She would end up returning the clothes and sample case in shame because she just didn't have the energy to leave the house in the morning . . . the stuffing, Nana would have called it.

Mrs. Scott seemed to know the problem. "You don't have to start big, you know. Just go to one house on the first day . . . one house a day for the first week. Believe it or not, the women are glad to see you. The kids're at school, the husbands are at work, and daytime TV is awful."

The women laughed, and suddenly Amy's mother was nodding her head quickly and saying "Okay, okay . . ."

Amy took Mrs. Scott to the door; she left it open and watched the Avon lady drive her shiny red car up the block to the stop sign and turn east toward town. Amy kept watch until the car was out of sight, and then she closed the door on the warm, clear day, and the must in the hall surrounded her. Suddenly she felt drained, the way she imagined her mother did most of the time. It was an effort to move away from the door and back down the hall to the kitchen. The morning had been a dream; the Avon lady had brought hope into the house, but she'd taken it away with her and nothing had changed. Amy would get to the kitchen door and see her mother back at the table with the bottle of liquor next to her coffee cup. Her teeth would be in the pocket of her robe, the TV would be on, and she'd be watching *Batman* and working her lips over her empty gums the way very old people did.

But the kitchen table was cleared except for the bottles and jars the Avon lady had left for samples, and Amy's mother was at the kitchen sink. She had let the dirty water out and was running fresh hot water in. She turned and smiled at Amy; her teeth were still in.

"What do you say, Chicken," she said happily. "Let's clean the house."

They scrubbed the kitchen floor, sink, windows, and cabinets. They pulled out Grandma's old Electrolux and vacuumed the living room carpet until the nap stood up. They vacuumed the furniture and drapes, then found a can of polish and rubbed the tables until they shone, and the room smelled of lemon oil. They washed the tile and floor in the bathroom. Amy polished the chrome. They stripped the beds, and Amy's mother piled the linens into the shopping cart.

They opened Amy's piggy bank and took out enough quarters to do the wash. Amy pulled the cart three blocks, along streets lined with tiny houses and scraps of front lawns covered with red-and-gold leaves, to the laundromat. Mrs. Gomez was on duty. She made sure the women didn't bully Amy, and Amy got her turn at the washers and dryers.

Amy pulled the cart home through warm air and falling leaves, inhaling the scent of clean blankets and humming to herself. She was going up the walk to the house when she saw something dark nestled in the leaves of the lawn next door. She left the cart, crossed the lawn, and kneeled in the leaves. A small bird lay on the top of the leaves under Mr.

Parker's picture window. Another bird once hit Mr. Parker's window, and that time Amy had taken it to their back porch so neighborhood cats couldn't get it. It had lain still as death for a few minutes, then it shuddered, got up, and staggered on its stalks of legs. After a few minutes it ruffled its feathers and flew up over the porch railing to the apple tree on Mr. Parker's property. It stayed on a low limb for a while, watching Amy (she imagined that it was thanking her), then it flew away.

But this little bird's head hung wrong; the beak was frozen open and its eyes were filled with blood. Suddenly she felt a chill. She shuddered and carried the bird back to her house where she lay the little body gently under the scraggly foundation shrubs.

Michael Kaslov looked around him. He didn't remember coming in here; he wasn't sure what time it was or even what day. It must be Saturday—the bars were closed on Sunday—and yesterday . . . he thought it was yesterday . . . that miserable nigger had fired him. *Him.* Who almost finished college, was almost a lawyer, and might have been a congressman or better. The nigger fired him because he was drunk on the job. It happened yesterday afternoon, he was sure of it. And he had had a few, maybe. But he wasn't drunk; witness the way he'd walked off the construction site, straight-backed and with the drying cement clinging to the knees of his trousers. That was the problem . . . he'd kneeled in the cement. But he couldn't *reach;* that was why he'd done it. Not because he was drunk. He'd tried to explain, but the motherfucker wouldn't listen. So he was out of a job, and after he paid the room rent and the installment on the truck, he had seventy-seven dollars in his wallet. Maybe less by now. He'd go to the can and count it later on.

He was drinking but he was still in control. He had to slow up, anyway. For one thing, he had to save a few bucks; for another, if he got falling-down, puking drunk, he couldn't stay angry, and anger was all that kept him alive today. Good, solid, righteous anger; at the nigger, but first and foremost at that bitch who'd ruined his life.

He'd had those drinks yesterday noon because of her. He'd run into Dale Simmons, who used to live in those miserable hills that rolled away into oblivion. Dale Simmons was a turd hillbilly not fit to kiss Michael's ass, and now he had a gray suit with a vest, a gold wristwatch, and a Buick special the same color as his suit . . . as if he changed cars when he changed clothes.

The sight of him climbing out of that sleek car on the Post Road made Michael stagger with rage. But that wasn't all of it. Dale Simmons had news; he'd shaken Michael's hand and asked to buy him lunch because they hadn't seen each other for so long. Michael tried to get out of it. He couldn't remember if he'd taken a shower that morning—he knew he hadn't shaved; it was no day to have lunch with a businessman in a gray suit. He said he only had forty-five minutes for lunch, he had to be back on the job. He'd lied and said he was foreman and he had to set an example for the men. But Simmons grabbed his arm and pulled him along the street toward Bosco's. Michael only went because Bosco's was just a gin mill; Simmons would be the one out of place in Bosco's. They had hamburgers and fries. Dale drank beer, and for once, so did Michael; until Dale gave him the big news.

Evvie's old bitch of a mother had died. Left the land to her daughter. Simmons had heard about the divorce. Seems Michael had pulled out a few months too soon; now she had that land and it was up for sale. Maybe sold by now. One hundred and sixty acres of Connecticut hills . . . Dale made a whistling sound that made Michael clench his teeth.

After all, Simmons crowed, all the biggies were moving to Connecticut to get away from New York taxes, dirt, crime, and graffiti. The only thing New York had worth more than warm piss were the roads. *Out* of the city, that is. In town, riding those streets was like biking up Mauna Loa during an eruption. So the big boys were getting out, moving east and north. Michael nodded, trying to look interested, although he didn't care if IBM, Xerox, and Union Carbide moved their corporate headquarters to the center of the Mindanao Deep.

Then Simmons said, "Bet a piece of land like that'll be worth a hundred and fifty, maybe two hundred thousand bucks. Yup . . . your ex-old lady's rich. . . ."

Rich.

That was on Friday, and now it was Saturday and he had seventy lousy bucks—maybe less by now—and she'd gotten him fired because after Dale Simmons's news he'd switched to shots and managed to get down four of them before he went back to the construction site. If she was rich, part of that money was his. She'd ruined his life and she owed him. And maybe his life wasn't ruined, after all. He was only thirty-three. If he could get fifty, sixty thousand out of her, he could get himself together, maybe go back to school. There was no statute of limitations on LSAT scores; there couldn't be.

For the first time in eight years he had hope. So he drank slowly and he planned. Maybe he'd take the kid. It was a cute kid, with black hair like its mother, and his big, dark Eastern eyes. Real cute. Little Amy, Amy girl. He hated the name, but he hadn't cared enough at the time to argue. But if he got himself together and went back to school, the kid would be better off with him, and he could change her name. It would be Natalie, after his mother. Natalie was the finest name he knew . . . only hill brats had names like Amy. Girls named Amy grew up to wait tables or work in a factory or on the streets of Bridgeport, but who ever heard of a hooker named Natalie?

He leaned on the bar, closed his eyes, and dreamed. He'd get the money, and the kid, and the bitch Evvie could go back to that diner in the hills where she belonged. He'd buy a light gray Buick special, and on an afternoon like this he'd drive the kid through the countryside to look at the leaves. They'd stop in a decent place for lunch together; he'd order lobster salad for her. The poor thing probably never tasted lobster before. People at other tables would stare at the handsome man and his beautiful daughter, and they'd envy him. Michael Kaslov would come into his own.

All he had to do was get the money.

He ordered another shot, this time with water, and sipped slowly. He felt good, better than he had in years. She'd give him the money and his life would open like a bud in springtime. She'd give it all to him because she was scared pissless of him. With good reason, he thought. If she didn't come across, he'd kill her.

A crash in the kitchen woke Amy up, and she jumped out of bed. It was ten-thirty; she'd been asleep an hour. She went out on the landing and heard her father's voice. She cowered back against the bedroom door, then she heard her mother weeping, and she made herself go down the stairs to the kitchen.

The lights were on. He yelled, "No money? You buy a hundred bucks worth of this shit and tell me there's no money? You lying bitch . . ." His voice scaled up into a falsetto, mimicking a woman's. "Under-makeup moisturizer . . ." There was another crash—he was breaking the Avon bottles. The hideous soprano screeched, "Cream glow foundation, Gardenia bubble bath . . ." More crashing. Then in his own voice he screamed "Bubble bath. I'm fucking starving and you're buying bubble bath. . . ."

Amy got to the kitchen door. The floor was covered with broken glass. The bottle with the crystal bird on top, her favorite, was on the floor with the others. The bottle was smashed, the wings broken off the bird. Her mother was kneeling on the floor, palms flat. The beige makeup and green bubble bath leaked across the red linoleum mottled with black. Amy whimpered, but he didn't hear her.

"Where, bitch? Where's my money?" he wailed.

He grabbed a pink glass jar off the table and pitched it against a cabinet. The glass was thick; it didn't break. That enraged him more. He picked up the jar and put it on the counter. Holding it on its side with one hand, he rummaged through the tool drawer with the other. He was looking for the hammer!

He'd smashed her mother's front teeth out with that hammer. This time he would knock out the rest of them or worse. Amy cried out. He glanced at her and went on scrabbling in the drawer. Then, with a cry of triumph, he pulled the hammer out of the drawer and raised it over the pink jar.

"No," Amy cried.

He whirled at her, holding the hammer.

"Shut up or *you'll* get this," he yelled.

He brought the hammer down on the jar; it cracked. He hit it again, and it smashed across the counter. He giggled and scooped up cream and glass in one hand and, still holding the hammer in the other, advanced on Amy's mother.

"No, Michael," she whimpered, "there's glass . . . please, Mickey—"

He grabbed a fistful of her hair, yanked her head back, and started smearing cream and glass into her hair. Broken glass cut his hand; blood mixed with the cream in the hair.

"Where's the money?" he said softly. He sounded seductive, sinuous, "C'mon, Evvie, where's the money . . ."

She sobbed weakly. He let her go and grabbed another bottle off the table. He opened it and poured the contents in a thick, white stream over her head.

"Where? Evvie. There's enough for both of us. Tell me where."

The Avon bottles were gone, and he picked up the garbage bag. He was going to throw garbage on her mother; the teabags and the morning's coffee grounds, a few crusts of bread, and the syrup left in a can of peaches were in that bag, and he was going to pour it all on her mother. The cool wind blew in Amy's ears, reached behind her eyes, and turned liquid, like it had before. Her whole head was cold; her eyes floated in iced oil. She made a sound she'd never heard herself make before, part growl, part screech; an animal sound, something like Mr. Parker's cat yowling. But it sounded like a dog howling, too, a pig squealing, a cow bellowing; it was like wild cats on TV, snarling into the camera. A shark might make that sound if it made any sound at all. It was wild and unidentifiable; as if the souls of a hundred dead animals possessed Amy and their voices came roaring up her throat and out of her mouth.

It startled her father. He jumped backward and dropped the bag. He looked scared and raised the hammer over his head to hit her if she came for him. Amy didn't care. She tucked her head into her shoulders and charged across the room at him. But her mother was faster than she was. She leaped up and grabbed Amy around the middle and lifted her off the floor. Amy struggled but her mother's grip was solid. She heaved Amy across the room, got the door to the broom closet open, and shoved Amy inside. Then she shut the door and locked it with the old-fashioned straight key that must have been used when the cubbyhole was a pantry.

The closet was pitch dark. Then a thin shaft of light came through the keyhole and Amy knew that her mother had pulled the key out. She would put it in her pocket or down the drain or even try to swallow it. Anything so her father couldn't open the door and hurt Amy.

But now her mother was alone with him.

"Bitch . . ." he screamed. "She's my little girl." The metal hammer head hit the pantry door.

Amy heard glass crunching. Her mother was trying to get away, and he was going after her. Amy heard the hammer hit wood again, then metal. The stove or the old sink. Then it hit something else with a muffled crunch, and something soft hit the floor.

Amy kneeled and looked through the keyhole.

She saw her father's legs. His shoes were covered with lotion; a few pieces of glass sparkled on the brushed leather. Her mother was on the floor, her pink robe spread in the mess, and blood ran out of her black hair.

Her father's hand dropped, and Amy saw the hammer. The head was bloody.

"Evvie?" he said.

Her mother raised her head and Amy saw her face. Her eyes were wrong; they weren't looking in the same direction. Then, as Amy watched, blood filled one eye like the dead bird's.

"Evvie?" her father said softly.

Her mother didn't answer. She lowered her head slowly and carefully so her cheek rested in the lotion and glass on the floor. Amy saw the hammer fall out of her father's hand and land on the floor next to her mother. He groaned, his feet backed away from the body on the floor.

"Oh shit," he said, "Evvie . . ."

Nothing from her mother.

He made whimpering noises, but he didn't say any words. Then his feet moved out of sight. She heard him cross the kitchen, open and close the back door, and his footsteps went down the wooden stairs of the back porch to the cement walk that went around the side of the house to the street. She couldn't hear him after that. The room was quiet.

She banged on the door. "Mommy," she screamed.

Her mother tried to lift her head again. She got it a few inches off the floor. Her eyes were even worse now. One looked in the direction of the refrigerator; the other was so glazed with blood, Amy couldn't see the pupil. Her mother stretched out her arm. Her hand was closed, but Amy saw metal gleam through her mother's fingers. She was clutching the key; she was trying to get to the broom closet and let Amy out.

"Mommy," Amy meant to cry out, but there wasn't a sound. She knew that her mother heard her, anyway. She felt the word lurch out of her head, through the door, and into her mother's mind.

Amy called again without making any noise, and this time her mother's body shuddered and she dug her elbows against the floor, trying to pull herself forward. But they slipped in the mess on the floor. Amy could see her mother's face for another few seconds. It was blank, then her head sank straight down on the floor, her nose and mouth crushed flat, and her hair fell forward.

Amy tried the silent calling again, but this time nothing happened. She tried again and again, but her mother didn't move.

TWO

SHE GOT THIRSTY before she got hungry. She remembered
the streams that ran out of the hill behind Nana's house.
Bright, freezing springs came up out of the ground, ran between the rocks, gathered into the little brook that ran
through the pasture and emptied into the farm pond. At this
time of year it was slow. Leaves got caught against the rocks
and made yellow-and-red islands on the water. In winter the
surface froze and water ran under the ice, and in spring it
was a cataract. Water coated the rocks on the hills, the ground
was spongy, and the water was full of mud and winter debris.
It turned sluggish in July; dragonflies and water fleas rode
the surface, and she could put her feet in the stream. She
dreamed that the stream flowed through the broom closet
and out the door. She drank from it and washed her face in
it.

She thought she fell asleep. When she came to, she had
to go. She tried hard to hold it in; she whimpered at the
keyhole and then looked out. Her mother still didn't move,
and she knew by now that she wouldn't. She didn't think her
mother was dead—she didn't let that word into her mind—
but she knew her mother wasn't going to let her out of the
closet so she could go to the bathroom and get a glass of
water.

No one knew Amy was here. It was Saturday night, maybe Sunday morning by now. On Monday they'd mark her absent at school and call the house. The same would happen on Tuesday, and maybe by Wednesday they'd send a truant officer, or maybe the police, to find out what had happened to her.

She crawled away from the keyhole and peed in the farthest corner of the broom closet. She didn't go back to the keyhole. She didn't want to see what was out there. She sat with her back against the wall, halfway between the door and the corner she'd had to use, and tried to go back to sleep. She couldn't live until Wednesday.

The cold liquid in her head, or whatever it was, was gone. Her face was warm to the touch; her eyes stopped feeling like iced marbles rolling in her head. She thought of the split second when she'd called her mother silently. She didn't know what had happened, except she knew that her mother had heard her. Her mother's whole body had shuddered, and she'd made a last try to get to Amy. Maybe she had touched something in her mother's head. Or her mother had touched something in hers. If her mother was truly . . . gone . . . (That other word swam around in the dark, almost visible in the closet; she would see it floating in the dark next to the Electrolux and vacuum-cleaner bags on the far wall if she let herself.) If her mother was truly gone . . . maybe that had been the instant when her mother's soul had left her body (that's what Nana said happened), and it was her mother's spirit on its way to heaven that had touched Amy's mind. Except that she had the feeling that *she* had done it, not her mother, and that it had something to do with the cold windfluid inside her head.

She drew her knees up and wrapped her arms around them. It must be getting on for morning because the heat had come on and the closet was warm. Thirst was hot in her throat; her lips and tongue were dry. She thought her gums would dry out and her teeth would rattle in her mouth like loose bones. She closed her eyes and hoped she would die while she slept.

Michael rolled over in bed and tried to sit up. His head pounded; he was afraid that he'd throw up. He lay back, then tried again. He made it up, then swung his legs over and put his feet on the cold floor.

"Some binge," he muttered.

Lousy dreams too. He tried to remember them because his own dreams fascinated him. He wrote some of them down in case he ever got enough dough to start seeing a shrink. This one was especially vivid. He was in the Bridge Street house, the kitchen floor was covered with blood and some kind of colored stuff, mostly white. He wondered what it symbolized; the blood was blood, the white creamy stuff might be semen. It would be fun to discuss it—more than fun. He needed to talk to someone because the rest of the dream was really horrible. There had been a black-haired woman lying facedown in the mess because he'd hit her with a hammer. He supposed it was Evvie. His aggressions were coming out at last, he thought. It was time; he'd swallowed too much shit as it was.

He put his hands against the thin, shelflike mattress to push himself to his feet. His palms stung, and he jerked them off the mattress and looked at them. They were crisscrossed with cuts and covered with dried blood. He must have fallen down on a patch of gravel somewhere and skinned his hands. He didn't remember; he knew that blackouts were a bad sign. Maybe he'd try AA, after all. He'd talk to Jonathan's doctor about it. Maybe today.

He got a whiff of his own sour smell and his mouth tasted like tidal mud. He needed a shower.

He took his towel off the rack. It was dirty; the linens on his bed were gray. If his father saw how he lived, the old man would die all over again. He had to get himself cleaned up, go to Limekiln, see Jonathan and the doctor. He'd go to AA tomorrow and try to get back a little ground in his life. Last night—the blackout, the cuts on his hands, the dream of the mess and dead woman that kept swooping in on him— scared him.

He went to the door, wearing only his Jockey shorts. It was Sunday and Miss Lester might see him. Let her, he thought, grinning to himself. If she turned up in the hall, he'd dangle his member in front of her and give her the first and only thrill of her miserable old-maid life. But the hall was empty. He went to the bathroom and tried the door. It was locked, and he heard water running. He pounded on the door.

"Hold your horses," Old Man Rimer yelled.

He leaned against the wall and waited. The other roomers' doors stayed closed. A lot of them were up and out by now: at church or off to the nicer suburbs to see their kids. He was the only one in the whole house under sixty, but the place was cheap and clean (except for his room), and the old ladies doted on him. He played canasta with them occasionally and always managed to win a few bucks. The old men didn't care for him much, and he thought that Old Man Rimer loathed him.

He heard water gurgle out of the sink, the door opened, and Mr. Rimer appeared. He was wearing a spotless Indian-blanket robe and carried his towel and soap dish. He stopped when he saw Michael and looked him up and down with an expression of total disgust.

"You smell like a pig, Kaslov. You should cover yourself, there're ladies in this house."

"And a good morning to you too," Michael said.

Rimer passed him and went down the hall, leaving behind smells of shaving lotion and soap.

Michael ducked into the bathroom. He stood under the shower until the hot water ran out, then stood under the cold for a few seconds. He came out, dried himself, and brushed his teeth until his gums bled. He wrapped his towel around his middle and went back to his room. It was Sunday; visiting day at Limekiln. But the doctor who was treating Jonathan might be there, anyway. His name was Hall, and Michael sort of liked him.

He drove north, into the hills, to Limekiln. He usually liked to drive—his body relaxed—the scenery was a rolling diorama that printed itself on his mind without effort. But today the dream wouldn't let him alone. He had one horrible second when it seemed to be a memory, not a dream. But he knew he hadn't gone to the house on Bridge Street, and he certainly hadn't left Evvie lying in a pool of blood and goo on the kitchen floor. He'd never hurt Evvie, not really. He wasn't one of those protein-starved hillbillies with the watery eyes and pasty skin who could barely read or write. They were the wife beaters of the world, not him. He'd read John Stuart Mill, Oliver Wendell Holmes, and scored in the seven hundreds on his LSATs. Not the stuff of which wife beaters are made. Listing his accomplishments made him feel better; the nightmare faded and he finished the trip north to Limekiln feeling relatively peaceful.

"Michael, you look . . . very tired," Jonathan said.

Jonathan would never tell Michael that he looked lousy, but Michael knew he did. His skin was gray, his eyes were bloodshot even though he had used Visine.

"Had a wild night," Michael said.

"Nooky?" Jonathan whispered reverently.

"Nooky," Michael said.

"Tell me," Jonathan pleaded.

Michael pulled his bright red, molded plastic chair closer to Jonathan, who was sitting on a flowered couch. They were in the lounge of the Limekiln State Psychiatric Facility; behind Jonathan, big windows with mesh inside the glass looked out on acres of lawn, a ring of trees, and the Connecticut hills in the distance. They were the beginning of the Berkshires and the Catskills; little hills that made a spine running north to the Adirondacks and farther north to the Laurentians. It was pretty out here, and Michael knew that Jonathan loved this room; he sat in front of the windows staring out at the changing leaves and the hills. It was a nice place. They kept it clean, the staff was polite and seemed kind, and Jonathan was as happy here as he could be anywhere. Their father would be pleased if he could see where his son had wound up. It was better than the private place and now and then Michael would kid himself that Jonathan was getting better. That someday he'd come out, get a job, a wife, have a kid . . .

Michael's hangover abated. The vague, sick headache he'd had all morning eased, and he started describing to Jonathan the night he'd spent with Norma Warren of New Canaan. It wasn't a total lie; he'd never get away with telling Jonathan a total lie. There *was* a Norma Warren, and he screwed her regularly, along with Mary Calisher of Weston and Barbara Cohn of Southport . . . the list went on. All suburban housewives whose kids went to school and stayed late for hockey practice or the drama club and whose husbands were in Houston or Cleveland or in town having dinner with a client and spending the night with their secretaries or the cute little girl who ran the Xerox machine. Michael listened to the women's sad stories, then screwed them in his best style. The encounters weren't much fun, but the women paid him (more than he'd ever made on construction or working Christmases at Caldor's). Not in cash, he wasn't that low yet. They paid him to clean the yard, do some cabinetry, fix leaky pipes. He charged way more than the jobs were worth, but the women knew what they were paying for and there were no complaints.

He could see Norma Warren tonight if he wanted to; her husband really was out of town, and her son had gone back to Dartmouth. But she was a raddled forty-five and he'd had a lousy night . . .

. . . *beating his wife to death.*

The thought was in his mind before he could stop it. He prayed Jonathan wouldn't notice, and he tried to concentrate on some vivid sexual detail to distract Jonathan. It didn't work.

Jonathan turned white, his eyes got that awful, blank look, as if they were about to roll back in his head, and he grabbed Michael. Michael tried to free himself, but Jonathan's grip was iron. Michael didn't want to struggle too hard. The lounge was full of patients and visitors. If Jonathan got out of hand, the orderly at the door would get help, and two of them would drag Jonathan out the door while the other patients watched with eyes full of crazy spite.

"Oh, my God," Jonathan whispered.

Michael kept talking desperately. "Then she wanted us to stand in front of the mirror . . . "

Jonathan's grip got tighter, his hands turned to claws of steel, the nails dug into Michael's skin, and he rocked back and forth on the couch and Michael had to rock with him. A few of the people in the lounge noticed and stopped talking. On the TV in the corner the Indians were getting ready to butcher Custer one more time; the music peaked, the red-skins rode over the rise; hundreds of horses' hooves thudded in the lounge, war cries screamed through the TV speaker, and Jonathan wailed, "Michael, what did you do? My God . . . what did you do?"

A tall, thin man wearing the chinos and untucked-in sport shirt that all the male patients wore ran to the TV and switched it off so they could all hear. The orderly at the door unhooked his radio and talked into it, and Jonathan cried, "No, Michael . . . no . . . " The lounge was quiet, the visitors looked embarrassed, the patients grinned, a few of them laughed, but Jonathan started to cry.

"I was afraid it would happen." Jonathan sobbed. "First the little birds, then the raccoon at camp, then the puppy. Did you smother it or break its neck? I don't remember. Daddy said it was only a violent streak . . . boys will be boys. But he was wrong. You liked killing. . . . " His hand swept the room. "They like killing. . . . "

Michael prayed that the other orderly would get there soon.

"Poor puppy." Jonathan wept hopelessly. "It stayed warm afterward, and I held it until Daddy took it away from me. By then it was getting cold and stiff . . . Michael, why'd you kill it?"

There wasn't a sound in the lounge. The patients looked at Michael, waiting for an answer. The visitors stared at the walls or out of the windows in a frenzy of embarrassment. It was almost funny. The crazies wanted to know why Michael had killed the puppy; the sane people didn't care.

"It was an accident," Michael choked.

Suddenly Jonathan's voice changed. "The little girl's in the closet," he shrieked, "the door's locked, and blackness is a blanket. She can't swallow . . . her mouth burns, her throat is full of sand . . ."

The other orderly raced through the door, and the two of them advanced on Jonathan.

"But," Jonathan wailed, "the worst is *outside* the door. There's blood in her hair and other stuff . . . what is it? Her body will swell soon, the little girl'll see. No . . ."

The orderlies grabbed him and hauled him to his feet.

One said, "We have to go upstairs now, Jon."

But Jonathan jerked back his head and screeched, "Murder . . ."

The orderly threw Michael a look of sympathy, and together they pulled Jonathan across the room toward the door.

"Daddy says that cruelty to animals is the worst crime." Jonathan sobbed at the orderlies; they nodded. Then, at the door, Jonathan wrenched his head around to look back over his shoulder.

"It's not a dream, Michael, she's really dead. They'll find her and come after you. Run, Michael . . . run. Get away . . . run . . ."

They dragged him out, and one of the visitors got up and closed the door after them.

Michael's hand shook as he deposited coins and dialed the number of the house on Bridge Street. He let it ring seven times, then he gave up and went back to the bar. There was no answer because it was a lovely, warm fall day and the bitch had taken the kid up to Newton to gloat over her hundred and sixty acres worth half a million dollars.

But Evvie didn't have a car.

So what? She could rent one. She was rich. Maybe she'd

bought one by now. A light gray Buick with red upholstery. How long does it take to buy a car when you've got hundreds of thousands of dollars? But the explanation didn't relieve him. He picked up the shot that Timmy had set next to the beer and sipped. It was his first of the day, and the hair on his arms lifted. He would call again in a little while, and if there was still no answer, he'd drive by . . . maybe . . . just to be sure that everything was okay. He picked up the beer chaser; it was cold and smooth and slid down his throat like silk. Everything was coming into perspective. . . .

But Jonathan knew about Evvie. . . .

The first time that Jonathan had known what he couldn't, he was nineteen and Michael was fourteen; their mother had just died, the business with the animals (all accidents, no matter what Jonathan thought) was in the past. Michael was a pretty kid with dark, wavy hair and eyes that had a slight slant to them. His mother's eyes, his father had said. He worked for his father in the afternoons delivering and picking up cleaning in the neighborhood. It was the end of August, the pavement got so hot by afternoon that he could feel it through the soles of his sneakers, and the plastic that covered the freshly cleaned clothes left damp marks where it clung to his skin.

He was bringing a silk dress to Mrs. Shapiro. She had called that morning to say that she needed it today, to wear to a dinner party. Michael waited while his father pressed the dress himself. It was pure silk, and his Dad wouldn't trust it to Nicky, the big, sweaty man with the bony face who did most of the pressing.

Michael brought the dress on his bike, holding it high in the air in its plastic wrap with one hand, maneuvering the bike with the other. Mrs. Shapiro lived on one of the quiet, pretty streets, away from the highway. It was hot, the street was empty, the leaves on the trees hung still. He biked up the Shapiros' drive to the kitchen door and rang. Nothing happened; the kitchen window was open and the house was dark and silent. He rang again and heard Mrs. Shapiro call from inside the house.

"Come in, Michael, the door's open."

Careful not to let the dress touch the ground, he opened the door and went inside the dark kitchen. It was a little cooler.

"Where should I put the dress?" he yelled.

Mrs. Shapiro appeared at the door from the dining room. She was wearing a robe of some filmy see-through stuff, and she wasn't wearing anything under it. He gasped, and his arm sagged so that the hem of the dress touched the floor. She crossed the kitchen quickly.

"Careful," she said, taking the dress away from him. She held it up but didn't move back. She was standing close; he could smell her cologne and the spray she used on her hair. Her arm was raised, holding the dress clear of the floor, and the pull of her position lifted one breast so high the nipple peeked out of the fold of her robe. Michael jumped back from her, and she laughed softly and threw the dress any which way across the table.

His face was so hot, his cheeks hurt, and he was suddenly afraid that he would wet his pants. His eyes went to the exposed nipple, and Mrs. Shapiro laughed again and folded the robe back so her whole breast was exposed.

"Would you like to touch?" she said softly.

He couldn't answer. She grabbed his hand and brought it to her bare skin, and with the other hand she caught hold of his belt buckle.

Michael got home about four-thirty. It had cooled down; clouds were piling up in the sky, and the curtains in the living room moved in a damp breeze. Jonathan was sitting at the round table in the dining area with the chessboard laid out, and he looked up when Michael came in the back door. He waved and started to turn back to the board. Suddenly he froze where he was, his head turned again, very smoothly, as if his neck were oiled, and he stared at Michael.

Michael didn't like the look. It was blank, but something

else, too, that Michael couldn't describe then (or now, either, for that matter), and he got a feeling that his brother's eyes were about to roll back in their sockets until nothing showed but squishy white orbs.

Then, his voice sounding rusty and unused, like the hinge on a coffin lid swinging open for the first time in a hundred years, Jonathan said, "Her hair is red; so are her nails. They're long, and they scratched your back. It was wonderful. Her tits are like marble, her mouth like warm pudding . . . it was wonderful. You'll go back again, she'll do it all again . . . ooh . . . "

Jonathan's eyes rolled, and Michael thought his brother was going to faint. He wanted to pass out, too, because he knew that Jonathan had never met Mrs. Shapiro, and Mrs. Shapiro hadn't called here to tell Jonathan that her hair was red, her tits solid, and that she'd spent the afternoon screwing Michael.

Timmy brought Michael another shot and refilled his beer. This time the liquor went down just right and the trembling in his middle eased a little.

It hadn't ended with Mrs. Shapiro. Jonathan had known everything important that ever happened to Michael without being told. He knew when Cindy Rush walked out on Michael, and he was waiting up to comfort Michael, who got so drunk, he literally crawled into the house on his hands and knees. (Cindy married Herb Gould, who became a pharmacist and now owned a chain of discount drugstores strung out along the Post Road from Westport to New London.) Jonathan knew about the LSAT scores before anyone told him. He was in Crescent Park by then, and when Michael walked in on visiting day, Jonathan leaped out of the chair and stared at his brother with that blank, white look that made Michael think of flat land covered with snow, and he'd said in his rusty graveyard voice, "Seven-twenty on LSATs. Seven-twenty. Congratulations."

Their father had been there, too, but he didn't say anything. They never talked about Jonathan's gift. No, *gift* was the wrong word. Gifts were good and this . . . thing . . . had driven Jonathan mad.

He knew about Evvie.

But that didn't make it true. Jonathan was telepathic, not clairvoyant. Michael had had a nightmare, Jonathan knew the content of it. That's all.

But Jonathan didn't know it was a dream. He couldn't tell his *own* dreams from reality, much less Michael's. He felt the horror and pity of it, as if it were real. Jonathan always felt the horror and pity . . . witness the scene this afternoon because a rambunctious puppy had gotten its neck broken twenty-five years ago. And out of this pathological tenderness poor Jonathan had imagined the blanket of darkness, and the thirst like sand in the kid's throat.

It made sense, and Michael finished his drink and called Norma Warren in New Canaan.

"Oh, baby," she breathed into the phone. "I've been waiting for you all day. . . . . "

Just the sound of her voice made everything normal again. He had another drink for the road, then drove down toward New Canaan. He didn't believe any of Jonathan's shit; there was nothing for the cops to find. Michael was just a day laborer who could have been a lawyer on his way to lay a middle-aged lady who needed some comfort. Everything just like always. Except that when he came to the Route 7 exit that would take him south to New Canaan and Norma Warren, he passed it and kept driving west.

THREE

THEY GAVE JONATHAN a shot, naturally, and he floated. He had seen the sun go its full path in the sky; he saw the moon rise and sink. He saw the seasons pass; snow blew in his open window and covered the blanket on his bed, and when he finally started to come to, he could swear it was April and the finches had come back and were tapping on the window to be let in.

He opened his eyes; the room was dark. He went to the window. There was a trace of light in the sky, but he knew it couldn't still be Sunday. They gave him the shot on Sunday, and it usually kept him out for a long time. It must be Monday or Tuesday evening.

He scrabbled in his bedside drawer and found his watch. It had stopped at three o'clock, but he didn't know which day. He went to the door of his room, hoping that he wasn't too late for supper because he was starving.

The hall was empty, but he heard distant voices and smelled brown gravy. His mouth watered, and he hurried to the elevator that would take him to the basement dining room.

The elevator guard, Mr. Crystal, had just slid the doors closed when thirst hit Jonathan. It was horrible; there was dry dirt in his mouth, his cheeks sank against his teeth from lack of moisture; his skin was turning to paper. He groaned, and Mr. Crystal looked sharply at him over his shoulder.

"Water . . . " Jonathan mumbled.

They reached the basement, the guard opened the door, and Jonathan staggered out into the corridor searching for the water fountain. He'd forgotten where it was. There was a soft-drink machine—7-Up was almost like water, at least it was white, and he searched his pockets desperately for change. He found what he needed. The machine dropped a paper cup, cold, fizzy liquid filled it. He gulped the drink down but it wasn't enough. He didn't have any more change. Mr. Crystal was standing at the open elevator watching suspiciously. If Mr. Crystal got worried, they'd take Jonathan back upstairs and he'd miss supper. He couldn't bear that, because now he was almost as hungry as he was thirsty. The smells coming from the dining room were driving him nuts.

He giggled at that, and Mr. Crystal took a step out of the elevator toward him. Jonathan put on as calm a smile as he could and said, "I was thinking that hunger would drive me nuts . . . but I *am* nuts."

Mr. Crystal laughed, and Jonathan went on to the dining room. He found the water fountain tucked behind a jog in the wall. He stopped and took huge slurps. . . .

Amy dreamed that her mother took her to the yard-goods store in Trumbull. The tables were covered with bolts of colored silk and velvets. Her mother unrolled one bolt of crimson cloth and held it to her face; it matched the color of the blood that filled her eye. Amy nodded that it was perfect. There was a chrome water fountain in the back of the store. Amy waited as long as she could, then she left her mother, walked slowly and casually between the tables of cloth, like a lady even though her tongue blistered and burned, and she pressed the foot pedal on the fountain and watched the stream of water arc into the silver basin . . . .

Jonathan was still thirsty; he drank milk, more water, cajoled a glass of ginger ale out of the fat woman behind the steam table, even had a cup of tea, but the thirst wouldn't quit. He had read that certain poisons did that. Warfarin drove rats mad with thirst; they ran out of their nests searching for water, bleeding from their mouths and eyes. Then they collapsed and bled to death in an agony of thirst. He couldn't remember where he'd read such a disgusting thing. He knew no one had fed him warfarin. They sort of liked him in here, as much as they could be said to like anybody.

He'd had more than enough to drink by now. His bladder felt like a balloon. But the thirst was unrelenting. Then he realized that it wasn't *he* who was thirsty. He put his spoon down next to his Tuesday night dinner of Salisbury steak and canned gravy and tried to concentrate.

Sunday—he thought it had been Sunday—came back to him. The pictures in Michael's mind . . . the sister-in-law he'd never known, lying on the kitchen floor with blood in her hair; the closed, locked broom closet with his niece trapped inside.

The woman was dead but the little girl wasn't. He couldn't believe what was happening at first because he'd never met the child. He understood that Michael wouldn't bring her here to see her crazy uncle, but it was very confusing because he never got "rays" (he called them "rays") from someone he'd never met. But now he was getting something from behind that closet door, and it was thirst . . . and blackness.

The blackness wasn't total. A stream of light came through a hole. It was—he pushed his mind harder; he felt his forehead crease—it was a keyhole in the door. There was a wooden wall; his eyes were used to the dark now, like hers (poor baby). He saw a broom hanging, a dust mop and a vacuum cleaner and an ironing board with strawberries printed on the cover. He smelled lemon oil and excrement, and he put his hands flat against either side of his head. He moaned against his will . . . the little girl was trying to hold it, but she couldn't. She crawled . . . he crawled with her . . . to the darkest recesses of the closet.

He felt her relief and shame as she crawled away from the mess she'd made, breathing through her mouth. She went back to the door but she didn't look out again. She knew what was out there; she didn't want to see it again. She closed her eyes; Jonathan closed his. She wanted to die.

"Kaslov . . ."

Perkins was shaking his arm, and Jonathan opened his eyes.

"Don't you want that?"

Perkins nodded at the Salisbury steak. Jonathan looked down at his plate. It was Amy who was hungry and thirsty, not him. He shoved the full plate over to Perkins. Perkins beamed and picked up his plastic spoon. The matron rushed over to the table.

"You can't give your dinner away, Jonathan," she said.

"But I don't want it and he does."

It was reasonable, but Miss Crain was not a reasonable woman. She was scrawny with colorless eyes and white eyelashes, and the only thing he ever got from her mind was a squeal of weak, ugly anger. He wanted to like her, as he wanted to like everybody. But he failed, and some nights he would try himself for disliking Miss Crain and Dr. Morgan and Rex McMahon . . . and he would find himself guilty on all counts.

She pulled the dish away from Perkins and set it firmly back in front of Jonathan. Poor Perkins looked miserable.

"You are not to waste food," said Miss Crain.

Jonathan started to say that he wasn't wasting it by giving it to Perkins, then he realized how stupid it was to argue about who would eat his supper while a little girl was dying of thirst and hunger, alone in the dark, with nothing to look at but her mother's corpse.

He had to do something.

He picked up his spoon and dug into the Salisbury steak.

Miss Crain started to turn away, and as calmly as he could, Jonathan said, "It's very important that I speak to Dr. Hall tonight." To show his goodwill he took a huge bite of the chopped meat and chewed calmly.

Miss Crain said, "You'll see Dr. Hall when you're scheduled to."

He felt panic rising. If he didn't control it, they'd give him another shot, and by the time he came to, the little girl would be dead. He forced himself to take another bite of Salisbury steak.

"That's not until tomorrow," he said, chewing. He paused and swallowed. "It will be too late by then."

"Too late for what?" Miss Crain sneered.

"To do anything about this important thing."

She walked away.

"Please," he called after her.

This time his voice shook, and even he heard hysteria in it. She stopped and eyed him, and he made himself grin pleadingly like the old yellow dog that used to belong to Mr. Samuels the stationmaster. He tried to remember the dog's name and what had become of it, then he stopped himself. The dog wasn't important. Only the little girl was. Miss Crain came back to the table.

"It's six-thirty, Dr. Hall is home with his family. What could be important enough to disturb him?" She spoke softly, not kindly. Jonathan knew she wasn't a kind woman. But she wasn't stupid, and she'd been working with crazy people for years. Since before he came here. She wouldn't be easy to manipulate, and he'd have to be very, very careful. He put his fork down next to his plate and tried a different approach. He hated to take the time because the little girl was getting weaker every minute, but he knew that if he was too forceful, if he showed a hint of desperation, Miss Crain would dig in.

He said, "I wonder if I could let Perkins have my dessert, Miss Crain. Those shots do tend to take the appetite away, and he's still hungry."

Miss Crain's eyes narrowed, but she nodded, and Jonathan put the plastic bowl of some kind of apple mixture in front of Perkins. Perkins gave a whoop, grabbed his spoon, and dug in.

"About Dr. Hall," Jonathan said.

"About Dr. Hall," Miss Crain said snidely.

"I wish there were something I could say to convince you how important it is for me to see Dr. Hall tonight." He not only spoke sanely but *was* sane for a second. She knew it; he knew she knew it. He also knew she did not like it. He wondered if she disliked all sane people, or only sane men, or only him when he was sane. He was getting off the track again, and he pulled himself back with an effort.

"I don't like to use words like life and death, Miss Crain, but I assure you that they're not too extreme. Not extreme at all." She stared at him for a moment, then turned away.

He stood up from the table; he felt the panic slipping out of grasp, and he fought as hard as he could. Perkins went on slurping up the dessert, watching with bright eyes that twitched from Jonathan to Miss Crain and back again. Jonathan kept his voice low and urgent but still in control. The effort was making him sweat; moisture covered his upper lip.

"Just call Dr. Hall, please. I would offer you anything . . . if I had anything to offer. Just call him and tell him that Jonathan has had a ray and there's an emergency. He'll understand. Just call him and tell him that much. . . ."

She was moving away; he had to stop her. "Just those few words, Miss Crain. If he doesn't think it's important, he can go right back to his dinner." She didn't even stop. He wanted to scream and turn the table over. He might have, but poor Perkins was still eating; Annie Crory was mushing her food around, mixing the apple with the gravy, meat, and potatoes, and he could see the mess on the floor that Samson would have to clean up. So he didn't.

If only he could control her. Telepathy, or whatever it was that was wrong with him, was useless bullshit. Only control mattered. Controlling Miss Crain.

Suddenly he thought,
Amy could do it.

Dale Ferris turned out the light and Jonathan waited. A
few minutes later Dale's breathing was even and Jonathan
got out of bed and went to the door. It still wasn't locked.
They weren't dangerous at Limekiln. Violent, all right . . .
but that was toward pieces of furniture, plates, glasses, themselves. Not toward other people. He slipped out into the hall
and closed the door behind him.

Marty was on duty; thank God it was Marty. He saw
Jonathan, laid his book down and stood up.

"Johnny?" Marty asked softly.

Jonathan went down the hall and stood in front of the
desk. He didn't know what to say.

"You okay, old man?" Marty asked.

"No. I need to see Dr. Hall."

"He'll be here tomorrow."

"Tomorrow's too late."

Marty looked confused. Jonathan felt his confusion and
was sorry. He liked Marty; Marty liked him. He knew a lot
about Marty Vespa. His folks had been killed in a car crash
when Marty was seven, and an aunt and uncle took him to
live in their Victorian house in Norwalk. It had a big, white-
tiled bathroom with a tub on a platform. The uncle was a
shit; he liked beating Marty, and he'd take the kid into the
bathroom and hit him with his belt . . . buckle end first. He
drew blood occasionally, and Marty still remembered it spattered on the white-tiled floor. The whirlpool at Limekiln was
in a white-tiled room, and standing guard in there was agony
for Marty. Jonathan hated when Marty was on duty in the
whirlpool because he felt what Marty felt. Marty could have
been a shit like his uncle, but he was a nice man. He adored
his wife. Jonathan had never seen her, but he knew that she
was short and had bleached blond hair, round brown eyes,
and a soft, warm behind, like a pillow. Everything should
have been great, but Marty was jealous of his own son. The

little boy was three, and Marty felt terrible about competing with his son for his wife's attention. But he couldn't help it. Jonathan did his best to behave when Marty was on duty, and he was sorry now that he was going to cause trouble for Marty; at the same time he was glad Marty was here. Marty had imagination; he might break the rules.

"Why's tomorrow too late?" Marty asked.

Jonathan sank to his knees and started to cry very softly. He didn't want to raise a rumpus and alert Miss Crain. Marty rushed around the desk and bent over Jonathan.

"Whatsa matter, fella? You gonna let go?"

Jonathan nodded.

"I'll get Miss Crain."

Jonathan grabbed the hem of Marty's orderly coat.

"No. Not Miss Crain. Dr. Hall. I've got to see Dr. Hall."

"C'mon," Marty said. "It's almost eleven. I can't call Dr. Hall."

Jonathan pleaded. "Marty, I've never lied to you. Marty, look at me . . . please. I'm not crazy this second, I swear. Just look at me. Am I crazy?"

Marty smiled sadly at Jonathan. "Yes, sport. Crazy as a bedbug."

Jonathan slid back quickly along the floor out of Marty's reach.

"If you don't call Dr. Hall, if you get Miss Crain . . . " He didn't know what to threaten with. All he had going for him was his certain knowledge that Marty Vespa was a softy. It might be enough, and suddenly Jonathan got an idea. It was awful, it almost made him sick, and he didn't know if he could do it, but he had to try.

He raised his hand to his own head and grabbed a fistful of his hair. He stared at Marty. "Call Dr. Hall, Marty. I beg you."

"Oh, Jesus, Jonathan. Oh, shit . . . don't."

The hair was coarse and thick in Jonathan's hand. It was black like his mother's hair, like the little girl's. Just pulling one hair took a real tug and made his eyes water. He held his

breath and yanked with all of his might. He felt it tear free,
then nothing for a second; then the patch on his head was on
fire and tears of pain streamed down his face. Marty turned
dead white, and Jonathan brought his hand down in front of
his face. He'd done it, all right. His hand held a clump of hair
with shreds of scalp clinging to it. He laid it on the floor in
front of his knees. It looked like a tiny dead animal. Marty
looked ready to throw up and faint, and Jonathan wasn't far
behind him, but he couldn't let go yet.

"I'll pull it all out," Jonathan said clearly, "every fucking
strand, unless you call Dr. Hall. I swear it." It was a lie, the
pain was terrible, the patch was wet, and he could feel blood
seeping across his head.

Marty backed up until his butt hit the desk, and Jonathan
reached and grabbed another fistful of hair.

"Oh, God," Marty said, "Stop . . . "

He picked up the phone.

"Dr. Hall," Jonathan said.

'Yes—shit, yes." Marty moaned.

Jonathan was scared for some reason. Marty led him
down the halls lit only with a night-light. The corridors
rolled away and ended in blackness; they passed the lounge,
the floor was covered with moonlight, the rest of the room
was full of shadows that moved as they passed the door. Jonathan couldn't remember if he'd ever been downstairs like
this at night. He didn't think so. The dark didn't usually
bother him, but it did tonight. Something was wrong. Not
here at Limekiln . . . something was wrong inside that closet.
He tried to reach the little girl again, but all he got was
coldness. She must've passed out. He did know that she was
still alive.

He walked on with Marty next to him, and the closer he
got to the door of Dr. Hall's office, the worse his fear got. He
was sweating, his hands were trembling, his heart pounded,
and the torn patch on his head throbbed. He tried to pretend
that Marty was taking him to the kitchen to raid the icebox

because he'd never finished his supper. It didn't work, and when they got in sight of the door of Dr. Hall's office and Jonathan saw the streak of light under the closed door, his fear turned to terror, and he almost broke away from Marty and ran back up the stairs to his room. That was what he wanted to do, he realized. He wanted to jump into his bed and pull the covers over his head. That was truly crazy. He'd threatened and cajoled, he'd pulled out his own hair and would probably be in pain for days and have a bald spot for the rest of his life, all to tell Dr. Hall about the little girl trapped in the closet. Now that he was about to save her, he was terrified and wanted to run away. It was because of something about her or around her. Something cold inside that closet.

Marty knocked softly and opened the door. And there, at last, was Dr. Hall. He was wearing a turtleneck sweater and no jacket. He looked tired but not annoyed, and just seeing him made Jonathan feel better for a second.

"I'm sorry, Doc," Marty said. "I didn't know what else to do."

Dr. Hall looked at Jonathan and spoke to Marty. "It's okay, Vespa. I'm sure you did the right thing."

Jonathan felt Marty's relief.

"Want me to hang around?" Marty asked.

Dr. Hall shook his head. "I'll buzz when we're done."

Marty went out and closed the door, and Dr. Hall folded his hands and leaned forward on his desk.

"What happened, Jonathan?"

Jonathan told him. It didn't take long—only about five minutes—which was shocking, since Jonathan had been living with it for so long now. Dr. Hall listened without moving or asking questions. When Jonathan was finished, Dr. Hall raised his hands, locked them behind his head, and leaned back in his chair. It was a characteristic gesture, designed to be casual, hopefully calming. But Jonathan wasn't fooled. Dr. Hall was confused and horrified and didn't know what to say or do next.

"You have to call the police," Jonathan said weakly. "The little girl is dying. . . ." He didn't mention that other feeling he'd had out in the hall . . . that there was something in there with her. It sounded crazy, even to him.

"Are you sure, Jonathan?"

Jonathan nodded.

"I don't want it to be true," said Dr. Hall quietly. "It's too hideous."

"I can't help that," Jonathan pointed out.

"Your brother thinks it's a dream. Maybe—"

Jonathan shook his head firmly. "He has to think that. He'll wind up in the bed next to mine if he doesn't. That's how Michael gets out of things—" Jonathan stopped for a second, feeling the weight of the dead puppy in his hands. "He killed our dog. Two weeks later he had convinced himself it was the dog's own fault, and now he says it was an accident. Not just *says*, Doctor, *believes*. This time he says he never hurt his wife, it was a dream, part of the DTs. I've told you he drinks."

"Yes, you have."

"In a way . . . at least for Michael . . . it *was* a dream."

"Go on."

"We don't have time."

Dr. Hall sat upright in his chair, all pretense of relaxation gone. "You're sure, Jonathan?"

Jonathan bent his head so Hall could see the bare, bloody patch on his scalp. "That sure," he said.

Hall swallowed hard. He had no idea how anyone could do such a thing to themselves, and he marveled at Jonathan. Madness was like Shakespeare's Cleopatra; time could not wither, nor use stale its infinite variety. Jonathan was crazy. He was also one of the nicest men Hall had ever known. He was also exactly what he claimed to be . . . telepathic.

Hall picked up the phone, got an outside line, and dialed the operator.

Hall had not believed it for a long time. Like Malkin at

Crescent where Jonathan was first committed, Hall thought that the claim to telepathy was simply part of Jonathan's sickness. But Jonathan puzzled him. Every psychotic Hall had even known talked, thought, and cared about one thing and one thing only. Themselves. Not that they were selfish; some were idiotically generous. But when you got inside the generosity, down to its bottom, there it was every time . . . like a ghost that wouldn't be exorcised . . . and sometimes Hall actually thought he could see it . . . the specter of total self-involvement standing pale and glittering in some corner of his office. But not with Jonathan. If it was there, Hall never found it, not even an inkling, and that puzzled him. He'd called Malkin at Crescent. Malkin was overworked, overpaid, had a private practice, and wrote popular-psych books to help people get more self-involved. Hall didn't respect him, and after he'd talked to him a couple of times about Jonathan, he didn't like him.

Malkin insisted that the telepathy claim was crap. He got annoyed when Hall wouldn't accept that on his say-so. Telepathy was crap, ESP was crap, all psi phenomena were crap, said Malkin. By the end of the conversation Hall was grinning into the phone because he almost expected Malkin to say,

"Psychiatry is crap."

After that, Hall went over Jonathan's file very carefully. Listened to the tapes with Malkin and the tapes of his own sessions with Jonathan and that same puzzling caring about other people—what they thought and felt, what frightened them, angered them, made them happy—was always there. Not just in the talking but in Jonathan's actual reactions. He seemed to have driven himself to true compassion (enough to put anyone around the bend, thought Hall at the time), and there were times when Hall would have sworn that Jonathan was looking through someone else's eyes. Of course, that didn't mean that Jonathan was telepathic, only incredibly perceptive and unfortunately sensitive to what he perceived. Then Jonathan told Hall something that he couldn't possibly know, and it turned out to be true.

Ida Barnes was a day nurse. She was big, competent, and very much in love with a man fifteen years younger than she was. Jonathan knew (so did everybody else at Limekiln). But Jonathan also knew that Ida and her lover lived in the house that Ida's mother had died in, and there were nights—more and more of them lately—when Ida's mother's ghost looked down from the attic, through the ceiling of the bedroom where she'd died, and watched with tears running down her transparent face as Ida and her young man made love.

It was ruining Ida. She couldn't sleep; she was having trouble keeping up with her job. She and her lover changed bedrooms; the face still appeared, especially on Friday nights for some reason, and watched them twining and untwining on the bed. Ida stopped making love to her young man. He really loved her and he cajoled, then threatened. Ida couldn't do it. The man packed up and left, and Ida was alone.

She had put the house up for sale; but that was in 1970, and no one was buying big old houses in New Milford back then. The ghost didn't leave with the young man, and Ida became convinced that her crime was so terrible, it never would. She hated going home. On summer nights she slept in her car. She was starting to break, and Jonathan wept for her in Hall's office and pleaded with him to help poor Ida Barnes. The ghost was real . . . at least to Ida. Jonathan had seen it glimmering in Ida's mind. The spirit was malevolent, it wanted Ida dead. Ida knew it; she was going to give in to it. Hall had listened and tried to comfort Jonathan. He didn't actually believe any of it, but Jonathan's worry was so vivid, Hall decided he'd have a talk with Ida Barnes. Just a general discussion to see if she was doing all right. He even made an appointment to see her a few days later. But the morning after the session with Jonathan, Ida Barnes locked herself in her garage, stuffed the cracks in the door with rags, and started her car.

Jonathan had screamed and cried all morning. He broke his hand trying to smash it through the window. They sedated him and kept him strapped to his bed until Hall came in in the afternoon. By then Barnes was late for work, and Hall stood over Jonathan's bed watching the drugged man. Jonathan's face was white, his eyes rolled under his closed lids, and suddenly Hall knew, with a cold jab, as if someone had stuck ice cubes down the back of his shirt, that Jonathan was right. He ran back to his office and grabbed the phone. His hands shook; the skin on his arms and the back of his neck shriveled and crept. He called the state police and waited with his heart hammering in his throat because he was going way out on a limb on the say-so of one incurable loony.

She was dead by the time the cops got there. But Jonathan had known for hours. They could have saved her if they'd listened. But all they did, with all their smarts, was give him a giant jolt of Librium and tie him to his bed.

After that, Hall decided to give Jonathan the card and color tests for telepathy. But Jonathan would not let him. He said the test would only confirm what Hall already knew, and no one else would believe, no matter what the tests showed.

They didn't have to break down the door of the Kaslov house; it was unlocked. They walked in and turned on the overhead light in the hall. Lieutenant Joseph Levin looked around. The floor tile was worn but clean. The house smelled of polish and perfume and spoiled meat. He and Baker glanced at each other.

"What smells?" Rails asked. Rails was young and smooth-faced and had only been on the force for seven months. Levin didn't want him to be the one to find it.

"You go outside, check around the yard."

"What should I look for?"

Levin looked helplessly at Baker; Baker said, "Signs of forced entry."

They waited until Rails went out the front door, then

Baker climbed the stairs and Levin went into the living room. It was shabby but clean here too. He admired Mrs. Kaslov's housekeeping. He left the lights on and went back out into the hall. The kitchen door was straight ahead. It was closed, but he saw a streak of light under it. He took a few steps; the smell got stronger. He leaned against the wall for a second with his head down; then he took a deep breath and pushed open the door.

He slipped and grabbed the doorjamb. He looked down; the floor was covered with thick liquids of different colors. He'd slipped in a blob of white lotion-type stuff. Some other stuff was green, some beige and looked like face makeup. The room reeked of competing perfumes, but the other smell was there; stronger than it had been in the hall. Broken glass glittered around his feet. He took another step; the soles of his shoes crunched the glass. He moved along the wall a foot, then saw the woman's body.

"Oh, shit," he whispered.

The doctor from Limekiln had told him what he'd find, and he should have been prepared. But it was a weird call, and Levin had hoped that the doctor was mistaken or drunk.

He leaned against the wall and called, "Baker . . ."

He heard Baker come to the head of the stairs.

"It's in here," Levin yelled, "the kitchen."

He heard Baker on the stairs and then in the hall. He felt like a fool, cowering against the wall, and he forced himself to move out, across the floor to the body. He stood over it for a second, then looked around for a phone. There was no point in feeling around for pulse; she was dead and had been for a couple of days anyway.

He saw the wall phone over the counter and went to it as Baker shoved open the door.

"Watch it," Levin yelled, "there's some slippery junk all over the floor."

Baker moved slowly into the room as Levin talked into the phone. He saw the body, froze, and turned dead white. Levin covered the mouthpiece.

"Don't fucking faint on me . . . open the goddamn door, get some air."

Baker raced across the room and yanked the kitchen door open. Levin noticed that it wasn't locked, either. Baker stuck his head outside, and Levin heard him taking big gulps of fresh air. Levin ordered a homicide crew, and Baker's head came back in the room. He was still pale but not sick-white.

"Why homicide?" he asked.

Levin covered the mouthpiece again. "The back of her head's bashed in and there's a bloody hammer on the floor."

Just then Rails appeared at the open back door.

"No sign . . . " he started, then he saw the body. Baker and Levin didn't know what to expect, but the kid just paled, then turned around with military precision and marched down off the porch.

"What do we do now?" Baker asked.

Levin was a lieutenant, Baker would carry out his orders. But Levin had none to give. He didn't know what to do, either. Suddenly Baker cried, "The kid. We gotta find the kid."

Levin had forgotten about the kid. There was no way Dr. Hall could have known about a child locked in a closet for days, unless he'd locked it in there himself. Highly unlikely that he'd do that, then call the police. The whole thing was unlikely, Levin thought.

But Hall had been right about the dead woman.

"The guy said it was in a closet."

Levin had seen a closet in the hall, and there was one here on the other side of the kitchen. He crossed the floor carefully, walking wide around the corpse, to the door. He tried the handle; it was locked, the key was gone. It was an old-fashioned lock, and he could have forced the tongue back easily, but molding on the edge of the door covered the slit. He pried at the molding with the tips of his fingers. It was an old house, well built. The molding was probably nailed and glued, or whatever they did back in the thirties, and it was on there to stay. He banged on the door and called.

"Anyone in there?"

There was no answer. He squatted down and looked through the keyhole. The closet was dark. He stood up.

"Maybe the key's in here. I'll look. You check the hall closet and the ones upstairs."

Baker rushed out of the room, and Levin started opening drawers. He found a bunch of keys. None of them were labeled, but they weren't the right type. If he could find a needle-nosed plier, he could unlock the door, but the Kazlovs didn't keep one. He found a screwdriver and left it out on the counter in case he had to pry the molding off, after all.

He thought he heard a rustle, and he stopped and stared at the closet door. It was quiet again. Baker came back.

"Nothing up there."

Levin nodded at the broom closet door and started to say that the kid must be in there, but he'd need help to get the door open, when he saw the glitter of metal in the corpse's closed fist.

"Oh, shit," he said softly.

Baker saw where Levin was looking, and he turned white again.

"It could be the key," Levin said.

Baker shook his head. "I can't do it, Joe. I mean it, I *can't* do it."

Levin came close to the body and squatted next to it. Behind him, Baker moaned, and Levin tried a trick that Lem Gooding had told him to do years ago . . . .

Lem had been on the NYPD for twenty years before he took his pension and got a job up here. He had once told Levin, "If it's bad—not that it'll happen, mind you—this is country, almost, and the people have space. They ain't sittin' on each other's heads. But people can lose it anywhere. And if they do and it's really bad, why, then, you've just got to empty your mind. I mean, totally. And turn off your senses. You can do it, Joe. Christ knows I've done it. I remember once we found these little girls about seven—their mommy had smothered them and dumped them in a tub full of water and Drāno . . . " He had seen the look on Levin's face and had taken pity on him. "Point is," he went on, "just shut yourself down. Sometimes singing helps. Any song."

Levin tried to blank out his mind, to imagine that the tips of his fingers were wood and his sense of smell was dead, and he reached out toward the swollen hand. He started to hum. He knew several songs but couldn't think of one this minute except "Waltzing Matilda." He hummed it, and as his hand touched the corpse's, he started singing the words.

"Joe, you okay?" Baker cried.

Levin sang softly and desperately.

" 'You'll come a waltzing Matilda with me . . . ' "

Gooding was right, people lost it up here just like they did anywhere, and by now Levin had seen it all, or almost all. He wasn't a kid. But this one was the kind of bad that Gooding meant. Not the gore . . . he'd seen worse than this. Old people who had died up in some shack in the hills and lain on their kitchen floor or in their beds for days or weeks before anyone found them. And accidents on the new highway with people twisted up in the wreckage of their cars. He'd seen a couple of kids murdered by their fathers; wives by their husbands. (No husbands murdered by their wives yet, but times were changing, and he imagined that was in the cards too.) He'd seen one mother shot in the face by her own son, and brothers stabbed by brothers. All bad. But there was something truly horrible about this one. Maybe because she was a young woman, and he could tell that a few days ago she'd been pretty, and her black hair had been clean and shining. Then someone—the husband probably, he'd bet on the husband—had come in here and smashed her bottles of makeup and the lotions she used to keep her skin soft and smeared the stuff in her hair, spilled garbage on the floor, and smashed her head in with a hammer.

He was as angry as he was sick, angry and full of pity. He concentrated on the words of the song.

" ' . . . And he sang as he sat and waited by the billa-bong . . . ' "

Behind him, the kitchen door opened. "Who's singing?" Rails asked. He sounded terrified.

Levin touched the dead hand and the trick was working because he felt nothing. But if the hand was stiff and the key locked in it, he'd have to pry the fingers open or break them back, and then nothing would protect him. He could sing the last act of *Turandot* or a medley of Shubert songs, but if he had to crack open those fishy green fingers, he would be sick. It was all right, though. He lifted the hand, the fingers fell open like fringe, and the key to the closet hit the floor with a ring.

Hall and Jonathan waited for the police to call. Out in the hall the big old grandfather clock struck midnight, and Dr. Hall jumped, then smiled at Jonathan. "I almost dozed off."

They were quiet, then Hall said, "You told me that it *was* a dream for your brother. What do you mean?"

Jonathan did not want to talk about Michael. Michael was done for.

"What did you mean?" Hall asked again.

He owed Hall an explanation; he owed Hall everything. Hall waited, Jonathan finished the last of the cookies that Marty had brought up from the kitchen, gulped down the milk. Hall was still waiting, but Jonathan didn't know what to say. He could tell him that Michael was mean, but that wasn't true. Mean or selfish implied intent toward other people, but Michael's intentions never had anything to do with anybody else. Still Hall waited, and finally Jonathan said, "We were on this bus one day. I don't remember where we were going; probably to the movies. That's all kids did in those days . . . go to the movies. So we're on this bus. Our mother's dead by then, and this . . . thing . . . had already happened to me. We're riding along, swaying with the bus, like the other people, not thinking about much of anything, and suddenly I get this feeling that poor Mickey's scared of something, and I look over at him."

As he talked, Jonathan carefully brushed cookie crumbs into his palm and put them into Dr. Hall's ashtray. He kept his eyes on the desktop and the empty cookie plate.

"Mickey's face is white, and he's chewing his underlip. So I ask him what's wrong, but he only shakes his head and goes on chewing his lip. At first I don't get anything but the fear. A little kid's fear, although Michael was fifteen at the time. Then I realize that the other people on the bus are scaring him and I look around us. But they're just people on a bus on a Saturday, you know. Women with string bags, wearing little hats . . . they all wore hats back then . . . men in heavy jackets, some with boots. Just going their own way, not even knowing that Michael was there. And suddenly it hits me that that's what's frightening the kid. There they are, some forty or fifty people or however many you get on a bus, going about their business, not caring if Michael Kaslov lives or dies. And they're all *real*. That scares Michael. They're separate, and worst of all, they are as important to themselves as Michael is to himself, and that terrifies Michael."

Jonathan raised his eyes. "You see, he was a beautiful little boy; he's a beautiful man. We all spoiled him. My dad worst of all. Even the other kids spoiled him, especially little girls. Then women spoiled him. Women are greedy of beauty. Anyway, he gets this feeling, I guess for the first time in his life, about those people on the bus . . . the *others* . . . and it scares the shit out of him. I hoped it would start something good. That he wouldn't forget what he knew that second. But he pushes it down, and I feel him doing it. So there we are, two kids riding the Post Road on a chilly Saturday, and I know that my brother's making ghosts out of all of us in his mind. Turning us into dreams. We aren't even planets revolving around him. We're wisps of smoke, mist on a cool morning . . . dreams . . . He could not *murder* his wife . . . she never existed."

Jonathan stared fixedly at Hall.

"Jonathan?"

Jonathan hugged himself.

"Cold," he said, "freezing." He hugged himself closer. "You'd better stop them."

"What are you talking about?"

Jonathan didn't know what to tell him. He was too cold to talk. He thought of mammoths trapped in ice, ax heads in the snow, worms crawling through freezing mud and bones in a graveyard. He made a sound but no words; his tongue was frozen. The cold was in the closet. Something had gotten into the closet or the little girl had brought it in with her, and it had gotten bigger, turned solid, and grew old and invincible in three days. They were letting her out, *it* was coming out with her, and Jonathan moaned.

He heard the key to the closet scratch in the lock, the knob turned, but she didn't notice. She was staring at that wall with the broom and mop, and her mind was freezing and empty.

The door was going to open.

"Don't," Jonathan cried.

"Jonathan . . . "

Jonathan didn't hear him. It was too late. The door was opening smoothly . . . no creaky hinges, no sound of maniacal laughter, but there should be. Now the door was open; light filled the closet. A low, pleasant voice spoke to the little girl, and she knew someone was there, even though she couldn't see or hear. Strong hands touched her, lifted her.

"No," Jonathan shrieked. The office door banged open and Marty raced in.

It was too late; she was cradled against a big solid chest, and the little girl and the ghastly cold thing—whatever it was —were carried together out of the closet and into the kitchen.

FOUR

LEVIN HAD NEVER felt so sorry for anyone in his life. He carried her out of the kitchen, shielding her face so she wouldn't see the body on the floor. He carried her into the living room and laid her gently on the couch. She didn't seem to see him. She didn't blink.

Her lips were swollen and cracked. He propped her up with one of the back pillows, then went into the kitchen and filled a glass of water. The kitchen was empty except for the corpse. Baker must have gotten out of there; he was probably standing at the car with Rails, waiting for the homicide crew —all two of them—and the ambulance.

Levin carried the water back to the living room. She had not moved. One arm dangled off the end of the couch, white and boneless-looking. He brought the glass over, put the rim against her puffy lips, and tipped it slightly. Water dribbled down her chin; her tongue was swollen and maybe her throat was, too, so she couldn't swallow. He dipped his fingers into the water and wet her lips with it. She didn't try to lick it. He had a horrible feeling that she was going to die right in front of him. He had read about concentration camp inmates who'd survived for years, only to die a day or two after the camps were liberated. Their veins had collapsed and the medics couldn't find any way to feed them. He lifted the limp arm and looked at the underside, but he didn't know what collapsed veins looked like.

He leaned over and looked into her eyes. They were empty.

"How long were you in there, honey?" he asked softly.

He heard sirens; the backup and the ambulance were in the block. She didn't seem to hear the noise.

"What's your name?"

No response.

He sat back on his haunches, holding the glass of water.

"Don't die," he commanded her softly. "Hang on a couple of minutes more, kid. Don't die."

The sirens screamed up to the front of the house and stopped, red lights flashed along the windows, and the front door crashed open.

"In here," he yelled.

Two men in white charged into the living room. Her eyes were still open, pulse still beat in her neck, and Levin wanted to collapse with relief.

One medic knelt on the floor next to her. He snapped his fingers in front of her face; nothing happened. He clapped, then he broke a vial of something and waved it under her nose. She blinked several times in succession. Levin saw tears fill her eyes, but they didn't focus. The other medic stood at the door looking helpless.

The first medic ran his fingertips expertly along her lips, looked into her mouth, raised an eyelid, and flashed a pencil light. He said, without looking up at Levin, "Where was she?"

"Broom closet."

"How long?"

"I don't know," Levin answered. "A couple of days, maybe three."

The medic pinched the skin on her arm and said softly, "Son of a bitch, son of a fucking bitch." He barked at medic two. "Get me saline and five-percent glucose. Don't forget the tubing."

The second medic raced out, and medic one, muttering obscenities, pulled open the dirty nightie, listened at her chest, then took her pulse. Levin watched silently. The medic opened his bag and took out a syringe.

"What are you giving her?" Levin asked.

"Epinephrine. She's in shock. We got a thready pulse."

"Will she live?" Levin asked. He couldn't bear to hear the answer because he had the feeling that if this nice-looking young man with the spiky blond hair and pink skin told him that the little girl was done for, Levin would throttle him and break the windows and every piece of furniture in the house.

The medic glared up at him. "How the fuck should I know?"

Levin wanted to talk to someone, but the house was dark and silent, and Jeannie was asleep. Her face looked smooth, peaceful, and young. One flannel-covered shoulder stuck up out of the comforter, and he reached out to touch it, then stopped. She'd listen to his horror story, all right, and she'd cry. Which would be great because it would keep him from crying. But he'd get over it (maybe) and he knew she wouldn't. Not for a long time, anyway. It wasn't fair, and he let his hand fall to his side without touching her, and he went into the bathroom to undress so he wouldn't disturb her. He meant to get right into bed, but he knew he wouldn't sleep. He put on his robe and slippers, left the bedroom, and went down the hall to the stairs. Greta's door was open; her night-light, shaped like a green pig, cast a dim light, throwing shadows across the walls and making the corners black and impenetrable. He thought the shadows would be scarier than plain dark, but Greta wouldn't sleep without the light.

Her room was pretty; Jeannie had chosen everything carefully. The curtains were frilly white with butterflies and flowers printed on the fabric, the walls were light yellow, and the comforter matched the curtains. He knew her closet and the drawers were full of clean clothes, most of them new. Her shoes were clean (except the sneakers), her toy chest overflowed, and the white bookcase was full of picture books. She was safe, warm, and looked after.

"You're lucky, baby," he whispered at the half-open door, and went down the stairs to the kitchen.

He poured himself a glass of milk and tore open a carton of Fig Newtons. It was after one when he finished the snack, and he called the hospital. A Dr. Brewer took the call.

"Yes, Lieutenant, what can I do for you?"

Levin wanted to shout at him to keep Amy Kaslov alive, but he spoke mildly. "I just wanted to know how she was doing."

"She's not responding."

"But is she going to make it?" Levin asked.

"She'll live if that's what you mean," Brewer said.

Levin wanted to be alone with her, but Dr. Brewer leaned against the wall near the door. He was tall and thin; his white coat hung from his shoulder like a drape. His face was expressionless, but Levin could feel him watching.

Her eyes were open and blank. He touched her shoulder.

"Amy?" She didn't hear him.

He leaned over the bed, and his eyes looked directly into hers. Her eyes roved his face, then looked at the ceiling, at the wall. She didn't see him.

"Amy?" he whispered. She blinked, the movement startled him, and her eyes went back to their aimless, unseeing wandering. He looked away.

"She doesn't see me."

"No," Brewer said.

"Why?"

Brewer shrugged. "Shock, I suppose. Some kind of protective psychological membrane. Your partner said there was an old-fashioned keyhole in the closet door. She probably saw her mother beaten to death. She won't want to see anything after that. Not for a while, anyway."

"How long?"

Brewer did not answer.

"I asked—"

"I heard you, Lieutenant. I don't know. Maybe a few days, maybe a week. Maybe a long time."

"What's a long time?"

"Years," Brewer said softly, and as Brewer said that, the little girl's eyes focused for an instant and looked into Levin's. Suddenly Levin was freezing, and he wanted to yell at Brewer to put the goddamn radiator on and throw him a blanket, before he froze to death. But he couldn't talk. He had read in stories that people's blood ran cold, and some poor bastard in the Bible (or somewhere) had his tongue cleave to the roof of his mouth. All bullshit, Levin would have said a second ago. But not now, because it was happening to him, and he knew that a radiator or a blanket wouldn't help . . . nothing would.

All at once his hand moved without his knowing it was going to. It moved slowly and deliberately, and he watched in horrified fascination because he didn't know what it was going to do, and he didn't think he could stop it. He made a sound of some kind, and he heard Brewer move closer. His hand kept going, numb and shaking with cold. It picked up the pitcher of crushed ice on the table next to her bed and poured cold water in a glass with a bent straw in it. Then he put the pitcher down and picked up the glass. The hair on his arms stood up stiff, the skin on his neck crept, and the hand . . . his hand . . . brought the glass and straw to the little girl's mouth, and it held it there. The little girl's white, cracked lips, with their shredded skin, sucked in the straw, and she sipped.

"She's drinking," he croaked.

Brewer said, "She's not comatose. She can drink on her own. Eat, too, probably."

She closed her eyes, and the cold stopped as suddenly as it had started. He put the glass back on the table. Brewer touched his shoulder and Levin jumped.

"You okay?" Brewer asked.

No, Levin wanted to yell. How did he know she wanted water? He didn't even know that the pitcher was on the table. Except that he did, he told himself. There was always a pitcher of crushed ice on hospital bed tables.

"You look a little green," Brewer said. "Let's get a cup of coffee."

The snack bar was in the basement. Brewer brought cups of scalding, sour coffee to the table along with two slices of dry pound cake.

Levin wrapped his hands around the cup for warmth, even though he wasn't cold anymore. On the contrary, he had started to sweat, and he felt like he used to when he and Morgan Donahue would sneak into old Mr. Blair's icehouse on blazing July afternoons. First the cold was blessed, and they played in the straw among the huge, blue blocks of ice. Then, before they knew it, their fingers were cold and they started to shiver. But they'd gone to too much trouble to sneak in here, and they had to stay until they just couldn't stand it anymore. When they came outside, everything looked white and the heat was a wall. They shivered harder for a few minutes, then they started to sweat until their polo shirts and shorts were soaked and their wet underwear stuck in their crotches. He had had three colds that summer, and Morgan five.

His shirt was sticking to his back now, the way it had after coming out of the icehouse. Sweat ran down his sides, and he squirmed in the chrome-and-vinyl chair.

Brewer had said something; Levin didn't hear what. Then Brewer asked, "Are you okay, Lieutenant?"

Levin burned his tongue on the coffee and said that he was fine.

"I asked if you knew who killed the woman."

"The husband, probably. Woman across the street saw his truck parked out front from ten to eleven or so on Saturday night. Eve Kaslov was killed about that time. And there're fresh prints on the hammer; we'll know whose they are by afternoon. But you can put your money on the husband."

"Have you brought him in yet?"

"No, but we will. Stupid bastard skipped in the same truck, apparently."

"I don't get it," Brewer said.

"Get what? It happens all the time, even up here. Fathers kill kids. Mothers too. Brothers kill each other, children kill their parents. Don't you read the papers?"

"I don't mean that. I mean, why'd the woman wait so long to call you?"

"What woman?"

"The woman across the street. She hears a woman getting beaten to death, then waits three days to call the cops. I don't get it."

"She didn't call."

"Who did? And why did they wait so long . . ."

"That's a good question. I should have asked it."

Levin stood up. His thigh hit the table edge and knocked the Styrofoam cup over. Grayish-brown liquid ran steaming across the plastic top. He took a wrinkled card out of his pocket and put it on the table in front of Brewer. Coffee soaked the edge.

"My home phone's on there too," Levin said. "Call me when the kid comes around."

It had rained all night; wind blew the trees bare. Wet leaves made the roads slick, and Levin had to drive slowly. It took him over an hour to get to Limekiln. The state asylum was in a pretty spot, the foothills of the Berkshires, the brochures would call it. The building itself looked like an old-time mountain resort; the kind that was abandoned in the fifties because it was huge, hard to heat, and looked gloomy and haunted unless the sun was shining right on it.

He parked at the front steps and got out of the car. A short man wearing a sport shirt and heavy cardigan yelled, "No parking. You see that sign, no parking."

Levin flashed his badge at the man and started up the steps.

"I don't care," the man wailed. "You can't park there."

Levin ignored him. The man started to sob. "Oh, my God, the steps are blocked. What'll I do . . . ?"

Levin raced up the last few steps and through the double doors into the lobby. He looked back; the man was standing on the stone steps with his face in his hands, the wind whipping at his sweater. An orderly was with him, touching his shoulder gently. Levin turned around. The lobby was enormous. There was a fine old wooden counter with a switchboard behind it and a wall of empty cubbyholes that must have held keys and messages for long-departed guests.

A fiftyish woman with fuzzy red hair and thick glasses sat at the switchboard reading a paperback. Levin showed the badge.

"Lieutenant Levin, state police. A Dr. Hall called us from here late last night. I have to speak to him."

"Dr. Hall is here," she said. "I'm sure he'll be able to see you shortly. Would you like to sit down?"

She motioned to a bank of benches built into the walls, with old, thin cushions on the seat. It was hard, the back was cold, and he sat stiffly, waiting. The lobby was empty except for the woman, but he heard distant noises. He'd never been out here before, and he half expected babbling, screams, and crazy laughter, but the noises were normal enough; muffled voices talking, the sound of a typewriter, a door closing. He heard footsteps, and a big man about thirty came into the lobby. He had a coarse but nice face, and the muscles in his arms and shoulders strained the white linen coat he wore. The woman behind the desk said, "This is Lieutenant Levin, Marty. He's here to see Dr. Hall."

"Right this way," said the big man. Levin followed him out of the lobby and down a wood-floored hallway. The floor was waxed, the wall was half paneled. They passed a big room with TV going and huge windows looking out on the grounds. A few people clustered around the TV, and four women sat at a table playing cards. They passed the room, and went into a hall that was long and dark, except for gray afternoon light coming through an old-fashioned window at the end. It looked to be fifty feet away, and he realized that the place was even bigger than it seemed from the outside.

The orderly led him to a door and knocked softly. Then he opened it, and Levin stepped through into a bare outer office. He crossed it to an open door.

A man behind an old oak desk stood up. He was much shorter than Levin, and he had a small head and delicate features. His hair was straight and sandy, and his skin pale and fine-grained for a man. He would have been pretty except for a good solid jaw and mouth. He smiled and held out his hand.

"Jeffrey Hall," he said.

Levin shook it and introduced himself.

Hall said, "Thank God the child is all right. I called the station at Bridgeton this morning and they told me she was alive when you found her—"

Levin interrupted. "Why did you call us?"

Hall sat down behind the desk and leaned his forehead on his hand. He seemed to be staring hard at a pencil.

"How did you know about the woman and the little girl?" Levin asked. Hall did not answer.

"Dr. Hall . . ."

"I'm going to tell you," Hall said quietly. "I'm just trying to figure out how to do it. It doesn't matter though, because you're not going to believe me."

Levin was startled, the office was silent, and outside, down that long, gloomy hallway somewhere, a big clock struck four. It was getting dark; the daylight coming through the window behind the doctor's desk seemed tarnished. The polished furniture, waxed floor, and the worn Turkish rug under his feet acquired a glow. The room, the man behind the desk, the whole place suddenly seemed unreal, and he wanted to get out of there; back down the stone steps, past the nut who wept when he parked in front of them, and home to his wife. But he was too curious. His worst failing, his mother had told him once. He could have been a lawyer or a doctor or a CPA, because he was handsome and smart and they'd saved money for his college. But he had to be a cop because cops saw things that no one else did. Cops saw everything. His curiosity ruined his career chances, his mother had told him. His curiosity would probably ruin his whole life and get him killed in the bargain.

The old lady understood her son, and Levin knew that the rug under his feet could catch fire, and he would stay put until Hall told him how he had known that Eve Kaslov was dead and her daughter locked in the broom closet.

Hall said, "A patient told me."

"How did the patient know?" Levin asked.

"This is the part you won't believe. I'd lie, but I can't think of one that'll make sense. Besides, I've wanted to say it out loud for a long time now. Years. This is a good chance, don't you think? I mean, you're a cop, not a fellow shrink. You might think I'm bananas, but you won't noise it around at psych meetings."

Things were getting bizarre. Levin stayed quiet because he didn't know what else to do. Hall took a breath and said, "He knew because he saw it in someone's mind."

Levin thought he'd heard wrong, then he didn't know what to think. Maybe Hall had been with crazies for too many years. Levin looked at his hands, then past Hall at a color photograph of one of those incredible Connecticut views from Roxbury or Woodbury or Southbury, where the land falls away and hills undulate east, some twenty or thirty miles to Long Island Sound. Finally he made himself look at Hall, right into the man's eyes.

"Okay, Doctor," he said, keeping his voice neutral. "He saw it in somebody's mind."

The days were getting short, it was dark when Levin left Limekiln. Black shadows crouched along the shoulder of the road; bare tree branches were skinny claws shaking in the wind. He flicked on the brights to drive back the shadows. For the first time in his life he'd heard more than he wanted to know, and he wanted to rush home, climb into bed, and pull the covers over his head. He'd felt that way when he was eight and he and Tom Sparry had seen their first Wolfman movie.

He had just pulled into his street when he remembered that the house was empty. Tonight was the General Starr School Harvest Festival, and he'd promised his daughter that he would be there. She'd been working on the costume up in the attic for weeks, and tonight was the unveiling. She would look for him.

The program was supposed to start at seven. It was ten after by the time he parked in the school lot and walked quickly through the front door. But the auditorium doors were still propped open, the lights were on, and Jeannie was craning around, looking for him. She saw him and waved, and he started down the aisle. Half the people in town were there. He knew most of them and they knew him. Bobby Everett stopped him with another light-bulb joke. Levin laughed dutifully and was aware that another night, after any day but this one, he would have laughed easily and heartily. Then Bobby invited him to stop down at his roadhouse off of I 84 for an afternoon beer. On the house, of course. Next Miss Cole, who taught eighth-grade music, stopped him to complain again about the Grogans' six cats, who yowled all night and "did their business" all over her herb garden. He promised to talk to the Grogans and moved on. Then Sam Albright caught his arm and told him that he'd pulled in a shitload of hubbard squash, and if Levin stopped by, he could load up enough for the whole winter. Assuming anybody in the family could stand hubbard squash. Albright's kids hated it. Levin laughed again, a small, phony giggle that didn't sound like him at all, and he told Albright that he'd get the free squash down Paulie and Greta's gullets somehow.

Finally he slid into the seat Jeannie had saved for him. He kissed her and reached around her to touch Paulie's shoulder. Paulie glanced at his father uninterestedly, then looked back at the stage.

Levin sat back. He was used to Paulie's rebuffs; he knew

that his son didn't like him very much. Jeannie said it was just a stage the boy was going through. All fourteen-year-old boys hated and feared their fathers and wanted their power for themselves. Levin didn't believe it. He had always loved *his* father. The old man had been dead three years and Levin still missed him. Besides, he didn't think that Paulie liked his mother much, either. In fact, Paulie didn't seem to like anybody, the coterie of boys he hung around with. They were Westerly boys from nice families. They'd been Paulie's friends since kindergarten, and Levin had watched them grow. But he'd never liked them much, except for Timmy. Levin had always had a soft spot for Timmy Cassini.

Finally the auditorium lights dimmed, the curtain jerked open, and the Harvest Festival began. The children were dressed as vegetables. he wouldn't have recognized Greta, except that he knew from bits of felt and papier-mâché he'd seen around the house that she would be green. So she was, covered from head to foot in a sheath of green shaped to look like a pea pod. She had even painted her sneakers green to match. It was a good costume; it looked more realistic and carefully made than the ear of corn next to her, or the tomato. It wasn't quite as good as the pumpkin, but Levin was sure that the mother had helped whoever was under the pumpkin, and Greta had done hers all alone, except for a few frantic phone calls to her best friend Cissy Simms for advice.

Applause erupted from the audience; there were whistles and calls of bravo. The fathers tried to outshout each other, and Levin joined them, yelling "Bravo, peapod." He started to enjoy himself, then the applause and shouting simmered down, and the first third-grader, a little girl wearing a balloon of dark purple, stepped to the front of the stage.

"I am an eggplant," she said. And went on to tell the audience where she was grown in Litchfield County, Connecticut, in what quantity, how much was used locally, how much shipped away. Greta came after the tomato. Her voice was steady, and Levin could hear that she was trying to make it deeper.

He had never heard Amy Kaslov's voice. She had not made a sound when he carried her out of the closet. She didn't whimper when the young medic stuck the IV needle in the back of her hand. She was silent in the hospital. Maybe she would stay mute, as well as blind, for a long time. Years, Brewer had said. Maybe she never would speak again. She looked like her uncle. Same dark hair and slightly slanted eyes; the Slav look that came to Hartford and New Haven with the Ukrainians and Poles who'd come to work in wire plants, hat factories, and witch-hazel distilleries back around the turn of the century. They were handsome people, and Levin supposed that Jonathan Kaslov was a good-looking man. But his face had frightened Levin.

First off, Levin knew the man was crazy. That alone scared him. Madness frightened most people. He'd read that the crazies who screamed, cried, laughed, and sang to themselves on the New York streets were never mugged because madness scared muggers more than a gun or a vicious dog. He didn't blame them. And then, if just knowing about his madness hadn't been enough, there had been that bare patch on Kaslov's head. It was raw and weeping and starting to scab. He had leaned forward to talk, Levin saw the scraped, bare patch that looked like rats had gotten at Kaslov's scalp, and Levin felt his gorge rise.

But Kaslov sounded quite reasonable. "I didn't mean to wait three days," he said.

"He was drugged," Hall explained.

Then it was Kaslov's turn. "You see, I had a sort of fit when I realized what my brother had done. They sedated me, of course. It was the normal thing to do. But I was more or less out for a long time, except for seeing the seasons change. Which, of course, I didn't really see. I told Dr. Hall as soon as I was . . . conscious. Or almost as soon. And he called you at once."

Levin didn't know what to say. Hall went along with all the bullshit for some reason. Maybe he'd been treating Jonathan Kaslov for too long, and through the years he'd come to believe it; probably wanted to believe it. Most people wanted to believe garbage like this and Levin was disgusted, but he didn't show it. He said calmly, "You mean that your brother confessed to you . . ."

"Oh, no. He didn't even know that he'd done it. He had buried the whole thing, thought he'd fallen down and scratched his hands when he was drunk and that what he'd done to his wife and daughter was a dream."

"So he told you his dream and you believed it," Levin said. Levin was sure that he had the answer now. Michael Kaslov had come here, told his brother that he'd hit his wife with a hammer and left his daughter locked in a broom closet, and Jonathan Kaslov went bonkers. An appropriate enough reaction, Levin thought, no matter how nuts the guy was. So they drugged him out, and when he came to two days later, he sucked in his buddy-therapist Hall, saying he'd read his brother's mind, and finally the police were called. It made sense and satisfied Levin. He stood up to leave.

"But he didn't tell me his dream," Kaslov said. "He didn't *tell* me anything."

Levin looked at the pale man and wanted to cry for Amy Kaslov. This poor, sad nut and the killer father were the only family that she had.

The instant Levin thought about Amy, Jonathan Kaslov's body shuddered, and his eyes fixed on Levin. They were piercing and blank at the same time, and Levin reached up behind him for the doorknob. He'd never seen anyone look like that before. The blankness wasn't the kind that Levin had seen when he'd interrupted somebody's daydream. The blankness in Kaslov's eyes was total, as if a wall had come down behind his face or he'd been struck blind on the spot. The eyes didn't move; Levin turned the knob, ready to shove the door open behind him and get the hell out of there.

He got the door open a little. A rush of cool air from the outer office hit the back of his neck and made him shiver. The blank eyes watching him widened a little. "Don't do it, Mr. Levin. Don't take her home with you."

He had thought it. Only fractionally, only for a second as he'd come out of the hospital this morning, but he had thought it. He knew that they'd put her in a foster home. They'd pay the foster family, and some of them were decent folk, trying to help out. But some just wanted the money or worse. They'd stint on food, they'd ignore her if she was lucky, beat her if she wasn't. There might be some son of a bitch who liked little girls—it had happened before—and he'd do things to her and make her do things to him. As Levin had left the hospital this morning Amy Kaslov's alternatives had come to him in a flash, and they were all lousy. Then, for some reason, he saw her in his kitchen. Jeannie loved little girls; Greta wanted a sister. It wouldn't hurt Paulie to have a stranger around who hadn't gotten into the habit of indulging him. Levin wouldn't mind having her around, either. He would never forget the pity he'd felt when he had carried her out of the closet; besides, he was curious about what she would be like. Of course, they couldn't take in a comatose child who couldn't see, hear or speak and had to stay hooked up to an IV. But if she came out of it, she would simply be an orphan child who needed a place to live and food and affection, and help to forget that she'd seen her father murder her mother.

Jeannie could do it. Jeannie's love and decency were stronger than all the small-time evils on earth. He'd suspected as much after their first date when she'd saved half of her after-the-movie hamburger to feed a lame raccoon that was hanging around Sutter Road. They had driven back to the spot where she usually saw the raccoon, and in the headlights of his father's car Levin saw a small, furry body on the side of the road. He kept going, hoping she wouldn't see it, but she did. She made him stop, got out, and went up to the raccoon, and after a second of cursing his luck (he'd planned a heavy necking session up in the hills overlooking the few lights of Bridgeton), he followed her. She squatted down next to the small body, holding out the sandwich, hoping maybe that it was only stunned.

"It's dead," Levin said.

A boy came out of a shacky house and crossed the road. He was carrying a .22 rifle, and his eyes were mean in the moonlight.

"I put it out of its misery," the boy said.

Jeannie had looked at him, then at the gun, then at the coon. Levin was very curious to see what she'd say. He was sure that she'd be angry. "Someone should put *you* out of your misery," she'd tell the boy. Or, "All you son-of-a-bitch rednecks know how to do is kill." But Jeannie didn't get angry. Levin saw tears shine on her cheeks in the summer moonlight. "I brought him some food," she said softly.

The boy's voice softened too. "He just would've died, anyways. No way he could forage for himself." He looked at the sandwich she held. She noticed and said, "Would you like it? We've just eaten and it would be a shame to waste it."

Yessiree, guys and gals, Levin had thought this morning as he pushed open the door of Millbridge Hospital, Jeannie Jacobs Levin would be the best thing that could happen to Amy Kaslov.

"You're wrong," Jonathan Kaslov said softly. Then Kaslov grabbed the handles of his chair and pushed himself half upright. The light shone on the scabrous patch of bare scalp, his dead eyes stared into Levin's, and he intoned, "Why was it so cold in the room, Mr. Levin? How did she make you give her a glass of water without asking for it?"

Levin had smashed open the door and charged across the outer office into the long, gloomy hallway.

Amy had heard voices; they were far away and rose and fell like the ocean. She didn't recognize them and she didn't listen. She didn't think she could hear them even if she wanted to. She dreamed, and at first the dreams were lovely. She went fishing with her mother; they were on Candlewood and pulled in a little round flatfish. A sunfish, her mother said, but too small to keep, and Amy was delighted. She held the fish tenderly, gently pried the hook from its mouth, then slipped it over the side back into the water. The little fish floated, and Amy was afraid it was dead; but then it gave splash and sliced down through the water, out of sight. In another dream Nana was alive, and they were having a picnic near the rushing stream. It was snowing, but the snow was soft and warm and there was no wind. Then the dream changed; she was watching a man split wood; the air was full of splinters and it was getting cold and dark. She wanted to go back to the house where Nana had cocoa waiting. She asked the man, and he looked down at her, his ax raised over his head. His face was smooth and featureless, as though he wore a stocking mask. The ax trembled against the sky, and features started to form out of the gauze of his face. Amy got scared. She knew that face would be the worst thing she had ever seen, and she whimpered and tried to run. . . .

"Amy."

This voice was familiar; it was a good voice, but the dream kept on.

Her feet were glued to the ground, she couldn't move, and all the time that face was coming out of the oblivion, getting clearer and more horrible. She pulled at her own legs, trying to unstick them, but it was no use. She put her hands over her eyes and heard the ax whoosh down at her. It hit her wrists and chopped her hands off. She felt them slide down the front of her body and hit the ground with a plop.

"Amy," the nice voice called again, and she came to. Her eyes focused; she saw a wall and the dream monster at the same time. It had her father's face. Then all she saw was the wall with a colored print of Mickey Mouse on it, smiling at her. He was an old friend; she'd adored him when she was very young, and she smiled back. She turned her head and saw Mrs. Scott, the Avon Lady, sitting next to her bed.

"Hello," Mrs. Scott said.

"Hello." Amy's voice sounded rusty, and she cleared her throat. "Did you bring the clothes for my mother?" she asked.

Mrs. Scott looked miserable.

She said, "I went to the house yesterday. There was a police notice on the door, so I called them, and they told me that you were here."

Amy looked around to see where "here" was. The room was unfamiliar: the walls were gray-green; there was an empty bed next to hers with an open curtain hanging from a track on the ceiling. Next to her bed was a long window that looked out on a bare tree. The gold-and-red leaves were gone; winter was starting.

When Nana was sick last summer, Amy visited her once. Nana's room was like this one, except that there were more beds.

"I'm in a hospital," she said.

Mrs. Scott nodded. "The police brought you here on Tuesday night. You've been . . . sleeping since then. The doctor wasn't sure when you'd wake up or what you would remember when you did."

Amy gazed at Mickey Mouse. He seemed to be encouraging her. It wasn't any use, anyway; she must remember or go back to sleep. But the dreams were as bad as reality: she had no place to hide, and she let herself remember. She saw the wall in the closet with the word *dead* superimposed over the broom and ironing board. She smelled lemon polish and saw her mother's pitiful walleye, full of blood. She looked through the keyhole again and saw her mother's body swelling like a rotting orange on the kitchen floor.

"I remember everything," she said tonelessly. Her voice made Betty Scott think of an answering machine, and she could not take anymore. She'd done all she could, and she knew she'd cry like a baby tonight as she put away the clothes that she'd meant to give Eve Kaslov. She said she'd get the doctor and left before she started crying. The last thing in the world Amy Kaslov needed was someone weeping over her who wasn't going to help her.

Amy watched the door after Mrs. Scott left, hoping she'd be right back. Time went by. She heard bells ping, phones ring, and voices floated up and down the hall. But Mrs. Scott didn't come back.

A man wearing a white coat stopped in the door of her room. She supposed he was the doctor.

He was tall and thin, with a thin face and a thin mouth that had a mole next to it. His eyes, behind thick glasses, were blue, like her mother's. He pulled over the chair that Mrs. Scott had sat down in.

"I just spoke to your friend, Betty Scott. She said you were back with us."

"Is she coming to see me again?"

"She didn't say. Amy, I have some questions to ask you. The answers will help us make you better. Can you answer them?" She nodded, and he asked her some simple things first: how old she was; whether she'd had measles, mumps, chicken pox, and so on (she'd had all except mumps and scarlet fever). Then he asked her if she'd ever fainted before, and that was harder to answer. She almost told him about the time her father threw her against the wall, but that wasn't like fainting, so she said that no, she had never fainted.

She thought of telling him about the cold feeling and the fact that she felt different since she'd been in the closet. She wanted to tell him about that second when her mind had touched her mother's and her mother had tried one more time to get to her, even though she was almost dead. She wanted to ask him what could have happened to make the cold feeling so much stronger, but before she could speak, he said, "You've been through a lot, Amy."

They both realized the understatement at the same time. Amy gave a hard giggle, and the doctor grinned and put his hands over his eyes. He took them away and said, "You're going to need help to get better. There's a man here who can help you. You'll see him tomorrow. Today you rest and try to eat. They're bringing a TV up here for you, okay?"

They had a TV at home, and Amy asked, "When can I go home?"

The doctor looked miserable the way Mrs. Scott had

done, and Amy knew that she had no home. They only rented the house and the rent was always late. Sears had come for the refrigerator by now, and there was nothing left at home but the TV and her clothes. The TV was old; the clothes weren't the best things that ever happened, either. She wanted to cry but she was too tired, and she knew tears would make her head ache. The doctor stood up and went to the door. He paused and looked back at her and thought, *It's a shitty, fucking, lousy break, kid. You're over the worst, believe it or not. If you hadn't come out of it, we'd have had to feed and water you like some kind of plant and turn you over and over so your flesh wouldn't rot off your bones. It's shitty, lousy, and rotten, and I'm sorry, but welcome back, anyway . . . .*

F I V E

CHARLES MORAN READ Amy Kaslov's file from nine-thirty until ten, when she was due in his office. It wasn't the worst he'd ever read; four years ago he had tried to treat a ten-year-old girl who'd been gang-raped in Bridgeport by a bunch of teenage boys. She stopped talking on that day and hadn't spoken again. Moran didn't know if she ever would. Then he'd seen a twelve-year-old boy who'd watched his father ground to hamburger in a threshing machine. The kid had tried to kill himself twice (slicing up his poor, thin inner arms both times with a dull razor blade). His mother had found him in time, but Moran wouldn't give six cents for the boy's chances of making it to fifteen. Those two were his worst, but Amy Kaslov was a doozy okay . . . right up there with the top ten.

He closed the folder and disconnected the tape machine earplug. The second Brandenberg came through the speaker and filled the office. He had an impulse to leave it on. He and the kid could sit here in silence, listening to Bach. It wasn't such a bad idea because he had no idea what he was going to say to her, and no plan for treating her. When he was fresh out of school, he always made plans; he would read the jargon-filled reports, "intuit" the diagnosis, and know exactly how to handle every child. Only he was almost always wrong. So he gave up the plans.

He ejected the Bach tape, labeled a new tape "Amy Kaslov," and put it into the machine. There was a Raggedy Ann doll in the supply closet, along with a Tonka truck, a GI Joe set (with most of the equipment missing by now), a toy train, and a dollhouse. But Amy Kaslov was eight; too old for most of that crap. He opened his bottom drawer and looked through his comic book file. It was pretty decimated. He pulled out a Classic Comic of *Tale of Two Cities*. He wished he had a Sheena comic; *Sheena, Queen of the Jungle*, had broken the ice between him and a lot of little girls. But the Sheenas were all gone. He would send Evans out to get some more this afternoon.

He shoved papers to the side, rescued a memo that fluttered to the floor, cleared a small space on top of his desk, and opened the comic. The first picture he saw was Sidney Carton with a bottle of wine tilted to his lips. Not the most fortunate start: Brewer had told him that the father was an alcoholic. He opened the drawer to look for a better one, but the door opened and Evans wheeled in a slight, pale child.

"We're still a little weak on our pins," Evans said briskly. "We should be able to walk in tomorrow." Then she left them alone.

He gave himself a second to look at her, and let her look at him. She was a pretty kid; with a few more pounds on her and a little fresh air to give her face some color, she'd be beautiful. He was startled by her prettiness. It was almost adult, and he had the feeling that if he saw her again in twenty years, he would recognize her. She would probably be a knockout by then.

He didn't feel like smiling, so he didn't. "Hi, kid."

"Hi."

"I'm Dr. Moran. I know who you are."

She didn't say anything.

"How was breakfast?" he asked. He liked to start with a question that they both knew could be answered. He was patient; he would ask such questions for months if he had to.

But time was the problem with cases like Amy Kaslov's. She was here on the state, and hospitals were expensive, even a shit-kicking backwater like Millbridge General, and in a few days, a week at the most, she would have to go. She was too old to be adopted; the social workers would know it was stupid to try. She'd go to some foster family or the orphan facility in New Britain. Either way he wouldn't be able to see her more than once a month. So he had to work fast with her, picking his way through the minefield of their sessions in double time. He had a much bigger chance of stepping wrong, but if she was going to blow, it was better for her to blow here and now. Even so, he'd keep it small for a while.

She said, "The food was all mashed up. I couldn't tell what it was."

"You haven't had anything solid for a while; good food might make you sick. Not that you'll get any here, anyway." (The old chestnut about the food, he thought with a touch of self-loathing. But it worked: sometimes.)

Amy didn't answer. He picked up the comic.

"Ever see this one?"

She shook her head.

"I bet you like Sheena."

She shook her head again.

"No? What is your favorite?"

"I can't remember."

No access that way. He tried to think. He was gentle, he knew his instincts were good, his touch firm and gentle. On bad days, like this one was going to be, he was sorry that he wasn't a neurosurgeon instead of a psychiatrist.

"You don't like comics?" he asked lamely.

She looked at her hands. She wasn't being surly. He didn't know what to do or say; she probably sensed it and was a little embarrassed for him. That wouldn't do—he had to get through just a little. He never lied to kids; they got enough lies from everybody else. He said, "I don't know what to do now."

She gave a surprised grin and nodded at him.

He went on.

"If you were grown-up, we could go out and have a couple of drinks and relax together. It's harder when you're a kid."

"I guess so."

"Why don't we try to talk, anyway? It'll get easier once we start."

"What should we talk about?"

He considered.

"We could talk about school, and your friends and teachers, and what you like to watch on TV, and what your favorite ice cream is . . . a lot of BS like that."

She was smiling broadly now; a totally gorgeous smile that made her wan little face so lovely, he wanted to hug her. He got up, came around his desk, and leaning awkwardly over her, he put his arms around her. He felt her stiffen, then she let go and pushed her face against his chest and started to cry. He picked her up easily in his arms and held her against him with her feet dangling down the front of his body. She wrapped her arms around his neck and her legs around his middle and sobbed. He carried her like he carried his infant son when he woke up in the middle of the night and Mary was too exhausted to cope. He carried her back and forth across the floor of the office until her sobs peaked into violent tearing sounds.

Evans opened the door a crack and peered in. Moran shook his head at her to leave them alone, and she stepped back and closed the door. Amy's sobs calmed down, then turned to whimpers, and he put her gently, in a sitting position, on the couch. She clutched his hand, then let him go. He went to the desk and brought back a box of Kleenex.

"We could talk about a lot of crap and waste a lot of time," he said while she wiped her eyes and nose.

"No," she said, shaking her head firmly.

"So why don't we start with the worst and talk about your mother."

Suddenly the room turned cold. It wasn't wind coming through the single pane of glass or a draft under the door. It was a solid block of indescribable cold, as if he'd fallen through a hole in the earth and come up in the middle of a lake of dry ice. He smelled ozone and thought his fingers would break off if he moved them. With the cold came a piercing terror worse than anything he'd ever felt—the time he'd almost drowned in Elmer Jones's pool; the time he'd totaled his dad's car on the LIE at two in the morning after a night of beer and rye, and thought he was surely one-hundred-percent dead, and wound up with a broken finger and a bunch of strained muscles; the time in the Yale–New Haven ER that that scrawny hillbilly, wired to the teeth on something, pulled a snub-nosed pistol out of nowhere and pointed it square in the middle of his face, then forgot to pull the safety and stood there trying to squeeze the trigger, raving and sobbing until Bob Simmons hit him with an IV carousel—all the times in Charles Moran's thirty-eight years that he'd been really scared, because he knew he was nanoseconds from death, were nothing to the terror that enveloped him with this abysmal coldness.

He felt his mouth open, he heard himself make a gagging sound, and then it was over and the cold was gone. His fingers moved, his skin warmed up, and he started to sweat. He looked around his little office as if he'd never seen it before. Nothing had changed: the indoor-outdoor carpeting dyed the color of rusting metal still had the worn spot by the door, his black plastic couch held his butt stiffly, his desk, the piles of paper, the unopened Classic comic, the misty autumn morning . . . and the little girl . . . were all there.

"I can't describe it," Moran told Ernie Sykes. "I'm in my office trying to get through to an eight-year-old, and the next second, I'm in deep space . . . " He shuddered.

"Eat your soup," Sykes said.

Moran spooned at it. It was split pea, homemade and delicious, but he wasn't hungry. They were in a diner on Connecticut 50, halfway between Millbridge and Yale–New Haven where Sykes worked. Rain ran down the window next

to their table, plonked off the cars in the parking lot. Moran
gave up and put his spoon down. Gail, their regular waitress,
came to the table.

"Something wrong with the soup?"

"No. It's delicious. I'm coming down with something, I
think."

Gail nodded. "You and everybody else. I'm waiting for
them to declare a plague alert and shut down the state."

Moran laughed dutifully. Sykes smiled, then ordered a
cheeseburger and coffee. Moran ordered coffee.

"Okay," Sykes said. "So it was cold."

"Not just cold."

"Okay, deep space. What about it?"

"I don't know."

"Hell you don't," Sykes said. The burger came and he
took a big bite. "You're trying to say something, Charlie, so
say it."

"You'll think I'm crazy."

Sykes laughed. "I'm an experimental psychologist with
two Ph.D.s. I'm not going to think you're 'crazy.' "

"Why not? Sometimes people just are."

"Sure. But I'm a pro. I'll find a fancier word."

Moran drank his coffee. Sykes finished the burger and
shoved his plate away. The rain beat on the black pavement
and pounded on the roof of the old diner, and Sykes waited.
Calm, patient Ernie Sykes, who believed in his heart of
hearts that mind was chemistry and was spending his profes-
sional life trying to prove it. He was Moran's best friend, the
only school buddy Moran still saw.

"Okay, Ernie, here goes. I think the kid did it to me."

Sykes said, "You're right. I think you're crazy."

"I mean it, Ernie."

"How'd she do it?"

"I don't know. Neither does she."

"You talked about it?"

"I couldn't not. But I was scared."

"Of her?" Sykes asked.

Moran nodded miserably.

"I asked her if she'd felt something odd, and she said that she did. It was like a soft, cold breeze inside of her head but not like a breeze, maybe a liquid. No, not that, either. I'm quoting her verbatim on the cold feeling inside her head." Sykes nodded at him to go on. "That's all she could say about how it felt, except that it wasn't unpleasant. She said it was like washing her face on a hot day. Then she told me that it had happened before. The first time was when her father hit her in the face with a beer mug; gave her a scar. It happened again, much worse, when she saw her father in the kitchen looking for a hammer to hit her mother with. The feeling was very strong. She tried to get to her father to stop him, but her mother intercepted her and shoved her into the closet to protect her from the father. I told her that she was lucky her mother had done that, because if she hadn't, her father might have hit her with the hammer too. She just looked at me for a second, and I kept thinking of that bone-eating cold and tried not to shake. Then she said, 'I could have stopped him.' "

He shivered; the hand holding his coffeecup shook and he put it down.

"Are you cold now?" Sykes asked. Moran shook his head.

"I wasn't cold by then, either, but that . . . terror—I can't describe it any other way, Ernie—that terror started to come back because I believed her."

"You believed that an eight-year-old could stop a grown man?"

"I believed that that little girl could stop anything or anybody on earth."

"You're spooked, Charlie," Sykes said gently.

"Of course I'm spooked. What the fuck have we been talking about but me being spooked?"

"Okay, take it easy. Is that all of it?"

"No," Moran said.

"Christ, I can't wait. What else?"

"She said that she touched her mother's mind."

Sykes groaned.

"She said it, Ernie. Her mother was on the floor, and she knew she was dying because her eye was filled with blood."

Sykes paled, but Moran went on. "She said her mother was facedown on the kitchen floor, clutching the key to the closet. The kid screamed, but it didn't work. Then she said that a thought leapt out of her head, and she felt it touch— her word, not mine—touch her mother's. Her mother struggled with her last bit of life to get to her. But it was too late."

Sykes played with a teaspoon. "Well?" Moran demanded.

"What if I said that this kid hypnotized herself, and you along with her?"

"I'd listen. I'll listen to anything."

"*Did* she hypnotize you?" Sykes asked.

"I don't know."

"It doesn't matter. We go with the molecules, Charlie. Molecules are everything."

For the first time that lunch hour Moran smiled. "You believe me."

"If the spectrometer and the immunoassay believe you, so will I. Now, I'll need blood and some tissue. I'd like a spinal, too, but you can't justify—"

"I don't have to. They did a tap while she was in cloud land."

"You got the stuff?"

"No, but I'll get it."

Levin stood in the doorway of her room. She looked small and lost in the hospital bed, and her face was still very thin and pale.

"I heard you were awake," he said. "Can I come in?"

She nodded. He came into the room and pulled a molded plastic chair over to the bed. Her hair was neatly braided now; a brand-new teddy bear lay in the crook of her arm. They'd brought in a TV for her and she was watching a soap opera. He didn't approve of kids watching that crap, but there wasn't much on in the afternoons.

He'd decided to come here as soon as he heard she was awake. He'd given up his lunch hour, and he was hungry and tired. There'd been a bad one on rotten Route 7; two kids were dead, and a truck driver for Finast would probably never walk again. Levin had spent the morning reading the accident report, looking at the pictures, and listening to a nasty, oily insurance man with long sideburns telling him to get the parents to sign the release because a child's life wasn't worth that much dough since children didn't support anybody. It had been a truly miserable morning, and Levin planned to try to forget it by eating a big, sloppy sausage grinder for lunch, washed down with a couple of beers. But halfway to Nino's on 202, he'd turned off and come here, even though he wasn't in any frame of mind to cheer up a sick kid.

She turned off the TV and waited.

He said, "I'm Lieutenant Joseph Levin."

She smiled at him, and for the first time she spoke to him. Her voice was soft, a little hard to hear. "Dr. Brewer said you found me in the closet. He said you saved my life."

Levin didn't know what to say.

She said, "Thank you," and she held out her hand. He was confused for a second, then he realized that she wanted to shake . . . by way of thanking him. Tears stung his eyes and he took her hand. It was small and warm and he wanted to hold it. But he made himself shake firmly and let go.

"How're they treating you?" he asked. His voice was hoarse.

"Oh, nice," she said. "Three squares a day. Tommy Sloane, my grandma's friend, says that's all that matters. Three squares a day."

"It's important okay."

"They gave me the TV to watch too. It's great. I never saw color TV before. Do you have one?"

"Yes."

"I thought Marcus Welby was blond. But his hair's gray. I guess he's an old man."

"I guess so," Levin said. His stomach growled, and she giggled and said, "I bet you're hungry. You shouldn't miss your lunch."

"No. I just wanted to see how you were doing."

"Fine. Ann gave me this . . . she's a nurse." She held up the bear. "I'm trying to find a name for him. Do you know a good name?"

"I called my teddy bear Little."

"Little what?"

"Just Little."

She held the bear against her cheek. "Little," she crooned. He stood up.

"It was nice meeting you, Mr. Levin," she said.

"Call me Joe," he croaked, and he started for the door.

"Will you come back?"

He had no intention of coming back. He should not have come here today. He should be at the counter at Nino's right now, sopping up red gravy with the crust of his grinder, but he said, "Maybe."

She spoke quickly. "Someone's going to be in the next bed tonight. A little girl's having her appendix out. That must be awful."

"Awful," Levin said.

"But you can come and see me, anyway, if you like. They have visiting hours from twelve to five and from seven to nine."

He nodded and almost ran out of the room and down the hall. Tears had spilled out of his eyes and down his cheeks. He wiped them away but they wouldn't stop, and he wasn't going to ride down in an elevator full of people who would stare covertly at him and wonder which of the people he loved was dead or dying. He found the stairwell and walked down five flights to the lobby.

The state child welfare agency had an office right there in Millbridge General, which was the largest hospital in the area. He found the office, got the necessary foster care forms, and started filling them out.

Halfway through page six he stopped and tried to think why he was doing this. He should at least put words to his reason. He pitied her . . . his pity had become an ache in his throat and back; his eyes burned with pity. He was curious about her, too . . . he was even a little curious about the crazy uncle who said he could read people's minds.

But there was more than pity and curiosity. He was doing it for his family, especially Paulie, who was getting worse every day. Amy was helpless, she needed the Levins, even Paulie. Maybe Paulie would sense that and maybe, just maybe, he would pity the little girl and want to protect her. Maybe at long last he'd feel something positive, no matter how weak; and maybe one small decent spark would start another. They were a lot of maybes—and long shots, at that —but Levin was going to try.

Then he remembered the last time he'd seen Amy Kaslov. She had not asked for water; she could not even talk. Yet he gave it to her willessly without even knowing he was going to. He admitted to himself that the episode had frightened him then; not now. He thought he understood what had happened. He wanted to do *something* for her, and he couldn't give her love, a home, a live mother, so he did what he could. He gave her a glass of water, blindly and unthinkingly, like a robot. Even the cold seemed explainable now. He'd probably been on the verge of flu that had never materialized. None of it seemed very important, and he finished the forms, read them over carefully, and brought them back to the office.

The woman who ran the office was out to lunch, but the receptionist who took the forms was encouraging. She told him that Amy Kaslov's stay in the hospital was costing the state thousands; they wanted her out of Millbridge General, and his formal offer of foster care would be processed quickly and almost certainly favorably. Keeping a child in New Britain was cheaper than the hospital, she told him, but the expense was still astronomical. She looked at Levin, holding the forms he'd filled out, and she said, "A child's future shouldn't have a price tag on it, should it?"

He did not answer, and she shoved the forms into a box marked "M. Dyer" and told him to come back on Monday.

He did not tell his family what he wanted to do until Monday. He wasn't ashamed or embarrassed; he just didn't know how to do it. Finally, at seven Monday morning, when the kids were at the kitchen table waiting for breakfast, he blurted the whole thing out.

Jeannie got caught at the stove holding a bowl of Cream of Wheat. Steam rose lazily from it and disappeared; it seemed to him that nothing else was moving. He wondered for a second if they'd all stopped breathing from shock. He kept talking. He told them about the dead mother, the killer father, the little girl locked in the closet in the dark for the three days, only a few feet from her mother's body. It was awful stuff; he didn't think Greta should hear it, but he couldn't stop once he'd started.

Greta's eyes widened and seemed to bulge; two gigantic tears brimmed and rolled down her cheeks. Jeannie put the bowl of cereal down and leaned against the counter, and Paulie listened silently.

Levin went on and on, listing the horrors of Amy Kaslov's life. Suddenly he thought of his father. "One tragedy is a tragedy," the old man once said, "and two is a pity. After that it starts getting funny." It *was* almost funny, and against his will he remembered Thelma Ritter's line from *All About Eve.*

Everything but the bloodhounds yapping at her rear end.

His mouth twitched, and he was terrified that he'd break into hysterical giggles. He clasped his hands together so tightly they cramped, and the urge to laugh dissipated. He finished talking and looked around the kitchen table at his family. Greta was crying openly. There were tears in Jeannie's eyes. He risked looking at Paulie, not sure what he hoped to see. Paulie's face was stiff and impassive. He stared at his father for a moment, then stood up and went to the kitchen door.

Levin had vowed not to lose his temper with his son. "This is your decision, too, Paulie."

Paulie turned at the door and looked at them. His sister was crying; his mother was close to it. His father's mouth trembled with stubborn anger, and suddenly Paulie saw his favorite movie scene. In it a tall, thin man with a mean face and blond hair blasted away with a tommy gun. Paulie imagined the faces in front of him exploding as the shells ripped into them, splattering blood and flesh on the walls and cabinets.

"Do what you want," Paulie said. "You will, anyway."

It was hard for Levin to believe that the boy was only fourteen. He sounded like a mean old man.

"Let's talk about it," Levin said as gently as he could.

"Okay," Paulie said, "I don't want her here. So that's three against one. So what's to say?"

Jeannie made some meaningless noise that was half sigh, half sob, and Paulie walked out of the kitchen. Levin heard him in the hall; then he heard the front door open and close, and Paulie was gone.

Paulie was right, as usual; it was three against one. Paulie had cast his customary pall over them, but it didn't last long. Greta recovered first. She said she wanted Amy to sleep in her room, not one of the spare rooms. She vowed that Amy would have at least half of her toys because she was poor and wouldn't have many of her own. Half an hour later Levin left his wife and daughter at the kitchen table looking through the Read's catalogue for new clothes for Amy—if Amy wanted to come and live with them and the sovereign state of Connecticut would let her—and he drove to Millbridge Hospital to see Martha Dyer.

The door to Miss Dyer's office was open, and he knocked on the door frame and went in. The woman behind the desk told him that Miss Dyer was waiting for him.

Martha Dyer was a tall, lanky woman about fifty. Her face would have been homely except that her eyes were beautiful. He sat next to her desk, and she shuffled through the forms that he'd filled out on Wednesday.

"On the face of it there's no reason why the state shouldn't approve," Dyer said. "You'd get enough money to keep the child more or less decently, although from your financial statement you don't need it."

"I always need an extra hundred," he said lightly.

"Everyone does." She smiled at him. Her eyes were really wonderful. "But that's clearly not why you want the child. We have to send someone out to see your house, meet your wife, and so on. But I imagine it will be a formality in your case. Everything seems to be in order." She reshuffled the papers. "I haven't made any recommendation yet. I wanted to talk to you first."

Levin waited.

"I know you see this as a kind, perhaps noble thing that you're doing," Dyer said slowly, "and I don't want to insult you by suggesting that it's anything else. But you've never taken in children like this before and . . . " She hesitated, then said, "I'm going to speak frankly, Lieutenant Levin. Sometimes the nobility of middle-class exurbia is not in the best interest of the homeless child or the family that takes them in." Her words stunned him. She must have sensed it; she said, "I don't want to make you angry, Lieutenant, but you are taking a child into your home about whom you know nothing. You can't realize the lack of structure in some of these families. I'm not talking about sloth and alcoholism; I'm talking about a way of life totally without meaning, where anything can happen: beatings, murder, incest. You're a policeman, and perhaps I'm not telling you anything you don't know. But does your *family* know these things? And aren't they the ones who're going to have to deal with your good deed?"

He stood up.

"Thank you for the advice." His voice was tight with anger.

"I see you *are* angry, Lieutenant, and I'm sorry. But before we go any farther, I want you to take some time to remember that this child watched her father beat her mother to death. You could be taking a time bomb into your home."

"She's not a time bomb, Miss Dyer. She's a little girl."

She went on as if he hadn't spoken, and he thought that she was as used to middle-class righteous anger as she was to middle-class nobility. It didn't cut any ice with her.

"Then I want you to talk to Dr. Charles Moran on our staff. He's seen her once and will see her again next week. I've set up an appointment for next Monday at two, if that's convenient."

"Two o'clock Monday will be fine."

He stalked across her office to the door.

"Lieutenant?" He stopped. "Please think about what I've said."

He left her office and crossed the lobby to the gift store. He looked through the rack of stuffed animals and chose a plush seal with a bright blue bow around its neck. He paid for the toy, carried it back across the lobby, and took the elevator to Amy Kaslov's floor.

That night he told Jeannie that Amy was a beautiful child. "And gentle," he said. "Her voice is so soft, I could barely hear her. I kept having to ask her to say things again, and finally I gave up and pretended I heard what she said. It didn't matter, I got the gist of it. She would like to stay with us for a while. That's how she put it. Gutsy little kid. She made it sound like she was looking into her options and we seemed like the best choice for now. But only for now. She's got zilch. Her clothes were at the shelter in Millbridge and I went there and looked through the stuff afterward. . . ."

The clothes were wretched, and even as thin as she was, they looked too small for her. There were some blankets packed, too; they were clean and threadbare. A gray-faced woman with long, streaky wrinkles down her cheeks had watched Levin suspiciously as he'd gone through the stuff.

There were a couple of schoolbooks and a ragged copy of a picture book called *Chips a Dog*. Then, at the bottom of the carton, he found a small stack of report cards. He'd opened them, smiled at the grim-faced woman, and put the cards inside the Chips book. He signed for the books and left the rest behind.

"It's all rags, anyway," he told Jeannie. "We'll buy her new stuff. But the report cards're terrific, Jeannie. She's a bright kid."

He opened two and put them on the kitchen table in front of Jeannie. A neat line of *A*'s marched down the card in blue ink; at the bottom was one *B*. The same *B* appeared on both cards. "She doesn't do so well in gym," Jeannie said.

"The kid's probably been undernourished since she was born. She'll do better. And see what the teacher says about her math. . . ."

Jeannie read the note on the back.

> *Mr. and Mrs. Kaslov:*
> *Amy consistently scores over her classmates in mathematics. It seems to be a special talent with her. Perhaps she could forge ahead, given the opportunity. If you wish, I will be happy to talk to you about accelerated programs or special tutoring for Amy. Thank you, and best wishes,*
> *Selma Graves, M. A.*

"Miss Graves doesn't mention her social adjustment," Jeannie said.

"What is social adjustment?"

Jeannie shrugged. "How they get along with the other kids, I guess. Paulie's homeroom teacher writes a note about it with every report card."

"That's Paulie," Levin said bitterly.

He did tell Jeannie about the crazy uncle locked away in Limekiln. She would have found out, anyway. But not that the uncle claimed to be telepathic or psychic or whatever. Or about the uncle's warning. He also didn't tell her one other thing about Amy. Just as he was ready to leave her this afternoon, with the TV and the stuffed seal, she had asked him if they'd found her father yet.

He could have lied, but he thought she had a right to know, and he said, "They found him in Poughkeepsie. He'll be back in Bridgeton next week."

"Can I see him?"

He was startled. "You *want* to see him?"

"Oh, yes," she said. Her voice was perfectly clear for the first time. It was cold and musical, like thin ice breaking. It brought back Dyer's warning, and Kaslov's. He didn't tell Jeannie, but he couldn't get it out of his head, and early Saturday morning he finally admitted to himself that good report cards, a talent in math, and the pity he felt were not enough. Dyer had called her a time bomb. Dyer was no fool. The scene in that kitchen festered in his mind; it must be throbbing in Amy's like an abscess. He had to know more before he brought her home, and he had to know it soon.

Jeannie had already called Mo Stern to come and paint the spare room on Monday. She and Greta were out now, buying the paint. Jeannie had bought curtain fabric, the sewing machine was set up in the den, and Greta had picked Amy's new skirts, sweaters, slacks out of Read's catalogue. He couldn't come home on Friday without Amy Kaslov and tell them the deal was off because the kid was a time bomb. If the deal was off, it had to be now.

He was going to see Moran on Monday. But Levin couldn't turn his back on the kid on one man's say-so. He needed help. He sat in front of the TV, not seeing the golf tournament, until ten A.M. Then he went to the desk and called Selma Graves, who had signed Amy's report card, and Jeffrey Hall.

Hall lived in an old Colonial on fifteen or twenty acres in Roxbury. It was a beautiful spread, and as Levin drove up the long gravel drive from the road, he thought of trust funds, private clubs, and the trappings of old money. Mrs. Hall fit. She was a tall blond with bony legs, a long plain face, and radiant blue eyes. She led him through a lovely room, furnished with good Colonial furniture that looked like the real article, and into a book-lined study, complete with bow window, window seat, gorgeous view, and stone fireplace. Levin knew that Jeannie would go bananas over the place, and he felt a stab of envy for Hall.

Hall laid his book open across the arm of a leather armchair and stood to greet Levin. He looked prettier and more feminine than his wife and was a good three inches shorter.

Mrs. Hall (who would be called Bitsy or Muffy or some other absurdity) asked if they would like tea. They said they would, and she left them alone.

He told Hall about seeing Amy, about the report cards and the poor, sad junk at the shelter. He told him how excited his wife and daughter were about Amy coming to live with them, then he told Hall about Dyer's warning. "Dire Dyer," he said, trying to lighten the warning.

Only Hall didn't smile. He was quiet for a while, and Levin drank the tea Mrs. Hall had brought and waited. He'd driven fifteen miles to listen to Hall, not hear himself talk.

Finally Hall said, "Jonathan knew what you wanted to do, if you remember."

"I'm a pushover for kids, Doctor. Maybe it shows in my face."

"Maybe. But *he* warned you too."

Levin spoke patiently. "Look, I don't doubt your good will, Doctor, but I've seen the kid and told her she might come home with us. Maybe I shouldn't have . . . but I did. Impulse, pity, all sorts of things. My wife is probably home by now making new curtains for the kid's room, and my daughter is more excited than she was when she got her first Barbie doll. I can't let that come crashing down on the say-so of one lunatic who says he reads people's minds."

"I guess you can't," Hall said mildly.

"Tell me things I can believe," Levin pleaded. "Tell me

that Kaslov's crazies run in the family and she'll be around the bend like her uncle in a few years. Or tell me that what happened to her is so horrible that she can never get past it and she'll be a mental basket case all of her life. Tell me she'll be a drunk and killer like her father. Tell me something to hang a decision on."

"I can't. No one can predict the effect of those three days in the closet, and some children *are* like their fathers, but just as many aren't."

Levin thought for a sad second that Paulie would be nicer if he was like his father, and Levin would be nicer if he were like *his* father. "In other words," he said, "you can't advise me."

"I can't make your decision for you, and I can't give you what *you* would consider a sound reason for rejecting the child. I won't even try because I could be wrong, and I'd have kept a little girl from having a family and doomed her to the mercies of the state. Not that the state is unmerciful, only woefully incompetent."

He thanked Hall and stood up to leave. Then he remembered the last thing Amy had said to him on Thursday. "Doctor, why would Amy Kaslov want to see her father?"

Hall said, "I don't think she would."

"But she does. She asked me especially."

Hall shook his head. "I don't know, Lieutenant. If I were she I'd never want to see the son of a bitch again."

Levin was depressed and getting a headache when he drove out of Hall's long driveway and onto Route 67. Selma Graves was his last hope. She lived in a condo complex on the edge of New Milford. It was fairly new and shoddily built. There was a ratty tennis court with cracked clay and a small pool. The grounds were unkempt, the leaves hadn't been raked. As he parked and walked up a mud-spattered gravel walk to number 24, the sun broke through, but it was thin and silver and made the whole place look like carved metal.

Selma Graves didn't go with Cornwall Village Condominiums. She was short and lively-looking with round, flushed cheeks and fuzzy red hair that looked dyed. Her apartment was small, but it was clean and full of healthy houseplants. She offered him more tea or coffee. He refused. She said, "I've been thinking about Amy ever since you called this morning. I'm afraid I won't be much help."

His heart sank.

She went on, "I don't know much about her. Her parents never came to school, although I invited them several times. Not because of any problem with Amy. She wasn't a problem. But I thought she should have some accelerated training in math. She is very good at it. Maybe better than good. But I'm not good enough myself to be sure. In any case, the parents never showed up."

"You know how her mother died?"

"Yes. I would rather not talk about it. I don't mean to hide my head, but if I hear any more, I'll wind up in tears, and that won't do either of us any good, will it, Lieutenant?"

She had more sense than Hall or anyone else he'd talked to, and Levin relaxed a fraction for the first time in days. He told her what Dyer had said, and she put her head to the side and looked at him for a moment, then she said, "I go along with *you*. She's a little girl, not a time bomb. Professionals try to predict everything. It's arrogant, and they're usually wrong, anyway. Sometimes I think the psychologists and sociologists try to be real scientists with solutions that'll meet Koch's postulates. That's bullshit."

Levin didn't know what Koch's postulates were, but he was finally hearing some sense, and he wanted her to keep talking. She complied.

"She's a nice child, a little solitary but not isolated. I think she was self-conscious about her clothes. They were awful, and little girls begin to care about such things very young. She scores average in verbal skills and goes off the chart in math. You'll see that she gets a good education, maybe goes to college. That's probably more than her own parents would have done. As for your family . . . she's a child, not a wild animal. What happened will leave terrible scars, but I don't think she'll go berserk some night and murder you in your beds, do you?"

Levin shook his head.

"Then I honestly don't see the problem. I guess you care about her or you wouldn't have started all this. You said you pity her; that's not a bad start. I've wound up loving people I pitied. I'm sure you have too. As far as I can see, the only question is whether she likes you."

"She seems to. She said she wanted to come and live with me and my family."

"You mean, you've told her?"

Levin nodded.

Selma Graves was silent, but her cheeks turned even redder, and Levin got the feeling that the woman was angry.

Finally she said, "You gave her hope. You can't take it away now. I don't know what you're looking for or what you hoped to hear from me, Lieutenant, but according to every rule of decency, you've burned your bridges." She stood up and held out her hand to shake good-bye. But he grabbed it, and on a crazy impulse he raised it to his lips.

"Thanks, lady."

"For what?" she gasped.

"For settling it for me. You can drive yourself crazy, and most people are ready and willing to help you do it. But you talked sense, and you're right: I've burned my bridges. Thanks again."

The temperature dropped, the water on the road froze, and Moran told Sykes to spend the night. The roads to Shelton would be treacherous; the trip home would take hours.

Sykes called home and told his wife, Gloria. She was nice about it; she had a good book, she said. Besides, *Key Largo* was on the tube tonight. Mary Moran wanted to see *Key Largo* too. She put little Davey to bed, broke out a gigantic frozen pizza, and mixed a salad. After dinner she left the dishes for the men and went into the den to watch the movie.

Sykes went out to the mudroom where he'd hung his parka and came back with a white scroll of film, like photographic contact paper. He unrolled it, holding one end down with the sugar bowl, the other with the brandy bottle. It was a spectrograph. Moran hadn't seen one for years. The faint lines looked like gray snow against a white sky. Each gray section was neatly labeled, and Moran recognized all the components. There was nothing out of the ordinary on the film.

"So what?" he asked Sykes.

"So this." Sykes pointed to a section of plain white film.

"What?" Moran asked impatiently.

"Look, for Christ's sake. Just look."

Moran bent low over the white film on his kitchen table. He didn't see anything at first, then, like a print blossoming in developing fluid, as his eyes became accustomed to the faint glare of the light on the film, he saw faint, broken threads of light gray. The section was unlabeled.

"What is it?" Moran asked.

"I don't know. Neither does anyone in the lab; neither does the computer. It's never been identified, at least not in this country."

Moran hovered over the film. "You're sure."

"Look, if it's not on Yale's computer, where is it?"

"I don't know."

"Cambridge," Sykes said softly.

"Harvard?"

"No. Cambridge."

Moran had never sent anything to Cambridge. Neither had anyone else he knew. They had invented modern biochemistry at Cambridge; they had built the DNA molecule there. Cambridge was the court of last resort, the dark side of the moon. He was impressed and sat down slowly at the kitchen table.

"Will they know?"

"Maybe, but I don't think so. I think your little girl has

something floating around her basic body soup that no one's ever seen before."

"Where was it?"

"Spinal fluid. Stop looking glassy-eyed, Charlie, and try to think. This stuff, whatever it is, had a definite effect on her. The cold wind in her head or whatever it is."

Moran nodded.

"But that's only part of it, buddy. You felt it too. You mention the mother, the kid gets excited and out spills this stuff, whatever it is. She's cold. But then you feel what she feels."

"You mean she made me feel it."

"Not willfully. Was it willful?"

Moran shook his head.

"So what happened?" Sykes asked softly. It was a rhetorical question. Moran waited. "She transferred the cold to you, Charlie. That simple." For the first time Sykes let his excitement show. "Why not? They got a guy in Russia who can light lights by thinking about it. And a woman who can light matches and slide metal objects around. And the Russians ain't clowns. Liars and killers, maybe, but not clowns. In this country there's a guy—an ex-cop—who can see places he's never been and describe them. They've been trying to prove it is bullshit. They put the guy in a cage and put the locations in a safe and they're picked by computer. But the guy knows . . . he always knows. So why not a little down-home thought transference . . . *sense* transference. You felt what she felt."

Moran shook his head.

"Why not?" Sykes demanded.

"She said it was pleasant. What I felt wasn't pleasant. It was horrible."

"The cold? A touch of cold was horrible? Are you scared of the cold, like a four-year-old is scared of the dark?"

Moran shook his head.

"So it wasn't the cold that scared you, it was something else."

Moran was getting nervous. He suddenly wanted to

shove the spectrograph into the fireplace and forget the whole thing.

"I don't know," he said weakly.

"Something under the cold," Sykes prompted, "something presaged by the cold?"

Something under the cold. As if the cold were only a symptom, like a runny nose and achy joints. *Like plague spots and buboes.* But if that cold was only the beginning of something, Moran wanted to leave it unstarted.

"It was cold," he said, "that's all I know."

Moran had rehearsed what he would say to Levin. He picked a spot just to the right of Levin's head and speechified at it.

"It's an experience you and I can't begin to imagine," Moran told the spot on the wall. "All violence is not created equal, you know. Seeing violence between strangers is one thing; seeing violence between people you love is something else. And between your parents . . . " Moran trailed off, and his eyes shifted down to the top of his desk. Levin didn't say anything, and Moran started up again.

"We have some cockamamie idea that suffering ennobles; it doesn't. Suffering callouses our feelings; brutality begets brutality."

Levin sighed audibly, and Moran blushed and finally looked into Levin's eyes. "I sound like Richard Nixon, don't I?"

Levin nodded.

"I'm sorry. I really don't want to say what I have to." He took a deep breath. "I'm not going to make a specific recommendation to Dyer, because all I have to go on is two sessions. In one she cried. In the second, this morning, she read a comic I was stupid enough to give her. A Sheena comic . . . " Moran laughed. "I guess the title of the comic is pretty irrelevant."

"Pretty," Levin said.

"Anyway, I'm not officially saying no to you because I

can't justify it. But I am saying it unofficially, Lieutenant. I don't think you should take this child into your home."

Levin gripped the arms of the chair. "You'll have to give me a reason."

Moran couldn't talk about supernatural cold or thought transference to this big, solid-looking man in the cheap suit that was just a fraction too small for him. Levin would laugh at him or sock him. Either way he wouldn't believe him. Moran barely believed it himself. He said, "I think the child's experience was too terrible to expect her to adjust to normal family life now."

He stopped again and twisted in his chair with tension and self-loathing. She hadn't really done anything except cry in his arms and read a comic book that he'd bought for her. And he was consigning her to New Britain where she would be regimented, badly fed, and miserably educated; where she would be raped by the time she was twelve and probably sent out at sixteen, fit for factory work, waitressing, or prostitution, depending on her character (whatever "character" was).

"You've got to do better than that," Levin said.

"I know. That's why I'm telling this to you, not Dyer. We did a couple of tests with her and nothing shows; there's no overt pathology that I can point to. It's just . . . a feeling, Lieutenant, but a strong one. There's something wrong with Amy Kaslov."

Levin stood up. "I saw that kitchen, Moran, you didn't. Of course there's something wrong with her. She'd be made of glass if there weren't. But what are we talking about? You think she'll be disruptive? Good. Families like ours—like most families—need disrupting. And I'm giving my wife and kids a chance to do something really decent. They won't get one often, and I don't want to deprive them. And no matter how insensitive or foolish we are with the kid, she'll be better off with us than with the state."

"What if you can't handle the disruption and have to give her up? Have you thought what that'll do to her?"

"Yes. It'll be awful for her. But everything's awful for her, anyway. It'll make it hard for her to trust anyone again, but she already knows she can't trust her father, and she sure as shit can't trust her luck. What could my family and I do to her that would be any worse than New Britain?"

The moment had come, and Moran knew that he had to put his ass on the table or shut his mouth for all time. He could actually feel the words in his throat: *She's dangerous.* Dangerous, why? Levin would ask. Dangerous to whom? Moran didn't know.

"You won't listen to me?" Moran asked hopelessly.

"You haven't said anything."

Moran could talk about the Brand-X substance in the spinal fluid that Sykes had packed up and shipped to Cambridge this morning. But it sounded like science fiction even to him. He could arbitrarily say no, but Dyer would be up here demanding to know why, and Levin would appeal, and sooner or later he would have to tell them something. Of course, there might be an answer from Cambridge by then, but Sykes didn't have much hope of hearing from them before spring. Cambridge moved at its own pace; nobody rushed Cambridge. Even if they replied in time, what would they say? Brand-X component appeared in the child's spinal fluid . . . so what? Or Brand-X component did not exist; the gray lines were a laboratory artifact. Then Moran would look like the fool he was. He didn't mind that so much, but in the process of making himself the asshole of the year he would have ruined whatever slim chance Amy had of living a normal life.

He looked at the form in front of him on his cluttered desk. Blank spaces leaped out at him.

"Will you let her come for treatment?" he asked.

Levin nodded.

"The state will only pay part . . . "

"That's not a problem."

He picked up his pen and wrote that after preliminary tests and a brief examination, he could find no psychological

problem serious enough to deny Joseph and Jeanne Levin
... He was suddenly crushed by a depression so black, the
words on the form blurred. He thought of Robespierre signing Danton's death warrant, and Elizabeth signing Essex's.
A whole list of reluctant executioners and their victims
marched through his mind: Henry VIII and Thomas More;
Henry II and Thomas à Becket; Eisenhower and the Rosen-
bergs. He told himself that he was signing a recommendation
for foster care, not an execution order, and he finished the
form and handed it to Levin.

There was custard on Amy's dinner tray. But when she
finished the chicken and strained peas and mashed potatoes,
she was full and she left the custard. A few hours later she
was hungry again. She remembered the full custard cup, and
she was sorry she'd left it behind. She knew from experience
that if she asked for something to eat, they'd give her applesauce, and she didn't like applesauce. She wanted custard.

The hospital was quiet, visiting hours were over, and the
other people on the floor were sleeping or reading or watching TV. Joe Levin had brought her Chips book to her, and
she read it again. The illustrations were flocked, and the pictures of the dog were supposed to be fuzzy to the touch. But
most of the fuzz was worn away, and poor Chips felt slippery
and looked a little tacky. She loved the book, anyway, and
she put it carefully on the bedstand next to the teddy bear
that the nurse named Ann had given her.

She clicked on the TV, settled back against the cool,
plump pillows. She didn't mind being hungry; hunger kept
her mind occupied until she got interested in the program,
and that was good.

Gunsmoke was on. She watched for a few minutes, then
started to get sleepy. Matt talked to Chester, then there were
some bad guys; Doc came on, and Doc and Kitty were in the
saloon talking about Matt's trouble with the bad guys. Suddenly there was a close-up of Kitty. Amy had never watched
color TV before; the color showed how thick Kitty's makeup

was. It was plastered on her face; her eyes were lined in black, she was wearing layers of mascara, and suddenly Amy saw her mother's face with all Mrs. Scott's stuff on it. Her mother's face was smooth and masklike, like Kitty's, except that her mother was younger and prettier. Amy shut her eyes tightly and clenched her teeth. She tried to push the picture away; it hung on stubbornly. She tightened her fists on the blanket and tried to think of custard; rich, yellow, and thick. The coolness, which was refreshing and familiar by now, almost like an old friend, washed into the room, over her body, and through her head. She relaxed into it, and her mother's face faded. Amy concentrated on the custard.

Ann Boyer shivered behind the counter of the nursing station down the hall.

"Cold?" asked Sally Stein.

"Freezing. Are you cold?"

Sally shook her head.

"Maybe I'm coming down with something," Ann said. "I'll get my sweater." She pushed back her chair—it slid smoothly on ball casters—and stood up. She wrapped her arms around herself and walked toward the metal-doored locker set into the wall. Halfway there she stopped and stood ramrod-stiff in the middle of the floor. Her arms dropped to her sides.

"Ann?"

Ann turned, passed Sally as if she weren't there, and went around the counter and down the hall.

"Ann?" Sally called softly. Most of the room doors were open; some of the patients were sleeping. Ann stopped in front of the galley, pushed open the door, and went inside. Sally stood up and leaned over the counter. She heard the refrigerator open and close, and a minute later Ann came out of the galley carrying a cup of custard. She passed the nursing station blindly and went into 507. Sally looked at the board. It was blank; the Kaslov girl hadn't rung, and she hadn't called out, either. Sally would have heard her. Sally watched

507: Ann left the room, came back down the hall and around the counter to her desk. Sally stared at her. Ann's face was smooth, her eyes glassy.

"You didn't get your sweater," Sally said carefully.

"No. I'm not cold anymore."

"Why did you bring custard to 507?"

Ann looked up, surprised. "I thought Amy might want some."

Sally leaned on the counter and looked down the hall. Black shadows gaped in front of open doors; a pool of black lay on the floor in front of the lounge. Sally wanted to go down to 507 and see what was happening, but the hall was spooky and suddenly full of an eerie, whispery noise. She knew it was only the ventilators coming on, but she wasn't going down that hall, anyway, and she wasn't going into 507 because all at once she didn't want to be alone with Amy Kaslov.

Amy stared at the cup of custard in her hand. In the background Matt Dillon was finishing off the bad guys, but Amy wasn't watching anymore. She knew that something astounding had happened. She wanted custard, Ann brought it to her without being asked. There were lots of ordinary reasons why Ann should suddenly take it into her head to give Amy custard. Ann liked Amy; she visited her more than she did the other patients. Ann had brought her the little stuffed bear that was like the one she'd had when she was just a kid . . . and maybe Ann was in tune with Amy. Or maybe it was a coincidence. Ann felt like giving Amy custard at the exact minute that Amy wanted custard. It *could* have been like that, but Amy knew it wasn't. She had a hand in it somehow. It was frightening, like that second when she'd screamed at her mother from behind the closet door without making a sound and her mother had heard her. But it was exhilarating, too, like winning the race against Toni Russo last summer when everyone, Amy included, knew she was going to lose. She remembered the soles of Toni's sneakers flashing ahead of her on the track, then they were gone, and she didn't see the sneakers or Toni's legs pumping away in the lead. She didn't see anything but dot-shadows of leaves on the track and bursts of sun through the trees. Suddenly she broke through the ring of screaming girls at the finish line, and there was nothing ahead but the meadow. Toni was back there somewhere, and Amy had won. She kept running until she was in the high grass of the meadow, then she had stopped and stood, thrilled and trembling, sweat running down her face and sides in a flood. She didn't know how she won the race; she didn't even mean to. She didn't mean to make Ann bring her custard, either, yet here it was.

Her hands were trembling. She waited, trying to take in the finale of *Gunsmoke,* until the trembling stopped enough for her to eat without spilling clumps of slippery custard on her chest.

Paulie left Greta watching *The Return of the Mummy* and went upstairs. His mother was on the stepstool, measuring the windows in the spare room, and two unopened gallon cans of paint sat on newspapers on the floor. He watched for a minute, then went back downstairs. He stopped in the den doorway. The mummy had smashed through the French doors and was advancing on a screaming man who'd plastered himself against a wall and was uselessly firing a pistol at the bundle of rotting rags staggering toward him. Greta was scrunched against the back of the couch, her hands half covering her eyes.

He wanted to watch the movie, but he couldn't sit still long enough. He was restless and unhappy and didn't know how to make himself feel better. It was Saturday night—the girl would be here in less than a week. He didn't want her here, but he didn't know what to do about it. It was no good telling *them;* his mother would stroke his hair, which he hated, and tell him that everything would be all right once he got used to her. He would like her, and it would be fun having a new sister. His mother was lying. He didn't like

Greta—he didn't hate her, exactly—but he certainly didn't like her, and she was his real sister. His father wouldn't listen; he probably wouldn't even hear what Paulie said. His father seemed to be deaf whenever Paulie complained. He did hate his father.

He left the den again, went to the kitchen, and made himself a peanut butter sandwich. Eating helped a little, but soon the sandwich was gone and the restlessness was back. He left the kitchen and went through the door under the stairs and down into the basement. It was dim, damp, and musty-smelling. It matched his mood. He took a flashlight out of the cabinet and shone it into the corners. He saw a black hole at the bottom of the cabinet molding and crept up on it, keeping the light shining on it. He knelt down on the cold stone floor and shone the light directly into the hole. It looked empty; the mouse or chipmunk that had made the hole in the base of the cabinet was in the basement somewhere.

He moved quickly; he found a can of prepared Spackle and his father's spatula and smeared white plaster over the hole. The hole was tiny, he filled it in easily and smoothed over the outside. Then he squatted on his haunches next to the hole, his muscles tense, his skin tingling. He didn't have to wait long. A mouse came skittering out from under the washing machine and scrambled across the cold cement floor for the hole. Seconds before it reached the opening, it realized that the hole was closed, but it was too late. Paulie's hand flashed out and grabbed the mouse midsection and lifted it up. The mouse struggled, its sides heaved, its tiny eyes glazed with terror. Paulie could feel the little heart's hammering pulse. He carefully took hold of the tail and loosened his other hand. The mouse scrabbled free, then fell and hung by its tail, its feet clawing air.

Paulie watched the small, struggling body intently for a few minutes, then swung the mouse around over his head in two fast arcs and let go. The mouse hit the cement-block wall with a faint crunch and fell to the floor. Paulie walked over leisurely and examined it. It was still alive; the sides heaved erratically, and it made a sick peeping sound. Paulie raised his foot and brought it down on top of the mouse. He crushed it slowly, feeling the thin bones mash under under the sole of his shoe. He pushed until the middle of the mouse was flat against the floor and the little swollen head bulged out from under his shoe. He waited a minute, then lifted his foot and picked up the corpse by the tail. He carried it to a window high in the wall, opened the window, and shoved the mouse out into the window well. He put the flashlight back, turned out the overhead light, and, feeling calmer than he had all day, went back upstairs to watch the end of the movie.

S I X

THE LEVIN CHILDREN waited in the foyer for their first look at Amy. She clutched her teddy bear against her and was ashamed of doing it because she was too old for such toys, but she couldn't let go of it.

Suddenly Greta charged across the foyer, threw her arms around Amy, and kissed her wetly on the cheek.

"Wait till you see your room," Greta cried.

"Let her catch her breath," said Mrs. Levin. The boy stayed in the shadows at the far end of the foyer. Amy couldn't see him clearly, except that he looked very tall.

"I'd love to see the room," Amy said.

Greta grabbed Amy's shopping bag in one hand and Amy's hand in the other and pulled her up the stairs.

"Mommy finished the curtains last night; the comforter came this morning. It's all in yellow, like my room; do you like yellow?"

Amy nodded. They got to the door and Greta paused dramatically, then threw open the door. Amy caught her breath. Greta heard her and she laughed. "You like it."

It was the cleanest, prettiest room she'd ever seen. All

done in light yellow and white with white furniture. Greta charged across the room and pulled open another door. "The bathroom," she announced.

Amy approached it slowly. The walls and floor were shining pink tile, the shower curtain was real cloth with a plastic liner, not like the stained sheet of plastic covered with faded flamingoes that they'd had at home.

"We have to share it," Greta said. "Paulie has his own bathroom. So do Mom and Dad. We have three bathrooms in the house and a sink and toilet on the first floor," she said proudly.

Greta opened the other door. "This is my room."

Greta was their daughter, and Amy was only a guest, so she expected Greta's room to be magnificent. But it wasn't any larger or prettier than the one she was going to stay in. There was an overflowing toy chest in a corner, and the shelves on the wall were full of books and games.

"I would have put some of the toys in your room before you got here," Greta said, "but I thought it would be more fun if you picked them yourself."

Amy didn't know what to say. Greta crossed the room, opened a drawer, and pulled out a light blue sweater. "We couldn't get clothes yet, either. We didn't know what would fit. You can wear this tonight if you like. It's brand-new."

It was fuzzy and light; Amy held it tenderly.

"You and me and Mummy are going to Read's to get you clothes. Have you ever been to Read's?"

"No."

"We're going tomorrow. Then we'll have lunch at Swenson's. That's the best restaurant in Danbury. Have you been to Danbury?"

Amy shook her head.

"It's big," Greta said. "Not as big as Waterbury or Hartford; but I think it's nicer. Have you been to Waterbury or Hartford?"

Amy shook her head again.

"Where have you been?" Greta asked gently.

"To my grandmother's near Newton and to the beach

once and around my house. We live in Bridgeton." She stopped, confused, because she'd used the present tense. Greta hugged Amy again. "You live here now," she said firmly.

Greta was shorter than Amy and much plumper. Her hair was a smooth, dark blond, like Levin's, and her arms were fat and strong and held Amy firmly. Amy wanted to hug Greta back and return the kisses, but she was too shy and broke the embrace.

Greta showed her the clean towels and gave her a new bar of soap. She had her own drawer in the bathroom vanity with a comb and brush already in it. She washed and put on the sweater; it was the loveliest garment she'd ever worn. Greta was waiting for her in the hall. The house smelled of roasting chicken.

Greta took her hand and they started down the stairs together. Halfway down Greta stopped. "I hate my name," she said confidentially. "When we're alone, will you call me Dorothy?"

"Why Dorothy?" Amy asked.

"After the girl in *The Wizard of Oz*."

"Okay, Dorothy."

They went a few more steps, and this time it was Amy who stopped. Greta asked, "Do you have a name you want to be called?" Amy shook her head. She stopped on the stairs because Nana had told her that sometimes God treated us kindly, and when he did, it was important to thank him. She didn't know any prayers—her mother didn't believe in God and didn't like prayers—but it seemed important to do something, so she bowed her head the way she'd seen Nana do a thousand times and whispered, "Thank you."

Greta led her into a small dining room with a tablecloth, cloth napkins, and dishes that were clean and unchipped. It was better than Nana's at Christmas dinner.

"Today's your first day," Greta said, "so we didn't have to set the table. But we will from now on."

Amy nodded. It would be a pleasure to handle the clean linen and heavy silverware with carved handles. The forks at home had crooked tines and tasted metallic. Here, there were candles and fresh flowers on the sideboard.

Mrs. Levin came in carrying a big deep bowl of soup. It smelled wonderful. Amy's mouth watered.

"You two sit there," said Mrs. Levin.

Amy and Greta sat next to each other. Amy watched Greta lift her fork, unfold her napkin, and put it in her lap. Amy did the same.

Levin came in. "Hey, kid," he boomed, "that sweater looks terrific."

He sat down, and Mrs. Levin put the bowl at the far end of the table. Greta took Amy's hand under the table. Mrs. Levin started ladling the yellow soup with noodles into flowered soup bowls, and Amy thought that if she had died in that closet and her soul had gone to heaven the way Nana said your soul did, it would be like this.

Then she heard footsteps thump down the stairs and across the hall, and Paulie Levin came in the dining room.

He ignored her and took the seat on his father's right, across from Amy and Greta. Mrs. Levin put his soup bowl in front of him, and he picked up his spoon and started to eat without looking up at her or thanking her.

"Manners," Levin said sharply.

Paulie shot him a look of pure hatred and waited with his spoon poised arrogantly over the soup while Mrs. Levin lit the candles, sat down, and picked up her spoon. Paulie went to work on his soup.

Amy did everything that Greta did; pushing her spoon away from her in the bowl, making sure she didn't slurp. The soup was the best food she'd ever tasted, and she glanced across the table at Paulie to see if he was enjoying it too. He was staring at her with empty eyes, a small, mean grin playing around his mouth. The candles lost their glow for Amy, the soup was hot salt water, and for the first time since she'd walked into this house, she thought of the kitchen and her mother. She put the spoon down and looked at Levin. He noticed and smiled encouragingly at her.

"Is my father back from Poughkeepsie?" she asked.

Everyone was silent. She could feel their embarrassment.

"Yes," Levin said. "He's here."

"When can I see him?" she asked.

"I don't know, Amy. I'll find out."

Mrs. Levin said gently, "Eat your soup while it's hot, dear."

Amy glanced again at Paulie Levin. He was staring openly at her, still grinning. His hair and eyes were lighter than Greta's, and he had a high, pale forehead that made his face totally different from the rest of the family. His light eyes stared into hers, and she knew that he was glad that her father was in prison because he hated her.

All of a sudden ideas came to Amy that were more complicated and grown-up than any she'd ever had. She pitied Paulie Levin because when it came to hating, he was a piker; small, mean, and incompetent. But *she* wouldn't be. If he made her hate him, she would be very good at it, and she suddenly felt sorry for Paulie Levin. He must have seen the pity in her eyes or just sensed it, because the nasty little grin left his face and he stopped watching her.

On Monday Levin met Moran in a health-food restaurant for lunch. It was 1973, organic was in, and the place was crowded. Moran had saved a table, and he got up to greet Levin when he came in. He saw the way Levin looked at the place and the other customers.

"The food's really good," Moran said, "and you can stay awake for the rest of the day after lunch here. Only they don't serve liquor."

Levin didn't usually drink during the day, anyway, and the vegetable juice he ordered was spicy and very good. The lunch choices were something else; they sounded like feed for ruminants, and he looked helplessly at Moran. Moran laughed. "Try the eggplant casserole. It's good."

They gave their orders to a young girl wearing an ankle-length peasant skirt. She left them alone and Moran said, "Trouble with the kid already?"

If he'd sounded smug or I-told-you-so, Levin would have decked him. But his voice was gentle, his eyes concerned.

"I don't know if it's trouble. That's why I'm here. She wants to see her father."

Moran looked surprised. "Why?"

"I thought you could tell me."

Moran was quiet, then he asked, "Is everything else okay?"

"It's a honeymoon. She's a lovely kid. My daughter adores her. She's six months older than Amy, and it's made her absurdly protective. She acts like she's Amy's mother. My wife looks in on Amy every couple of hours during the night to make sure she's okay, and I think the kid's gained weight just in the past few days."

"What about your son?"

Levin looked grim. The waitress brought their food, and Levin tasted the eggplant. "It's good," he said.

"What about your son?" Moran asked again.

"My son's a creep, Doctor. He doesn't like her. No reflection on her; he doesn't like anybody."

Moran was shocked and tried not to show it. Levin went on. "A couple of years ago, I bought Paulie an air gun. You know the kind; lots of kids have them. They won't do much harm, but you can kill a bird with them or maybe a chipmunk. I had one when I was a kid, and after I'd killed my bird, the way I guess all little boys have to for some reason, I was sick. I put the gun away and never looked at it again. I think my father had just that in mind when he got me the gun. I had the same thing in mind when I got it for Paulie. We went out one Sunday . . . me with a walking stick and my field guide to mushrooms, and Paulie with his air gun, and sure enough, he shoots his bird. We went up to it and I was almost sick all over again, the way I'd been when I was a kid. The limp body, the ruffled feathers, that awful stillness when just an instant ago it could fly. But I was glad, too, in a way, because

I was sure Paulie would feel the same way, and now that lousy gun would wind up in the attic or at the October rummage sale. I looked at him, knowing that I would see pain, sorrow, and sickness and that he would try to hide it. I planned to be the best daddy in the world, and we would talk it out so he wouldn't be ashamed of being ashamed of killing the bird. Only, when I looked at his face, I saw nothing. Absolutely, totally, one-hundred-percent zilch. He looked carved. I would have thought the kid had died with the bird except that he blinked and had this gorgeous flush on his cheeks. He kicked the body out of the way and looked up into the trees. 'What're you looking for?' I ask him, knowing the answer and terrified of hearing. 'More birds,' he says."

Moran looked down at his plate of half-eaten rice, sprouts, and God knew what else. It was getting cold, rubbery at the edges. Soft conversation at the other tables made a pleasant background to this sad little conversation. He wondered if he should keep his mouth shut. Levin was not his patient; neither was his son. But he couldn't let it go; it just was not his way. He looked up at Levin and said quietly, "That's really a load of shit, isn't it, Lieutenant? You don't dislike your son because he shot a bird and wasn't eaten up with self-disgust and guilt. You're a cop. I imagine you carry something a whole lot more lethal than an air gun. Maybe you've shot a *man* or two in your time, never mind a bird. There's more to it than a dead bird."

"Such as?" Levin asked.

"All the shit things that happen between fathers and sons . . . two males trying to occupy the same space. Mostly jealousy on both sides. The father's afraid of being surpassed, supplanted. The son's afraid of being overridden, controlled. . . ."

"I've told myself all that crap."

"Won't wash?" Moran asked.

"No. I wouldn't like him if he were someone else's son. Wouldn't even try."

"*Do* you try?"

"I used to."

"And now?"

"Now I try . . . to be . . . ambivalent."

It was a terrible admission. Moran had to look away from the pain he saw in the other man's eyes. Levin turned his knife over on the table with a clink a couple of times, then shoved it away.

"Fuck this," he said. "What about Amy and her father?"

"*Can* she see him? I mean, will they let a child visit a man in prison?"

"Yes. He's in Longbury. The charge is murder two, and he can't raise bail, so he's not convicted of anything yet. They have to let him see her. Unless I forbid it. I guess I can do that legally, but I'm not sure I should. She'll have to see him sooner or later, anyway."

"Why?"

"She's the only witness. She'll have to testify at the trial. But why rush it? Why does she want to see the shit now?"

"Lieutenant, most kids love their parents more than anything on earth. More than they love themselves. I've seen lots of abused children. I've seen children whose parents came close to killing them. But they always want to go back to Mommy and Daddy."

"But he didn't hurt *her*. Not directly. He killed her mother."

"She might love him, anyway, Lieutenant," Moran said.

Levin attacked his eggplant. Moran watched him for a second, then said, "You talked about the honeymoon with your wife and kid. How was it for you?"

"Okay," Levin said.

"Just okay."

Levin shrugged.

"How do you feel about Amy?"

"She's . . . okay."

"You're bullshitting, Lieutenant. It's a honeymoon for you, too, isn't it?"

"I told you, she's an attractive kid. They spent Saturday

in Danbury, came home with a whole new wardrobe for her. Cost me a hundred or so, but Christ, it was worth it. They put on a kind of fashion show for me . . . Amy in all the new clothes. She didn't even look like the same kid." He pushed his fork around in the uneaten food. "She didn't thank me out loud, Moran. But I could see it in her eyes."

Moran smiled. "You should see your own eyes."

Levin blinked and looked away.

"Ever hear of Occam's razor, Lieutenant?"

"Yeah. Most cops have. He was an Irishman from the tenth century. Said the obvious answer is almost always the right one. Or something."

"Or something," Moran said gently. "So what's obvious? Amy wants to see her father. Why? Probably because she loves him, no matter what he's done." Moran paused. "Now we get to the second part. She probably loves him, and you probably know it. But you don't want her to see him. Why?"

"You're saying I'm jealous. That seems to be today's special."

"It's possible. You're the only one that knows."

Only Levin didn't know. He almost wanted to believe Moran because jealousy was easy to understand. But it didn't feel right.

He waited.

Amy and Greta went off every morning on the school bus together and came home swinging their book bags. They did their homework together. Greta was good at English and history; Amy was a whiz at math.

The girls took to sneaking into each other's rooms after lights out, and one Sunday morning he found them asleep in Amy's bed with their arms around each other.

Paulie ignored Amy, and she learned to ignore him. After the second week Levin gave up his long-shot hope that the little orphan girl would change his son and decided that he had been a naive schmuck. Helpless orphan girls reformed big bad boys in musicals and children's books.

Paulie stayed out a lot. When the weather got really bad

and the boys he kept company with (Levin couldn't call them friends) were around, they stayed in the basement. Levin didn't know what they did down there. He didn't want to.

Once a week Jeannie took Amy to Millbridge to see Moran. Amy's voice got stronger; loud noises no longer made her jump. She'd gained about five pounds and she was beautiful. At first Levin was afraid that Amy's prettiness would bother Greta, but it didn't. She wasn't that kind of kid and, he thought with great pride, she wouldn't be that kind of woman.

Everything would have been fine (excluding Paulie) except that every four days, as if she were keeping a schedule, Amy asked to see her father. Her manner was gentle, her voice soft, but under it Levin heard steel, and he knew the little girl wouldn't be distracted and just forget about it. Then the week before Thanksgiving it came to a head.

Amy was the ward of a police lieutenant, so they sent Baker and James Kennedy, a short, red-faced man from the DA's office, right to the house to get her deposition. They set up a tape recorder in the dining room. Jeannie and Greta were forbidden to come in, but Levin was there. He hovered at the sideboard in front of the window, feeling huge and helpless while Kennedy questioned her.

But she gave her answers calmly.

"I didn't see him hit her," Amy said, "I heard it."

Kennedy's Adam's apple bobbed, and Baker played with his pipe.

"Tell us what you did see," Kennedy said.

"I saw the floor with the mess, and broken glass, and the bottom of her robe, and his legs. She tried to get away from him, but he went after her, then I heard a sort of crunch. . . ."

Kennedy turned white and wiped his face, and Levin stared at the Christmas cactus on the sideboard. He felt sorry for Kennedy. He was a lawyer, not a cop. He'd only been with the DA's office for a year. He'd probably never heard a story like this before.

Amy said, "Then she fell down, and his hand"—she

stood up and let her arm drop to her side to show them—"hung down with the hammer in it . . ." Her voice had turned flat and dead; she sounded like a machine and her eyes were glassy. "It was all covered with blood."

The room was cold. Kennedy shivered and said, "Can you turn the heat up in here, Joe?"

Levin nodded and went out to the thermostat in the hall. It was set for sixty-eight and the thermometer read seventy. He turned it up to seventy-five and went back. Amy was sitting at the table again, in front of the recorder. The furnace blower came on; the room was warming up.

She said, "I don't know after that. He said her name, then ran out."

"You definitely saw the hammer in his hand?" Kennedy asked.

Amy nodded, and he pointed to the tape recorder's speaker. "Yes," she said into it. "Then he dropped it on the floor and he ran away." Now the room was getting too warm, but the men were done. Baker unplugged the recorder. Amy stared at Kennedy.

"My father's in jail, isn't he?"

"Yes." Kennedy avoided looking at her.

"What'll happen to him?" she asked.

"He'll be tried and sentenced if he's found guilty."

"Will they electrocute him?"

Kennedy had to wipe his face again. "We don't electrocute people anymore," he said.

"Will they hang him or something?" Amy asked.

"No. He's charged with second-degree murder. That doesn't carry the death penalty. We don't use the death penalty anymore, anyway."

"But he killed my mother," she said.

"He'll go to prison for a long time."

"Forever?"

Kennedy tucked the recorder under his arm and made for the door.

"Will he go to jail forever?" Amy asked again.

"I don't know, Amy," Kennedy said, opening the door. "I'll have this typed and sent over this afternoon, Joe. You're her guardian, you'll have to sign it."

Levin nodded, but he was staring at Amy.

Kennedy finally got out the door, and Baker rushed after him, leaving Amy and Levin alone in the dining room. It was quiet. Rain trickled through the downspout outside the window, the wind moaned around the house, and Amy stood perfectly still, staring at the closed door. He wanted to talk to her, but he didn't know what to say. After a minute she opened the door and went out into the hall. He heard her going up the stairs where Greta was certainly waiting breathlessly to hear what the men with the tape recorder wanted.

Levin went to the table. The rubber feet on the recorder and the men's fingers had left smudges on Jeannie's polished table, and he rubbed at it absently with the sleeve of his jacket. Occam and Charles Moran were full of shit. Amy didn't love her father; she hated him.

He was on the twelve-to-eight shift right before Thanksgiving, covering for Sal De Rosa. A few days after the deposition he came home at eight-thirty and found Amy sitting on the steps in the foyer waiting for him. The TV played in the background. Greta and Jeannie were in the den. Paulie was probably out with his buddies or upstairs staring at the ceiling or jerking off or whatever he did up there.

"Hi, Amy." He took off his coat and hung it in the front closet. He hadn't worn a uniform for years now and could have worked eight to four all the time if he wanted to. He was rising; there was the chance of a captaincy now that Larry Seymour was retiring. The rank and file liked Levin; the brass trusted him. The captaincy was a good bet, and he was feeling pleased with himself as he hung away his damp coat on that chilly November night.

"Joe," Amy said.

He turned to her. Her eyes were wide and unhappy. He sat down on the steps next to her and put his arm around her.

"What's the matter, honey?"

"When can I see my father?"

His arm stiffened around her. "Amy, why do you want to see your father?" He almost laughed out loud because he'd been puzzling and worrying at it for a month, and this was the first time he'd thought simply to ask her. It probably never occurred to Moran, either.

She said, "I don't know. He's . . . he's my father."

"The other day you sounded like you hated him, Amy."

"He's still my father."

Levin said, "What if he doesn't want to see you?"

"Doesn't he?"

"I don't know."

"Joe, will you ask him?" she pleaded.

Just like that . . . after a month of agonizing, should he or shouldn't he, she was giving him a way out. Kaslov had killed her mother and left Amy in a closet to die. That was enough to make a fiend feel guilty, and Kaslov wasn't a fiend. He was just a poor-slob drunk who'd beaten his wife to death without meaning to. According to Baker, who took Kaslov's testimony, the poor jerk didn't even remember doing it. Of course, Kaslov knew by now, and his guilt must be epic. Amy was the embodiment of that guilt, and she was probably the last person on earth Kaslov wanted to face. Levin would ask, Kaslov would say no, and that would be the end of it. Amy didn't realize any of this; she looked pleadingly at Levin, and he was suddenly shocked by the depth of his feeling for her. He tightened his arm around her thin shoulders and kissed the top of her head.

"Okay, Sweet Pea," he said. "I'll ask."

Longbury Prison was gray and hideous; it rambled across a small valley and looked like they had used every cement block on earth to build it. The visiting room was long, narrow, and cold. A table with a mesh grate bolted to it divided the prisoners from their visitors. Cardboard turkeys were tacked on the chipped light green walls to celebrate the season. The fluorescent light faded the bright colors; shadows from the bars on the windows streaked the turkeys in black. Amy's father would spend Thursday here, eating turkey roll and gummy stuffing with a spoon, and against his will, Levin felt sorry for the man.

The light over the door to the cell blocks blinked on, the guard at the high desk folded his newspaper away, and the door opened. Kaslov came in, followed by another guard. Levin had time to watch him while Kaslov gave his card to the guard at the desk. He was tall, and in spite of the prison grays and the sick pallor the fluorescent lights gave his skin, he was extremely handsome. Levin felt a pang of real jealousy for the first time. Not so much for Amy's sake as for his own. Levin knew that he was a good-looking man; he was as tall as Kaslov and bigger-boned. He was thirty-nine, but his body was firm, his hair was thick and still more dark blond than gray. His eyes were clear blue, and young women still flirted with him at neighborhood parties. Sometimes Jeannie called him a bull of a man; and when she said that, he felt young, virile, handsome. But Michael Kaslov was magnificent-looking, movie-star material, and Levin knew that women would blush when he looked at them and preen in a way that they never would for Levin.

Kaslov walked down the length of the table toward Levin. He was six years younger than Levin; he walked gracefully with perfect control, and Levin imagined the play of ropy muscles under the prison uniform.

Kaslov sat down on his side of the grate and smiled at Levin. His teeth were perfect, and Levin felt a depressing stab of hatred for the man. He was jealous, all right, because he knew that when Amy said "Father," this was the face she saw.

"They told me you have my daughter," Kaslov said.

Levin nodded.

"Is anything wrong with her. Is she okay?"

"She's fine," Levin said, and then, hating himself as well as Kaslov, he did something he never did; he tried to hurt the man on the other side of the grate.

"We've been feeding her up. We bought her all new clothes. Everything she had was rags, and she was down to about fifty pounds. But you should see her now."

Kaslov wasn't hurt; his eyes lit up, and then, with two words, he ruined everything.

"Can I?" he pleaded.

Levin didn't answer.

"Oh, please. Oh, sweet Christ, can I see my little girl?"

"She saw what you did to her mother, Kaslov."

That stopped him for a second, but then he seemed to gather himself and he said, "I'm still her father, Levin."

And there it was again, Levin thought. Moran, Amy, and now this matinee idol who'd killed his wife and almost killed his daughter . . . they all came back to the same thing, like dogs to their own vomit. He was her father.

Levin had never felt so old and defeated. He stood up and felt his knees creak. "I think she hates you, Kaslov. It may be a very unpleasant visit."

"She won't hate me if I can see her, talk to her, explain . . . please." He grabbed the grate, his fingers wrapped around the steel mesh. Miserably Levin noticed that even the man's hands were beautiful.

He said, "We'll see," and he nodded to the guard that the visit was over. Kaslov clutched the mesh. "You'll try, Lieutenant. Promise me you'll try," he called. Levin ignored him and went to the door. The guard buzzed, the door clicked open, and Levin went through it. Behind him Kaslov was still calling to him, "You'll try, won't you? Just try . . ."

Levin raced along the clangy corridors to the reception area with its cinder-block walls covered with peeling orange paint. He stopped at the door with his hand on the cold metal handle and looked out. The drive out was cracked, the field alongside was a no-man's-land of brown grass beaten down by wind, rain, and years of neglect. He could see the double cyclone fence in the distance, and an old, abandoned guard tower crumbling to an ugly ruin of cement and wire.

Kaslov wanted to see his daughter, she wanted to see him, and lying was the only way Levin could keep them apart; but he was a lousy liar and this lie would have to go on for years. His shoulders slumped, his hand dropped off the handle, and he turned to the guard.

"Who do I see to arrange a visit?" he asked.

Now that it was going to happen, Amy didn't want it to. She never had, and she didn't know why she kept on asking. It was too late; she couldn't back out. She wouldn't, anyway, because she had to see him. She didn't know why. The night Levin told her the visit was arranged for December 15, she dreamed about her father for the first time in months.

She was in the hospital bed, and his figure appeared in the doorway. He was huge, dressed in white, and had a stocking-mask face that she remembered from another dream. But she knew it was her father. He staggered into the room toward the bed. He carried the hammer, her mother's blood dripped off it onto the floor. He was going to hit Amy with it . . . kill her.

She was terrified; so was Greta; she was across the room cowering under the picture of Mickey Mouse. Greta tried to scream, but her voice was stuck with fear. Amy had nothing to fight with but the cup of custard. She waited until he had dragged himself almost to the edge of the bed. He raised the hammer, blood ran down his arm into the white sleeve of his jacket; it dripped on the white sheets of her bed. She forced herself to wait until he'd taken one more step, then she jerked the custard cup at him and custard flew out and hit him squarely in the face. He screamed and dropped the hammer. He clawed at the yellow stuff that filled his eyes. The custard spread, covered his face and ran down his neck. It dripped out the sleeve, and in a second his hand was covered with it.

Greta jumped up and down and thumped the wall, the picture of Mickey Mouse shook on its hook, and it looked like he was sharing Greta's jubilation.

"He's melting," Greta shrieked, "like the Wicked Witch in *Wizard of Oz* . . . he's melting . . ."

It was true. Her father writhed to the floor, his flesh melted, and Amy could see white bone gleaming through the custard. She screamed because he was her father and she hadn't meant to kill him, only to stop him from killing her. How could she know that a bit of custard would be lethal . . . ?

She woke up with a jerk. She was covered with sweat and lay awake for a long time before she dared to close her eyes again.

She told Moran as much of the dream as she could remember. After a moment he said, "You *can* hurt your father, Amy. I suppose that deep down you know that."

"How can I hurt him?"

"By rejecting him, by pretending that you don't love him."

"But I don't love him," she said. "He killed my mother and they're not going to do anything to him for it. They'll put him in jail for a while, but Greta and Cissy Simms told me that they don't keep them there long. They parole them. Cissy's father's a cop, too, so they know all about it."

"You don't think the years in prison are enough punishment?"

"No."

He thought he figured it out, and he smiled gently at her. "Do you think that showing him that you don't love him will punish him more?"

"But that's not all—" She stopped.

"What's not all?"

She didn't answer.

He asked her several times, but she shook her head. He could see that she really didn't know what else she could do to her father.

That night Moran had what he would have told one of his patients was an anxiety attack. He woke up gasping for breath, with a band of pressure around his chest like shrinking rawhide. It could have been a heart attack but there was no pain. He'd had an EKG in August and everything was fine. The tightness radiated out, his arms were numb, his throat constricted.

He rolled out of bed and stood up on shaky legs. There was no point waking Mary; she couldn't do anything for him. He took two Valium and went down to the kitchen. He opened a can of tuna fish and ate it standing at the counter. He'd read recently that tyrosamine was as effective a relaxant as benzodiazepine and tuna fish was full of tyrosamine. The Valium or tuna fish or both worked, and little by little the rawhide band that threatened to crush in his heart and lungs loosened; feeling came back into his arms.

He knew the source of the attack. One more time his moment had come to say something, and he was going to keep his mouth shut. He wasn't a coward, he told himself firmly, as firmly as he could, since his eyelids felt draggy, his head was heavy, his thoughts thick and slow. He wasn't going to talk because he didn't know what to say. Except that he did know . . .

"Don't let her go to Longbury . . . don't let her within ten miles of that poor jerk up there . . . don't . . ."

Jonathan sensed disaster. He could smell it, like sulfur before a heat storm. He was getting it from the kid, but he hadn't gotten anything from her since they carried her out of the closet.

He put his cards down.

"Gin again?" Perkins wailed.

Jonathan always won because he knew what was in the other hands. He'd won thousands at poker and hundreds of thousands at gin. If real money changed hands, he'd be rich. But it didn't, and he had nothing to spend the money on, anyway. Except for Marty Vespa, all the men he played with were crazy. They'd never pay. When Perkins lost too much, he hid in his room and wouldn't talk to Jonathan.

"No gin," Jonathan said. "I can't play anymore. You win."

Perkins stared wonderingly at Jonathan. He'd never won before.

Jonathan left the table and went to the window. A second ago he'd been a happy man. He knew it was absurd for a crazy man locked up in an asylum to be happy, but he had been. It was his favorite time of year; the days were drawing in, as the English said, and the lights were on by four. The grated electric fire glowed across the room, and even the huge lounge looked cozy. Some of the ladies were watching *Edge of Night*, and the voices and music in the background were soothing. Christmas was coming and people's thoughts weren't so bitter. Today was Monday—they were having meat loaf, his favorite. He'd been looking forward to dinner and feeling warm and content only a few seconds ago. He tried to get the feeling back.

"Jonathan?" Perkins wailed.

"I said you win. You finally fucking win. Go tell somebody."

Irma Crosby, one of the ladies in front of the TV, whirled around when she heard the word *fuck* and glared at Jonathan. He raised his hands in apology, and Irma went back to the program.

Perkins smiled uncertainly. "I really win?"

"You really do."

Perkins left the card table and walked jauntily across the lounge and out the door. He'd tell everyone he could find that he had finally beaten the invincible Kaslov. Jonathan turned back to the window, and his niece's thoughts and feelings swooped in at him. He tried to get rid of them; he stared at the horizon trying to remember what was on the other side of those hills. He hadn't crossed them for years, but he knew the little towns wouldn't change much. One-stoplight towns with a couple of churches, a bar, a dry-goods store. Nice little towns, full of nice people who ate their suppers with metal forks, made love in secret, and got children.

He missed children—and women, too, of course. Women more. Thinking about women usually drove everything else away, and he imagined that he was in the backseat of Michael's old Ford with Sally Grayson again. He had just slipped down his zipper and forced her half-willing hand inside his pants. He remembered her warm fingers on him and the sweat on her palm and the odd look of concentration that she'd gotten on her face as her slick hand touched him. He started to get an erection; he leaned his body against the windowsill to heighten the feeling and overcome the ugly, icy thoughts he was getting from his niece. He remembered Michael and Cindy in the front seat of the Ford. Michael could get Cindy to do anything to him, and Jonathan could see her head disappearing down into Michael's lap, and Michael's eyes closing . . . *Michael* . . .

She was going to see Michael, and she hated him.

Her hatred hit Jonathan like a moving wall. The erection collapsed, and he started to feel sick to his stomach. Michael was in danger; that was the disaster. He didn't want to know anymore, and for the billionth time in his life he prayed that it would go away and leave him alone. But it got worse. Now he saw his father standing behind the counter of the little dry-cleaning store. It was boiling hot; his father's thin face ran with sweat, his shoes were cut out at the sides to ease his bunions. His father stood behind that counter from seven in the morning (to catch the commuters) until seven at night every day but Sunday. After he closed the store he stayed at the pressing machine to get clothes pressed for special customers. His father had worked himself to death for his two sons. And now one was a certified, one-hundred-percent lunatic, and the other was a killer. But there was still hope for Michael. He didn't mean to kill his wife, so the sentence would be light. He could be out before he was forty. He'd be off the sauce by then, and maybe he'd get married again and have another kid besides this one strange, dangerous child. But if anything happened to Michael, their father's life and his miserable, sad little death before he was sixty would mean nothing, and Jonathan couldn't let that happen.

But he didn't even know what she was going to do; *she* didn't, either. She didn't know that she could do anything, but it was there, okay; buried under confusion and hatred and a funny kind of longing that he supposed all little girls had for their fathers.

He left the lounge and went up the hall to the pay phone, then realized that he didn't have a number to call.

He could get it, but on the phone he would be nothing to her but the disembodied voice of the crazy uncle she'd never laid eyes on.

He had to *see* Amy. But he was here, she was there. They never allowed children at Limekiln. It was an ironclad rule that even Dr. Hall couldn't break. Jonathan had to go to Amy.

The thought was outrageous. They wouldn't let him out, and even if they would, he didn't know where he was going or how to get there. He had no car, no money, nothing. He could do it, anyway—he was crazy, not stupid—and for once he could be crazy-crafty. A lot of them were.

He thought for a few minutes, then left the phone and went down to the end of the main hall. Another shorter hall branched off and led to the door to the basement. The staff lockers and showers were down there, and it was off-limits to patients. He looked at the door for a second, then walked past it to the first-floor linen closet. There were always a few tools in the closet: a screwdriver, pliers, maybe a wrench. He ducked into the closet, turned on the light, and found a small screwdriver to pry open lockers.

He went back through the forbidden door (which was never locked because of fire rules) and down the stairs to the basement. The locker room door was straight ahead; he stood to the side and peered around the door frame. The room was lined with metal lockers with a changing bench in the middle. Bob Snep was in there with one foot on the changing bench, tying a white shoe with his back to the door.

Jonathan looked around the landing and saw a heat detector sticking out of the wall near the ceiling. He glanced into the room. Snep was tying the other shoe. Jonathan stuck the screwdriver in his back pocket, went up a few stairs. He took out the Zippo that no one knew he had, pried up the wick with fingernails, and lit it. The flame blazed on the high wick. Jonathan stretched as high as he could, holding on to the stair rail, and held the lighter a few feet under the heat detector. Nothing happened. His arm started to tremble, the lighter got hot. He held on, even though his fingertips were burning, and the alarm went off. A siren rose, fell, rose again, and upstairs another siren joined in.

Jonathan leapt over the railing and into the dark well between the stairs and the wall. The sound was deafening, and he clenched his teeth (because he had a sudden impulse to raise his head and scream in tune with the sirens) and froze. Snep raced out of the locker room and up the stairs. The upstairs door opened and closed, then crashed open again. Snep yelled, "It's not down there. I just came up. . . ."

The door swished closed and Jonathan ran for the locker room. Snep's locker was open. He must have banged it to, and the door hit and bounced back. Inside the locker was Snep's overcoat, a sport jacket, a pair of brown trousers with a shiny seat, and his street shoes. Jonathan couldn't take the coat, even though it was cold outside. Snep might come back to lock up and he'd see it was gone. Jonathan searched the pockets. In the coat he found a pack of cigarettes and a Mars bar. In the jacket he found Snep's wallet with thirty dollars in it, and his keys. The orderly's keys would open almost any door in the building.

Jonathan took all the keys and the money and left the locker room. There was a steel door at the end of the basement corridor. If it faced the way he thought it did, it would lead to the rock garden (Dr. Hall's pride) and the employee parking lot.

Jonathan ran to it; the lock was stamped De Met, Omaha. He found the De Met key on Snep's ring and opened the door just like that. He stood still with the door half open, the cold, damp air blowing around him. Maybe the door was alarmed, but no one would hear it over the bedlam of the sirens. He still couldn't believe it, and he waited for someone to come rushing down the stairs and pull him back inside. No one came; the sirens screamed on.

Jonathan still hesitated, but there was nothing to stay for, so he stepped outside and let the door close. He had a moment of panic when he heard it lock from the other side, and he knew he couldn't get back in. He stepped back and looked up at the big dreary building. All the windows were lit; the bricks sweated in the fog. There were hundreds of rooms in the place; rooms where the patients slept, where they bathed, where they were dunked in the whirlpool and hooked up to machines and jolted back to earth. There were linen closets with hundreds of bed sheets, pillows, straps to hold them down, and shrouds to cover them when they died. There were a thousand cabinets full of drug bottles and hypos, bandages, pills, and straitjackets. He supposed it was a dreadful place, but it had been his home for a long time.

The kitchen fan blew out into the fog, and Jonathan smelled the meat loaf he would have had for dinner, and he longed to be back on the other side of that door. But he turned away, went to the parking lot, and tried Snep's keys on the car with the least dew on it. They worked, and he slid into the driver's seat.

He started the motor, put the car in reverse, and turned around into the drive. It ended in a small, back guardhouse with a wooden bar across the road. He slowed up, but no one came out. Mr. Cermak was the guard here; he was probably running across the front lawn to see the fire. Jonathan heard more sirens, this time in the distance, and he knew that the Sharon volunteer fire department was on its way to save Limekiln. One more time he hesitated, then he put the car in second, floored the accelerator, and the little Ford crashed through the wooden barrier and out onto the road. He put the car in drive and turned away from the sirens. He could go in any direction he wanted to; he could stop in a diner, buy coffee, use a pay phone, say hello to people on the street. For the first time in years he was free.

He parked across from 114 Windy Ridge Road at two-thirty the next afternoon. It had been absurdly easy. Last night he had found a motel room for seventeen dollars near Torrington. He thought it would be dreary, but it was clean, had thick towels, carpeting, a color TV, and an assortment of local phone books. He supposed the phone books were for traveling salesmen. He bought two hamburgers at the White Castle across the street and watched the color TV. It was a real revelation after the huge old Magnavox at Limekiln with its perpetual snowstorm behind the screen. When the late show started, he went to the phone books.

His brother's house was in Bridgeton. Levin had been sent to find the body and let the child out, so he must be stationed near Bridgeton. The Bridgeton book also contained numbers for Havens Mill, Millbridge, Stockton, and Westerly. He prayed that Levin wasn't the kind who lived fifty miles from where he worked, and he looked down the line of *L*'s with his heart pounding. He found it first time, J. Levin, 114 Windy Ridge, Westerly.

Now he was parked across the road from the home of the Westerly Levins—probably, hopefully, please God . . . the right Levins. The house was painted white with green shutters. It looked roomy, not huge. The grass had been fed and was still green, the ornamentals were trim and healthy-looking. He would have bet that there was a vegetable garden in the back, tilled for winter and covered with straw. His niece was lucky to live in a house like this . . . then he laughed out loud and thought that her luck had been a long time changing. It was Wednesday, she would be at school, and he supposed she would be home sometime between now and four.

A small squall came up, rain spattered the windshield, the black ash tree he was parked under dripped rain on the roof of the car. He turned on the radio, then feared for Snep's battery and turned it off. At ten after three a school bus lumbered into the road, flashed its red lights, and stopped. Jonathan's heart pounded; his hands started to sweat. The lights blinked off, the school bus pulled away, and he saw two little girls on the path to the Levin house. One was blond, one dark. They both carried book bags. He jerked open the car door and jumped out into the road.

"Amy!" he yelled.

Both girls turned. He raced across the road and stopped a few feet from them. The dark girl was very thin and had Michael's eyes.

"Amy," he said again, softly this time. He'd traveled forty miles to see her, but it felt like thousands. The men who'd flown to the moon had not gone one inch farther than he had come to stand here in front of this child.

The blond girl plucked at the strap of Amy's book bag.

"C'mon. We're not supposed to talk to anyone we don't know."

Amy didn't move.

"I'm your Uncle Jonathan," he said, "your father's brother."

"Amy," the blond girl said, "come inside."

Amy stared at him without moving. The little blond girl (she was kind of pudgy and very cute, and Jonathan got good, sunny feelings from her, except this instant he knew she was scared of him) said, "I'll get Mother."

She ran up the stairs and into the house, and Jonathan thanked her silently for leaving him alone with his niece. She was pale and thin but pretty, and looked like Michael and maybe a little like Jonathan.

He knelt down; the pavement was cold and damp, and he started to shiver. He knew that she noticed that he didn't have a coat, and he felt her feel sorry for him. That wouldn't do; they had to understand each other, not just feel things.

Eye contact was usually painful for him and he tried to avoid it, but this time he made himself look right into the little girl's eyes. At first he just got snatches of thoughts in pictures, a broken doll in a dusty attic, a field behind a farmhouse; he saw Mickey Mouse and the face of the girl who'd just run away and of a nice-looking woman who might be the woman inside the house. The pictures changed and darkened. He saw blood on the kitchen floor and running out of a woman's black hair. He saw his brother looking drunk. The sickening hatred he'd felt back at Limekiln hit him again, and suddenly he was frightened and wanted to run away from her. He made himself stay on his knees in front of her, holding that excruciating eye contact. He said, "He didn't mean to do it. It was like an accident. He did not remember. He did not even know you were in the closet."

She stared at him without speaking.

"I tell you, he didn't mean it," Jonathan wailed.

A white face appeared at a first-floor window, then disappeared. Amy's thoughts changed and came in words, *I suppose he didn't mean to knock my mother's teeth out and scar my face . . . .*

Jonathan noticed the thin white scar cutting through her eyebrow.

I suppose he didn't mean to leave us with no food and no money to pay for the refrigerator. He didn't mean to get drunk and throw me against the wall. He didn't mean to break the Avon lady's bottles and throw garbage on my mother. I suppose he didn't mean to hit my mother with the hammer.

"He was drunk," Jonathan cried. "He was out of control."

It was hopeless. She was only eight; she couldn't know what he was talking about. He grabbed her arms, and the front door of the house opened and a lovely-looking woman came out on the stoop.

"Leave that child alone," she yelled.

"I'm Jonathan Kaslov," Jonathan yelled back, "I'm Amy's uncle. How do, ma'am. This is the first time Amy and I've had a chance to talk."

"I've called the police," the woman cried.

He heard sirens somewhere on another road. Their time was almost up.

He looked back at Amy. "Listen to me." His hands tightened on her arms; she didn't squirm or try to get away. "My father was a good man. He was your grandfather. He loved his sons. If something happens to Michael, it'll be as if your poor grandfather never lived. Do you understand?"

He felt confusion. She didn't want to do anything to Michael. Mostly she didn't know that she could.

But he knew. That cold thing that came out of the closet with her was still there, no kidding himself about that. It was stronger than ever. She knew it was there too. But she didn't know what it was and neither did he. He *did* know that it wasn't a separate thing. It was not like a worm or bacteria, or some other opportunistic organism that invaded her body because she was too frightened and grief-stricken to fight it off. It had gotten strong in the closet, maybe invincible—it felt invincible—but it had always been part of her, like the timbre of her voice, the color of her eyes . . . like his . . . ability . . . was part of him. Maybe seeing what she saw just made way for it, the way he supposed his mother's dying had made way for the thing in him to come out.

He always thought of it as "the thing," but it needed a name. Dr. Hall called it an "ability," trying to make it seem ordinary. But that was too small a word. An ability didn't drive people mad like it had Jonathan; it didn't freeze people in their tracks and make little girls like Amy fearsome (and she was fearsome, no kidding himself about that, either). He threw out *ability* and rummaged in his mind for a word. He'd read articles in old magazines in the lounge that mentioned "psi talent," a catchall phrase for a panoply of "things." But that sounded petty too. And this might be dreadful, wonderful, supremely inconvenient, but it wasn't petty. He thought of the word *power*, and while that was too grand (maybe), it was better than any of the others. He and Amy shared a power in their minds. Hers was different; but it was like his, too, and maybe she had inherited it from him or maybe it came down to both of them from some distant forebear who had gone quietly crazy in some tiny Black Sea village a hundred years ago. He didn't know, of course. He never would. But for the first time in seventeen years since that afternoon he had seen Mrs. Shapiro in his brother's mind—since he had been an incorporeal observer to that incredibly exciting and nasty sex scene between his little brother and the midde-aged woman—Jonathan was not alone.

He pulled Amy close to him; her arms flew around his neck and they hugged each other. He could almost feel whatever it was coming out of the fog in her mind. He could almost see it, then he thought he could, then he did . . . it was . . . a cup of custard. He laughed, and she giggled against his neck. Someone grabbed his collar and yanked him to his feet.

"He's my uncle," Amy cried. But the policeman ignored her. He hauled Jonathan down the path, stood him against the squad car chuffing away at the curb, and searched him. The other cop went up the path to talk to Mrs. Levin. The cop shoved Jonathan into the car and locked it. Amy stood in the middle of the neat path watching Jonathan through the car window. He wanted to open the window and ask her about custard (of all the insane and ridiculous things), but there was no window crank or door handle inside the car. It was over. He couldn't stop whatever was going to happen tomorrow. She couldn't, either. Poor Michael had to face the music on his own.

Suddenly Jonathan wanted to tell her things that had nothing to do with Michael; he wanted to tell her that life was ugly and cruel and control meant nothing; no one could control ugliness . . . it was built in . . . a given, like death. But there were small pleasures; you could get through the garbage if you concentrated on the small pleasures.

The cops came back; one got in the front, the other got in back with Jonathan and said something about his rights. He told the cop that the only right he wanted now was a chance to share his wisdom with his niece.

"She's an orphan, you know," he said.

The cops looked at each other, then the car pulled out into the road and Amy waved good-bye.

The cardboard turkeys were gone; a big cutout of Santa Claus and his reindeer replaced them. Someone had put up a shredded-looking cellophane Christmas tree with tarnished tinsel on it. It stood sad and unlit under the window on the visitors' side. The visitors' room at Longbury was as gloomy as before, and Levin wasn't going to leave her alone here.

"Where will he come from?" Amy asked.

"The door with the light over it."

She fixed her eyes on it. She had looked fine when they left this morning. Her clothes were new, her hair was brushed till it shone like coal, and Greta insisted that she wear a red satin hair ribbon. In fact, she had looked gorgeous when they left the house. But now her little face was pale and strained; dark circles had appeared like magic under her eyes.

Five minutes later, at two exactly, the light blinked on, the door opened, and Michael Kaslov came through it. A guard followed.

Kaslov beamed at Amy, gave the desk guard his card, and came toward her. He was still smiling, and Levin thought the man's gall was bottomless.

Amy was riveted on him; her look was so concentrated it was almost theatrical, and Levin thought of Miranda. . . .

Oh, brave new world that has such people in it.

But then he noticed that the room was perceptibly colder. He draped Amy's coat around her shoulders and shoved his hands into his jacket pocket. Kaslov got to them, sat down, and looked at his daughter for a long time. Then he said softly, almost seductively, "Hi, baby."

He leaned forward and put his lips against the grate in a kiss gesture. Any other man would have looked absurd doing that, but Kaslov looked beautiful. He waited for her to kiss him back, but she didn't move or make a sound. He waited with his lips pursed against the cold metal, and Levin almost felt sorry for him—and annoyed at Amy. It was stupid to be here if she was going to sit like stone for the next half hour.

Kaslov finally gave up, drew back, and just looked at her for a moment. She stared back, her eyes wide and blank. Levin wondered if she even saw him.

Kaslov said, "They told me what I did."

Amy blinked. The temperature in the room dropped by the second, and Levin saw the guard at the desk put his hands under his arms to warm them up. The other guard took a section of the desk guard's newspapers and leaned at ease against the wall to read.

Kaslov said, "I didn't mean it, Amy. I wouldn't have hurt her. Not really. I don't even remember it. I wouldn't hurt you, honey. You're my little girl."

It sounded like bullshit, but Levin saw tears in Michael Kaslov's eyes.

Kaslov said, "Even grown-ups can't control themselves all the time. Just like kids. You remember when you did things you didn't want to because you just couldn't help it? You remember that, don't you?"

No answer from Amy.

Kaslov smiled. "I bet you remember other things, though. I bet you remember the picnics at Nana's, and the time I took you into the woods so you could go, and you almost sat in the yellow jacket nest. I bet you remember that. I grabbed you up, and we ran out of there with those yellow jackets bombing after us. You remember we had to jump in the stream to keep them from getting us, and then I dried you off and you spent the rest of the day wearing the picnic blanket. But you didn't get stung, honey. And you remember the time we found the bird nest in the raspberries and I took you back there every Sunday until the baby birds hatched out. You remember that, don't you?"

Amy was blinking at him. Her eyes lost the fixed look; her face was getting some color. She was listening, she was remembering, and Levin was almost sorry.

Kaslov laughed softly. "And you remember how we stood in line in the snowstorm to see *Mary Poppins,* and it was so crowded that you had to sit in my lap for two and a

half hours and my legs fell asleep and when I tried to stand,
I fell down in the aisle and you had to help me up? I bet I'd
still be lying in the aisle of the Town House Cinema if it
weren't for my girl."

She blushed like a girl in love and looked at her hands.

"And you remember the time that Tom Sloane taught
you to say *shit,* and you came out with it at Sunday dinner
and I thought Nana was going to faint."

She gave a quick giggle and covered her mouth, and
Levin felt the tension and coldness in the room breaking
apart like ice floes in May.

Kaslov laughed with her; his eyes shone, and his face
was so beautiful, Levin couldn't bear to look at him.

"You know what we're going to do when I get out of
here, baby?"

Amy shook her head, and Levin mourned her resolve to
keep on hating the son of a bitch no matter what.

"We're gonna go and get you a lobster!" Kaslov raised
his hand. "My word, Amy, I don't care what it costs. My little
girl's gonna have lobster. I bet you never tasted lobster. You
tasted shrimp once. You remember that?"

Amy shook her head again.

"You said that poor little shrimp was the ugliest thing
you ever saw. You said nothing that looked so ooky could
taste good. But you were brave and you tried it, and it was
delicious. You remember how good that shrimp was?"

"Yes," Amy said, so softly Levin could barely hear her.

Then Kaslov said, "Trust me, Chicken, it won't . . . " and
the air seemed to shut down and turn to ice. Kaslov stopped
in mid-sentence, as if she'd slapped him. He stared at her,
aghast, for a long time, then very slowly, like a sick old man,
he pulled himself to his feet. He made a small sound, a sort
of cough, like an *ahem,* as if they were having a tea party and
he wanted to interrupt the conversation but very genteelly.
Kaslov and his daughter stared at each other. All the color
drained out of Kaslov's face: his eyes were black holes; his
mouth was a black slash across the bottom of his face. The

slash worked, and Kaslov's voice came through it. It was low, hoarse, and without intonation.

"Amy, don't."

Don't what? Levin's mind screamed. The child hadn't done anything except turn as pale as her father. Her eyes were narrow, and she was frowning, as if she were concentrating.

Kaslov stepped away from the table, then he turned around. Levin thought of an old movie line . . .

Slowly he turned.

It was from a comedy—Abbott and Costello—definitely a comedy, not a horror show. Only suddenly this *was* a horror show and Levin didn't know why.

Kaslov began to move across the room, dragging one foot like a man who'd had a stroke. He wasn't actually walking, he was moving himself toward the guard, who leaned against the wall reading the *Hartford Courant*. The guard looked up. His mouth made a circle of surprise, and Kaslov's hand darted out—it looked huge and white, a monster hand, not a man's—and grabbed the guard by the neck. Levin saw the veins pop in the back; the tendons bulged as Kaslov squeezed the guard's neck in one hand. The guard's face swelled. He choked, and the guard at the desk looked up.

With his free hand Kaslov tore the snap loose on the guard's holster, ripped the gun out, and let the guard go. The man fell back against the wall, then slid down to the floor, his face purple, his paper crumpling around him.

The desk guard pulled out the huge pump gun he kept under the counter and aimed at Kaslov. Kaslov tried to aim back at him, but even from the side Levin could see that Kaslov's aim was way off. The desk guard saw it too.

"Drop it, Kaslov," the desk guard screamed.

Kaslov raised his arm straight out, still way off aim, and pulled the safety. It came off with a clack and he fired. The bullet buried itself harmlessly in the cinder block. The desk guard fired back over Kaslov's head. Part of the wall and the

cardboard Santa disintegrated, and the air was full of pow-
dered cement and cardboard.

Kaslov tried to right his aim, but his movements were
slow and jerky, like a robot getting confused instructions
through faulty wiring. This time the aim was better. Still not
on target but definitely better, and of course the desk guard
couldn't chance it. He lowered the pump gun and shot Kaslov in the chest. His body flew back and hit the wall, but he
stayed on his feet and didn't drop the gun. His face was
green, his eyes went from blank to empty, and Levin thought
he was already dead, but he was raising his arm again in that
infernal, unwilling, jerky way, to get another bead on the
guard.

"Oh, shit," the desk guard sobbed, "fucking shit," and
he shot Kaslov in the gut. Kaslov's blood exploded across the
walls and the floor. A stench filled the room and he settled to
the floor. He sat without moving for an instant, then, bent
like a fetus, he tilted over, fell on what was left of his side,
and dropped the gun.

Cordite stung Levin's eyes; tears ran out of them and
blinded him; through the smoke he saw Amy crumpled over
across the top of the table. He cried out and pulled her upright. He thought a shot went wrong and hit her. She didn't
move. He lifted her in his arms, laid her across the table, and
looked at the front of her body. Then he rolled her to the side
and looked at her back. But there was no blood. Her breath
was ragged but regular. She had fainted.

SEVEN

MORAN WAS SCARED, lost, angry, and bitter. He was lost in Westerly trying to find Levin's place, and he was bitter because he hated all Connecticut towns tonight. They couldn't even put up road signs and streetlights.

He took another wrong turn, wound up back in Westerly Center, and pulled into the Amoco station. Everything else in town was shut up, the main street was dark. But he didn't have to see the town; he knew it was quaint, neat, pretty, and phony. It was like a thousand towns dotted across inland Connecticut and Massachusetts, and tonight he hated them all.

Vermont, New Hampshire, Maine seemed realer; maybe because the winters were so lousy or because there were still farmers there and people who sold things to farmers. The mountains started there; the wilderness. But tonight he wanted to go back to New York. He longed for his mother's old neighborhood out in Flatbush. There the streetlights lit streets, they didn't just decorate them. The bar at the end of his mother's block was open until two in the morning, and it was never empty; the street noise was constant and soothing, like waves on a beach.

But here the roads were dark and empty, as if the people

were reverse vampires who could only come out in the light of day. Except, of course, for the poor slob in the open Amoco station. Moran crossed the lit gas-pump island, hurried through the shadows and into the small, freezing office. The kid in the office tilted his chair on its back legs and stared past Moran as if loath to admit his existence . . . the usual exurban casualness that went with the beards, beer, pickup trucks, and, in this kid's case, pimples and a leather jacket.

Moran felt murderous. He wanted to tell the kid that if he kept on swilling beer, he'd have as many pimples on his ass as he had on his face and his dick would fall off. But he managed to announce mildly, if a little squeakily, that he was lost. The kid gave him a really nice smile, put his beer can down, and told him how to find Windy Ridge. The directions were clear, and Moran realized where he'd gone wrong. He tried to give the kid a dollar, but another surprise . . . the kid wouldn't take it.

He left the station and headed back out of town one more time. The kid's niceness should have made him feel better but it didn't. He didn't think anything would.

He felt guilty because he'd had a hunch something would happen and hadn't done anything about it. But what could he have done? he asked himself desperately. Eight-year-old girls didn't kill their fathers . . . and certainly not in the visitors' room of the county prison. He was being stupid, superstitious, and a total twat, as Sykes would say. But he couldn't help it.

He was angry at Amy because she had no right to attract so much horror. Amy Kaslov belonged in Calcutta or some miserable village in eastern Russia, not in western Connecticut where life was supposed to be as distressing as an IBM training film.

He took the turn the kid told him to and found himself in another development of builders' Colonials on two-plus acres; he supposed it was Windy Ridge. The street sign was gone; maybe it never existed or, more likely, the local youths had knocked it down. The poor little creeps had no subway cars to deface and no one to get annoyed at graffiti, anyway. Sometimes they got up the balls to bash in mailboxes, but it was stupid, small-time vandalism, and tonight Moran wanted the real thing. He wanted to see gutted pay phones and "Jose Sucks" spray-painted across the tiles of the West Fourth Street subway station. Tonight he wanted exurbia to take its pretty houses, overpriced grocery stores, and exorbitant antique shops and stuff them up its collective ass.

His rage was getting away from him, and by the time he pulled into the driveway at 114, he was shaking. He wanted to sit in the car for a couple of minutes to calm down, but the front door crashed open as soon as he killed the motor, and Levin's huge figure appeared in the light from the foyer.

"Moran?"

"Yeah," Moran called, and he climbed out of his car and went up the path (that looked like the path to his house) and into the foyer (like his foyer) and followed Levin through a standard dining room to a standard kitchen.

He put his bag on the kitchen table and collapsed into a Colonial-type chair that he happened to know was sold at Ethan Allen for seventy-five dollars. He wanted to put his head on his arms and weep with bitterness. Then he saw Jeannie Levin, standing uncertainly at the stove. She was pretty, very pale right now, and she was twisting her hands. There was no Connecticut smug in that woman's eyes, and suddenly all of Moran's anger dissipated and he was ashamed of himself.

"Would you like some coffee?" she asked softly.

He nodded. Not because he wanted coffee—he'd had seven cups already today—but because those poor, twisting hands needed something to do.

He turned to Levin.

"How is she?"

"Awful," Levin said. He looked like he was controlling tears.

"Tell me what happened," Moran said gently.

Levin started talking. Jeannie served the coffee and gave Moran a slice of really good nut cake. Levin told about Kaslov grabbing the first guard's gun and the second guard pulling the pump gun and firing the killing shot that left Kaslov's guts slithering halfway across the floor, and Moran actually got dizzy. He gulped the strong, hot coffee, burned the roof of his mouth, and the faintness eased. He realized that Levin had stopped talking.

"She fainted?" Moran said.

Levin nodded.

"How much did she see?" Moran asked.

"I don't know."

"Then what happened?"

"The doctor at the prison gave her a shot, and she seemed okay. Out of it but okay. And I thought the best thing would be to get her home. Then, just this side of Millbridge, she seemed to come around, and she asked me—very calmly, mind you—if her father had been shot. Shit, Doc, she sounded fine or I would have said no or made up some kind of story. But I wasn't feeling so hot, either, and I said yes. Then she asked, 'Is he dead?' and I said yes, and then . . . she started to cry. I never heard crying like that. I thought she'd tear her throat out, honest to God. I pulled over. It was so cold in the car, I couldn't drive, anyway, and I put my arms around her to warm her a little, to stop that horrible crying. It was like holding a steel rod, Moran. I thought she was having a fit; I even thought of socking her just to stop her before she choked on her own tongue or something. But I held her and rocked her for a long time. Finally she got quiet; too quiet, which was almost as bad. She sat bolt upright with her eyes open, staring at nothing. I brought her home and we got her undressed and into bed, and she's there now. She closed her eyes at some point, but she won't open them or make a sound, so I called you. . . ."

Moran finished the coffee and stood up. Jeannie Levin said, "Her room's upstairs, first door on the right."

He nodded and climbed the carpeted stairs, carrying his bag. At the top he stopped for a second and thought, *I don't know what to do about this*. Then he turned right.

The door was open. Amy was lying on the bed in a pretty

room with yellow walls, flowered curtains, and a comforter to match. Her black hair spread like spilled ink on the pillow. He realized that her hair was magnificent—the most beautiful head of hair he'd ever seen—and he had a sudden feeling that he'd never forget how it looked, fanned out on the white linen. Visions of that hair would come back to him when he was an old man.

A little girl sat in a small chair next to the bed. She was reading aloud from a book with a brightly colored cover. Greta Levin watching over Amy.

He knocked on the doorjamb and Greta looked up.

She was a pretty kid with round cheeks and dark blond hair like her father. But she looked almost plain compared to Amy.

"Are you the doctor?" she asked.

"Yes," Moran said softly.

"Don't whisper," Greta said, "she can't hear you. She won't open her eyes, either. Something happened to her father."

"I know."

"Is he dead?"

The Levins should have told Greta that the father was dead, but of course they didn't. People lied to children about death; they lied to them about everything. Moran wasn't going to do that.

"Yes, Greta, he's dead."

She shut the book and clutched it against her chest. "Oh, Amy," she said softly, and she rocked back and forth in the chair for a moment. Then she looked up at Moran. There were tears in her blue eyes. "She wanted to see him so bad. She pretended she didn't, but I knew. She wore her best clothes, she let me put a ribbon in her hair. She'd never wear a ribbon before. She said she hated him, but I knew better. She said he was ugly. He looked like Dracula. But I didn't believe that, either. I understood why she said it, though. He killed her mother."

Moran nodded.

"Maybe she'll be glad he's dead when she thinks about it. But I wouldn't be. Would you?"

"No," Moran said softly.

"I knew he couldn't look like Dracula. Amy's so pretty. Ugly fathers don't have pretty daughters, do they?"

"Not usually."

"I kept after her, and finally she said he didn't look like that. He looked like his brother. That's Amy's Uncle Jonathan. He's handsome. Like a movie star. Except that he's got this bare patch on his head." She pointed to the side of her own head, then added with some relish, "And the hair all around it is white. Yuk!"

"When did you see Amy's uncle?"

"He came here yesterday. He scared me and my mother. Mother called the cops and they came and took him away. But he didn't hurt Amy, he just wanted to talk to her. He told her about her grandfather, but she didn't really understand what he meant. But she said she was glad to see him. He's her *blood* relative." Her eyes went to Moran's bag; suddenly she was suspicious. "What are you going to do to Amy?"

"I'm going to try to wake her up. It would be better if you left us alone for a few minutes, Greta."

Her suspicion deepened. "Are you going to take her to the hospital?"

He had the feeling that if he said yes, this plump, pretty little girl would try to put him out of the room bodily. He raised his hand in the gesture of swearing that most kids understood. "No," he said, "I promise."

"She'll get scared if she opens her eyes and doesn't see me."

"I'll tell her you're close by. You'll be sure to stay close by in case I need you?"

Greta nodded gravely and stood up. She put the book on Amy's bed table, hitched her flannel robe up around her, and came to the door. She stopped next to Moran and looked back at Amy.

"She's going to feel awful," Greta said with true sadness;

amazing for a nine-year-old. "She really loved her daddy, no matter what she said. I knew that."

She wiped her eyes again and said, "I'll be right down the hall there if you need me."

"Thank you," Moran said. She left the room, and he waited until she was in her room, then closed the door. He was alone with the strange, beautiful child on the bed. He went close and looked down at her. Her eyes rolled under the lids. Her thin arm was draped over a newish teddy bear. The chair Greta had vacated was too small for Moran's butt, and he sat on the edge of the bed. The mattress tilted; Amy's eyelids fluttered but didn't open.

He said, "Come out of it, Amy."

She squeezed her eyes tightly. He knew she wasn't faking, exactly. She really, truly, absolutely didn't want to see what was out here, and he didn't blame her. But it wasn't like last time; she wasn't in shock, there was no hint of a coma. He sighed and lifted her arm and took the teddy bear, then let her arm fall back on the cover.

"Come on, Amy. If you keep this up, they're going to send you to the hospital." He hated to threaten, but it wasn't idle. The people downstairs were badly scared. They'd already taken more responsibility and shown more guts than he would have in their place. Amy's next stop was Millbridge General. That was the last thing on earth she needed.

"I mean it, Amy."

She opened her eyes. They were red, swollen, and so full of pain he flinched back before he could stop himself.

"I killed him," she said flatly.

"Nonsense."

She shook her head.

"How, Amy? How did you kill him?"

"I made the guard shoot him."

Fear filled his mouth in a sour flood; his armpits were clammy and he clung to the teddy bear.

"How did you make him shoot your father, Amy?"

"I don't know."

"You'd better know. I'm not going to listen to you unless you talk sense."

"It was like before. I told you I thought my mother tried to get to me because I made her . . . and then there was the time with Ann and the custard. I told you about that."

Moran nodded.

"It was the same with the guard," Amy said.

Moran was quiet. Sykes had suggested thought transference, and maybe, as outlandish as it seemed, maybe that *was* what happened to Moran at that first session with Amy. And maybe Amy had somehow transferred the thought of custard from her mind to nurse Ann's, and so it occurred to nurse Ann that Amy might like some custard. Okay; and not particularly scary, even if it was true. He thought of the children's old refrain that he'd always loved for its defiance and gallantry. "Sticks and stones will break my bones, but names will never hurt me." Thought didn't kill people. Even if she'd made that guard see his own gun plugging away at her father, because that was what she wanted to happen, that didn't mean the guard would do it. Everybody thought lots of things they didn't do. Even some kind of ultra-fantastic hypnotic ability wouldn't explain it because people truly would not do anything under hypnosis that they wouldn't do anyway. That was absolutely, one-hundred-percent documented. The guard couldn't be hypnotized into shooting Kaslov. Kaslov couldn't be hypnotized into grabbing the gun or into some insane attempt to escape or commit suicide.

None of it washed.

"Amy, tell me what happened."

"He was getting me to remember nice things, and I did. But I didn't want to."

"Why?"

"Because I wasn't so mad at him when I remembered, and I wanted to be."

He nodded at her to go on.

"He talked about picnics and movies and lobster, and I started to feel almost nice, you know?"

"Yes."

"Then . . . then he called me Chicken! And it all came back."

"What's so terrible about calling you chicken?"

She kept her head down and spoke very softly. "That's what my mother called me. It was her . . ."

"Her pet name?"

"Yes. He called me Chicken, and that cold came through my head, only it didn't feel good this time, not exactly bad but not good. It was too much . . ."

"Too cold?"

"I guess so. But exciting, too, and scary. I can't explain."

He wanted to grab her, shake her, make her explain. Cold, exciting, scary . . . "Like what?" he wanted to shout at her. Like getting to the top of Everest and not knowing if you're going to get down? Like getting elected president of the United States and not knowing why you ran in the first place? Like starting to come for the sixth time and not knowing if you're going to live through it? Like what Amy . . .

He clutched the teddy and stroked it shakily.

"Never mind explaining, Amy. Just tell me what happened."

"The cold happened. And something seemed to break loose. He stood up and said, 'Amy, don't,' and I would have stopped if I could. But it was loose and wouldn't come back. I looked away from him at the guard against the wall. He was reading the paper and he had a gun strapped to his side. Then it was so cold . . . and I couldn't stand it, and . . . I don't know after that. Joe said I fainted, and I guess that's right. It was like they turned out all the lights, and when they turned them on again, I was in Joe's car and he told me that my daddy"—hot, agonizing looking tears rolled out of her red eyes—"was dead. The guard shot him. I made him do it."

"Amy," he said quietly, "which guard did you make shoot your father?"

"I told you. He was against the wall reading a paper. . . ."

Moran laughed, and Amy looked at him as if he'd gone

crazy. He didn't blame her. He put his arms around her and pulled her against him. He rocked her in his arms for a second, then let her go.

"Amy, Amy." He moaned, keeping his voice down as much as he could. "I'm sorry about your poor father. Truly, honey. But you didn't do it. It was the *other* guard who shot your father."

"What other guard?"

"The one behind the desk. Joe told me there was a guard behind a high desk. You remember?"

"Yes. But I didn't look at him. He wasn't the one . . . he didn't even have a gun."

"Yes, he did, Amy. It was under his desk. Joe said it was a pump gun. Joe wouldn't lie about it; Joe doesn't know the things you've told me. About your mother and the custard. He wouldn't lie to protect you, honey. He told the truth. It was the other guard, Amy. You didn't kill your father, honey."

He saw hope flare into her eyes, and he felt like the prince in a fairy tale. He'd kissed her and talked to her. And what he had said was so clear and honest that the evil spell was broken forever and the princess was awake. Of course, it wasn't like that; he didn't know what the spell was or even if it existed. He *did* know that it was over. Amy Kaslov hadn't killed her father with thought transference or any other such bullshit. He'd been a fool to listen to Sykes, and if Ernie was in the room right now, Moran would have punched his eyes out. Only he wouldn't, because he suddenly felt too good.

"Amy, I'm going to get Greta. I promised."

"Wait. Are you sure . . . "

"Yup . . . " Her eyes jerked past him, to the door, and he turned around. A tall boy, about fifteen, had opened the door. He was pale with a high forehead that people associated with intelligence. He stared at Amy for a second, then looked at Moran.

"I'm Paul Levin, how do you do." He spoke too politely for an American kid his age.

"How do you do," Moran said with equal politeness. "I'm Dr. Moran."

"Is Amy better?" Paulie asked.

Moran turned to her, smiling. "Are you, honey?"

"Much better," she said. She didn't take her eyes off Paulie.

"I'm so glad, Amy." The boy smiled. It wasn't a pleasant smile, but Moran thought that the smile Amy gave him back was positively horrifying. Then he realized that he was backsliding, telling himself ghost stories at the bedside of a sick child. That was inexcusable. If he had a thirst for horror, he should make Mary go with him to see *Night of the Living Dead* and stop dressing this little girl in his sick fantasies. He'd probably seen too much during the past couple of years; he needed to do a little work on himself now. He'd ask Ernie Sykes to recommend someone.

He went to get Greta, and when he came back, Paulie was gone and Amy was up and putting on a flowered flannel robe, just like Greta's. Greta thought she should stay in bed, but Amy wanted to go downstairs to see Joe and Jeannie. Moran gave permission and trailed the children downstairs to the kitchen.

The Levins were almost as elated as he was with her recovery. She still looked haunted, but she hadn't seen her father for a long time before today; and then only intermittently between binges. Besides, he had beaten her up a couple of times and killed her mother, so her grief must certainly be moderate. Besides, having your father die was one thing, thinking that you killed him was something else, and he thought that Amy Kaslov was probably the most relieved child on earth tonight.

Moran left the four of them in the kitchen together (Paulie had disappeared). Jeannie had brought out a quart of chocolate ice cream, and Amy and Greta were getting out bowls and spoons.

He drove slowly; the way that had seemed so circuitous only an hour ago was smooth and easy now. He passed back through Westerly and smiled an apology at the lit office of the Amoco station. In fact, he apologized to the whole town of Westerly, which now looked terrific to him, and drove on through with no wrong turns, right to the highway.

It was almost nine when he got home. Mary was in the kitchen baking David's first birthday cake. She found a recipe for a cake made in sections and decorated to look like a train, and he knew she was at the counter struggling with it. He called to her, hung his coat up, and went into the den to warm up in front of the fire.

Ernie Sykes sat up out of the depths of Moran's easy chair.

"Hi, Charlie." Sykes grinned, and the light and shadow from the fire made his face almost demonic.

"I heard from Cambridge," he said.

Paulie was on the landing, listening to them in the kitchen. Eating the ice cream had turned into a kind of celebration, and his father sounded young, happy, affectionate. Since *she* came, his father acted like a cross between St. Francis and Santa Claus. But Paulie knew the truth; his father had muscles like bricks. He carried a gun and he'd shot a couple of punks who held up a gas station. One of them died. He got a citation for that; it hung on the wall in the den. That was the other side of big Sugar Daddy Joe Levin. Paulie's face burned as he listened from his dark post halfway up the stairs.

"Want some chocolate sauce, Sweet Pea?" his father asked.

Sweet Pea was the bitch, and she must have nodded because Paulie heard the refrigerator door open again.

"How about you, Princess?" His father again. Princess was Greta, but he'd asked Amy first, and the point was not lost on Paulie. He thought of going down there just to ruin their party. He *would* ruin it, too, and he let himself be sorry for a second. He almost wished it was different, but he knew what would happen. He would get his ice cream, but his father's voice would take on its patient, dealing-with-Paulie tone, and his mother's pretty smile would waver, the corners of her mouth would tremble with strain. The bitch would fix her strange, dark eyes on some corner of the kitchen, or on her ice cream and chocolate sauce, and she wouldn't look at him. Only Greta would be glad to see him, but Greta was glad to see everybody, like a good-natured dog.

He turned away and went back upstairs. He could call one of the guys and go out somewhere; he could turn on the stereo, roll a joint, and stare at the ceiling and let his thoughts sail up through the roof, out of this house, and go anywhere they wanted to. He didn't need ice cream or company, or affection, or anything from the people in the kitchen. But when he got to the top of the stairs, he turned away from his own room and went into his parents' room.

The room was neat, dim, chilly. The bed was huge and smooth. He used to come in here on Sunday mornings a long time ago. His mother would be downstairs feeding Greta then and making breakfast, his father would still be in bed with his back turned to the empty half of the bed and his shoulder jutting up out of the bedclothes like a mountain. Paulie would crawl into the bed and nestle against his father's back. His father would feel him there and turn and envelop Paulie in his huge arms. Paulie wasn't sure when things had changed; it happened little by little until, when Paulie was about eleven, he realized that his father didn't like him anymore. Paulie knew it wasn't any one thing that he'd done, it was *him*.

Paulie backed out of his parents' room, closed the door, and started back to his room. Amy's door was open, and on impulse he went into her room. He'd never been in here alone before. Everything in it . . . the books, toys, everything . . . had been bought with his father's money. He looked around quickly; his father had spent hundreds on her. Maybe some of the money he'd been saving for Paulie's college. He opened the closet and looked at the clothes his father had bought. They hung neatly from the bar, a few pairs of shoes sat on the floor, her jeans hung from a hook on the wall. Suddenly it hit him like a sledgehammer that the clothes were really hers, no matter who had paid for them. They smelled like her, they carried the imprint of her body. The shoes were worn to the shape of her feet, the heels slanted to accommodate the way she walked.

Suddenly he knew in a deep-down way that he hadn't before, that Amy Kaslov was here to stay. Shock drove him away from the closet to the middle of the room, and he stood there, helpless and angrier than he'd ever been in his life. He clenched his teeth until his jaw ached; a vein in his forehead throbbed like a bad tooth. He had prayed from the start that she would leave; today there'd been a chance. She had lost it after they shot her killer father (and too fucking bad it hadn't been her guts splattered all over the place), and they talked about sending her back to the hospital. But that doctor came and must have given her a shot or something, and now she was sitting downstairs eating ice cream like Queen Shit while Paulie's father waited on her.

Paulie tried to think. She was a charity case and an orphan with no one to protect her. Greta said that her uncle was crazy and had a bald patch on his head with white hair around it. It had scared Greta; everything scared Greta, so she wouldn't be able to protect Amy and the uncle was back in the loony bin where he belonged. Of course, she had his mother and father to watch out for her . . . especially his father. He wasn't ready to take on his father yet (someday maybe, not now). But even his father couldn't protect Amy from things he didn't know about.

Paulie thought of Len Brachman. He was a sort of a friend of Paulie's, one of the four guys who'd bought matching fake leather jackets from Korvette's last spring with money they'd saved out of their allowances. They were a clique, held together by things that Paulie already knew were stupid. They smoked grass in the basement, carried switchblades that they'd bought off Sam Curtin when he graduated, and stole beer from their fathers' caches. Len was a short kid who wore glasses and had a face full of pimples. Len hated his father too. He told them that his father had driven his brother out of the house and they hadn't heard from him except for one lousy Christmas card in '72, postmarked Miami. Len missed his brother, and someday he was going to get out of that house and go to Miami, too, because now his father was making *his* life hell. "You just wait," he'd told the other boys, "I'm saving my dough, and the day I turn seventeen, out I go, just like Frank."

Paulie pitied and despised Len, but right now he was grateful to him because he'd given him an idea. Old Man Brachman made life hell for Frank, and Frank took off. He was making life hell for Len, and Len couldn't wait until he was old enough to leave. If Paulie made Amy Kaslov's life in this house miserable, she'd want to leave. If he made it hell, she'd want to leave so badly that they'd have to let her go.

She wasn't adopted. She was a foster child. This was her foster home and she could leave anytime. His father had made that clear. Paulie knew that eight-year-old girls couldn't get on a bus or hitch a ride to Miami. But there were orphanages for people like Amy, and other foster homes. Not in Westerly. Westerly wasn't that kind of place. She'd have to go to Waterbury or Hartford or Danbury, where there were bohunks and Polacks and spades. Lots of freeloaders to keep her company.

The next question was how to do it. It had to be gradual and constant. Not one big sudden thing but lots of little things. He looked around the room for a way to start.

She had brought three things into this house with her; they were all she had in the world that truly belonged to her, and Paulie reasoned that they would be very important to her. There was a book, a stuffed seal that his father had bought her (so it really didn't count), and the teddy bear sitting on the bed next to her pillow. He didn't know where she got it; it was just a cheapo Woolworth stuffed toy with acrylic fur and a thin ribbon around its neck. But she slept with it, she watched TV with it tucked in the crook of her arm, and he'd seen her whisper to it. The teddy bear was a good start, so he went up to the bed and reached out for it. The bear's black shoe-button eyes seemed to look into his, and suddenly he remembered that insulting look of pity she'd given him her first night in this house. His skin felt cool and damp, as if the room were full of fog, and he jerked his hand away from the toy and stared at it for a second. It was just a lousy teddy bear, and he told himself he was being brainless and gutless like his sister, Greta.

He grabbed the stuffed animal and left the room.

Later they came upstairs, and Paulie opened his door a crack and listened.

Amy called to Greta, "Did you see Little?"

Paulie glanced back into his room. The bear's eyes glittered at him. He looked away.

"No," Greta answered. "Maybe you left him downstairs. We'll look tomorrow. You go to bed now. The doctor said you have to rest."

He kept listening, and he heard Amy moving around the room, looking for the bear. Then he heard water run in their bathroom and the toilet flushed. Then it was quiet. She must have been too tired to go on looking, and she gave up for now. He opened his door wider and went out into the hall. The light under her door was out. He grabbed the bear, digging his fingers into the fur and stuffing as if he could hurt it, and carried it downstairs.

Sykes sat with the large white envelope from Cambridge cradled in his lap. Moran saw the foreign stamps and postal markings and looked up at his old friend. The firelight was playing tricks; Sykes's normally pleasant, broad face was shadowed, and he looked old and malevolent.

"Aren't you going to ask me what's in the envelope?" Sykes asked.

"I don't want to know," Moran said. He meant it too. Until Evans had wheeled Amy Kaslov into his office in October, he'd been a happy man. He hadn't realized how happy at the time. He loved his work, his wife, his kid, and if the stolid smugness of inland Connecticut got on his nerves sometimes, he would tell himself that at least his kid could go to public school here without getting stabbed for his lunch money. That was enough to recommend the smuggest, phoniest place on earth. He'd been just fine until last October, and he was going to be fine again. He didn't want to know any more about strange spinal fluid components, thought transference, or Cambridge. Sykes leaned forward. The strange shadows slid away from his face.

"Still spooked, Charlie?" Sykes asked gently.

"No. I just got unspooked and I want to stay that way!"

"Charlie, we're not telling ghost stories here. You gotta hear, whether you want to or not."

"Why?"

"Because it's real. They found something in the spinal fluid. A couple of guys at Karolinska in Sweden had isolated it a few months ago and gave it a name . . . 5 Hydroxyintoleacetic acid. 5-HIAA for short. But they had to use an X-ray microscope to find a substance in normal people that we saw on a spectrograph. Spectrographs are pretty crude creatures nowadays."

"So what?" Moran said.

Sykes looked at him for a moment, then he put the hateful white envelope on the low table between them and stood up. Sykes knew this room almost as well as he did. They had spent hours in here, talking in front of the fire, watching games on the tube, arguing the merits of organic gardening. It was a good room, full of pleasant memories. One night Moran and Mary had inadvertently gotten drunk watching a full-scale, back-to-back repeat of *The Forsythe Saga* in this room and wound up making spectacular love on the floor because the couch didn't seem big enough to contain their passion. Now his wonderful wife was alone in the kitchen struggling with their kid's first birthday cake, and he wanted to be back there helping her, not sitting in his favorite room that was strangely cold and dark tonight, in spite of the fire, arguing with his best friend about the mysterious components of a child's spinal fluid.

Sykes went to the cabinet under the built-in bookcases and came back with the bottle of cheap brandy and two of the balloon glasses that were kept there. He poured stiff shots for both of them, handed a glass to Moran, and said, "You know, Charlie, you sound like one of the villagers in a Frankenstein movie. 'Zere are zings no man should tamper vit . . . ' " Moran smiled in spite of himself.

Sykes said, "What's scaring you?"

"I'm not scared. I told you I just got unscared."

"And I'm telling you that you're full of shit. You're petrified. Admit it and tell me why."

He was going to protest again, then he realized that his heart was pounding, his palms were slimy with sweat. He drank down half of the brandy in a gulp and leaned back.

"Okay," he said. "Her father was killed this afternoon. Shot by a guard at Longbury. She was there when it happened."

Sykes whistled. "Christ, the poor little bitch."

"Yeah."

They were quiet for a moment, then Sykes said, "Go on, Charlie. Why did that scare you?"

Then Moran told him the rest. He spoke calmly, finished the first shot, and poured and drank a hefty second. He lost the feeling in his upper lip, a sure sign that he was getting high. He told Sykes about the nurse and the custard. It was almost funny, and he thought Sykes would grin but he didn't. He told him about how scared he'd been that somehow Amy Kaslov was responsible for her father's death; he got to the visit to the Levin house. . . .

"Then it turned out she didn't even know which guard had shot him. It was that ridiculous. . . . " Moran tried to smile, but he knew it came out as a stiff grimace. Sykes didn't smile back.

"So you concluded . . . "

"I concluded that you and I are a couple of assholes. *Thought transference* . . . what bullshit."

Sykes's eyes went to the white envelope on the table.

"I don't care what Cambridge says," Moran cried, "it's bullshit. But even if it isn't . . . sticks and stones . . . "

"What?" Sykes asked.

Moran chanted, " 'Sticks and stones will break my bones, but names will never hurt me.' "

"Apropos of what?"

"Apropos of the fact that no matter what you or Cambridge found in that sample, thoughts don't kill."

"Oh, but they do. You and I know people whose thoughts drove them to suicide, hemorrhaging ulcers, heart attacks, strokes, and God knows what else. We could probably cite sixty or seventy of them, all killed by their thoughts."

"*Their* thoughts, not somebody else's."

"Then why were you scared, Charlie?"

Moran ignored the question and poured them more brandy.

Sykes swilled his down, and Moran realized he must be getting pretty high too. Nice. They'd get plastered and pass out, and he couldn't wait because he couldn't see any other satisfactory end to this discussion.

"Look," Sykes said thickly, "you're a pro. I don't know what kind of physician you are, but I know you're a good psychiatrist. People trust you because you don't lie to them or to yourself. At least, not usually. So let's get it out, ass on the table. Fair, white truth, in the name of medicine and science. What do you think happened to that girl's father?"

"She killed him."

Moran hiccuped with shock at what he'd said. The night wind rattled the windowpanes, the fire was dying. He should stoke it up, but he couldn't move.

Sykes watched him for a long time. Then Sykes sank back into the chair, and the shadows crossed his face again.

"You're not laughing," Moran said.

"Not yet. How did she kill him, Charlie?"

"I don't know. But she didn't think him into a bleeding ulcer or suicide. She didn't think him into anything."

"Thought transference isn't our only choice."

"Choice of what?"

"Of psi phenomena," Sykes said.

"And what the fuck are they?"

Sykes grinned. "You'd know if you read sci fi, Charlie. There's a whole laundry list of them. Telekinesis, tele-hypnosis, pyrokinesis, telepathy, good old thought transfer-ence—" Sykes stopped suddenly, then said, "And mental domination."

EIGHT

THE TEDDY BEAR was only fake fur and stuffing, but Amy had the awful feeling that it was cold, lonely, gathering dust, and waiting for her. Greta seemed to understand without Amy having to tell her, and she searched almost as desperately as Amy did. They had to stop for Saturday breakfast.

Greta said, "Don't worry, we'll look after breakfast. We'll find it."

Paulie had taken off early on his bike. He was probably going to the parking lot at the Grand Union in town to meet his friends. Joe was on duty until three, so there was just the three of them.

Jeannie had made pancakes, and when they got to the kitchen, they were served up, dripping with butter. They looked delicious, but Amy couldn't eat much.

Jeannie looked at the food on Amy's plate. "Honey, I know I'll find the teddy when I vacuum. He's probably under a couch or stuck behind some pillows."

Amy nodded.

"And if we don't find him, Amy, if he's really disappeared—things do that sometimes—then we'll get you a new one."

Amy knew that they would: the biggest, most expensive

teddy bear in Connecticut. Joe would order one made out of real fur if Amy wanted it. No one had ever treated her like that in her life (her mother would have, but she never had the means), and Amy loved Jeannie and Joe for feeling like that about her. But that particular teddy bear was the only thing on earth that actually belonged to her, except for the Chips book.

Jeannie left them to do the dishes and went upstairs. It was the day to change linens and put out fresh towels. Greta and Amy cleaned up the kitchen, then went back upstairs to go on looking. They finished in Amy's room and moved on to Greta's; but by now Amy was sure that they wouldn't find it. It had disappeared the way Jeannie said some things just did.

They searched carefully, trying not to make a mess that they'd have to pick up later. They went through the drawers, closet, the toy chest, and looked behind the shelves and bed table. There was nowhere left to look, and Greta gave up and flopped on the bed. Amy didn't want to cry; she'd cried all day yesterday. She didn't want to think about yesterday, either.

Greta said, "Hey, you know what's on the ten o'clock movie?"

It was five to ten.

"No," Amy said.

"*The Thing*! It's all about this vegetable shaped like a man that comes to earth in a spaceship. Come watch, Ame. Maybe it'll make you feel better."

Maybe it would; besides, she didn't want to sit up here alone and brood about the bear (or worse . . . worst of all . . . think about yesterday), and she followed Greta downstairs to the den. She tried to watch for a while, but she kept seeing the bear's bright black eyes; only in her mind they looked frightened and expectant, like a child lost in a store waiting for its mother to come and find it.

The movie wasn't helping; her face felt hot and dry and she couldn't sit still. She had to change clothes soon, anyway. Jeannie was taking them to the new Family Restaurant on

Route 202 for lunch. After that they were going to Cissy's, and Joe would pick them up before dinner.

"I'll go wash now," Amy said, "so you can have the bathroom."

"Don't be long. The best part's coming soon. The ice melts and the creature gets out. . . . "

The words stuck with Amy as she climbed back up the stairs.

The ice melts . . . the creature gets out. The phrase sounded familiar, as if she'd heard it before, or as if it should have some special meaning to her. The rhythm of the words was soothing . . . *the ice melts* . . . she remembered the cold wind in her head yesterday before she could stop herself. She ran into the bathroom and ran the water hard and splashed her face. Then she wet the clean washcloth that Jeannie had put out for her and held it against her eyes for a minute. She combed her hair, changed out of her jeans and into a skirt and sweater. She tried to match the colors, but she wasn't very good at it. If she got it wrong, Greta would help her pick something else. There was time to change if she had to.

She looked hopelessly in Greta's room one last time, then she came out into the hallway facing the closed door of Paulie's room.

On impulse she opened the door and went in. She'd never been in here before; she had never wanted to. She wasn't sure what she was doing in here now; she did not think the teddy bear was in here.

The room was neater than Greta's, as neat as Amy's. There were college pennants on the walls and a cork bulletin board with pictures of athletes. Mostly football players. Sometimes Amy watched football with Joe on Sunday afternoons. Greta and Jeannie hated football, and they'd do some baking or watch the little black-and-white TV in the kitchen. Amy didn't care much for football, either, and in a way she would rather have been with Greta; but she loved the time alone with Joe, and she liked bringing him pretzels or potato chips or beer from the kitchen. Paulie never joined them. He was usually down the road at the Cassinis' or the Brachmans'. Maybe he watched the games there.

She recognized one player: Y. A. Tittle of the New York Giants, a huge man and a great quarterback, Joe'd said. But in this picture he was on his knees without his helmet. The other players were standing around him and he looked dazed. The photo was clipped from a newspaper; it must have been taken when he was hurt in some game. Sure enough, there was a thin line of blood running down the side of his pleasant-ugly face. She wondered why Paulie would put up a picture of a great player when he was hurt and on his knees. "Brought low," Nana would have said. It was a mean thing to do, even for Paulie, and suddenly she knew, as certainly as she knew it was Saturday, that Paulie had taken the teddy bear.

The knowledge was sudden and shocking. She looked around the room. She didn't think he'd be stupid enough to keep it in here. Mrs. Simmons might find it when she came to clean, or Jeannie might come in for something and see it. But she looked a little, anyway, because she didn't know what else to do. She opened a few of his drawers and found a tin box with a leather strap around it. It looked like a box in which he'd keep his secret treasures; but it was too flat to contain the teddy bear.

She left the room and stood in the hallway. She knew he'd taken it while she was downstairs eating ice cream last night. She remembered Dr. Moran holding it for a second, than putting it down. It had been on the bed when she and Greta and Dr. Moran left the room. He must have taken it then and hidden it.

She looked up. The stairs to the attic were hidden in the ceiling right above her. But they screeched when they were pulled down; he wouldn't have put it in the attic. Then it hit her that he wouldn't hide it anywhere. He didn't want to keep it for himself; it was hers and he hated her. He would destroy it. He couldn't set a fire out back to burn up a stuffed animal. He wouldn't put it in their garbage; the garbage pickup was on Wednesday, and one of them might find the bear anytime between now and then.

But he could put it in somebody else's garbage. He could have taken it with him this morning; maybe in a bag on his bike basket so no one would see it. And he could have stashed it in the Cassinis' or the Brachmans' garbage to wait for the Wednesday pickup. The Cassinis and the Brachmans weren't looking for a lost teddy bear, and it would stay there until Wednesday when Country Disposal would come with their mechanized truck, squash the teddy bear to bits, and take it to the dump.

A sob rose in Amy's throat. She pushed it down as hard as she could, composed herself, and went downstairs to watch the movie.

Amy waited until it was very late. Then she got up, got dressed, and went through the bathroom to check on Greta because she didn't want Greta to come into her room and find her gone. Greta was sound asleep. She lay on her back, her full lips puffed out with each breath. She looked very young, almost like a baby.

"Greta?" she said softly.

Greta didn't stir, and Amy smiled at her and left the room. She went downstairs, put on her jacket and gum boots, and went through the dining room into the kitchen. The rubber soles squeaked on the bare floor. She stopped and listened. The house was silent except for the chugging of the refrigerator motor.

She took Joe's big flashlight out of a cabinet, put the latch on the back door so she could get back in, then went out into the backyard. It was clear, the moon was full, and she could see without the flashlight.

The Cassinis lived three houses down, but the Brachman house was at the end of Windy Ridge, almost in the woods. He'd probably put it in their garbage. She passed behind the houses on Windy Ridge. The backyards yawned in the moonlight. Some were fenced, some had gardens like Jeannie's. They were black patches on the gray grass, like blankets covering the ground. A green light flickered in a window of the Chaffe house. Mrs. Collins told Jeannie that Mr. Chaffe drank, and she didn't know how Mrs. Chaffe put up with it. Last week poor Nan Chaffe came to the PTA with a bruised cheek and dark glasses. She said that she fell down, but Mrs. Collins knew that Mr. Chaffe had hit her. He must be the one who was awake; the green light was probably the TV, and Amy imagined him watching the late show and drinking all by himself while his family slept. She shuddered, her teeth started to chatter, and she longed to be back in bed, but she kept going.

The lots at the end of Windy Ridge were larger and wooded at the back. The bare trees cast scraggly shadows across the moonlit lawns; there were rustling and crackling noises in the woods, and the twigs breaking under her gum boots sounded like pistol shots to her. But nobody heard. The backs of the houses stayed dark. Everybody in Windy Ridge was asleep except for her and Mr. Chaffe. And maybe Mrs. Chaffe, cowering upstairs in terror, waiting for her husband to get drunk enough to come clumping up the stairs to bruise her other cheek . . . *or hit her with a hammer.*

Amy shrank inside her jacket and ran. She tripped once and almost fell down; the flashlight in her pocket banged her side and she slowed up. She reached the end of the development. There was nothing beyond but a thick strip of woods, and past that, the Morris farm, which had just been bought by some developers in Hartford. So she'd heard Cissy's father say this afternoon.

A few lots back a dog barked belatedly, then gave one halfhearted howl and shut up. She thought she was in the Brachman backyard, but she couldn't be sure. She didn't know how the back of the house looked, but she thought she'd recognize it from the front. She went along the end of the lot, marked by a line of junipers, and out onto the road. It looked like the Brachman house, but it was hard to tell in the moonlight. She looked down the curved road at the other houses. In daylight they were cheerful, neat, pretty places. Now they looked abandoned and ghastly. The fronts were gray, the windows were squares of liquid black, and they all looked alike.

But the Brachman house was the last, and this seemed to be it. She went back along the side of the house to the garbage bin. It was made of wooden slats, held fast against raccoons by a metal hasp. She unhooked it and lifted the top and started looking through the Brachmans' garbage for her lost teddy bear. Jeannie put the garbage into white plastic bags, so their cans were clean; but Mrs. Brachman used paper bags that split, and some of the garbage was just thrown in. The cans stank, the sides were slimy, and Amy felt her gorge rise.

She found the teddy bear in the middle can, resting in a nest of coffee grounds; his black plastic eyes were coated with grease; there was grease on his fur and cheese sauce on his ears and face.

She tried desperately to get him clean. She filled the laundry sink in the basement and sponged his fur with Oxydol.

"Amy?"

She whirled around, holding the dripping, smelly stuffed animal. Jeannie stood at the bottom of the basement stairs in her robe and slippers.

"What on earth . . . " Jeannie said.

"I found him in the garbage."

"*Our* garbage . . . "

Amy almost said yes, but they hadn't had cheese sauce this week and Jeannie might remember.

"Next door," she said. She wasn't used to lying. Her cheeks burned.

"How did he get into the Collins's garbage?"

"I don't know," Amy said.

Jeannie looked at her for a while. Amy's blush

deepened. Then Jeannie turned her attention to the teddy bear. "Poor Little," she said slowly.

Amy started to cry. Her eyes were still swollen from all the crying yesterday, and the tears burned. Jeannie took the bear in one hand and pulled Amy in close to her with the other.

"He'll be okay, honey. He's machine-washable. See, it says on the tag, 'Machine wash warm.' We'll use the minibasket and the gentle cycle and he'll be as good as new."

"Bleach . . ." Amy sobbed.

"No, bleach'll ruin him. Now you get the minibasket, I'll set the cycle." She kissed the top of Amy's head and let her go.

It was after one when they finished, and Jeannie took Amy back upstairs to bed. The bear was clean and sweet-smelling. The plastic eyes sparkled again. Jeannie tucked her in, kissed her, and left her alone. The moon was gone, the room was pitch dark. Amy held the bear and closed her eyes, but she couldn't sleep. She kept thinking.

Her grandmother had said that life was beautiful but full of small crimes. Transgressions, she called them. Amy could hear her high, thin, old lady's voice. "And every transgression must be put paid to or they'll multiply like pokeweed in May. And then, Amy girl, you're a sinner, surrounded by sinners, and your soul had better be at the bottom of the ocean."

Amy didn't understand about the bottom of the ocean part. She knew that taking her toy and putting it in the Brachmans' garbage was a small transgression. Killing her mother was a big one, but it had been put paid to, as Nana would say. Suddenly Amy could think about yesterday and her father. He'd paid for his trangression, and if Dr. Moran was wrong and she'd had some weird part in it, she'd have helped put paid to that huge crime. Her grandmother would have been happy with her. So would her mother.

The only question was what to do about Paulie and how to put paid to stealing her teddy bear.

Amy sat in front of Moran's desk, twisting the plaid skirt in her fingers. He didn't think she'd come today; it had snowed all night and into the morning. But the plows kept up with it and he got here all right, and by ten-thirty the snow fell in fat, lazy flakes that melted when they touched the pavement. Jeannie Levin hadn't called by ten forty-five to cancel; they were on their way and he was ambivalent, which he hated and knew he should be able to deal with. He didn't want to see Amy Kaslov, yet he couldn't wait until she walked through the door, and he was almost breathless by the time Evans buzzed to announce her. And then Amy came in, sat across from him, and started fidgeting, like any eight-year-old who had burdensome things to tell and didn't know how to start.

"Mental domination," Sykes had said on Friday. By the time he came out with that, Moran was well and truly on his way to getting plastered for the first time in months, and he'd giggled. The giggle didn't go with the atmosphere—with the wind hitting the house, the dying fire, the admission that he thought she'd killed her father—and Sykes looked startled.

"Where'd you get that?" Moran had asked, working hard not to slur his words.

"From a novel," Sykes said.

"What novel?"

"It was called *The Power*, and they made a movie out of it starring George Hamilton."

Moran laughed out loud.

Sykes ignored him. "The hero had a whole bunch of powers. Chief among them was mental domination."

Moran held his belly and leaned over in his chair laughing.

"I don't see what's so funny," Sykes said thickly. He poured two more shots, and Moran almost choked on his. He couldn't stop laughing. Sykes looked hurt, then he grinned, then laughed too. The laughter got out of control, they rocked

back and forth, the fire spit and crackled, their shadows
swayed on the wall as they leaned in and out of their chairs
howling with laughter.

They wiped their eyes and calmed down. Then Moran
said, "Mental domination," and they were off again. They
stopped finally and had another drink. It was almost midnight and Sykes got up to leave.

Moran was mightily relieved. He thought he understood
everything now. She was a beautiful kid, something out of a
fairy story. He'd told himself the truth tonight at her bedside,
albeit disguised, as the truth often is. In his mind she was
the princess in a thrall, and he was going to bring her out of
the caverns of all the horror she'd lived through and past the
dragons of her loneliness. He'd given her fairy-tale powers
in his mind, and somehow he'd dragged poor old Ernie into
it with him. It was all just premature male menopause (not
so premature, actually). Ernie needed some excitement in
his life, too; last summer, on a dead-hot night in this very
room, with the air conditioner struggling against the black
heat that seeped through the walls (and after another half
bottle of brandy), Sykes had admitted that he hadn't made
love to Gloria for months. Didn't seem to want to anymore.
So poor old Sykes needed some magic too. Why not? They
were both pushing forty, they worked hard and saw a lot of
pain, most of which they couldn't relieve. They were entitled
to manufacture a fairy tale or two to give life a little spice,
and Amy Kaslov had played princess for them. Harmless shit,
Moran thought.

But then, as Sykes was shrugging on his coat, ready to
drive (very slowly and carefully, he had promised) back to
Newtown, he had asked, "By the way, what's her name,
Charlie?"

The glow of the laughter and brandy dimmed.

"Why?" Moran asked warily.

"I'm going to put this into the computer. . . ." Sykes held
up the white envelope from Cambridge. He was taking it
with him! As if it still mattered, as if it still had validity. They

should have poured brandy on it and stuffed it into the fire-place.

Moran was quiet, Sykes looked confused.

"What gives, Charlie? No matter what kind of bullshit I've been spouting in my cups here, *this*"—he waved the envelope—"is still real. The kid's got unheard-of levels of some crap swimming around her neurons. Maybe it's a pre-cursor of chemically induced mania or depression. Maybe it'll give her a brain tumor or Parkinsonism . . . we can't just forget that it happened."

Moran felt betrayed. "Stick it in your computer . . . Stick it up your ass for all I care. Without names."

Sykes looked at him for a moment and must have seen the drunken stubbornness. He went out the door without a word and down the path to his car. Moran stood in the open door. He didn't want to fight with Ernie; Ernie was his best friend.

"Ernie," he cried. Sykes stopped. Moran yelled, "Take it slow."

Sykes had waved at him, so maybe it was all right. Moran looked up. It was a cold, clear night; the stars spilled over his head and he got dizzy. It stayed cold and clear through the weekend and into the week before Christmas. Then it clouded up on Tuesday and started to snow.

Amy had made it to Millbridge, through the snow, and now here she was. The object of all the speculation and fear, sitting on the other side of his desk, twisting the wool of her pretty plaid skirt in her fingers.

"You're going to ruin that skirt, Amy," he said gently.

She stopped and let her hands lay, palms up in her lap.

"What's the matter, sweetheart?" he asked. And he braced himself for a storm about her father.

But she said, "Paulie Levin stole my teddy bear and put it in a garbage can down the road."

He did not laugh but it wasn't easy.

"How do you know?" he asked.

"I found it. Jeannie washed it for me."

"What did Jeannie say about this?"

"I didn't tell her. I'm not a tattletale."

"Why do you think Paulie did that?"

"He hates me. He wants me out of the house." She paused and thought for a moment, then she said, "He's jealous because Joe likes me better than he likes him."

"I see. Well, you've got your teddy bear back, and I think you're right about how Joe feels about you. So I guess everything's pretty much okay. At least from your point of view."

Say something about your father, he thought. Please, mourn your poor shit of a father.

"But that isn't all," Amy said.

Moran waited.

"My grandmother said that you had to pay things back. So I tried to pay Paulie back."

Moran's heart leaped; his esophagus seemed to sail up his chest and lodge under his throat. Part of his mind was clear and distant. He even thought that he'd someday write an article on the physiology of terror, although it had probably been done long since. The other part of his mind was empty and on the verge of panic.

"How?" he choked.

"I went up to his room on Sunday afternoon. He was gone somewhere. He doesn't spend much time at home. Jeannie and Joe're getting him a motor scooter for Christmas. So he'll probably be gone most of the time. I think they're doing it on purpose. He makes them uncomfortable. He can't help himself, I guess."

She sounded sorry for Paulie Levin. Moran relaxed a little.

"Go on."

"Well, I went up there. I thought I'd steal something of his and hide it or put it into the fire. To put paid to what he did to Little, you understand?"

Moran nodded.

"I'd seen this tin box up there with a strap around it. I thought his favorite things would be in there. So I undid the strap and opened the box. And there was all this *junk*. An old knife that wouldn't open, some marbles, a long piece of something that looked like snakeskin. Some cards with pictures of baseball players, a broken watch. Then, under some of the junk I found this picture of Joe. He looked young, as young as my father. . . ."

Moran held his breath, but she went on easily.

"And he was wearing a uniform. He doesn't have to wear one anymore. He's too high up," she said proudly. "I knew that the picture was Paulie's favorite thing. It was worth taking it away from him. It would put paid to stealing Little. I started to do it . . . I even took it out of the box. Then . . . I couldn't because he didn't have that much, after all. The picture, those bits of junk, some other stuff. And he must've loved Joe to keep that picture of him hidden like that. He doesn't act like it, you know. He pretends to hate him. But when I saw the picture, I knew he didn't and I felt . . . I felt sorry for him. So I put it back and I didn't take anything, after all."

She sounded very unhappy.

"What's wrong with that, Amy?" he asked gently.

"My grandma said you have to punish . . . trans . . . trans . . ."

"Transgressions?"

She nodded. "Those're like crimes. She said if they're not punished, they get bigger and there's more of them. Like . . . weeds. You know what happens if you don't pull weeds."

"But what happens if you force yourself to take the picture of Joe, or something else that Paulie cares about?"

"I guess my grandma would say that if he gets hurt bullying me, he'll leave me alone." She sounded utterly confused, and Moran cursed the grandmother. She must have been one of those fundamentalist hill people whose hearts belonged to the Old Testament and thought that only sissies and fools turned the other cheek. But poor Amy wasn't so sure, and Moran's heart went out to her. She was asking one of the oldest questions on earth: How do you treat a bully?

Do you make your vengeance so terrible he won't dare hurt you again? Or do you shame him with your dignity, charm him with your kindness? Moran didn't know the answer to that one.

The snow got worse after she left. Patients canceled, and Moran decided to eat in, file some tapes, then go home. He'd stop at Korvette's, get the kid a toy; not that Davey needed one. Moran had heard that too many toys confused and spoiled children. Although he wasn't sure how you "spoiled" a kid. He'd probably find out if he didn't watch himself with Davey.

Evans went down to the cafeteria and came back with sloppy joe sandwiches. He put on a tape of Handel's Water Music and leaned over and took a big, messy bite out of the sandwich. Suddenly he heard Amy saying, "He had this junk and the picture of Joe, and I felt sorry for him."

Moran put the sandwich down on the waxed paper and sat back.

Paulie was their natural son, but Amy was a foster child, without rights or status, like the 1940s DP kids. And she knew it. But *she* felt sorry for *him.*

Moran knew pity came from power; Amy felt sorry for Paulie because she believed he was no match for her.

Moran's sandwich stopped tasting good; even the smell of it was bothersome. He wrapped it in waxed paper and threw it away. He was telling ghost stories again, but he couldn't help it.

He needed to talk to someone besides Ernie Sykes.

Moran was embarrassed and tried to make a joke of it. "Then Sykes . . . you remember Ernie Sykes?" he asked. Reed nodded and Moran went on. "Then Sykes said, 'Mental domination!' " He laughed phonily. Reed was quiet.

"Did you ever hear such bullshit?" Moran asked.

Reed said, "If you wanted to hear that mental domination was bullshit, you came to the wrong person."

N. Compton Reed had lived in the same rooming house

with Moran when they were in med school. There was a communal kitchen and they cooked their meals together. Reed was rich; he bought fresh fish and vegetables, steaks, and sliced rare roast beef. Moran had tuna fish and peanut butter. Reed noticed and insisted on sharing his food; Moran used to joke that N. Compton Reed saved him from rickets. Then, around their junior year, Reed announced he was giving up medicine to get a Ph.D. in psychology, specifically something called parapsychology. One night, over half a case of beer, Moran tried to talk him out of it. Reed was firm. "It's like magic," he'd said. "I love magic."

"Loving it doesn't make it true," Moran countered.

"It doesn't make it false, either," Reed answered. "Besides, I'm rich. I'll never have to make a living. So what the fuck?"

"What the fuck," Moran had finally agreed. It had been four in the morning; he had a pharmacology quiz at nine. "What the fuck."

Reed quit Yale and went to North Carolina where the study of parapsychology was as trendy as revivalism. Now, nine or ten years later, he was back.

His office was a cubbyhole at the ass end of campus; it was underground, with one window, high on the wall, opening onto a window well. Magic seemed to have gone out of fashion.

Moran said, "You still believe that stuff?"

"I never 'believed' it. I wanted to find out if it was true."

"And did you?"

"We studied seven thousand subjects in five years and found four telepaths. Honest to God, go to hell telepaths. Two of them are dead. One in the war, one on the highway. One was a drunk and itinerant dishwasher. He knew what he could do; called himself a sensitive. 'That and a buck'll get me a pint of Berrycup,' he used to say. Berrycup's a fruit-flavored wine. I think they even make it in orange." Reed shuddered. "He hung around for a while, then disappeared. Went back on the bum, I guess. The last one was an old woman who lived with her daughter in Raleigh. She was eighty-three and must've been beautiful once. Still was, in a way. But she was the meanest bitch I ever met. She said she saw inside our heads, knew us all for what we were, and she hated us. Reminded me of that old song . . ." He sang softly, on key, " 'My name it is Sam Hall, and I hate you one and all, yes, I hate you one and all, goddamn your eyes . . .' "

"But no mental dominants . . ."

"No."

Maybe because there's no such thing, Moran was going to say, but Reed said, "I did hear of one, a boy from East Germany. I heard about him from a man who heard about him in West Germany. So it's hearsay out of rumor. But I'll tell you about it if you like."

Moran didn't know if he wanted to hear it or not, but no one had knocked on Reed's door since Moran got here, or passed in the hall. The phone hadn't rung. Reed was probably dying just to talk, and it would be cruel not to listen.

"Sure," Moran said.

Reed brightened, took out cigarettes, and offered Moran one. Moran took it, Reed lit them up. Moran noticed that the lighter was slim and golden, probably a Dunhill. The rich didn't lie as much as other people, he thought; they had fewer axes to grind.

Reed said, "I heard it from a man named Dieter Strom. Dieter was from Frankfurt; before then, from East Berlin. He and his parents crossed over on the S Bahn a month before they closed the border. He said it wasn't a near miss, but it felt like one. He hated the East, he hated Russians, I think he even hated Germans.

"I met him five years ago, in the least likely place imaginable. The Purchase Golf Club and Resort; at a conference of clinical and experimental psychologists and psychiatrists. Do you play golf?"

Moran shook his head.

"Me, either," Reed said. "And I don't like golfers. They're smug, like people who drink buttermilk. Anyway,

the meeting was in May. The weather was perfect, and almost everyone was on the golf course from dawn to sunset.
No one came to sessions or seminars; papers were cut short
or not given; no one bothered with question sessions or
slides. It was sad, and I'd decided to leave after one day.
Then I noticed this man who'd been to sessions and had
eaten lunch in the almost empty coffee shop instead of the
clubhouse on the ninth tee. We got to talking, and discovered
we had two big things in common: we distrusted golfers and
believed in psi. It was a revelation. We talked and talked and
took our meals together. We skipped meetings and went for
long walks in one of the bits of woods left in southern West-
chester. We couldn't get enough time together . . . we practically fell in love. You see, when I talk about my work, people
either try not to grin or their eyes glaze. They humor me or
think I should be put away. Dieter had the same experience,
so you can imagine what joy it was to talk to someone who
took you seriously.

"We had four days together. We still correspond. Someday I hope to visit him or have him visit me . . .

"On the last night he told the story. It happened in East
Berlin, fourteen years ago . . ."

He paused and Moran thought, *Once upon a time* . . .

"In those days East Berlin was full of Russians. There
was still rubble in the streets, and the new buildings were so
shoddy, they had to put mesh cages on the facades to keep
bricks from falling on pedestrians. Russian ingenuity. We
were in the club dining room when Dieter told me the story;
it was paneled, the booths were red leather, the brass fixtures
were shined. But as he talked, the room disappeared, and I
saw East Berlin as it must have been in '59. A city like one of
those old European railroad stations; a vast stone cavern with
damp walls and a skylit ceiling fifty feet high, that let in
streaks of light like dirty fog.

"Somehow the Russians had heard about a Saxon boy
who could get people to 'do things.' The Russians have a low

threshold of disbelief when it comes to psi. Maybe state materialism makes it attractive. Anyway, Saxony was in East Germany, and they brought the boy, who was about eleven, to Berlin. He missed his mother and sister, wanted to go home, and refused to cooperate.

"For a while the Russians were kind to him. He had his own room, good food, a tutor. They told him they'd see his family never wanted for anything again if he'd go along. But the boy hung tough. Then the Russians did something really stupid and cruel. They told him they'd send him home if he strutted his stuff. It was a lie, of course. Imagine the use of such a power; imagine a mental dominant in an arms-control talk or infiltrated into a NATO planning session. Trouble is, mental domination's like germ warfare; great as long as the wind doesn't change. But the Russians were paranoid, just like now. They didn't bother with subtleties like changing winds. So they made their offer. Besides, I imagine it was half true. If he had no stuff to strut, they'd've sent him home."

"But he did?" Moran said.

Reed nodded and said "Dieter called him Gregory. . . ."

They'd won, but he had, too, Gregory thought. He'd give them what they wanted, but they had to send him home in return. Tit for tat. Not like it'd been for three months, with them expecting something for nothing. Now they'd pay and he'd perform.

"You ready?" Lutz said softly. He had his hand on the doorknob of the workroom. Behind it, the sergeant waited as he did every weekday, reading a Russian newspaper. He sat at a molded metal desk with a pile of clean paper on it. Lutz told Gregory that the Russian sergeant was only following orders. He didn't know why he was there or what the paper on the table in front of him was for. Today he'd find out. Gregory grinned in anticipation. Not because he wanted to hurt the sergeant, but he hadn't used the thing for so long, it was backing up in him, like waste in a privy. He couldn't wait to let it go; he was trembling with excitement as Lutz opened the door.

The sergeant ignored them as usual; behind him was a wall mirror, reflecting the sergeant's back, Gregory's and Lutz's faces, and the room. Gregory had read spy stories his sister brought home from the Kamenz library. He knew the mirror was two-way, and Colonel Yanov and Dr. Spilorov, in his dirty white coat, were back there watching. All the Russians were dirty and smelled of old sweat, except Colonel Yanov. He smelled of lilac cologne and Turkish cigarettes. He had black hair combed straight back from his forehead, dead black eyes like flints, and sallow skin. Gregory suspected that the colonel was not pure white and he tried to feel superior, but it was impossible. The colonel was a devil; the kind who'd wade through blood and keep his shoes shined, as Gregory's mother would say.

They'd be there today for sure, watching to see if Gregory would take the offer and make the poor sergeant eat the paper. . . .

"Eat paper," Moran cried. There was a joke about two Mexicans making each other eat horseshit at gunpoint. One was Pancho Villa, and the punch line was, *Do I know Pancho Villa! We had lunch together.* . . . Moran howled with laughter. Reed slapped the desk with the flat of his hand.

"It's not funny," he said. "They had to find a task he'd fight doing but wouldn't harm him. They could've come up with strangling a kitten, handling a rattlesnake, drinking Drāno. But they didn't. Ask yourself if they'd've been so careful in Langley or Washington, if the boy had been ours."

"Sorry," Moran said weakly. Reed went on with the story.

Lutz turned the knob and shoved the door open. There was the sergeant with his newspaper . . . there was the mirror, hiding the other Russians. Gregory came in, took his regular seat. Old magazines lay in a pile next to the chair.

Lutz didn't take his regular chair but stood by the door. Gregory glanced at the mirror. The sergeant must've sensed something because he closed his paper. Gregory smiled . . . and got ready. But he didn't feel anything. No spark, no exhilaration. Maybe he hadn't used it for too long and it had dried up, like the farm pond in August. They'd never believe him. They'd think he was still holding out. He'd never get home . . . they'd stand him up in front of the wall that ran along the back of this palace-turned-prison and shoot him. . . .

Then it stirred and he knew it was okay. He didn't need words. He didn't need anything but the picture of the big, doughy-faced sergeant with those slanty Slavic eyes chewing up paper like it was black bread with butter and salt. He saw it, but it was such a ridiculous vision, Gregory laughed, and the picture wavered. The two men stared at him, wondering what was so funny. Lutz raised his eyebrows; Gregory ignored him. He got the picture back, steadied it, like waiting for ripples on water to stop before you throw the next stone. Then he sort of lofted it out at the sergeant, the way he used to throw his balsa glider back home.

The sergeant went right on looking stolid and stupid; his eyes didn't widen, his eyebrows stayed in a thick black line that stretched almost all the way across his face. But slowly, carefully, he tore a strip off the first sheet of paper and stuffed it in his mouth. His eyes were disinterested, but he chewed in a kind of panic, probably sensing that if he didn't get the paper wet enough, he'd choke when he tried to swallow. Gregory gave him plenty of time. The sergeant was a Russian and dumb as they come (plus he smelled like the rest of them), but he'd never done Gregory any harm. The sergeant chewed and chewed, Gregory grinned over at Lutz, but Lutz stared, enthralled, at the sergeant's fat, wet-looking mouth. Gregory figured he'd had enough time by now, and sure enough, the sergeant's Adam's apple gave a giant bob and he swallowed. Then the sergeant blinked, and picked up his newspaper as if nothing had happened. Without the crinkly sound of paper being chewed, the room was totally silent.

Gregory looked at Lutz again, waiting for congratulations. Lutz looked scared. Then he smiled weakly, came over, and hugged Gregory the way Russians were always hugging each other.

There was a sort of celebration later. The colonel, a few of the soldiers and doctors, and, of course, Lutz and Gregory assembled in a room that opened off the marble-floored rotunda in front of the building. Gregory was allowed to have some wine, which made him dizzy. He hoped they wouldn't remember that he was only twelve and cut him off before he got really drunk. Getting drunk was something he could brag about when he got home. He didn't want to turn up at home with nothing to talk about.

Along with the wine and vodka they had herring and caviar, pickled eggs, chicken in jelly, stuffed eggs, and beet salad. It was a glorious spread. Gregory ate until his pants were tight. Then he picked up Lutz's hand to look at his wristwatch that ticked as loudly as a wall clock. It was almost nine. He should go to bed early to be fresh for the trip home. He didn't need to pack; the clothes belonged to the Russians, anyway, except for what he'd had on his back when he left home. He walked over to within a few feet of the colonel and stopped. The colonel had a glass of vodka in one hand, a toasted bread slice covered with caviar in the other. He shoved the toast neatly into his mouth, then swallowed the vodka in one gulp and stared down at Gregory. His hair looked like lacquer painted on his skull; his eyes were awful.

"What time am I supposed to leave tomorrow, sir?" Gregory asked, using his politest manner. The colonel continued to stare. Gregory thought he must have drunk a lot but didn't look drunk, just . . . dead. Gregory hated him, and now that he was leaving here, he let himself realize how much the colonel scared him.

"To go home," Gregory reminded him softly. "You remember?"

The colonel walked away, back toward the table of food.

Gregory followed right behind him. "Sir . . . it'd be best to leave early since the roads are bad, and you can't see the ruts at night. . . ."

Not a word from the colonel. Gregory almost tugged at the back of the colonel's lightweight tan jacket but restrained himself. Then he realized that everyone in the room was silent. He looked around. They were watching him trail after the colonel. The colonel got to the table, popped a stuffed egg into his mouth, and refilled his vodka glass. Then he deigned to look down at Gregory.

"We'll do some more tests," he said in German with that awful, spineless Russian accent.

"But you said if I showed you . . . I *did* show you."

"Not enough, boy. Not yet."

The colonel walked away from Gregory. No one moved or made a sound. Rage overcame Gregory; his heart hammered in his chest, he got dizzy, and had to hold on to the edge of the table; he occupied the same spot the colonel had just left; the smell of lilac cologne surrounded him. He whirled around to face the colonel's back.

"You said I could go home tomorrow," he called after the colonel. His voice shook with fury. The colonel stopped and turned; his thin lips twitched with mild surprise, his eyes stayed expressionless.

"I was wrong," the colonel said.

Gregory looked wildly around him. The scientists and orderlies who'd all claimed to be his friends were looking assiduously at their feet. Only Lutz's eyes met his; dear Lutz, the Jew from Leningrad who'd looked after Gregory these three lousy months. He told Gregory that Leningrad was the queen of cities; it made Paris look like a baboon's asshole. He told him his apartment was gorgeous, since parapsychologists (even Jew parapsychologists) were in favor with the regime. There was room for Gregory, he'd said as they'd walked together around the back courtyard on the first warm spring day. Someday Gregory would come to Leningrad and be Lutz's guest. He'd meet Lutz's mother, wife, and daughter, who was only a year younger than Gregory. A difficult age for boys . . . impossible for girls.

Gregory raced across the room to Lutz; the rest of the people forced themselves to talk and move around. They restarted forays to the buffet of food.

"He promised," Gregory whispered. "He said I could go home tomorrow."

Lutz's face was pale; he looked angry. "He lied, Grisha. You're leaving tomorrow but not to go home."

"Then where?" Gregory whispered.

"Moscow. They should have told you. I pleaded with them not to play you for a fool. I told them they can't isolate what's in your head from the rest of you . . . as if it were encapsulated. It's part of you, like the cowlick in your hair, the color of your eyes, the fact that you're male. Assholes . . ." He said the epithet in Russian, then switched to German. "We Russians are spoiled, Grisha, not with food or drink or anything worldly, but for centuries we've gotten our way without wit or luck or much of anything but doggedness and bloodletting, and we think we always can. But this time it won't work." Lutz raised his hands and touched Gregory's head lightly with his fingers, as if it were a very delicate and beautiful egg. "God knows what's in here or where it came from, he said in Russian, then back to German, "And they want to force it out of you, like they would information from a third-rate spy. They'll cajole and blackmail. Then off come the gloves and they'll probably beat you up. . . .

"But—big *but*, Grisha—if you do what they want, you'll be treated like a prince. You'll have your own apartment and car. You'll have good food, foreign clothes, beautiful women. . . . I know it doesn't mean much to you now, but some—"

He stopped suddenly and looked up. Gregory whirled around. The colonel had come back and stood a few feet away, staring at them. Gregory smelled the lilac and tobacco, and the loathing that overcame him was dizzying. He glared at the colonel and seemed to see him in a flash of illumination, as in a bomb explosion. The colonel's mustache glistened with wax; his black hair shone with oil; his uniform was immaculate; the crease on his trousers was steel-edged sharp. The picture was perfect. Without meaning to, before he even knew what was going to happen, Gregory imagined how those perfect trousers would look with a spreading stain across the crotch. The colonel would be mortified; it would be the best revenge Gregory could imagine. He still didn't mean to do it, but the picture came into his mind perfectly delineated. It didn't waver; he didn't have to loft it out, as he had this morning. It sailed on its own, and with a kind of shriveling horror that reminded him of falling into a pig swill when he was very young, and feeling the slimy stuff slithering along his arms and legs (a feeling that stayed with him for months after he'd been fished out and cleaned off), he felt the picture connect solidly with the colonel's mind.

For the first time he saw an expression in the colonel's eyes. It was sheer horror, a mirror of what Gregory was feeling. The colonel's legs slid closed, knees knocking, like a three-year-old trying not to wet his pants. But that was just what the colonel was doing; the stain spread across the front of his knife-creased pants, blotched the edge of his jacket, and ran down one leg to the cuff. The colonel stared down at himself. A drop of urine fell off the cuff of one trouser leg and dropped softly to the floor. Then the colonel made an indescribable noise, between a snarl and a bellow; his yellow face turned red; his flinty eyes bulged with rage. Gregory backed up until he was mashed against Lutz. He whimpered and covered his eyes, as he used to do when his father (who'd been dead about three years) would haul off and whack him one. He heard a snap, leather creaking, a loud click, and he opened his eyes. The colonel had his long, blue-black pistol out, pointing at Gregory's face.

But Gregory wasn't going to let the Slav son of a bitch shoot him in the head over a pair of piss-soaked pants. Gregory was only twelve, but he knew that was absurd, and this time he gave a command in words; in German because his Russian wasn't good enough and the colonel understood German fine.

The colonel blinked, then got a steady, ugly tic around

his eyes and mouth as he tried to fight. It was useless. He was the child, Gregory the man. The gun turned in his hand; the barrel was long, and he had to straighten his arm some. He pressed his lips shut, clenched his teeth, but slowly Gregory pried open the colonel's mouth, and slowly, with the colonel fighting madly, Gregory made him slide the muzzle between his teeth. In a split second plates of salad, glasses of champagne or vodka crashed to the floor as the men dropped them to unsnap holsters and get out guns. Lutz threw his arms around Gregory, trying to shield him. A shot hit Lutz and threw him sideways. He didn't let go of Gregory in time, and Gregory stumbled sideways with him.

Gregory was terrified; now he'd give anything to stop because they were going to kill him. He yelled for his mother as a bullet drilled into his chest from the side. He expected immense pain, but it was going to take too long to feel it; he'd probably be dead by the time shock turned to agony. He had another second or two, and he forgot about his mother, sister, home (the weeds would be growing up around the doorstep since he wasn't there to pull them). He took a tiny instant to curse Pastor Stoltz, their own pastor—good old Stoltz—who'd baptized Gregory and confirmed him . . . and sold him out for a chance to kiss Russian ass. Gregory hoped, with his second-to-last conscious thought, that Pastor Stoltz would burn in hell.

Another shot drilled into his cheek; he heard his teeth shatter, but still felt nothing. With his last bit of breath, his last instant of down-spiraling consciousness, he said silently, in German, *Pull the trigger, Colonel Yanov.*

He had the final satisfaction of hearing the blast of the colonel's gun and seeing the back of the colonel's head dissolve into a pink cloud of bone chunks and brain. . . .

They brought Michael Kaslov to the cemetery in a beige van. Dr. Hall had hired an Eastern Orthodox priest to come all the way up from Stamford. It was a nice gesture, Jonathan thought, especially after he'd escaped and left everyone with egg on their faces. But Michael hadn't been in church since he was confirmed; neither had Jonathan. God and religion seemed beside the point for the most part. But he was glad Dr. Hall had gone to the trouble, for his father's sake. The priest looked right for his job: he had a long, cadaverous face; a gray-and-black beard; and a mournful voice that was perfect for such a grim occasion. It *was* grim too. There were no flowers, except a small wreath from a woman in New Canaan; probably one of Michael's fuck buddies, as he called them. And no mourners, except for Jonathan, Dr. Hall, and Marty. Dr. Hall was there because he was Jonathan's friend; Marty was here in case Jonathan went to pieces over his brother's death and became uncontrollable. Jonathan wouldn't, but he couldn't explain this to them. They'd be shocked to know how he really felt.

The truth was that he was relieved. Poor Michael was spoiled, confused, and dogged by bad luck. But Jonathan knew better than anyone on earth that his brother was a son of a bitch, and it was wonderful not to have Michael's thoughts inside his head.

The priest crossed himself, and Jonathan followed suit. He didn't know any of the prayers, but the rhythm of the words was hypnotic, and he looked down at the ground under his feet. The pit of Michael's grave was brown mud; the coffin swung over it on a winch. The grass was still green between patches of wet snow. He looked up; the bare trees glistened, the wind had died, and it was quiet except for the priest's sonorous voice. It was a lovely spot on a hill overlooking Shelburne, miles from his father's little dry-cleaning store. His father had chosen this cemetery back in the forties, and he bought plots for himself, his wife, his two sons, and their wives. Now Michael was here to claim his place, and someday Jonathan would join him. The other two graves would not be used. Jonathan would never marry; Evvie Kaslov was buried somewhere else. Maybe Dr. Hall could help him find out where, and someday he'd write to Amy and tell her so she could put flowers on her mother's grave. It would be nice if she brought flowers here too. But she wouldn't because she had killed her father.

It wasn't a conscious act. She didn't decide to do it, and the second she put it into action, her body became her ally and she passed out. But the part of her mind where that incredible power lived was awake, alive, active. *It* had known exactly what to do. . . .

Grab the gun, Daddy, point it at the guard. Get it away . . . choke him . . . unsnap it . . . point it. Keep going, Daddy. . . .

She didn't see the other guard's gun, but she knew it was there, just as Jonathan or anybody knew that prison guards have guns whether you see them or not.

The priest dug the trowel into a hill of dirt, prayed some more, and spilled the contents of the trowel into the grave. In novels Jonathan had read that the dirt made a hollow sound on the top of the coffin. The writers did not lie. The dirt was damp and spilled in tiny pellets of mud. It hit the metal coffin lid and seemed to echo, as if there were nothing in the coffin, around it, or even under it. It was the hollowest, most depressing noise he'd ever heard. Suddenly he realized that he was the only one left who remembered Michael wearing his short blue pants and skinning his knees when he was six. Michael watching with a frown of concentration on his face as an earthworm oozed across his palm, through his fingers, and plopped to the ground. Michael trying not to cry at eight when he fell off his bike, trying not to cry at twenty-three when his father told him that he had to marry the hill girl.

The priest held out the trowel to Jonathan. Jonathan's eyes were swimming with tears as he took it and emptied it into the grave. Then it was over; the priest nodded at them, shook Jonathan's hand, and went down the path across the lawn to the green Chevy waiting on the road.

It was time to leave Michael for the last time, and Jonathan smothered a sob. He was alone, except for Amy. And what use was Amy? She couldn't come to see him; she couldn't call and talk to him on lonely Saturday afternoons. She was only a little girl (with a power).

He shivered. She was only eight. What would the power be like when she grew up? What would *she* be like? There were too many choices; they buzzed around in his head. She could be her father's daughter, living in a world where other people were ghosts without substance. She could be her mother (whatever her mother was like—lazy and decent, Jonathan suspected—not caring whether school kept or not, as Marty would say). She could be like her grandfather, who carried his burdens gallantly until they overwhelmed him. She could be like Jonathan, himself, riven with pity and driven mad by a power that was harmless to everybody but him. Only hers wasn't harmless.

NINE

AMY HID THE teddy bear and the *Chips* book in the knotted leg of her oldest pair of jeans and hung them in the back of the closet. If he did find and destroy them, she had the feeling that the black, shining eyes of the stuffed bear would haunt her forever. But it was only a toy, and she had to keep telling herself that Paulie was a real boy who loved his father (as she probably once loved hers a little deep down) and was hurt because he thought his father didn't love him.

He knew the teddy bear had been rescued; Jeannie talked about it, so did Greta, and every time after she'd been out of the house, she'd go right upstairs and check the leg of the jeans to be sure it was still there.

He gave up on the bear and tried other things. He squeezed toothpaste into her hairbrush. And one sleety morning in February they found the fuzzy blue sweater Greta had given her in the backyard under the clothesline. It had been there all night, and the raccoons had torn it to shreds. Then he stole her homework. She didn't think Paulie would go that far. Homework wasn't like toys and sweaters —and this was a report on George Washington that Greta had to help her write. She started to get mad, then she reminded herself that he was their own child. If there was a war between them, she would be the one to go.

The thought of leaving this house made her heart pound with fear. She would give up Little and her old *Chips* book if she had to. She would give up anything not to be sent away.

He must have known she was scared, because it got worse. He put mud in her book bag, short-sheeted her bed (only moving fast kept her from tearing one of Jeannie's good sheets). The stuffed seal was gone one day and Greta noticed.

"What happened to the seal?"

Amy wanted to cry. She wanted Greta to put her arms around her and tell her it would be okay; but to get comfort she would have to tell Greta about Paulie. Greta loved her a lot. Maybe more than she loved Paulie, but Paulie was her *brother* and she'd have to be on his side. Amy understood. If she had a brother, she would take his part, too, no matter what.

"Must be around somewheres," she said. "Mrs. Simmons probably vacuumed him and stuck him away somewhere."

Greta was satisfied and didn't ask about the seal again.

The winter ground on. Her toys and books disappeared. Her two other favorite sweaters were gone, along with the white, silky blouse with the ruffle around the neck that she'd planned to wear to Cissy's birthday party. One afternoon after school she found the ribbons that Greta had given her in a clump on the floor next to her bed. They were trampled and filthy. She tried to wash them in the bathroom sink, using hand soap, but the dirt was tarry and it caked the sink and dirtied the bar of soap. She wrapped the ruined ribbons in toilet paper and threw them in the wastebasket, praying that Greta wouldn't find them, then she scoured the sink and rinsed off the soap.

Her early furtiveness came back; Paulie was always grinning at her across the dinner table (he knew he was winning), and her appetite waned. Jeannie noticed and tried to tempt her with special food like the nut cake that she knew Amy loved. Amy tried to eat, but everything tasted like cotton and seemed to swell in her mouth until it was hard to swallow.

Joe worried about her, too, and paid even more attention to her, pulling her close to him on the couch in the evening after dinner to watch TV. His kindness only made things worse; she was terrified that she'd weaken and cry in front of him, and he'd insist on knowing what was wrong. Besides, Paulie saw the extra affection, and she knew it made him hate her even more (if that was possible).

Dr. Moran noticed, and she had to make up things to tell him when he asked her what was wrong. She told him that she had trouble at school. She hated history (that was the absolute truth); her English teacher didn't seem to like her (mostly the truth. Her English teacher was a wan woman with thin, mousy hair. She didn't care much about Amy, herself, but Amy had the feeling that Mrs. Snow hated Amy's hair). She told him that Greta paid more attention to Cissy than she did to Amy, and Amy was jealous (that was a bold lie and her cheeks burned when she said it. She had the feeling that Dr. Moran could look inside her head and knew when she was lying. But he didn't call her on it).

Mostly she told him that everything was "jes fine," like Grundoon in *Pogo*. Saying "jes fine" got Grundoon out of the worst scrapes.

It wasn't *all* terrible. Jeannie taught her to knit; she managed to learn enough American history to get a *B* (Greta got an *A*); and Mrs. Snow buried her envy of Amy's hair and gave her a *B* in English. And, of course, there was math. Sweet, simple, clear math, which had nothing to do with people liking or hating each other. There were no wars in math (like there were in history) and no families or feelings like there were in the things they read in English. In fact, there were no *people;* and the hour that she spent on math was the best part of Amy's day.

She lost so much weight that some of the clothes got too big. She stole safety pins from Jeannie's sewing basket and pinned in the waistbands of the skirts, hoping no one noticed.

One day in March Paulie almost went too far.

There were patches of snow on the ground, but the buds on the shrubs had gotten fat and fuzzy and the days were longer. It was still cold, and on this day the sky was gray. It was a Wednesday during spring vacation, and Jeannie took Greta to the dentist in Millbridge; Amy would have gone to keep Greta company because they both hated Dr. Cooper (not that he'd ever hurt Amy, but she had the feeling that he would sooner or later. Besides, the whole business was uncomfortable and degrading . . . sitting with your mouth open, spit running down your chin, and the cold metal mirror tapping against your teeth). But Amy had a cold, and Jeannie told Amy to stay home with Mrs. Simmons.

Mrs. Simmons had put the laundry into the machine and was vacuuming upstairs. Amy liked folding laundry, putting it away in neat piles in the linen closet and in the drawers upstairs, and she told Mrs. Simmons that she'd take the things out of the dryer.

"Would you, love?" Mrs. Simmons had a weird accent, not foreign exactly but not American, either. Jeannie said she was from England; Amy knew vaguely where England was.

Amy picked up the skirt of the robe she was wearing (she didn't get dressed because Jeannie said she had to take a nap this afternoon) and went down to the basement.

The basement was spotless like the rest of the house, and her house shoes didn't crunch across the floor the way they had in her old house in Bridgeton. There were no cobwebs, no dust-covered cardboard boxes with broken sides. But it was dreary, anyway. The table for folding laundry was covered with an old sheet pinned around the legs, and Amy emptied the dryer, put the next load of damp clothes from the washer into it, and pushed the start button. The dryer whirled. Upstairs, Mrs. Simmons started up the vacuum. Amy went to the table and started folding the clothes neatly. She enjoyed making the corners on the towels even and lining up the piles of underwear and handkerchiefs. Everything smelled clean; the fabrics were still warm from the dryer.

She didn't hear steps on the basement stairs over the dryer and vacuum upstairs; she didn't hear anything until Paulie's voice said, "Well, well . . . look who's here."

His voice was high and clear. She thought it was the worst sound she'd ever heard a human being make (except for her mother's grunt when the hammer hit her). Amy's heart thumped, and something inside her belly started beating like a second heart. Her palms got wet, but she kept on with what she was doing.

"She's a bohunk," Paulie said. Amy gasped. Her skin was on fire and she felt sweat pop out at her hairline. No one had ever called her a bohunk. She didn't know what it meant. But she knew it was nasty . . . like nigger or kike.

"Bohunk girls *like* to see, Timmy."

Timmy Cassini was there too.

"Go on, Timmy, show her," Paulie cried in his high, ugly voice.

She turned around. They were standing a few feet away, looking at her. No one had ever looked at her like that before. It made her aware of the fact that she was only wearing a robe and nightie; it made her so embarrassed that she was almost sick to her stomach. Timmy grinned. He was much shorter than Paulie but he looked older. He had black fuzz on his upper lip, and fuzz grew down the sides of his face near his ears. He had pimples, and his shoulders looked big under his plastic jacket. His grin widened, and she saw the glint of his teeth.

"Yeah," he said softly, eyeing her in that weird way. "You want to see."

"I don't want to see anything." She picked up a blue towel. She wanted to wrap it around herself because he was looking at her as if she didn't have any clothes on. But she was wearing her robe and nightgown; she was covered to her ankles.

"Go on, Timmy, show her," Paulie said.

"She'll tell," Timmy whined excitedly.

"Naw. She won't tell. She's scared to tell anything,

'cause she knows they'll throw her bohunk ass outta here if she makes trouble."

Paulie was smart; she had to give him that much. He knew she was scared and he knew why.

"You sure?" Timmy asked.

"Sure," Paulie said. "We can make her do anything we want."

She blinked.

Paulie took a step closer. Amy stepped back.

"Go on, Timmy," Paulie said, "then we'll get her to show us something."

"Leave me alone," Amy wailed. She prayed Mrs. Simmons would hear and come to her rescue. But the vacuum was going strong. She could scream, but they could tell Mrs. Simmons anything they wanted to; they could make it all her fault, and who would Mrs. Simmons believe . . . a bohunk orphan they'd taken in or the true Levin child? Amy whimpered and hated herself for being so scared. She didn't even know what they were going to do. Maybe nothing. Maybe they just wanted to make her cry. Another second or two and she'd oblige them. Then Timmy unbuckled his belt and opened his pants; he was wearing white underpants, like Joe's underpants on the table waiting to be folded. They had a front slit in them, so did Timmy's, and he reached into it and pulled out a red, meaty-looking thing. It was hard and stuck out like a rod. His grin widened; his eyes were half closed. He squeezed it, and the tip of it bulged.

"Make her touch it," he said softly. "Make her touch it."

Paulie grabbed her hand and pulled her toward Timmy. She struggled; she would die before she would touch that thing he was pointing at her. It looked hot, like it would burn her skin.

"Let me go," she pleaded.

Paulie giggled and hauled her closer, and suddenly, from every corner of the basement, the cool wind blew in at her; it sank into her ears, settled in her head, and turned silver and liquid. It felt magnificent; the flush left her face,

her skin was cool, the fear sweat dried, and she turned her
head away from the hideous protuberance sticking out of
Timmy Cassini's underpants and looked at Paulie. Right into
his eyes. She felt things that she could never have described.
She felt very old, as if she'd grown up in a second; she felt as
hard as the cement-block wall and even more impregnable.
With the cold came pity for Paulie Levin and his little boy's
tricks; and fear, not for what he could do to her or even for
what would happen to her if the Levins threw her out, but
fear for *him*, as if he were standing at the edge of a cliff in a
strong wind with his back facing the precipice and didn't
know that another few inches and he would fall backward
into space. This second, looking at Paulie was like watching
the scene in a horror movie when the star goes up the stairs
to the attic or into a dark room, while everybody in the audience knows the monster is hiding behind the door. The cold
settled in, and she stared at him without blinking.

He dropped her hand and whirled to look at Timmy.
Amy looked at Timmy too. His face had turned gray, making
the dark line on his lip thick and black like a streak of ink.
The thing in his hand shrank, and he stuffed it back inside
his underwear and zipped up his pants. He didn't take his
eyes off Amy, and Amy thought that as smart as Paulie was,
Timmy was much smarter, because he looked terrified. He
stepped back toward the stairs.

Paulie tried to give an arrogant laugh, but it came out as
a squeaky giggle.

"Let's go," Timmy said. "Leave her alone."

Suddenly (Thank God) the vacuum cleaner stopped.

"Hi, Paulie," Amy yelled as loud as she could, "what're
you doing down here?"

He jumped back and poor Timmy shivered.

"Let's get out of here," Timmy whined.

Mrs. Simmons opened the basement door. "You down
there, Paulie. Come up here and leave Amy alone. She's got
all that folding to do."

Timmy ran up the stairs; Paulie followed slowly. Halfway up he turned, and his eyes bored into hers. He was

starting a staring contest, like a lot of kids did at school. It was too silly and small to bother, and Amy looked away. He clumped up the rest of the stairs and left her with the laundry to fold and her sour triumph, which she knew hadn't changed anything.

The next day she and Greta got off the school bus, and Paulie and three others—Len somebody, Bobby somebody, and Timmy—were waiting. They let Greta pass and go up the walk, but when Amy tried, they closed in, narrowing the path to almost nothing. Greta stopped at the front door, Amy hoped she'd run inside and get Jeannie.

Timmy Cassini stared at his feet, but the others watched her with mean little smiles on their faces. The bus chugged away; she was alone with them except for Greta, who looked tiny and helpless way up by the front door. Amy tried not to be scared; it was just a tease, she told herself. It was really dumb for high school boys to be teasing little kids like her. They should be having Cokes with girls, asking them to movies, worrying about football and who they'd take to the prom. But Paulie must have told them what happened in the basement yesterday, and it stirred them up somehow.

Cringing drove boys wild; she must not cringe. It wasn't easy because she was scared. Greta called to her, but Amy's mouth was dry. She didn't even try to answer.

The boys closed in tighter, their smiles got slyer, meaner. They reminded her of how Timmy and Paulie had looked in the basement yesterday, and suddenly she was terrified they were all going to open their pants and stick themselves out at her. But false spring had ended; it was only the end of March and wind whipped the still bare trees. They wouldn't want to open their pants in the cold; besides, Jeannie or one of the other Windy Ridge ladies might look out the window and see them. So she was safe; all she had to do was get past them.

There was a tiny path between them that she could pass through, like the gauntlet heroes sometimes had to run in movies. But she'd have to touch them as she passed and they were sort of leading with their hips (Timmy excepted). In spite of their grins they looked like they wanted to murder her. Len wasn't very nice-looking; he had spots (Jeannie called them zits) and some scraggly black hairs growing out of his jaw, and his eyes were blank-looking and didn't go with the grin on his mouth, so his face looked split in half. Oil shone on his nose and forehead, even in the cold. But Bobby was handsome with clear skin and long, clean blond hair that blew softly in the wind. He leaned toward her; her head shrank into her shoulders turtle-fashion.

"Heard you got to see something special yesterday," Bobby said.

"She loved it," Paulie crowed softly.

"No . . ." she wailed, and Bobby chuckled.

"Sure you did. Pretty little thing like you could have lots of fun with a nice hot play toy like that," he said. She was going to have to run for it, but Bobby positioned himself so she couldn't get past him without brushing against the zipper in his pants. Maybe she'd sock him there with all her might. She'd never hit anyone really hard before. . . .

Then Greta shoved past the boys, grabbed Amy's hand, and yelled, "Leave her alone, you . . . you turds." The boys laughed and backed away. Greta tugged her up the walk to the house with the boys laughing after them.

Greta got the door open, pulled Amy inside, and slammed it shut. "Turds," she said. Amy looked through the sidelight and saw the boys moving away in a clump; the gauntlet was broken.

April came, and Paulie found the teddy bear and her *Chips* book.

Amy didn't know how he'd done it, but one night, after an almost glorious evening watching *The Wizard of Oz* on TV, she and Greta (a.k.a. Dorothy) went upstairs to bed. Amy reached into the leg of the jeans as she always did and felt nothing. She knew that they were gone, and she wasn't particularly surprised. She took the jeans out of the closet, anyway, and turned them inside out just to be sure. She unknotted the legs and shook them. But they were empty.

There was no point in searching; he wouldn't put them in the Brachmans' garbage again. He'd put them in the trash at school, or into one of the litter cans in the Grand Union parking lot. Maybe this time he had taken the risk and burned them somewhere out in the woods, way behind the house. It didn't matter, she wouldn't find them. She wasn't sure she had the energy to look, even if there was a chance.

She wasn't overwhelmed with grief or pain, but she felt a grinding sadness as it came home to her that she'd never, never see them again.

She went to bed and finally fell asleep. When she woke up, the pillowcase was wet. She had been crying in her sleep. It was still dark; everyone in the house was asleep. She got up and left her room. She prowled through the house in the dark, trying to think of something that would make her feel better. Nana had been right, after all, she decided. You let one single transgression go and pretty soon they drown you. She should have listened to Nana instead of Dr. Moran. She went into the kitchen, and in the faint light of the stove clock she found the box of Oreos and ate two, standing at the counter. She would hold out a little longer, but one more bad —really bad—thing, like Timmy Cassini showing his pecker (she had asked Cissy about the protuberance between a boy's legs, and Cissy informed her that it was called a pecker and had something nasty to do with having babies) or stealing anything else she cared about (although there was nothing left) and she would fight back, no matter what.

The decision made her feel better. She washed the Oreos down with gulps of milk right from the carton, then went back upstairs.

The overt war with Paulie broke out in June. But it really began in the middle of May when F. Gordon Swain came to see Levin.

PART II

THE GAUNTLET

TEN

F. GORDON SWAIN came exactly at eight, pulling into the driveway in a bandbox 1950s Jaguar. When Levin saw the car, he expected Mr. Swain to be wearing a leisure suit and to have the long sideburns that desperate middle-aged men affected these days, along with gold bracelets and facial hair. But F. Gordon Swain wore an old, well-cared-for three-piece suit that looked custom-made and had probably cost more than Levin made in a month. He was short with weak-looking blue eyes, thick glasses, thin sandy hair, and a chin that almost disappeared into his neck. He was the prototype of what Levin's father would have called a schlemiel. Yet his eyes were direct, his voice low-pitched and strong, and even though he had the Harvard–Yale upper-class accent that usually set Levin's teeth on edge, Swain didn't put Levin off at all. In fact, Levin found himself almost liking the man. He seemed precise without being fussy; he put his briefcase squarely on the coffee table and took the chair Levin indicated with neat movement.

Levin offered coffee, and the man accepted gratefully. He was pale and looked tired, and Levin wondered if he'd gotten his dinner yet tonight. He left the lawyer to bring the coffee and cake. Jeannie had them ready on the counter in the kitchen. She and the girls had finished clearing up after dinner, and they were in the den watching TV.

He brought the stuff into the living room and set the tray on the table, next to Mr. Swain's briefcase. Mr. Swain doctored the coffee with cream and sugar, took a few bites of cake, mentioned the weather and the war in Vietnam, then said, "I'm grateful for your time, Lieutenant. I'm a little reluctant to be here, but I felt that I must speak to you."

Levin's stomach muscles tightened. All afternoon since Swain had called and asked for tonight's appointment to discuss business that was "urgent, sensitive," and concerned Amy, Levin had been eaten up with curiosity. He couldn't imagine anything about Amy's mutilated life that could be urgent or sensitive to F. Gordon Swain, who was, Levin had found out a few hours ago, one of the most respected lawyers in central Connecticut.

Swain took a thin folder out of his briefcase and opened it.

"Amy Kaslov is your foster child, correct?"

Levin nodded.

"You are not her legal guardian."

"No."

"Do you have any plans to ask for guardianship?"

"I have plans to adopt Amy."

Swain raised his pale eyebrows. "That can be a complicated and expensive procedure."

"I know," Levin said.

"Well, maybe not *so* complicated," Swain said gently. "Her mother and father are dead. She appears to be quite alone in the world."

"She has an uncle."

"Ah, but he's not legally competent, I believe."

If Swain knew about the uncle, he knew a great deal about Amy. Levin's gut muscles tightened a notch.

Swain said, "Did the child ever mention her maternal grandmother . . . Edna Wooster Montgomery?"

Suddenly Levin had the mad feeling that this pleasant,

precise little man was going to reveal that Amy was the lost grand duchess of all the Russias and heir to the Romanov jewels and a Swiss bank account worth millions. He grinned, and surprisingly Mr. Swain grinned back.

Levin said, "She's mentioned her grandmother but not by name."

"Did she ever mention a farm up around Newton?"

"Yes."

"She certainly seems to be the right Amy Kaslov."

Levin laughed. "It's not a name like Mary Smith."

"No. Well, then, to the point. Mrs. Montgomery left that farm to her daughter, Eve Montgomery Kaslov, who died"— he consulted his folder—"in October."

"Yes," Levin said softly, "October."

"Since Mrs. Kaslov did not leave a will, the land would normally be divided between her husband and child. However, Mr. Kaslov died—"

"In December," Levin said shortly.

Swain clicked his tongue. "Poor child." He sat in a kind of reverie for a moment, then he said, "However, Mrs. Montgomery's will stipulates that if the land is still in her daughter's possession at the time of her death—which it was—then it goes to her granddaughter, Amy. The Amy you plan to adopt. In other words, the farm in Newton belongs to your ward."

Levin was startled. He never thought about who owned the farm Amy had mentioned a few times. She had come to him with nothing, and he almost preferred to think of her that way: destitute and dependent on him for everything. He was ashamed of himself, and he looked away from Swain as he asked, "How big is this farm?"

"One hundred and sixty acres."

Now Levin was stunned. It was positively grand.

"With a house in fairly decent repair and three outbuildings," Swain went on. "There is, of course, a problem. That's why I'm here."

"Of course," Levin said.

"I have been retained by Jason and Alwyn, Developers. They're a respectable company. They've built several shopping malls around Danbury and Bethel; decent enough places, not at all fly-by-night. They have empowered me to make you—as Amy's foster parent—an offer for the land. There are"—he consulted his folder again—"seven hundred and eighty-five dollars owed in back taxes. If they are not paid by June, the land will be sold. My clients feel that if you refuse their offer, they will be able to buy it cheaply at auction. So they have sent me here to make an offer and to urge you to accept. I'm afraid, however, that I find myself on the horns of a moral dilemma. Jason and Alwyn are my clients and I owe them my first allegiance, of course. . . ."

"Of course," Levin echoed again, wondering wildly what was coming.

"However, I find myself in the dubious and uncomfortable position of having to urge you not to take their offer. I expressed my reservations to Mr. Jason. He . . . I believe the phrase is, sloughed them off . . . thinking perhaps that my self-interest was equal to his. He was wrong."

"What is the offer?" Levin asked.

"One hundred thousand dollars."

Levin did not know what to say. His Sweet Pea—his little abused and abandoned orphan—was rich. It was like a fairy tale. Probably one of those lousy ones where the stepsisters get their eyes pecked out by doves or the poor maiden-cum-mermaid must traverse dry, ugly land in agony for the rest of her life.

"And what do you think *is* a fair offer?" he asked.

"There are several considerations. The appraised value of the land. The fact that before you can accept such an offer in Amy Kaslov's name, you must be appointed her legal guardian. That means lawyers' fees. Then there's upkeep. The place has been neglected. Mrs. Montgomery was ill for some time before she died. Mr. Montgomery, the child's grandfather, has been dead for years. So there's work to be done to bring the place back up to snuff. Nothing that major—"

"Mr. Swain, how low is the Jason–Alwyn offer set"

Mr. Swain took a breath. "The land and buildings have been appraised at one hundred and sixty thousand dollars. Appraisals tend to be low, as I'm sure you know. I think if you paid the back taxes and put another thousand or so into repairs, you could sell it for quite a bit more. Of course, the money would have to stay in trust for the child until she reaches her majority, but the trust would reimburse you for what you spend."

Swain looked deeply apologetic. "I think my clients are victims of a misconception, Lieutenant. They listened to key words, as people so often do. They heard *foster home* and *policeman*, and I think that they assumed you would not have the means to pay the taxes or do the repairs." He looked around the living room, "They were wrong. You appear to be comfortable, perhaps substantially so. That's not my business. I should add that the land is free and clear, except for the taxes owed. It has been in the Wooster family for generations. The Woosters are an old family in these parts, going back, I believe, to the Colonial wars . . ."

When Amy and Greta came down to breakfast on Sunday morning, May 21, she found an envelope on the table at her place. Joe was already there, Jeannie was at the stove, and Paulie was late.

She picked up the envelope. "What's this?" It was long and didn't look like a greeting card; besides, it wasn't her birthday. She looked up at Joe. His face was bright red and he was grinning. Jeannie looked at Amy over her shoulder from the stove. She grinned too. So it was a surprise. Greta looked bewildered and she shrugged. Greta was a worse liar than Amy; she really didn't know what was in the mysterious envelope.

"Open it," said Joe.

Just then Paulie came in and took his place across from

Amy. He didn't greet anyone. He started eating his toast and looking back impatiently at his mother for his eggs. She served him; no one else seemed interested in eating. Paulie started in without waiting for anyone else.

"Open it," Joe said again.

Paulie looked up, saw the envelope in Amy's hand. She knew he was curious, but he wouldn't deign to ask. Certainly he would not have anything to do with a surprise for Amy. At least not a nice surprise, and from the expressions on Jeannie's and Joe's faces, this one must be wonderful. She opened the envelope (it wasn't sealed, the flap was just tucked in) and drew out a long, folded piece of paper. The paper was slippery, like the photocopies that they made on the machine in the library. She opened it and tried to read. But the copy wasn't good, or the original was very old, because the background was all gray and the words were written in faded ink, in flowing handwriting.

"Read it out loud," Joe said.

She tried. "Know ye that on this, the nineteenth day of February, in the Year of our Lord—"

She stopped because the date was impossible. If it was a joke, she didn't get it.

"Go on," Joe urged.

"But it says 1762."

"That's right," said Joe happily. Jeannie laughed out loud, gave up at the stove, and sat down at her place at the table.

"Go on," Joe said.

She looked over at Greta. Greta looked dreamy.

"Seventeen sixty-two," Greta said softly.

They'd made a mistake. This was some kind of historical thing. They should have given it to Greta, not Amy. Greta knew all about the 1700s. She loved reading about the people back then and had pictures showing how the women dressed.

"Is this for me?" Amy asked.

"Absolutely, one hundred percent for you, Sweet Pea. Keep reading."

She did, in a halting voice, leaving out a lot of the words that were too faded to make out. The writing was really weird, with letters like *f*'s in places where there should have been an *s*. It seemed to have something to do with a piece of land. There was a pine tree. (Imagine, a pine tree from 1762. She wondered where the poor tree was by now. Long cut down, long since carved up into the floors or walls for houses that didn't exist anymore.) Then there was something about a stone wall and some numbers that seemed to refer to feet.

Then she saw the name: David Increase Wooster.

"Wooster." She said it out loud, drawing out the *o*'s as she tried to remember.

"Wooooster—" She stopped. Wooster had been Nana's name before she got married. Suddenly a whole flood of things came back to Amy. A pincushion embroidered with the initials EPW—that was Elvira Pingree Wooster, Amy's great-grandmother—and a whole set of napkins with the same initials on them that Nana used only at Christmas and Easter and washed by hand because she said that their old washing machine with the wringer would ruin them. Amy could see those napkins . . . they were yellowing, like the original of this piece of paper must be by now. She remembered some beautiful silverware engraved EWM—that was Nana—and how Nana had cried when she sold the whole box of it a long time after Grandpa died. She'd kept a couple of the big pieces; they were beautiful and heavy, heavier than the silver Jeannie used on Fridays, and they had those same wondrous initials: EWM. Edna Wooster Montgomery.

Amy stared at the piece of paper, tears filled her eyes, and she ducked her head. She thought she understood. This piece of paper had belonged to her Nana, and somehow Joe had gotten a hold of it, for Amy's sake. Because he somehow understood that she was bereft of all possessions and he wanted her to have something of her own. Of course, he couldn't *know* about the teddy bear or the *Chips* book and any of what went on with Paulie, but he understood, anyway.

And he had dug this up from somewhere, and now it was here in her hands.

She looked up.

"This was Grandma's," she said very softly.

Joe nodded; Paulie put down his fork and listened. She glanced at him, saw the interest in his eyes, and her heart sank. Then she rallied. She would protect this with her life. Better, she'd give it back to Joe for safekeeping. He could put it with his very important papers. Paulie wouldn't dare tamper with it.

"Where did you get it?" Greta asked her father. Amy smiled at her in gratitude. Greta always asked the right questions, and Amy was too overcome to think.

"Well, Princess, I got it at the town hall over in Newton."

Amy was confused again.

"But didn't my grandma have it?"

"Not exactly, although it did belong to her. That's not the real one, Amy. That's just a copy."

Her joy faded. She thought that she had something that her grandmother had touched, perhaps read once a week or once a year. It was just a piece of paper. She looked from it to Joe. He saw how bewildered she was.

"Amy, that's the deed to your grandmother's farm."

"Deed?"

"That's right. When your grandmother died, she left the farm to your mother. When your mother"—he took a deep breath—"died, she left the farm to you. And that's a copy of the deed. That proves that the farm belongs to you."

It was too much for her to take in. She felt the blood leave her head, and she was dizzy for a couple of seconds. She swallowed and breathed as best she could, and the dizziness went away.

"The farm . . ." she said. It wasn't exactly a question.

Joe beamed and his face looked like it was in a spotlight. Jeannie was laughing quietly to herself. Greta looked as confused as Amy, and Paulie was pale and chewed his lip.

"The farm belongs to you, Amy," Jeannie said.

Suddenly she connected the strangely written words with things she remembered. The stone wall . . . it was there. The brook was the brook that they'd had picnics next to and that she had dreamed about when she was locked in the closet. And the tree . . . the pine tree was still there! It was huge and old, and Nana was afraid that one of the branches would come down in a storm and stove in the roof of the shed. It was there! The needles under it were thick and yellow, and she remembered the soft rug that they made under her feet. She remembered how that tree smelled; this second she could actually smell it.

"How big?" Greta asked suspiciously. Bless Greta, because Amy wanted to know too. Not that it mattered. Even if it was on a few feet, it was land, with grass, and the tree, and maybe . . . maybe Nana's house.

"Very big," Joe said, "one hundred and sixty acres."

"How big is that?" Greta asked. Paulie leaned closer.

"Yes," Amy whispered, too overcome to talk out loud. "How big?"

Joe laughed uproariously. "The greed of these two," he crowed. Then he said, trying to sound serious and impressive, "Darlings, our piece of land is two acres. That's the front yard, the backyard, the bit of woods, and all the rest. Only two acres. Multiply that sixty times."

"Eighty times," Amy choked out. She was close to fainting.

"Eighty times!" Joe cried.

"And the house?" Amy managed to ask.

"The house, the barn, the shed . . ."

Greta leaped to her feet. "Oh, heavens!" she screeched, and she threw her arms around Amy. Joe went on with his list. "A brook, seventy-five acres of good timber, fences, grass, a path . . ."

Paulie's face was positively white.

Amy struggled to her feet so she could hug Greta back. They hung on to each other and danced around the kitchen in a wild polka. Amy realized that they were crushing the piece of paper—the deed—between them. "Wait . . ." She pulled back. The deed fell to the floor and they both looked at it. Amy picked it up and on impulse she handed it to Greta.

Greta carried it ceremoniously back to the table, laid it down, and began smoothing it, trying to get out the wrinkles.

Joe said, "It's only a copy, Princess. We'll get another one."

But Greta kept smoothing.

"Joe, how did you know about it?" Amy asked.

He told her about the lawyer who'd come to see him three weeks ago. She remembered the night when the man in the big old car came? She did. That was about her grandmother's farm. He would have told her right off, but there were a couple of things to clear up. He didn't tell her about the taxes. It didn't matter, because if everything went as planned, and there was no reason it shouldn't, she would legally be his child by next fall. As much his, in the eyes of the law, as Greta or Paulie. Much more the child of his heart than Paulie was.

She sank back down at the table, staring at him. The room was quiet. She didn't thank him; she didn't know what he had done for her. He was delighted with himself because he didn't want her to know. If there was a debt, it would be settled somehow, someday. Right now it didn't seem like she could ever owe him anything, because sometime in December—by the time that shitty war was over for good—he would be her father. Children didn't owe fathers; his own father had made that clear. Fathers owed children. Besides, this minute, the kitchen was a happier place than it had ever been. She made him feel good about himself; she showed him that his Greta, who was still industriously trying to get the wrinkles out of Amy's deed, was going to be one of the nicest people he'd ever known. Jeannie looked as young and pretty as she had on their wedding day.

Amy had brought a sort of dowry . . . a farm . . . land, water, trees. A place they could go to and walk across. An antidote to Windy Ridge with its ticky-tacky houses; a place with history. Amy had brought them riches.

Paulie stood up and crossed the kitchen.

Jeannie cried, "Paulie, don't you want your eggs?"

For once he answered politely. "No thanks, Mother." And he went out of the kitchen. Levin noticed that he was very pale and his bottom lip was red, as if he'd chewed it raw.

On May 25, Levin went to Swain's office in an imposing old Colonial on the Main Street of Washington to get the keys to the Wooster farmhouse.

"Don't expect too much," Swain warned him. "Mrs. Montgomery died last July, and the place has been empty since. It was up for sale for a while, and the broker told me that the windows were boarded up when Mrs. Kaslov died. It was taken off the market until the . . . ah . . . its legal status could be established."

"There's no question," Levin asked sharply, "Amy owns it?"

Swain smiled. The man had a truly charming smile; his eyes looked positively bright behind the Coke-bottle-bottom glasses. "She owns it, Lieutenant. It was very good of you to pay those taxes out of pocket like that. I hope the cost of repairs won't discourage you."

Levin thought of Greta and Amy polkaing around the kitchen.

"They won't," he said, and he laughed, "I don't think anything would at this point. You should have seen her face when she read that deed and realized what it was."

Levin took the afternoon off and drove down to Newton to see the place alone. He was curious first of all, but he wanted to be sure the place wasn't too much of a wreck. If the roof had fallen in or if kids had gotten in and vandalized it, he'd put off the family trip until repairs could be done.

It was still called the Wooster farm on the survey map. It was up a winding dirt road with a few houses on it. It was a

town road, so it would be scraped and plowed as necessary.
He had driven through Newton center, which was pretty
much like Westerly center, and like most of the towns around
here, but once away from the antique shops and old Colonials turned into offices and out into countryside, it was
beautiful. More beautiful than Westerly because the land
was not covered with that scrubby second growth that de-
faced most of Connecticut. It was still meadow, as most of
the state must have been a hundred years ago. The trees in
the woods he could see in the distance were old and thick-
trunked, not like the poor, scrawny things that grew like
weeds around Windy Ridge. He passed a house and looked
for landmarks on the survey map. A stone wall, a stream running under the road, and the next turn would be the Wooster
place. Amy's farm.

He came to it, expecting a driveway, but it was a rutted
dirt road leading across a field of overgrown pasture grass.

He turned in. The road wound, climbed, and kept climbing; the ruts were enormous, and the station wagon heaved
through them, groaning on its springs. At the end of the road
was the house, and he pulled up, stopped, and got out of the
car.

The house was a mess; the windows were boarded up as
Swain had warned him; the siding was painted shingle, but
the paint was worn away, exposing old wood, so it was hard
to tell what color it had been originally. The wooden back
porch had a dangerous slope to it; the stairs were rotted. He
went closer and realized that the rot was only surface. His
house sat on a cement-block foundation, like most of the
houses they threw up these days, but this foundation was
solid stone. The doorsills were in true; the roof was real
shake and so was the siding: fine, thick, old-time shakes that
would cost a fortune today.

He went carefully up the ruined steps to the porch. It
was almost a veranda, and from here he could see the side of
the building, and he realized that it was large and rambling
and that the Woosters must once have been prosperous. He

tried the door; it was locked and didn't look like it had ever been forced, so maybe the interior was intact. He had the key. He could open the door and find out, but he thought that Amy should be the first one to open the door and step over the solid threshold of her house.

He turned to go back and was arrested by the view. The house was on a hill coming up from the road. There were no other houses, nothing except the old barn and a shed with a collapsing roof. Amy's land stretched as far as he could see; the uncut field rolled to a line of old trees, and in the distance, almost hidden by the trees, the stream he'd crossed down by the road glittered in the sun. The wind blew; the air was damp, cool, and smelled of pine. It was the most beautiful place in the world, he decided. Almost—he grinned—almost good enough for his Sweet Pea.

He decided to wait until June 5 to take her to see the place. He consulted with Jeannie and they decided to make a picnic. They'd leave Westerly to get to Newton around eleven, and spend the day. They'd stop at one of the new family restaurants on their way back and give the kids hamburgers or fried shrimp. Greta and Amy loved that crap food, and Paulie didn't seem to care what he ate. Not that it mattered, anyway, because Levin was sure Paulie would not want to go.

He was wrong.

He knocked on the door of Paulie's room after dinner. He heard the little TV that they'd bought for him because he never wanted to watch the programs that anyone else wanted to see. Plays seemed to make him restless; he didn't think the sitcoms were funny. (Levin had to go along with him there, but Jeannie and the girls loved them.) In fact, he didn't seem to like much of anything that wasn't somehow assaultive; he watched hockey, football, and war movies. He would sit still for the occasional cop film, but only if there was plenty of violence. Levin stood outside his son's door, heard some kind of mayhem coming from the tube inside, and wondered what strange combination of genes had produced his Paulie. Levin's father had been the nicest, gentlest man on earth. His mother had been a bit of a trial, a whiner . . . the Queen of Kvetch his sister called her. But a harmless, ultimately gentle woman and very loving to him. Too loving, he supposed, because she ignored her daughter and carped almost constantly at her husband. Years after she had died (not long after Levin graduated from the academy), he found himself wondering if his father hadn't felt a touch of relief when the lid closed on his wife's coffin. Still, there was nothing about her to account for Paulie. Paulie was a throwback, but Levin would never know to what. Some Polish peasant who made life as wretched as he could for everyone around him and managed to pass on his meanness, hidden deep in some dormant gene, through the generations that followed him.

He rapped on the door. Nothing happened. He tried again and called, "Paulie, it's Dad, can I come in?"

He heard Paulie thump across the floor; the volume on the TV went down and Levin knocked again.

"Okay," Paulie yelled.

His voice had that special tone of the adolescent disturbed that made Levin want to kick the door in. But he opened the door and walked in.

Paulie was on his back on the bed with his arms crossed under his head.

Levin said, "I want to ask you something."

Paulie shrugged his crossed arms. "Ask," he said.

When Levin was away from his son, he could think about him more or less objectively. Never with liking but at least without anger. When he was in Paulie's presence, he was always controlling rage. It was boiling up in him now. He felt the blood rush to his head. He forced himself to walk slowly across the floor and sit in the desk chair near the bed.

"What's on?" he asked as conversationally as he could.

"Did you come up here to ask me what was on?"

Levin clenched his fist and swallowed. Maybe he should

do it; maybe the kid needed a good man-to-man beating. He noticed that his son's arms were muscled and the hair on his arms was thick and golden. He didn't shave yet, but fine, light hairs on his face were thickening, getting longer, and it wouldn't be long. It was a miserable time. If someone told Levin that he had to relive the years from thirteen to seventeen, he would cut his throat.

Remembering how miserable it had been sapped his anger, and his fists relaxed. Poor Paulie, he thought, poor miserable Paulie. He wished he could tell him that it would be all right. It would pass, he'd get grown, and someday . . . believe it or not . . . he'd be able to see the humor in these years, even if he would never, never remember them fondly.

The nightly news was on; the same thing that they were watching downstairs. Helicopters throbbed across the screen, then Walter Cronkite's kind, fatherly face appeared for some commentary, then back to the helicopters. Beneath them, to mark their progress, trees burned. Levin started to get engrossed, and he thought he might stay up here and he and his son could watch the news together, maybe even discuss the war. Paulie was bound to have some opinion of it. Everybody had an opinion on Vietnam. But Paulie wasn't going to let that happen.

"You said you wanted to ask me something."

"Yes. I thought we'd go up to the farm on Saturday. Look around. Maybe have a picnic. The weather's supposed to be nice . . . we'll have a good time."

He was waiting for his son to remind him that it was early June, the height of the black fly season, and a picnic in the country was the last thing Paulie would consider a good time. Levin braced himself, Paulie didn't say anything. Levin looked at him. He was still watching the screen (the commercial was on, a woman was being tried and found grindingly guilty for leaving a ring around her husband's collar). Paulie's high forehead was furrowed for a second, then his face relaxed.

"Saturday, huh?"

"Yeah."

"Okay."

Levin was shocked. "You *want* to go?"

"Sure."

"Hey, maybe we'll scare up the old baseball mitts and throw a few. Show the girls our stuff."

"Maybe," Paulie said noncommittally. He blinked, dismissing his father, and concentrated on the screen. They were showing game replays. The Mets looked as lousy as ever.

Levin went to the door and looked back. A sudden black premonition came out of nowhere, and all at once, for no reason he could imagine, he wanted to tell Paulie to forget the farm and the picnic. They'd stay home and toss a few around in the front yard. They'd pull out the barbecue, and Levin would let Paulie build the charcoal fire, and they'd have hot dogs or pizza or anything Paulie wanted. If he wanted, Levin would even take him into Millbridge to whatever horror show was on at the local theater. They'd do any and every one of Paulie's favorite things (or what used to be Paulie's favorite things), but they wouldn't go anywhere near that place in Newton. He paused at the door, waiting for the odd moment of darkness to pass, but it got worse.

He remembered Paulie at one. He had been a fat little kid with golden hair that was already thicker than most kids', and that fine, high forehead and the blue eyes. He remembered him rolling around, rubbery with all the baby fat, trying to sit up, crawl, walk. "Barb" had been his first word, and Jeannie and Levin had laughed like fools, making up stories about who Barb might be.

"Paulie," Levin said softly.

"Yeah." The boy didn't bother to look at him; he was long and lean, and his face was clean-lined, almost ascetic. But it was the same creature; that fat, adorable baby was in there somewhere.

Levin almost said, "I love you, Paulie," but just then, Paulie's eyes shifted, and he looked at his father. His eyes were cold.

"What?"

"Uh . . . we'll take some fried chicken, and maybe we can build a little fire and roast some weenies."

"Whatever you say," and Paulie's eyes went back to the screen and Levin left him alone.

Amy and Greta sat in the back, on the floor of the station wagon with the picnic basket. They'd all had a light breakfast because Jeannie got carsick and was convinced everybody else did, too, so by the time they turned onto 108, heading south toward Newton and Danbury, the smell of fried chicken and raw kosher hot dogs was driving Levin crazy with hunger.

Paulie half lay across the backseat looking out the window, but Levin thought that from the vantage point he'd chosen he couldn't see anything but sky and treetops. Still, even though Paulie steadfastly maintained his usual disinterest, he was with them. It was Saturday morning; the little girls and his son were together, they were going on a picnic, and anyone looking through the car windows would describe them as a happy family. And maybe they were.

Levin heard a heavy scraping in the back. "What's that?" he asked, looking in the rearview mirror.

Paulie didn't budge.

"The gas can's in our way," Greta said.

"There's plenty of room back there," Jeannie said. "You be careful with that can."

"But we can't stretch our legs out," Greta cried.

Amy said, "My knees're gonna freeze bent."

Levin and Jeannie grinned at each other. Levin called to the back, "Okay, slide it over against the backseat. Both of you do it, it's heavy." He wasn't sure how heavy. He hadn't filled it for a couple of months, but he thought it was almost full. He kept it in the back in case he passed a driver who'd run out of gas on one of the roads. It happened a lot. Not to him; he was a well organized man, he had never let himself run out of gas.

"And after that, pass me a drumstick."

"Joe, it's only ten-thirty," Jeannie cried.

Levin looked in the rearview mirror. Both girls' heads showed over the backseat; they were looking at Jeannie, waiting for instructions. He knew they would take their orders from Jeannie, not him.

He made a mock moan of agony. "I'm starving."

"You'll get sick," Jeannie said.

"I won't get sick."

"Then I will," Jeannie said.

He glanced at her. Just thinking about eating a fried chicken leg in the swaying car made her pale.

"Okay, I'll starve."

"I'm sorry," Jeannie said. But she didn't relent and he didn't blame her. They didn't want to start this gorgeous day by having to pull over so poor Jeannie could throw up at the side of the road. He tried to think about something besides food. In the back the girls started to sing; Greta couldn't keep a tune without Amy, but Amy, like a lot of people who had a bent for math, had good pitch and kept them both in tune. They were singing a popular song about holding hands. Their voices were high and light and filled the car with their sweet sound. He prayed to hear Paulie's voice join in, but it didn't. He looked back; Paulie's eyes were closed; his face was relaxed, young, handsome; and for a second Levin's heart lifted. They *were* a family, on their way to a picnic.

Half an hour later they crossed the brook.

"It starts here," he said.

He looked in the mirror. Amy was kneeling up at the back window, holding on to the sides of the car. Greta crawled over and looked over her shoulder. They were passing woods along the side of the road. Jeannie looked out of the window; even Paulie heaved himself upright to see.

They came to the dirt road. The pasture undulated upward from the road. The long grass was light green and gold in the sunlight.

Next to him he heard Jeannie catch her breath. He looked back at Amy again. She was frozen at the window.

The car heaved up the road (barely a road, more like a track) and pulled up next to the house. The house looked shabby and beautiful at the same time; the almost paintless shingles glowed in the sun, and the boards over the windows were hideous.

Greta was the first one out; she clambered out through the tailgate and made a comic little bow to Amy.

"Your palace!" she cried.

Amy played it to the hilt. She crawled out through the tailgate with as much dignity as possible, held the sides of her jeans out with both hands as if it were a skirt, and made a deep bow back to Greta.

"Thank you, Dorothy."

Dorothy?

Levin glanced at Greta; she blushed but looked delighted. Amy took Greta's hand, and together they faced the house.

"It's big," Greta said uncertainly.

"It's a mess," Amy said happily.

"Be careful of those stairs," Jeannie called. The girls crept up the steps, uttering fake little screams of fear. They looked ridiculous and wonderful. Jeannie stood next to the car and turned to face out across the fields. "Oh, Joe," she whispered, "it's magnificent."

"I know."

"Where does it end?" Paulie asked, leaning out of the car, looking back over the fields.

"You can't see the end," Levin said proudly. "And the agent told me that it's bordered on three sides by Audubon land. Forever wild."

"Nobody else's dogs," Jeannie said softly.

"Or kids, or swimming pools, or stereos," Levin said.

Paulie looked at them grimly. "You sound like it belongs to you. It belongs to her." He jerked his head toward Amy, and once again Levin was amazed at the power of his son's malevolence. He could have sworn that the sun dipped behind a cloud for a second. But the sky was perfectly cloudless; the moment of darkness was in Levin's mind. He said, as gently as he could, "Amy's part of the family, Paulie. Maybe she'll let us use it when we want to."

Paulie didn't answer. Jeannie looked from one to the other, as always stymied and frightened by the tension between her husband and their son.

Amy called from the porch, "The door's locked."

The tension broke, Levin reached into his pocket and held up the key.

"Let's pull off a couple of the boards first," he said, "so we'll have some light. The electricity's off."

"Okay," Amy yelled, "but I remember there's a gaslight inside."

The gaslight turned out to be an old kerosene lamp with a carved bronze base, a hand-blown chimney, and a hand-painted bowl. The kind of thing they charged two hundred dollars for at Esther's Antiques in Westerly center. It was a beautiful thing; Jeannie dusted it carefully with her handkerchief and ran her fingers over the carved metal figures, smoothed with age. Amy watched her in the light from one of the unboarded windows.

"You like it," she said.

"It's beautiful, Amy."

"It's yours."

"No, honey."

"Yes," Amy pleaded. "This house is mine, and everything in it, isn't it?"

Jeannie nodded.

"Then I can give this to you because you gave me—" She stopped. She had the feeling that there weren't enough hours or pieces of paper anywhere to list what Jeannie had given her "Please take it," she said softly. "Mrs. Collins'll go crazy when she sees it."

Jeannie laughed. "You notice a lot, don't you, honey?"

Amy said, "Please. I know where there's lots of nice things. Things for everybody. I want to . . ." She ran out of words or voice—she wasn't sure which—and she was quiet.

After a minute Jeannie said formally, "I'll take it for now. But someday you'll get married and have your own home. You'll take it back then, okay?"

"Yes . . ." Jeannie was saying a lot with this speech; she was telling Amy that they would still know each other when Amy was old enough to get married. It was a marvelous thought, but Amy wasn't so sure. "You'll take it for now, anyway," Amy said. "It'll look nice on the big round table in the living room."

From another room of the house Greta yelled, "Amy, come look at this!"

They explored the house. The kitchen was 1930s modern, except for the refrigerator, which was a Sears Coldspot, vintage 1960. There was no dishwasher; the deep double sink was unchipped. There were only two bathrooms, not enough by 1973 standards for a house this size (they counted ten rooms), and the fixtures in them were old, but outwardly in good repair. They couldn't tell how the toilets worked because the pump ran on electricity. Three of the bedrooms were small, two were very large with bow windows and window seats with drawers built into them.

But the downstairs was really the best part. Amy had never thought the house was big, but now, after Joe and Jeannie's house, Nana's downstairs looked enormous. The ceilings were high; the beams showed in the kitchen. The living room had many paned windows and a tile fireplace. Amy realized that the room was almost twice as long as the living room in Windy Ridge. There were French doors at one end, and Amy thought they'd let in a lot of light when the boards were gone. As it was, the big room was dim and green, as if it were underwater. Some of Nana's furniture was left, but most of it had been sold a long time ago. Amy thought she remembered the high-backed chair and the metal fireback. The delicate desk-table looked familiar; so did the footstool. But everything else was strange. She had been in this room a hundred times since she was a baby, and she was disgusted with herself for not remembering more. It was full of treasures, anyway, and she gave Jeannie a tarnished mirror in a gilt frame and set the footstool aside for Joe.

Wood splintered outside, and Joe pried a board off the French doors. Sunlight shone through the aperture; dust sparkled in the air. The room looked more real, infinitely shabbier.

"Joe," Jeannie said, "come in here, look at this."

He pried another board loose, Jeannie pulled one door open, and Joe stepped through into the living room. He looked around in amazement.

"Joe, this wasn't a *farm*house," Jeannie said.

"Yes, it was," Amy said. "My Grandpa farmed until he died. He grew vegetables and cows; he cut wood out back and sold it. Nana told me."

"I mean, it's an estate house, Amy."

Amy looked at Greta, and Greta explained, "People don't have estates much anymore. They have to be very rich."

"But my folks were very poor," Amy said.

"Not always, honey," said Jeannie. "Not always. Oh, Joe, look at the floor!"

Amy and Greta looked down too. It was just a dusty wooden floor with big planks it it. Amy didn't think it was nearly as nice as the neat, narrow-slatted floor in the house in Windy Ridge.

"And the fireplace," Jeannie said. Joe went over to it and looked up the chimney.

"Did you see the fireback?" he asked.

Jeannie nodded.

"That's been there all the time," Amy said importantly. "I remember it."

She insisted that Joe take the footstool and kept looking for the right present for Greta. They found it upstairs in what had been her grandmother's room. It was an old porcelain doll with silky hair and a lace gown. The lace was yellow but not torn. She blew dust off the lovely china face and turned to Greta. "This is yours, Dorothy," she said softly. She thought it was the nicest thing in the house. Greta took it slowly.

"Nice . . ." she said, trying to sound casual, but her cheeks got red.

"We can wash the lace by hand, I bet," Amy said. "It'll probably come out good as new."

"Do you think it's from the 1700s?" Greta asked.

"I wouldn't be surprised." Amy said firmly.

She realized that there was nothing for Paulie. He wouldn't want anything from her house, anyway. She looked out of the bedroom window and saw him walking across the pasture toward the brook and trees.

He was in agony. It was almost physical. His breath hitched in his chest; he was afraid that he would cry. He got to the brook and looked back. He couldn't see the house.

He turned away and looked into the brook. The water rushed past his feet, grass overhung the bank, ferns grew alongside. He saw flashes of little fish, and tears actually filled his eyes. She owned the water, the rocks, the grass and fish. In one swoop she'd sailed up over his head and out of his power to hurt her. He couldn't drain the brook; he couldn't kill all those fish or destroy the rock, the grass, the trees. She had everything. The house, the land, his father. She'd never leave now . . . unless she knew.

"Knew what?" he asked out loud, not sure what he was thinking.

Knew that he hated her so much that they couldn't live in the same house? But she already knew that and she'd stayed, anyway. Now she had this place, and his mother and father loved it already. They might give her up but never this. He almost didn't blame them. He knew his father would brag to Lester Baker; his mother would lord the hundred-and-sixty-acre-plus farmhouse over Mrs. Collins. Except that his mother said it wasn't a farmhouse but an estate . . . what bullshit. He giggled to himself. Who ever heard of a bohunk estate? Still, it would give his mother ammunition in her war with Mrs. Collins that Paulie knew instinctively the women were engaged in, although they would never admit it. His father was fighting the same kind of war with Lester Baker

and probably with that Larry Seymour. Everybody against
everybody . . . like him against Amy. But *they* lied to themselves and he didn't. The question was what to do now.

He had heard all the moaning and carrying on about
pieces of silver and some rags of napkins and tablecloths and
oh, shit, didn't they just cream themselves over a kerosene
lamp. How he hated them; how he hated that rat-eyed little
bitch. He almost couldn't bear it, except that it felt good in a
way. It was exciting.

The question still was: What to do now?

He had watched her through the break in the window
boards, opening drawers, touching things. She showed Greta
a dusty, ragged pincushion that had been her great-grandmother's. She bragged about some books that her great-
grandfather had collected (miserable-looking things covered
with dust).

His face was on fire; he scooped water up in his hands
and splashed it on his face and drank from the stream; his
belly was empty, his mouth tasted sour. They couldn't eat
until they'd seen and exclaimed over everything, then they'd
bring their fried chicken and hot dogs down here; they'd
build a fire and leave everything in the house unguarded.

"So what?" he asked out loud, dangling his fingers in the
water.

He couldn't steal a whole houseful of that crap and spirit
it away or hide it in the woods. So he was back to his same
question: What to do now?

Out of nowhere came a vision of the gas can in his father's car. With it he saw boards on the windows that were
so dry, they splintered as his father pried them off. He saw
the old wooden porch around the back of the house, the leaning stairs, the wood-shake roof, the bare, wood-shake siding.
When his father went through the French doors into the
house, Paulie had gotten a glimpse of old, dusty curtains.

He had taken the teddy bear and the *Chips* book down
to the dump on burning day and stayed to watch the fire lit.
A stupid-looking man with small eyes, a pitted face, and a

hairline that almost started at his eyebrows had asked Paulie
why he was throwing his toys away. Inspired, Paulie had
answered, "Because they're kid stuff." The man had smiled
indulgently and let him stay while the incinerator was lit. He
didn't actually see the book and toy burn, but he saw the
smoke come up out the incinerator chimney and almost ob-
scure the trees on the far side of the dump. He watched the
sea gulls, who came this far inland for their share of garbage,
scream and wheel away from the smoke. The man stood next
to him as the fire raged in the cement-block building. The
fire reached a peak, Paulie heard it roar, and the ash from the
smoke fell on his shoulders. He had thanked the man, gotten
on his bike, and ridden away.

He felt let down; he thought burning her stuff would be
more fun. He had one bad second as he rode into the Grand
Union parking lot to meet Timmy and Len, when he saw the
teddy bear's black eyes on the road in front of him. They
were bright black, in spite of the fire and soot. He could
almost see them now: he shivered, and in his mind he heard
his own voice, faint but definite, saying, *Let it go, Paul. She
ain't so bad. Let it go . . .*

The fish—her fish—skimmed under the ripples of the
brook. His father called it a brook, but it was a proper stream.
Somewhere east of here, it emptied into the Housatonic or
even the Connecticut.

The voice in his mind got stronger. . . .

Let it go.

What would happen if he let it go? They'd bring home
all that old-lady crap, and every couple of weeks they'd come
back here, have picnics, and start to fix up the house. Everybody around here fixed up houses. It was all they seemed to
care about. They'd fix up the house, come here every chance
they got. He could come, too, if he wanted . . .

What's so terrible about that? the voice asked.

He didn't have an answer, but it *was* terrible. It was
unbearable. His father was proud of the place. You'd think
he built it for her himself. If something happened to that

house, then the land would just be land . . . like the empty fields of the Morris farm behind Windy Ridge. A great big piece of nothing—zilch and *nada*—and that would take care of his father and maybe her too.

The voice came again. *She's here to stay, fucko, no matter what you do to that house.*

Okay, he accepted it. But she didn't have to have every single fucking thing worth having on this earth: his father's love, that house, silver and linens, and fine old furniture. She didn't have to have it all.

He came out of the trees and looked up at the house. It was beautiful, and for a second he almost felt sorry for it. If it has been his, he would cherish it forever. He'd repaint the outside, redo the floors, buy carpet and curtains . . . do all that stupid cuntish stuff that they did in these parts. If it were his, he would love it, but it wasn't.

The basement was the only spooky part of the house, the walls were stone, Joe examined them. "Looks to be a yard thick," he said proudly. But Amy thought the basement was ghastly. Greta must have agreed because she clutched the doll protectively against her chest and drew closer to Amy. There were no windows. The floor was dirt; tramped down for so many years by so many feet, it felt as hard as the cement in the basement of the Windy Ridge house.

"What's this?" Jeannie asked. She was looking at the ugly old washer; it was yellow enamel with a roller-wringer stuck up on the top. Nana always complained that it never worked right.

"The washing machine," Amy said.

"Heavens." Jeannie examined it. "It looks antediluvian."

Amy had no idea what the word meant, but it sounded right and she nodded. "Grandma hated it."

"I don't blame her," Jeannie said.

"What's in here?" Joe called. He was at the other end of the basement; in the darkest part. He opened a creaking wooden door. The light from upstairs couldn't penetrate, and the recess behind the door was black. Greta grabbed Amy's hand. "There could be *anything* in there," she whispered.

"Bats, spiders, snakes . . ." Amy whispered back.

Greta gave an excited giggle and squeezed Amy's hand hard. Suddenly Amy remembered the creaking door opening a long time ago. It wasn't creepy then; Nana was with her wearing a yellow apron with blue flowers on it. Nana turned on the light bulb that hung from the ceiling, and Amy remembered bright colors and shining glass, like the bottles that the Avon lady had brought to the house in Bridgeton.

She let go of Greta's hand, went to the door, and peered into the blackness.

"Joe, you got the flashlight?"

"Sure, Sweet Pea." He clicked it on and turned it into the recess. Glass jars shone; colors exploded through the glass.

"Oh, God," Jeannie said, "more wonders."

Jars of tomatoes, green beans, squash, and brilliantly colored combinations of peaches, apples, pears, and cherries shone in the thin beam of light. Amy remembered her grandmother in a whole series of flowered aprons, stirring the big black pot that must still be upstairs somewhere, filling the jars, then boiling them until they were sealed. The autumn before last she'd let Amy help her peel and dice fruit and vegetables; Amy stirred the brine for pickles while her mother sat at the kitchen table, smoking and watching. Poor Mama, Amy thought before she could stop herself, she never helped much. She tried, but she'd cut her finger on the knife or drop a jar or touch the lid wrong, so it had to be sterilized all over again. Amy wasn't as clumsy as her mother, and the last autumn before Nana died, they had done ripe and green tomatoes and Amy got to peel the tomatoes. It was not even two years ago, but it seemed like it had happened to someone else and longer ago than she could imagine. It might as well have happened in the year her ancestor bought this place: 1762.

"I helped can some of it," Amy said.

"Is it still good?" Joe asked.

Jeannie stepped into the cupboard and took down a jar. Amy recognized brandied peaches made from Nana's secret recipe that won a prize at a fair a million, million years ago. Jeannie pressed the tin top.

"Perfect," she said. She tested a few more. "Perfect."

It was hot in the sun. They unloaded the back of the car and carried the food and the portable grill down to the brook in the shade of the trees. Paulie was down there waiting for them. He helped his father set up the grill and spread the charcoal in it. They had the good, fat kind of hot dogs, not like the pale, skinny things Amy's mother used to cook. Jeannie had brought baked beans, potato salad, fried chicken, and a dozen brownies. They ate the chicken while the hot dogs were cooking. They had a couple of plastic bottles of bug-off in case the flies attacked, but the day was enchanted and the flies left them alone. Finally the hot dogs were ready; Amy smeared two with mustard and piccalilli. Joe ate his with sauerkraut on it, and she decided that she'd try the third one that way. She noticed that Paulie wasn't around. She wondered where he was, then decided he'd probably gone into the woods to go to the bathroom.

She ate until her belly stuck out and her jeans almost fit again. She and Greta helped Jeannie pack up what they didn't eat and put it in the hamper. They spilled water on the fire, dumped the wet coals under the trees, and rinsed out the grill. Paulie still didn't come back. No one said anything.

Joe lay down under an old maple. He said that by angling himself right he could see the hills on the other side of the highway. He rolled his jacket up under his head and fell asleep. Jeannie sat in the folding lawn chair that they'd brought, turned her face to the patch of sun coming through the trees, and closed her eyes. Greta and Amy took off their shoes and socks, stood in the stream, and tried to catch the minnows with their hands.

"I smell something burning," Amy said.

Greta sniffed. "Must be some of the charcoal." They picked through the sodden remains, but they were cold. The smell got worse, and Amy left the shade of the trees and looked up at the house. She didn't see anything, but the smell was stronger than ever.

"I'm going up to see."

"Put your shoes on," Greta cried. "The grass'll cut."

For once Amy didn't listen to her. She started up the gradual slope of the pasture toward the house. "Wait," Greta called. Amy glanced back; Greta was sitting on the ground struggling with her socks and shoes. Amy looked toward the house and saw a thin trail of black smoke seep up over the roof and dirty sky. She ran.

The stubble in the grass stabbed her feet, and she was sorry she hadn't stopped for her shoes. Then the smoke thickened and she forget everything and ran like she had the day, summers ago, when she beat ol' Toni Russo. Trees flashed by; grass slashed at her ankles. She was going as fast as the water in the brook; the sky sailed over her head. She passed a thicket; an animal jumped and scooted through the grass ahead of her. She thought she'd been running for hours and covered miles, but the house looked as far away as ever, except that the smell of burning was much stronger. She heard glass break; a dagger of flame stabbed out through a space in the window boards. Smoke leaked out everywhere, her eyes teared, she heard wood crackle, and smelled tar and gasoline.

Gasoline! And Paulie had been gone for an hour or more. She tore through the pasture; splinters of dried scrub stuck in her feet, she kept going. She got to the car and fell against it, gasping for breath. She looked inside. The gas can was not there.

Inside the house, something gave a crack, muffled by the walls, and fell. She ran around the side. The poor, old porch leaned crazily; the window that Joe had unboarded was broken; flames ate at the wooden frame. She felt heat and saw it radiating in waves off the roof, seeping out the sides of the house.

She raced around the porch to the back steps and stopped.

Paulie was on the porch. The kitchen door was open; he was backlit by fire. The floor was burning. Everything was still there but covered in flames; Nana's pine table was charring, the old cabinets that Nana oiled every spring blistered and snapped. Another window broke, and she knew from the sound that it was in the living room. So the curtains were gone, the chair, the lamp that Jeannie liked. Everything . . .

She looked up at Paulie. He was watching her, his face quiet. He didn't look arrogant or happy or anything.

"It's too late," he said almost gently. "You'll burn to death if you go in there."

"Nooo," she screamed.

Burning chunks of kitchen ceiling fell behind him, the jars in the basement started exploding like firecrackers, and birds screamed up out of the trees and flapped away. A foul, black billow of smoke from burning linoleum blew out the sizzling doorway, and Amy thought of all the other things in there she hadn't remembered until now; the spoon rest shaped like a tulip that had sat next to the stove all her life. And the ivory lace curtain in her Nana's bedroom, and Nana's aprons, some calico, some gingham, washed, ironed, folded away in a kitchen drawer, waiting. There were albums of photographs in the living-room secretary, with snaps of her Nana as a young girl, and her mother's baby pictures, and pictures of her mother holding Amy when she was a baby. They must be ash by now.

Rage knotted her stomach. She opened her mouth to howl, as she had when her father found the hammer the night her mother died. But nothing came out. Words came to her instead. . . .

If I'd burn to death in there, Paulie Levin, so would you.
Out loud she said, "Go back, Paulie."

The cool wind had come without her noticing. Paulie shivered in spite of the heat blasting from the fire.

"Go back," she whispered.

* * *

Jonathan reached out for the cup and saucer. His hand shook, and old Mrs. Cole's hand shook too. She was eighty in the shade, and her poor old crooked fingers practically bent back on themselves from the arthritis. The cup and saucer slipped out of their trembling grasp and crashed to the floor.

"Oh, dear," said Mrs. Cole.

"Oh, dear," Jonathan echoed, staring stupidly at the broken china. He slid out of the chair to his knees and started picking up the pieces. A splintered edge knicked his thumb and blood welled up in a bubble. Fantastically red, the meniscus bulged, and he waited for it to break.

Suddenly, he smelled smoke.

Out of the corner of his eye he saw white trousers; Marty had come over to help. The smoke smell intensified, got worse, and Jonathan's eyes teared. He heard the crackle of flames and felt Amy try to howl with rage and pain. The muscles in her neck strained, but no sound came out. He'd howl for her—it was the least he could do—and he opened his mouth and let it rip. Marty grabbed him and hauled him to his feet. Next Ol' Mart would try to get him out of there, but Jonathan felt mad strength pour through him. He heard Amy whisper *go back, Paulie* and he broke free and ran . . .

Paulie grabbed hold of the porch railing to stop himself, but his fingers slipped on the old wood, splinters dug under his nails, and he let go of the railing. There was nothing left to hold on to. A few more steps and he was in the burning kitchen. In a second the fire would eat off his clothes and hair and split open his skin like a ham rind. Water would run out of his flesh and he would twist, curl, char. His eyes would turn black, his tongue would broil. . . .

It was awful, but Amy couldn't stop. The satisfaction was so intense it almost hurt. This was what revenge was like . . . this was why people spent so much time and trouble getting their own back. . . .

The dark part of her had come out; the part her grandma called the devil. He was even in her grandma. The old lady would catch woodchucks in a cage trap for eating up her garden, then drown them in the stream. They would run around the bottom of the cage squealing in terror as the water rose over their paws and wet the fur on their underbellies. . . .

"Paulieee!" Jeannie's voice rang across the pasture. "Pauliee!" she screamed.

Amy whirled around. Jeannie was running through the grass. She stumbled on a hillock, righted herself, kept coming. Jeannie was his mother. Amy's mother would have gone into a burning house after *her;* Jeannie'd go in there after Paulie. She would choke in the smoke searching for her son; flames that consumed Paulie would burn off Jeannie's clothes and hair. The roof might cave in; burning beams could fall on her. The cool wind stopped as suddenly as it had started. Heat and smoke blasted Amy, and she whirled back and faced the burning house. She couldn't see Paulie through the wall of smoke and thought the fire had gotten him already and it was too late to get him back. Joe still must be sleeping in the chair by the stream. She'd have to stop Jeannie herself; Greta'd help her if she got there in time; she was only a few feet behind Jeannie, her plump legs pumping through the grass. Then Amy saw a dark shape in the doorway, and Paulie burst through the smoke and ran across the porch. He stumbled down the slanting steps, threw himself in the grass, and rolled back and forth beating at himself. Jeannie reached him, fell down next to him, and helped him roll, slapping at his shirt and trousers. His hair was singed; his shirt was covered with black burn holes.

Jeannie screamed at him, "What were you doing in there? What were you doing!"

Greta flopped down next to them. "Trying to put out the fire," she cried.

Amy turned away from them and looked out over the pasture. Joe was finally coming, puffing up from the stream as fast as he could. She turned away from him, too, and looked up at what was left of the house. The roof gave a *whumpf* and sagged, exposing the chimney. Its stones were turning black; it stuck up awkwardly from the ruined roof. She started crying hopelessly.

Paulie had won. He'd burned down Nana's house, the gas can had probably burned up with everything else, and no one would ever know what he'd done. She couldn't snitch on him. If she did, they would wonder why she had not called for help but stood calmly in the grass waiting for him to burn to death. Telling would be like opening a swollen can, something Nana said never, never to do.

Coughs racked Paulie's body.

If only Jeannie hadn't yelled . . . *Next time, Paulie,* Amy thought, wiping tears and soot off her face. *Next time.*

ELEVEN

THE DOOR OPENED and a woman in a maid's uniform glared at Marty Vespa's pale face, then at his rumpled raincoat. It was warm, supposed to go into the nineties tomorrow. No one wore a raincoat on a night like this, but Marty's whites were covered with Jonathan's blood and he had to keep the coat on.

"I gotta see Dr. Hall," Marty said.

"The Halls have guests. They're just sitting down to dinner."

"Please. I'm from the hospital. There's been trouble. Just tell him it's about Jonathan. He'll want to know. I swear."

She hesitated, then held the door open and let him into the hall. She didn't offer to take the coat, thank God, but disappeared down the hall. Marty waited. The hall was huge, almost bigger than his whole house. Grand stairs curved up one side; real paintings lined the walls.

Jeffrey Hall, looking very pretty in a tux, came through a set of double doors and along the hall.

"What happened?" Hall asked.

"Jon tried to bash his head in. Almost did it too. We called Severn and he came and cleaned him up. He said he's

236

okay, he didn't lose consciousness, but he's crying for you . . ."

Hall took Marty's arm. "Let me get you a drink."

Hall led him into a wonderful room with a fireplace and leather furniture. Real leather, Marty bet, not like the Naugahyde in his aunt's house that made his ass sweat summer and winter. He sank down on one of the couches flanking the fireplace. Sweat ran down his face and neck; his shirt was soaked.

"I got Jon's blood on me, Doc. But I gotta take this coat off."

"Sure."

Marty shrugged out of it, Hall caught his breath, and Marty looked down at himself. He was covered with blood.

"It looks bad," Marty said, "but it was mostly scraped skin. 'S okay."

Hall brought over a snifter half full of brandy. Marty took a slug, leaned back, and said, "Today was tea day . . ."

"Oh, shit."

"Yeah. And they were all there . . . "

Once a month, seven or eight of the oldest, richest women of Sharon, Connecticut, threw a tea party for Limekiln inmates. They pulled up in their limos, and chauffeurs brought in platters of cakes, cookies, and finger sandwiches with the crusts cut off. Then came a silver tea service that Marty thought was probably worth enough to refurnish the whole building. Tables were set up; the old ladies sat behind them to dispense the goodies. Boiling water went into the big carved silver pot; the tea steeped and its rich smell filled the lounge. Everything was ready and the patients poured in. The teas were always calm; the old ladies were so polite, so soft-spoken, it was hard not to respond in kind, Marty thought. Jonathan was their favorite, probably because he was so handsome but also because he asked the old ladies questions and listened to the answers, and Marty had the feeling that no one listened to these old broads much anymore. Their kids came up from Stamford or Greenwich or

New York, or down from Pittsfield, Springfield, or Boston to make sure they weren't cut out of wills, not to listen.

But Jonathan listened. And they told him about their gardens, their servants, and family troubles and about the parties they gave and went to. Jonathan loved the party talk; they'd tell him about young women at the parties, his eyes would glow, and Marty knew his dear, nuts patient-friend was imagining himself with his hand—or even his head— up the skirt of one of Mrs. Cole's or Mrs. Dever's guests. If the old ladies got a whiff of the sexuality, they didn't mind. Today Mrs. Cole told Jonathan about her grand-daughter's wedding, which was planned for outside, and had everyone on tenterhooks in case it rained. But it didn't— the party went off without a hitch. Mrs. Cole's great-niece was there; she had long blond hair and wore a gray silk frock that barely covered her thighs. Jonathan smiled beatif-ically and reached for the cup and saucer Mrs. Cole held out.

"I don't know what happened," Marty told Hall. "I heard china break, saw the cup on the floor, and came over to help. Jon was bending over it, picking up the pieces. Then he cut himself. It was one of those little slices that bleed a bucket, and he stared at the blood running down the side of his hand, dripping on the floor, and I knew from the look in his eyes we were in for trouble. Then he threw back his head and howled."

"He what?"

"Howled. Like a dog at its master's grave."

Marty shivered. "I never heard a human being make a sound like that, Doc. Even at Limekiln. It froze me . . . froze us all. Nothing in that lounge moved, except for the flowers and ribbons on the old ladies' hats trembling. The rest of the nuts sat there with their teacups and saucers and plates of cakes and sandwiches, grinning because they knew there was going to be a scene. Crazy people aren't any nicer than sane people, are they?"

"No."

"Then Jonathan stopped howling and looked straight ahead at nothing. Except he was seeing something, okay? You know that look he gets . . . "

"Yes."

"Then he jumped up and I grabbed him. But I couldn't hold him, Doc. He had that crazy strength, you know?"

Hall nodded.

"He pulled free, as if I were a ten-year-old who'd been sick. He stood still for a second. Then he ran full-speed for the fireplace and crashed into it headfirst. It's stone, the stone's jagged . . . Christ, what a sound it made. Like gravel crunching. He reeled back; blood ran down his face. I thought he'd fall. His eyes rolled, then he smashed his head into the stone again. One of the old ladies screamed and fainted across the table, her little straw hat fell off. And then I got to him. By then he was dazed and not so strong anymore. He tried to smash his head against the stone again, but I held him. Then he fell to his knees and I knelt with him. He went limp and I cradled his head against my chest and got blood all over me.

"Silverstein finally got there, and we got him upstairs, into the bath. Then Severn came and cleaned him up. He kept crying for you. I tried to ignore him, Doc, but he had that look. And then I remembered Ida Barnes. Me 'n' the guys who were there then never talk about it. But we all knew what happened. Shit, I helped strap him down that day; Silverstein pulled his hand back out of the broken window before he cut an artery. We know but never talk. What's to say?"

"Nothing."

"But you gotta listen to him when he looks like that, don't you?"

Jonathan heard her say *Next time, next time,* and he woke up with a jerk. Down the hall crazy Mac Trapper was calling, "They're crawlin' on me, they're crawlin' on me." He didn't sound panicked, not even especially upset. More

like a sportscaster calling a game . . . they're crawlin' on me
. . . *the Lakers have the ball.* Mac did it every night; same
words, same tone. Jonathan was used to it; that wouldn't
wake him up. Only Amy could do that with her *Next time,
next time.* The boy was alive, Amy was okay, everything
should be fine, except for that infernal next-time business.
She was rocking back and forth on something, probably her
little bed, whispering the words over and over to herself. She
didn't know what she meant exactly. Neither did Jonathan
. . . but the words frightened him, and he forgot the restraints
and tried to sit up. Nylon mesh yanked him back, and he
collapsed on the bed on his back. At the same time an itch
like red ants crawling started in his crotch.

"They're crawlin' on me," called Mac Trapper.

Mac never said what was crawling on him.

Maybe it was ants; like the creatures crawling over Jonathan's balls, creeping into his perineum. He tried to imagine he was outside under the big old beech tree . . . his
favorite tree on earth . . . in the cool moonlight, scratching
himself with ragged fingernails. It didn't work.

Next time, Amy chanted softly to herself.

The itch got worse. Marty'd put the call button right next
to his hand but if he rang, Miss Crain would come. She'd
never undo the straps, he'd never ask her to scratch his
crotch. That was the game: itch (ants) ten, Jonathan nothing.

He closed his eyes and tried to float. Impossible. Just to
make things worse, along with the itch and Amy whispering
those terrifying words over and over, the scrapes on his forehead started burning. He was so miserable, it was almost
funny. He'd hack it another minute, then he'd ring for Crain
and scream until she undid the straps or called Silverstein.
He'd let Silverstein scratch his crotch. It'd be embarrassing
but better than this. He inched his hand over to the bell.

Next time . . . Amy made a prayer of the words.

He touched the bell, put his thumb on the button, and
just then the door opened and Marty and Jeffrey Hall came
in. Marty wore a rumpled raincoat over his whites; Dr. Hall
had on a tux. Jonathan thought he looked terrific.

He forgot the straps again and tried to sit up. They yanked, and he crashed backward in a burst of creaking bedsprings.

"Take 'em off," he cried. "Oh, Marty, please. My balls're on fire."

Hall nodded, Marty came over and undid the straps, and Jonathan scratched right in front of them. He was usually a modest man, but he couldn't help himself. The relief was incredible. He grinned up at Marty stupidly.

"Better, Sport?" Marty asked gently.

"Oh, God."

Marty shook his head at Jonathan, but his expression was tender.

"Take it easy," he said, and went out, leaving Hall and Jonathan alone together. Hall came over to the bed, helped Jonathan sit up, and pushed pillows up behind him. Then he pulled over one of the million or so molded plastic chairs in the place and sat down. He looked at Jonathan's forehead for a moment. "It'll look like shit for a week or so, but I don't think it'll scar," he said.

Jonathan nodded.

"Okay," Hall said, "why'd you do it?"

Jonathan's mind raced. He was mad, not stupid; he could think fast when he had to. *Next time* was coming because Paulie Levin was the shit of all time, and Jonathan was the only one who could stop it. Except he couldn't. He was a helpless maniac, but Jeffrey Hall had money, credentials, freedom. He could call Joseph Levin and say, "Your son is in danger, Amy must leave your house." Of course, it couldn't be put that baldly, but Hall'd think of the right words. And Hall would do it all if—big *if*—he believed in the danger. So Jonathan had to convince him. It sounded impossible, but Jonathan had a track record. There was Ida Barnes, the dead woman on the kitchen floor, and Amy saved from the closet. Hall might listen if Jonathan could find a way to say it.

It was getting late. Hall must be getting impatient, but he didn't show it. He asked softly, "Why'd you try to brain yourself, Jon?"

"I didn't try to brain myself. I tried to knock myself out so I wouldn't see a boy burn to death."

"What boy?" Hall asked calmly. But he wasn't calm; he was shocked and starting to get scared. Join the club, Jonathan thought. Aloud he said, "I don't want to start with that. I don't know where to start."

"How about the beginning?"

Simple, except that was the closet and the cold whatsis that came to life and gathered strength during those three days in there with Amy. It was way too vague and horror-story-sounding, and he searched for some better beginning. Life was a mess; events had no logic. Then he thought of the cup of custard. Nothing could be more banal, mundane, more intrinsically believable than a cup of hospital custard.

Hall went right to his office, unlocked and opened the door. The janitor had drawn the blinds, the anteroom was pitch black, and he heard something scrabble off to his right. His heart thudded. He felt like he was eight again, waking up from a nightmare in a sweat and lying with his eyes wide and staring in the dark, because he knew that *it* was still in the room with him and would see him if he moved or closed his eyes.

Hall inched his hand up the wall in a thrall of childish fear and flicked the light switch. The room was empty, ugly, normal. Rats from the century-old stone basement had not come up to chew on patient folders; no patient who had made the transition from harmless to murderous was waiting behind the desk with a knife.

Hall cursed Jonathan and went through the anteroom to his office. The blinds were up in here, the room was full of moonlight. He went to the desk and sat down. He didn't know what to do. He wanted to go home and forget the whole thing, but the little girl in the closet was alive because he had the guts to believe Jonathan Kaslov, and Ida Barnes was dead because he didn't. If he let this go, the day would come when he'd pick up the paper and read that Paul Levin, son of Captain Joseph Levin, had burned to death or drowned or fallen in front of a truck. But he couldn't go to Joseph Levin with nothing but the mad fairy tale he'd just heard. Levin would kick the shit out of him, and Hall wouldn't blame him.

He sat back and looked up at the ceiling; moonlight reflected greenly on the dirty ivory paint. He knew Jonathan was not lying, but that didn't make any of it true. Hall didn't even know for sure that there'd been a fire; he could find out that much.

He thought for a moment, then called the *News-Times* in Danbury. It was a fairly respectable paper, they must have a night desk. As the phone rang thirty miles south he thought of the little town-city rotting in the hills. The wire mills and hat factories were gone; the conglomerates talked about opening headquarters down there, but it hadn't happened yet and there was nothing left of Danbury's nineteenth-century prosperity except the fair. He'd gone when he was a kid; it had been one of the sweetest memories of his youth. There were farms and farmers around Danbury back then. The men wore suit coats and overalls and had creased faces and bright blue eyes. The women were plump and wore flowered dresses, and he remembered them having a kind of smooth, glowing skin you didn't see anymore. The midway had been clean; the air smelled of fresh straw, cinnamon, cowshit. The rides had been dinky, but not the food, and he'd spend the day eating homemade sausage, blue-ribbon apple pie, sweet and dill pickles, homemade candy, and fried chicken and had never gotten sick.

He went back with his daughter Marcy a couple of years ago to show her the great Danbury fair. The hills were the same; still green that time of year with a few patches of early turned birches shining in the sun; everything else had changed. The midway was dirty; the stall floors were covered with sticky Astroturf. Down-at-the-heels carny pitchmen ran crooked games, sold blenders and T-shirts with dirty sayings on them, and the air smelled of moldy straw and overcooked sugar. The farmers and their wives, the prize pig, and five-hundred-pound pumpkin were gone. He'd wanted to weep, but Marcy didn't know any different and she had a good time. She even bought a T-shirt with Fuck Communism printed on the front over a clenched fist.

A pleasant-sounding woman picked up the phone at the Danbury paper and said she'd check their reports to see if there'd been a farmhouse fire this afternoon. Hall waited, praying that Jonathan had just had an hallucination. Hall knew how to deal with hallucinations.

She came back on a few minutes later. "There was a fire in Newton this afternoon," she said. "An old farmhouse burned to the ground. Part of it had been built in the eighteenth century and it was sort of a local landmark. Pity."

"Pity," Hall echoed.

Jonathan told himself he'd done all he could. Hall would find some way to get her out of there. She'd go to an institution. It'd be awful for her, but she'd survive and that was all that mattered. She was a beautiful kid. She'd be a pretty woman. Even if she just wound up as a diner waitress or factory worker, men would notice that lovely face and she'd get married, have a couple of kids. His father and mother . . . Michael and even Jonathan himself . . . would stay alive through her. All he had to do now was relax, forget, go back to his regular life of walks, TV, Perkins's books, playing gin . . . and watching the clock for dinnertime to come around.

But Hall couldn't just walk into the Levin house and drag Amy out. He needed background, evidence, information to convince Levin. That would take time, and there was not much left. This second Paul Levin must be trying to figure out what else to do to her. *Next time* was in the works, and Jonathan had to warn Amy to lie low no matter what that monstrous kid did.

But Jonathan couldn't see her and he was afraid to call. Even if they let her talk to him, he might hear her voice, lose it, and not get out a coherent sentence. He had not talked to anyone but Michael on the phone for ten years now.

He *could* write her a letter.

It was such an exciting thought, he sat bolt upright in bed. It was very late, the moon had set behind the trees, the room was dark. He was still in the solitary they'd put him in and didn't have to worry about waking Ferris. Amy was sleeping; he'd stopped getting those words from her, but he still felt her grief and loneliness.

"Poor baby," he whispered to himself. "Poor nipper."

He'd try to write his warning obliquely so she alone would understand. There was still some of the old hotel stationery around with a blue letterhead on thick cream-colored paper. Miss Crain kept it in her desk and probably would not let him have any of it. But Marty could get him some tomorrow.

Suddenly he couldn't wait until tomorrow; writing to Amy would be almost as good as seeing her. He could imagine her sitting next to him as he wrote, listening gravely to his warning and all the things he'd wanted to tell her that day in front of the Levin house.

He got up and went down the hall to the nurse's desk. The floor was quiet, and Miss Crain was reading the Sunday funnies. He was startled; he thought she'd only read editorials, bitchy columns, and want ads to make sure she was making as much as all the other nuthouse nurses. But here she was with funnies spread out over her desk and a nice look on her face. He knocked on the doorjamb; she looked up and her expression soured.

"Yes, Jonathan?"

"Do you read *Pogo*?" he asked.

"What do you want, Kaslov?"

"How about *BC*, with the clams and the Midnight Skulker—"

"Kaslov!"

He didn't mean to tweak her. Softly he said, "I really love *BC*." She smiled at him. It was just a tiny twitch of her mouth, but it was a smile. He smiled back. "Could I have some of the Limekiln stationery, Miss Crain? I want to write a letter to my niece."

"I didn't know you had a niece."

"Yes. She's an orphan now, living in a foster home. I'm her only living relative, and I thought she'd like to get a letter from me." Only a beast could resist that story, and Miss Crain might be a grim soul most of the time, but she was no beast (not like Paulie Levin). She pushed the paper forward, opened her drawer, and pulled out a few sheets of the precious stationery.

"Do you have a pen?" she asked.

"No."

"Here." She handed him one of the clear plastic ones that showed the ink level. He thanked her and went to the door. She said, "'I like *BC* too."

"Gonna take a sentimental journey," the voice on the radio sang. Hall sang softly with it: " 'Gonna set my heart at ease.' "

He took another gulp of bourbon. He was on his fourth, the house was silent, the guests had gone, Babs was in bed.

" 'Gonna take a sentimental journey,' " he sang. He had a pleasant voice—especially when he was drunk, he thought. He should have been a crooner. But then he'd be out of a job. It was the age of the screamer, the Age of Aquarius, whatever that meant.

"Pops?" Marcy called from the study doorway.

He snapped off the radio guiltily and put his glass on the table next to him. She came into the room. "Celebrating?" she asked kindly.

"Sleeping medicine," he said thickly.

She laughed. "Oh, Daddy, you're a shrink. You can get something better than hooch."

"There is nothing better than hooch." He still heard the song in his head: "Seven, that's the time we leave, at seven . . ."

"Want a drink?" he asked her. She shook her head. He was glad his daughter did not want a slug of bourbon at two in the morning. At least she was considerate enough to say she didn't. She was a good girl, even though she'd probably had plenty of liquor or grass tonight and had spent the last hour screwing Whit Hutchins in the back of his daddy's Caddy. But she'd come home from Smith with a four point for the year, and she had a right to get a little stoned, have some sex. She looked beautiful, in spite of the ragged jeans she wore nowadays and the seemingly endless collection of T-shirts advertising garages and pizzerias in the Midwest. For dress-up she put on a headband. She had it on now; her blond hair, which was the exact color and texture of his, fell over it. She flopped down on the sofa across from him; the same one Marty Vespa'd sat in a few hours ago in his blood-stained whites.

"You okay, Pops?"

He wasn't okay but couldn't imagine how he'd explain. Maybe he could just say, "I've got this patient who reads minds, who's got a niece that can . . ." What? He didn't know what to call it.

He looked at Marcy. "Do you still read that out-of-this-world crap you used to?"

She laughed. "Aficionados call it occult fiction."

"Do you believe in it?"

"I do while I'm reading it. It wouldn't be any fun if I didn't."

"And the rest of the time?"

"I don't think about it. It's not exactly great literature."

"What about the stories of people . . . with powers?"

"What powers?"

He pretended to think, then he said, "The power to make other people do things they don't want to."

"You mean mental domination."

"Yesss . . ." he said, drawing out the *s*, making it sibilant. "Do you believe in mental domination?"

"You gotta be kidding," she said.

The temperature had started to climb even before dawn; by nine on Sunday morning it was over seventy; by ten-thirty, when Levin pulled into the lot of the Newton police station—a converted bungalow just off the main street—it was pushing ninety. Haze made the air hard to breathe; the tarmac was soft under his feet.

The lobby was not air-conditioned; it was paneled in old knotty pine that had turned yellow over the years. The desk-man had his feet up, the Sunday papers were spread all over the desk, and he was reading the sports section. He half closed the paper and looked at Levin over it. Levin handed him his card. The cop saw the name and title, shoved the paper out of his way, and stood up smartly. "Captain . . . a pleasure. Patrolman Guiterez. A pleasure, sir."

They shook.

"Chief Borchers asked to see me," Levin said.

"Yes . . . I'll tell him you're here."

The cop left the newspaper-covered desk unmanned and went down a short knotty-pine-paneled hall. Levin sat down next to a small Formica table with some magazines on it. He thought only town cop stations in the boonies would have magazines around. He picked up one—an August 1970 *Ladies' Home Journal* with most of the pages torn out—then put it back on the table.

Chief Borchers of the Newton police had called him this morning and asked if he could talk to him about the fire.

"Sure," Levin had said, "what about the fire?"

"I'd rather not say on the phone," Borchers answered. "Can you come here?"

Levin said he could; he wanted to get out of the house, anyway. A pall hung over his home that was almost as black as when Jeannie's parents were killed in a plane crash coming back from Hawaii after their first vacation in years. He'd thought at least they were coming, not going. At least they'd had their two weeks of sun, fun, orchids and mai tais before the bony finger pointed at them and the two hundred and some other poor souls on that plane.

Amy and Paulie had mostly kept to their rooms since last night. Amy did not cry, Greta cried for her; she wandered through the house like a small, plump ghost with tears running down her face.

Paulie had a few blistering burns on his face, back, and arms; smoke had harshened his voice so he sounded like a three-pack-a-day rummy. The intern at Newton Hospital ER said he'd be hoarse for a few days, more susceptible to colds for a week or so, and recommended he stay in bed until Wednesday. Paulie was very, very subdued as the intern smeared salve on the burns and gave him a shot.

Amy didn't come down for breakfast. Greta brought a tray up for her, then brought it back with the food untouched, and Levin went up to try to comfort her. And so when Chief Borchers had called this morning, Levin was standing in front of Amy's closed door. He heard the bed creak in rhythm and realized she was rocking herself back and forth. Pity, like the pity he'd felt when he carried her out of the closet, came over him. He'd tell her that the important part—the land, with the trees, stream, and rolling pasture—was still hers. And maybe, if they saved dough, made a real effort, they could rebuild the place and someday maybe she and her husband and kids would live there like her forebears had.

He had raised his hand to knock—he never went into the kids' rooms without knocking—when Jeannie called him to the phone . . .

The cop came back to the lobby, smiling brilliantly. His black sideburns were bushier than would be allowed on the state force, even in the days of the flower children.

"The chief's waiting for you, Captain. First door on your left, down the hall."

Levin went down a short hallway paneled in old knotty pine. To his right was a washroom with the door open; to his left, a half glass door with Daniel Borchers, CHIEF painted on it in old-fashioned gilt letters. Levin grinned to himself. The place was silent. No one had gone in or out since he'd gotten here; the phone had not rung. Borchers and the cop in the front and a couple of guys who were home watching the game, or scraping down barbecues for later, probably comprised the entire Newton police force; the chief and the non-chiefs. Levin knocked. Borchers called to him to come in and Levin opened the door. A blast of freezing air hit him in the face and he started sneezing. Borchers stood up and held a box of Kleenex out to him. Gratefully Levin pulled out a couple of sheets, wiped his nose and eyes.

"It's this dinosaur," Borchers said, nodding at a huge old air conditioner that took up most of one window. "It only works on high. We're getting new ones." He smiled at Levin and put out his hand. "Dan Borchers," he said. They shook, and Levin sat in an old-fashioned, slat-backed oak chair. Borchers said, "You'd left by the time I got out there yesterday. I guess your son was a mite hurt."

"He's okay," Levin said.

"Glad to hear it." Borchers sat back down; he was as tall as Levin but much, much thinner. He had a long face with deep creases running the length of his cheeks; his skin was tanned and his hair, eyebrows, and eyelashes were sun-bleached almost white. He was about sixty with a rugged country look that Levin's mother would have dubbed redneck and dismissed. But Levin saw intelligence in Chief Borchers's eyes and noticed that the man's desk was clear, the *in* box empty, the *out* box full. The office was spotless, and there was an air of quiet competence about the place.

Borchers took out a pack of cigarettes, offered it to Levin, and Levin shook his head. Borchers lit up and sat silently for a moment, watching the freezing wind from the old air conditioner tear the smoke to shreds. Then he looked into Levin's eyes. "Sorry," he said, "been in a reverie since the fire yesterday. I've been passing the Wooster place all my life, and now it's gone. Makes me feel old, which I am. Makes me aware of my mortality, which I try to forget.

"I knew the Woosters," he went on, "knew *of* them as well. Family once had dough. The great granddaddy owned a bank in town and a little trunk railway that ran from Hartford to the coast, back around the turn of the century. They also owned a couple of mills of one sort or another. Part of the great New England industrial boom. Lots of families around here had dough then. My own included, though we were small-time compared to the Woosters. Everything went bust in twenty-nine. Hoover went through central Connecticut like Sherman through Georgia. Left us with nothing but land and taxes and fuck-all to pay the taxes with. We managed, though; hung on to the land. My daddy voted Republican all his life, anyway; me too. Figure that if you can."

Levin didn't respond. Borchers said, "Sorry for all the jawing, Captain. What I have to tell you ain't pleasant, and it's hard to spit it out. We know how the fire started."

"How?" Levin asked.

Borchers got up, went to a door, and opened it to show a neat closet with a black slicker hanging on a hook and shelves of office supplies. A black, beat-up-looking thing sat on the floor. Borchers picked it up by a blackened wire handle and held it up.

Levin looked blankly at it. Borchers licked a finger and ran it down the side of the thing. Black streaked away, showing red underneath; Levin saw it had a spout.

"It's a gas can," Levin said.

"*Your* gas can, I think. I carry one, in case some fool runs out at an intersection or highway entrance. I guessed you do the same."

Levin stared at the can.

"Someone who was with you yesterday at your picnic poured the ten gallons, or whatever was left in this can, all over the Wooster house and lit it up. It was an old, dried-out house; a tired, uncared-for house—Miz Wooster-Montgomery being down on her luck these many years—and it must've caught like tinder in August. . . ."

Until this moment, Levin thought, he had never even imagined the depth of his son's viciousness.

Until this moment, Joseph Welch had said to Joseph McCarthy during the famous hearings twenty years ago, *I had not gauged your recklessness and cruelty.* Levin knew how the old man felt.

But then Borchers got it wrong. He said, "We think it was the little girl you took in. Edna Wooster's granddaughter."

"No, it wasn't," Levin said evenly.

Borchers came back to his desk and sat down. "I know how you feel, Captain. Taking in that child was an act of kindness, of Christian charity. And then to have her repay you like this, sort of like the serpent in the fable—"

"It wasn't Amy," Levin thundered.

Borchers sat back, stunned for a second. He recovered and said with dignity, "No need to shout, Captain. The fire was set; no doubt about that. If she didn't do it, who did?"

"My son."

Borchers paled under his tan. "Why?" he cried.

Because he got the worst of some lousy gene pool, Levin thought. *Because we toilet-trained him too early, weaned him too late . . . who the fuck knows why.* Aloud he said, "Because he's jealous of the girl, hates her. The house— that lovely house belonging to her—must've driven him crazy."

Borchers looked very sad.

"I guess you know your own son."

"I do," Levin said.

"I'm sorrier than I can say. How old's the boy?"

"Fifteen."

"Terrible age," Borchers said. "My own son went through it too; booze, shoplifting, fucking around, and general first-class snot. Gave me the worst eight years of my life. Then he got to be twenty and just changed, like a caterpillar changing to a butterfly. Now he's a good man; fine husband and father. Owns an electrical contracting company in town here; makes more than I ever did. Hard, having your son outdo you that way. But I got past it; so did he. And now my boy's my best friend, and I believe I'm his. Same'll happen to you and your boy someday. You'll see. But we're talking about arson. Can't send him home to his mommy with a paddle on the fanny for arson. Unless . . ." Levin waited. Borchers lit a new cigarette from the butt of the old one, then said, "It was your ward's house. No one was hurt. We could stay out of it . . . if you say so."

Levin tried to think. He wanted Paulie shamed, punished, hurt, but Paulie was a juvenile, the law'd do zilch.

In the meantime Jeannie'd have to face her friends' sympathy and secret glee, and the kids at school would taunt Greta and Amy. Having his son tried for arson, even in juvenile court, wouldn't do his career any good, either, though he hated himself for even thinking of that.

"What would you do if you were me?" Levin asked.

Borchers looked at him through blue smoke. "I'd leave the cops out of it. Beat the shit out of the kid and hope for the best," he said.

Levin crashed through the door of Paulie's room. The lock tongue snapped through the door frame, and the door banged back so hard it broke the stop and knicked the wall. Paulie was in bed. Levin held up the blackened gas can Borchers gave him, and Paulie cowered. Levin dropped the can, raced across the room, and yanked the sheet down. Paulie was wearing pajamas; beige cotton clung to him, outlining the muscles in his legs and chest. He was almost a man. Levin grabbed him by the hair and pulled. Paulie shrieked, Levin pulled him out of bed by the hair and shoved his head down over the gas can.

"Why?" Levin yelled.

He jerked the boy's head up so he could see his face. Pulling on his hair had brought tears to his eyes. His face was pale and he looked very young. The tears ran down his cheeks. Levin had not seen him cry for years. Paulie's fifth birthday was the last time he could remember. Jeannie'd rented one of those helium tanks and bought a bunch of balloons, and all the kids got their balloons filled in the backyard. Paulie'd gotten the biggest reddest one, because it was his birthday, and he'd carried it around most of the day, protecting it from the other kids. But Len Brachman had been a little son of a bitch even then, and he'd punched the balloon out of Paulie's arms. It escaped and sailed in the wind toward the trees at the end of the yard and Paulie'd run after it wildly. He almost caught the string, but he'd tripped on something and fallen on his face. Levin remembered slamming down the vodka and tonic he'd been mixing for the adult end of the party under the awning they'd also rented and running across the grass to pick up his son. Paulie'd skinned his knees and hit something sharp on the root in the grass and sliced his chin. (A faint scar was still there.) Tears had run down his face, like they were doing now, and spit drooled out of his mouth, mixing with the blood from the cut, as he'd watched his grand balloon sail up over the trees to get lost in the glare of sunshine.

That had been this same boy, but now Paulie's eyes were blank in spite of the tears. They looked like the dead, scum-covered pond at the old Williams' place.

"Why?" Levin cried. "Were you jealous of her? Was that it?"

Jealousy was normal. It'd attacked Levin a million times in his life: when he was a boy and his father showed too much affection to his sister; and later, whenever Jeannie's eyes rested on another man for longer than a second. And only a few months ago, when he'd seen Michael Kaslov. He'd been jealous of Burt Scanlon when he made captain before Levin, and of Baker when his son got accepted at Williams after finishing first in his class at Millbridge High. Levin would understand jealousy. If Paulie cried like he had the day he'd lost his balloon, sobbed that he'd been jealous and couldn't help what he'd done and was sorry . . .

But Paulie stared at him with those scum-covered pond eyes and sneered. "Jealous of a freeloading bohunk? Gimme a break." And Levin punched him with everything he had. He felt his son's lips split against his knuckles, blood ran out of his mouth and dripped on his pajamas.

"Let's try again," Levin said softly. Paulie's legs collapsed, and Levin held him up by his hair. "Why?" Levin asked.

"Fuck yourself," Paulie said.

Levin hit him again, felt his nose flatten, and pulled back his arm for another punch. Vaguely, through the pink haze that seemed to film his eyes, he knew he better stop before he killed the kid, but his muscles ached to keep punching. Feeling bone smack against his knuckles, skin split under his fist, was irresistible.

"Joe . . . no," Jeannie cried.

He looked over his shoulder. Jeannie and the girls stood in the doorway. Jeannie's face was white; Greta was crying. Amy watched calmly. He dropped his arm, relaxed his fist. He said, "He set the fire, Jeannie. He burned the house down."

Jeannie gasped and went even whiter. Greta hiccuped with shock and stopped crying. Only Amy didn't show any surprise. Maybe she knew about it already.

He twisted Paulie's head around to face Amy. "Tell her you're sorry," Levin said. It was so inadequate, it was funny, but he didn't know what else to do. He shook Paulie's head by the hair. The fresh pain brought some life to the boy's glazed eyes. "Say it," Levin thundered.

"Sorry," Paulie mumbled through bloody lips.

"Again!"

"Sorry . . ."

Levin let go of Paulie's hair, and Paulie crumpled to the floor. Levin faced Amy. Her eyes were almost as blank as Paulie's. He was afraid he'd bawl if he stayed here another second, and he pushed past Jeannie and the girls and out the door of the room.

Amy heard his feet pounding down the stairs; then the front door opened and closed. He'd probably drive for a while to blow off steam. Her father used to do that. Then maybe he'd stop in one of the bars around and hoist a few; just like her dad. But it was okay. Joe'd never hit Jeannie or Greta or her.

Jeannie crossed the room to where Paulie lay in a heap, getting blood all over the nice hooked rug. She knelt down next to him, then looked up. "One of you call Dr. Corcoran."

Greta leaped, like she'd been released from a slingshot, and ran down the hall to the phone in the master bedroom. Amy watched Jeannie help Paulie stagger to his feet. His face was a mess; his nose and one eye were swelling up; a splotch of blood stained the white of the eye. He was hurt and he'd said he was sorry, but she knew he wasn't. Next time he would be.

Paulie looked down at Amy. He didn't remember coming into her room, he didn't remember anything after the Doc had given him that horse-pill painkiller called Percodan. He didn't even know how long he'd been standing here.

She slept on her side with her folded hands tucked under one cheek. Her mass of hair lay across the pillow like an oil spill. People said she was pretty; Bobby Whitman thought she was a doll. He'd show her a real good time if she were just a few years older, he'd said with nasty yearning. Paulie didn't understand; she looked ugly to him; alien. A little like Russ Thomas, the albino in class. Russ was weird as shit, with blotchy, white-on-pink skin, beige freckles, and eyes so light you could barely see the irises. She looked just as weird with the moonlight making slashes of her slanty eyes, hollowing out the spaces under her cheekbones. His head started throbbing.

He didn't know what was next on the agenda for little Sweet Pea. Her toys, books, nice clothes . . . house—most of all the house . . . were gone. He'd poured the gasoline around yesterday until the old house reeked. He'd made a thin trail of gas up the stairs and along the landing. It'd burn good up here; there were strawlike rugs around that reminded him of rugs in the summer cabin in Vermont they'd rented for a couple of summers. And there were lace curtains and bedspreads. He'd gone back downstairs breathing through his mouth because of the fumes, and trailed the stream of gas around the dining room table and out into the kitchen. The kitchen was supposed to be the heart of a house. This one'd burn nicely; the linoleum was coming up near the door; the wood on the cabinets, counter, and table looked old and dried out. He splashed the rest of the gas on the floor, across the counter, and shook the can to get the last drops; then he'd pulled out his matches and paused.

Through the fumes that were almost visible he looked down the length of the kitchen, past the short jog in the pantry to the dining room.

Then he thought again, *Let it go.*

It was a nice old house. It'd stood here for over a hundred years before he was even born. But things happened to houses, he thought. There were chimney fires, kitchen grease flare-ups, lightning strikes. He had told himself he was just a bolt of lightning and he'd lit the match and tossed it gently into the stream of gasoline near the door. He meant to run right outside to get the can back in his father's car. But the flames streaking across the linoleum, licking at the cabinet fronts and counter tops and running up the leg of the old table, were mesmerizing; the smell of burning gas and varnish intoxicating. The countertop blistered, snapped, started to burn merrily, and he literally had to pull his eyes away from the sight. He realized that sweat from the heat was running down his face. He was breathing in smoke; his throat started to burn. He finally turned away from the fire to the door, saw her running across the pasture to the house, and stepped out onto the porch, swinging the gas can by the wire handle. "No," she'd screamed. He could still hear it. He'd said something back, and the next thing he remembered, he was dashing off the porch and rolling in the grass to put out cinders that had stuck to him. Everything in between was blank.

Now, he backed away from her bed. The floor creaked, and he froze; but she didn't move. He left the room, closed the door quickly, and went back to his room. He lay down and rested his pounding head against the pillow and suddenly remembered standing in front of the blazing fire on a warm June day shivering with cold. With the memory came a tremor of real terror, and he thought again, *Let it go*.

But he couldn't. He didn't know why, he just couldn't.

TWELVE

MARTHA DYER WAS quiet, and Hall waited. He still had jitters from the mad story Jonathan Kaslov had told him Saturday night, even though he kept telling himself—about every five minutes—that it was garbage. But belief had taken hold of him over the weekend and hung on, like the Lamprey eels that he'd read were killing the fish in the Great Lakes by grabbing on to the fish's side and sawing through its flesh to its guts.

He'd told Dyer he needed information about the girl named Amy Kaslov, who'd been found in Bridgeton; they'd have brought her here instead of Bridgeton Hospital because Bridgeton was too small to cope with psychogenic coma.

Dyer had said, "Yes, they brought her here and we placed her. Is something wrong?"

Hall had a lie ready. "No, one of my patients is her uncle. He wants to know more about her, and I think knowing would be good for him. I didn't want to trouble the foster parents. They know the uncle's in Limekiln but probably don't want to be reminded of it. I thought someone here might have some information about her."

Then Dyer found the folder with AMY KASLOV typed on the tab. Seeing that name on an official file deepened Hall's jitters.

"She sees one of our staff psychiatrists once a week," Dyer had said. "She came here under terrible circumstances. Continued therapy was a condition of her placement."

"I see. Could I speak to the psychiatrist?"

Now Dyer thought about his request while Hall waited. If she refused to give him the name, he was stuck. He couldn't go to Joseph Levin with nothing but the nuts story he'd gotten from Jonathan. He couldn't say, "I've got this feeling that clings to me like a Lake Michigan eel that you'd better get rid of your foster child."

Dyer looked up, her lovely eyes resting on him a moment. "We don't like giving out information about foster children, but I don't see what harm it would do for you to speak to the doctor. He doesn't have to tell you anything he doesn't want to. His name's Charles Moran. His office is here, upstairs."

He thanked her and stood up. She said, "Did you ever see her?"

He shook his head.

"She's a beautiful child," Dyer said. "Not Ivory Snow pretty—beautiful. It can be a problem, you know. The other children get jealous. Average is best, isn't it, Doctor?"

"I don't know."

"It is," she said bitterly.

He left the office and went to the bank of elevators to look at the directory. Charles Moran, M.D., P.C., had Suite 502. He was an office physician, so Hall would have to make an appointment to see him. But he wasn't ready yet. First he was going to the big computer at Yale to see if he could get a chart or a piece of printed paper—an aid like the detail men used to push drugs—anything that Moran could touch, read (crumple up and throw in his face). Hall didn't have much hope, but he was going, anyway, because he didn't know what else to do.

He drove south. It was clouding up; rain was predicted for later, and the heat wave was supposed to break tonight. He took back roads—trees made it cooler—and the sur-

roundings were pleasant for a while. Then he got to the out-
skirts of the city, and gas stations, fast-food joints, and little
hold-out houses with peeling paint and sagging front porches
crammed the roadside. He was getting close to the water—
the port of New Haven on the Sound—but it was hotter.
Building facades soaked up the heat; the city was a furnace.

He parked in a staff lot and entered the drowsing Geor-
gian Quadrangle. Summer school hadn't started yet, the
paths were empty, and the grass was browning out from heat
and lack of rain. He was sweating heavily by the time he got
inside the building. His faculty card was ten years out of
date, but it got him past the front-door watchman and down
to the computer room.

It was cold down here; the graduate assistants who min-
istered to the machine wore sweaters. The computer itself
hulked behind a glass wall at the end of a long basement
room with slimy green cinder-block walls. The cold chilled
Hall's soaked shirt; it clung to his back under his jacket. He
filled out a request form and looked around the room, trying
to pick the oldest, most understanding looking of the GAs.
He chose one about thirty with full, pink cheeks and thin-
ning brown hair. His desk nameplate said he was Alan Fried.

Hall brought the request form to him and sat tensely in
the straight-backed chair next to the desk as Alan Fried read
the form. Hall watched his eyes travel down the sheet to the
line designated "Subject (Use Headings from *Index Medicus*
or *Scientific Abstracts*, if possible)." He looked up at Hall.

"Mental domination? Are you kidding?" he asked.

But Hall had picked well. Alan Fried had not leapt to his
feet shouting "Mental domination? Are you out of your mind,
asshole? This is Yale . . . we're doing real science down here
. . . take this crap to the *National Enquirer.*"

"I'm not kidding," Hall said. "I have a patient who
thinks he has such a power. Calls himself Magnus Mind. I
thought it'd help if I knew something about it. If there's
anything to know."

"It's your nickel," Fried shrugged.

The GA typed on his console keyboard, and Hall watched the screen. It stayed blank and he thought he'd stumped the big computer, which was supposed to have something on everything. But then the mechanism gave a faint tap, lines of green-glow type started running across the screen, and the GA said proudly, "There it is—mental domination. This baby's got everything."

Amy crept into Moran's office like an old lady and sagged into the chair. Her hands lay limply, palms up in her lap, as if she didn't have the energy to clasp them or to grab and twist the fabric of her skirt as she sometimes did when she was upset.

He was shocked. On Saturday she'd seen her grandmother's house for the first time since the old lady died; a picnic had been arranged so the whole family could see it together. She didn't remember much about the place she'd told him, but it'd come back the instant she saw it again. It'd be like seeing her grandma again, and that'd be a little like seeing her mother.

Moran had not liked that train of thought, but she sounded so happy, he let it go. She'd promised to bring him a present from the house. A momentum, she'd called it. "Memento," he'd corrected her gently. He'd told Mary later, and they laughed indulgently at the error. He didn't tell his wife how much he wanted that "momentum." It would be a token of Amy's affection, and he'd probably keep it the rest of his life, whatever it was. He'd been looking forward to seeing her happy and full of news of the house; descriptions of furniture, drapes, and all the odds and ends (some nice, some dreadful) that collect in a family through a century or so.

Now here she was without the memento, looking like a truck had hit her. He waited for her to say something, but she was silent. It went on for a long time, then he said her name softly. She jumped slightly, clasped her hands, and stared at them.

"Where's my 'momentum'?" he asked.

"I couldn't get it," she said in a high, one-level voice. "Paulie burned the house down. There's nothing left. Besides, you said it was *memento,* not *momentum.*"

He caught his breath, then silently cursed Jeannie Levin for not telling him. But that was his fault. In the beginning he'd told her he wanted to hear everything straight from Amy, without adult interpretations.

"Did he mean to burn it down?" Moran asked.

"Oh, yes. He stood on the back porch swinging the gas can, brazen as brass. He meant it, okay."

"Then he'll be punished for it, Amy."

It was poor consolation, but it was all he could think of. She twisted her hands, looked at the arrangement, and said, "No, as a matter of fact, he won't."

"Of course he will," Moran said. "He committed arson. Arson's a crime."

"Sure. But he's a cop's son, and it'd be terrible if he went to jail. So Joe fixed it with the other cops. That's what Greta says, and she usually figures things out pretty well. He'll get away with it, like my daddy got away with killing my mother."

She looked up at him with a cold, sly look that he'd never seen before.

"He almost didn't, though."

"What do you mean, Amy?"

"I almost got him. Almost got him for good and all. Almost sent him back in there to fry!"

"Horsefeathers!" Moran cried.

"It's true! I told him to go, and he was going, okay, dragging himself backward like a dying crab. Like my daddy that time you wouldn't believe me about. Oh, he was going, and I knew how it'd be when he got back in the kitchen and the fire got him. His hair'd burn off, his skin'd pop open. . . ."

The room got cold.

"Amy . . ." Moran cried.

She kept on, "And all the water'd run out of him in a

gush, and his eyes'd burn black and crunchy, and his
tongue'd burn to the top of his mouth. . . ."

It was freezing. Moran's neck was a block of ice, his teeth
were ice carvings. He couldn't move; he didn't think he was
breathing. The terror he'd almost forgotten about came back,
he knew that he was done for. She'd make him crash back
through the window to fall seven stories to the steaming
pavement in the hospital lot. Or maybe she'd have him cut
his throat with his old, silver letter opener. It was dull, it
would take all his strength to jam it into his neck. He fought
the abysmal cold, pried his mouth open, and screeched,
"Amy!"

She focused on him, blinked, and the cold stopped. The
room was normal again; chilly sweat streamed down his face.
He could move his neck, flex his fingers. She stared at him a
second, bowed her head, and started crying. He stood up
carefully and came around the desk to her. He didn't know
why; he was afraid of her, didn't want to touch her. Yet here
he was, less than a foot from her. Her small, thin hand snaked
out, grabbed his hand, and the next thing he knew, he was
on his knees next to her and she was sobbing against his
chest. At first his arms hung stiffly at his sides, knuckles graz-
ing the carpet. Then slowly he raised his arms and put them
around her.

He had just told himself another living-color horror fan-
tasy about this little girl . . . for all the same reasons as before.
Middle age was rushing in on him, his life was full of a
thousand disappointments he hadn't even let himself think
about yet. He was tired, bored, and all the other things men
get to be when they're looking down the barrel of forty. But
there *was* something magical about her. All the stuff about
her mad uncle, murdered mother, and blasted-to-death father
might be par for the course in some neighborhoods. But here
in Millbridge, Connecticut—or even out in Flatbush—Amy
Kaslov was as exotic as a creature from the canals of Mars.

So he knew why *he*'d made up the cold and terror; and
for the first time he thought he knew why *she* was doing it,

and they were going to lay the ghost, exorcise the demon, right now.

Half an hour later he led her out into the waiting room where Jeannie Levin was sitting stiffly, leafing through last month's *House and Garden*. Amy's eyes had life to them, there was color in her face again, and he allowed himself to be a little proud.

Jeannie Levin looked up. Moran said, "Can I speak to you a moment? I've asked Amy and she doesn't mind. Right, Amy?"

Amy nodded and sat down to wait. She opened the Sheena comic he'd just given her and started to read almost eagerly. Jeannie saw the change in her and smiled at Moran.

"In here," he said.

He followed Jeannie Levin into the office and shut the door. She sat in the side chair—the patient chair was fairly small—and looked around her. She'd never been in here before and he watched her eyes travel over the walls with the Disney prints, a bright clown painting, an old sepia of the Grand Canyon, and a print of a hideous Dutch still-life with two slaughtered ducks lying limp-necked on a table covered with metallic looking fruit and flowers. Her eyes stopped on it.

"That's awful," she said.

"I know. But it fascinates the children. And it's a useful contrast to Mickey Mouse and Donald Duck. Walt Disney didn't write the script for my patients, Mrs. Levin."

She looked away from the dead-bird print to take in the cluttered desk, the open closet with the drug cabinet and toys and comics piled in front of it. She smiled, the white lines of strain around her eyes smoothed out, and he thought what a pretty, neat-looking woman she was.

"You can say anything in here, can't you?" she said. "Anything goes."

"I hope so."

She settled her purse in her lap. "She told you about the house," she said.

He nodded. "She also told me that your son will not be prosecuted for arson."

She looked away, and a half memory tugged at him. He tried to catch it but couldn't.

He said, "It's not my business. I'd probably do the same if it was my son. Amy's in better shape now. She's yelled out some of her rage and grief and she cried. Much better. But she has to go back to your house . . . with your son. She hates him, he hates her; they should not be together."

"I'm not giving her up, if that's what you mean," she cried. "She's mine."

"Then keep them apart. I mean it. Strictly apart."

"How?"

"I don't know. But she's made up some pretty terrible fantasies, and they're getting worse. Plus, she's losing ground physically. Her clothes are hanging on her. I don't know where she'd go if she left your house. . . ."

"That's out of the question," she said.

"But if it keeps on," he said, talking over her, "if I hear of one more incident of grand or petit torture against her in that house, I'm taking her away from you."

"Can you do that?" she cried.

"With difficulty, since it'd mean she'd go back on the state, and they won't like that. But they don't like abuse either and that's what we're talking about. Child abuse, Mrs. Levin, in neat, pretty little Westerly. I don't know the extent of it—neither do you, probably. But I'll find out and if it goes on, I will take her away. She's headed for a breakdown, and I can't let it happen to her. She's too nice a little girl. So take me at my word, Mrs. Levin: Keep them apart. I don't care how."

Her lips trembled; from her purse she pulled one of that collection of washed, ironed, delicately wrought hankies that Amy carried, too, and put it to her lips. It was an old-time, totally feminine gesture that went right to his heart. He looked away from her.

"I'll try," she said.

"Don't try. Do it. If you want to keep her."

She held the hanky another moment, then put it carefully back in her bag. He noticed that the bag was a gaily colored straw thing with raffia daisies embroidered on the front like the bag Mary had brought home from a vacation in St. Maarten, years and years ago. Jeannie Levin closed the purse and looked at Moran with dry, clear eyes full of purpose, and suddenly he knew he'd run up against the real strength in the Levin house, that he'd hate being on the wrong side of Jeannie Levin in a fight.

He said, "There's something wrong with your son. He's not my patient, Amy is. Partisanship is part of doctoring, so *she*'s my concern. Still . . . he's a shit, Mrs. Levin. You should do something about him, Amy aside. I suppose there're nicer ways to say all this, but I find nicer is always less clear."

She nodded and stood up, hiking the bag over her shoulder.

"I'll do it," she said.

They shook hands and she left the office. He waited until he heard the outer door open and close, then he stood up, and took the pile of new comics he'd bought this morning to the closet where he piled them on top of the old comics, next to the Barbie doll with no wardrobe, the GI Joe with no equipment; in front of a drug cabinet full of Thorazine, Tranxene, Librium, lithium. His back cramped, and he thought he should bend more carefully at his age. Then the phone rang, he straightened up gingerly and easily, and almost lazily the memory he'd tried to get when Jeannie Levin was here slid into his mind. Amy had said, "He'll get away with it, like my daddy got away with killing my mother." But her father had not gotten away with it; he was dead.

The back pain intensified and Moran hobbled over to answer the phone, expecting Evans to tell him that his next patient, Johnny Mengies, was there. Johnny was the scariest kid ever, and there was nothing magical about him. He was Amy's age, and last year he'd stabbed his father in the arm with a paring knife. It was deliberate, but he was so young,

the court remanded him to his parents' custody on the condition he see a psychiatrist twice a week. That had been a
year ago, and by now Moran knew that little Johnny had
grabbed the paring knife because he couldn't reach the
chef's knife or the cleaver. He'd stabbed his father in the arm
because the man had seen the slash coming and raised his
arm to protect himself. Johnny had been aiming for his daddy's gut.

If Paulie Levin was like little Johnny Mengies, no one
could help him. Such people were born, not made, although
Moran hated admitting it because it went against everything
he'd been taught and wanted to believe. But by now he knew
there were a few—a special few—who could be called acts
of nature, like earthquakes, tornadoes, hurricanes. The DNA
helix spun, locked, and Johnny Mengies (and Paulie Levin?)
got the monster protein.

He picked up the phone, holding his back firmly with
the flat of his hand. But Evans did not announce Johnny
Mengies and his mother, instead she told him that a Dr. Jeffrey Hall was calling.

Amy grabbed the bag of groceries and hurried up the
path after Jeannie. She got to the back steps, looked up, and
saw a shadow in Paulie's window. He was watching her. She
ducked her head so he wouldn't think she was spying and
hurried into the kitchen. Jeannie had held the screen door
open for her, then let it go, and it swished shut. The house
seemed to close in around Amy; she could feel Paulie's presence, almost smell it, like the faint, half-nasty, half-fascinat-
ing cat smell in Mrs. Tangry's big old house up the block
from their house in Bridgeton.

He was right above her in his superneat room with the
pennants and new nine-inch color TV, listening to her move
around down here. The thought drained her. She leaned
against the counter and tried to recapture the feeling she'd
had in Dr. Moran's office. She'd cried her heart out, then felt
empty and sort of clean. And much, much better. Especially

after they'd talked. Dr. Moran had asked her why she thought she could make Paulie Levin burn himself to death.

"I just know it," she'd told him.

It sounded babyish, like being asked why this or that, and answering, "Jes 'cause." But he didn't get impatient with her. He'd smiled and said gently, "People just know all sorts of bullshit, Amy. People just know the universe was created in six days and Laetrile cures cancer. Time was they just knew the earth was flat, tomatoes were poisonous and lead could be turned into gold."

She didn't understand every word, but she got the drift okay. Not long ago she'd just known that the stork brought babies, and if you washed your hair too much, you'd never grow breasts.

Then he'd asked, "If you *could* do it, Amy, why's he still alive?"

She told him about Jeannie yelling *Paulie*. Paulie was Jeannie's son; Jeannie'd try to save him and get hurt, maybe burned up. As soon as Amy had put that together, the cold and the other *thing* just stopped. So Paulie didn't have to stay in there anymore, and he'd raced out through the smoke and fallen in the grass. It had seemed real, then. But today, as she told Dr. Moran, it sounded lame, like the excuses poor, dumb Rory Blanchard gave Mrs. Lowenstein for not having his homework done. Rory was ten and still in fourth grade.

As if he'd read her mind (which she sometimes thought he did), Dr. Moran had said gently, "It sounds pretty lame, Amy."

She didn't answer, and he'd said, "You know, kids have no real power. So they make up games where they control things. That's what you've done, honey. You've made up a fantastical power for yourself so you won't feel so helpless. . . ."

Helpless. The word hit home. Helplessness was horrible. Her father used to scream at her mother, "I'm helpless. You and that fucking hill brat (meaning Amy) make me helpless." Then he'd run out of the house and it'd be quiet. Her mother turned on the TV, made some supper, took out the bottle of vodka. After a couple of drinks her mother would mutter, *"He's* helpless! What about me?" She'd cry, and Amy'd sit in the kitchen watching TV but not hearing it . . . feeling helpless.

She pushed herself away from the counter and started helping Jeannie put the groceries away. Jeannie had splurged and bought raspberries at a dollar and a half a carton. She washed a couple of them and gave them to Amy. They were delicious; Amy remembered her mother couldn't eat raspberries because the seeds got stuck under her false teeth. There were lots of things her mother could not eat after she got those teeth.

Then Amy sat down at the kitchen table to watch Jeannie cook. Paulie's presence didn't seem as strong in the kitchen as in the rest of the house, so she'd just stay in here until Greta got home from school. But then Mrs. Carver tapped on the screen door and Jeannie let her in and put up water for tea. Amy would like to have stayed, anyway, but she knew that Mrs. Carver would rather be alone with Jeannie, so Amy left the kitchen, crossed the dining room to the foyer, and paused a second at the foot of the stairs. His TV was a faint rumble from down here; he had to go back to school tomorrow; so did she. But school was almost over for the year. She wondered if they'd have a last-day homeroom party, like they used to have in her old school.

It was after two; Greta'd be home soon. Since the boys had tried to make Amy run the gauntlet, she was afraid to go out without Greta. Amy went into the den and turned on the TV: a space cartoon came on with creatures blasting each other with swords made of rays. She flipped channels, but everything looked pretty dumb. She went back to the spacemen and started to doze.

"Amy," Greta hissed from the doorway.

Amy turned around; Greta was holding a long ivory-colored envelope.

"Amy, you got a letter," she whispered. "It was in the box with the other mail. I thought maybe you wouldn't want Mom and Dad to see it. I think it's from your crazy uncle."

Amy was stunned. She'd never gotten a letter; in Bridgeton they'd gotten bills, some Christmas cards from her mom's high school buddies, and a yearly calendar from Gomez's Laundromat. But this had her name on it in slanting, grownup writing. On the back was written, "Kaslov, Limekiln, Sharon, Conn." The envelope paper was thick and rough, almost like cloth.

Greta shut the den door while Amy examined the envelope. "Open it," Greta whispered. " 'Less . . ."

" 'Less what?"

"You don't want me to read it."

Amy wasn't sure. Her uncle was nuts; he could write anything. Yet she'd gotten the feeling that one time she'd seen him out front that he liked her very much. He'd probably try not to embarrass her. Besides, Greta was her best friend; they lived together, like sisters. Greta's feelings would be hurt if Amy didn't let her read the letter. It was a risk, but she had to take it.

"Sure you can read it," she said.

Greta sat next to her on the couch. Amy tried to pry the envelope flap open without tearing it, but the glue was too good, and it ripped across the return address her uncle had written. She pulled out two thick ivory-colored sheets of paper with LIMEKILN IN THE BERKSHIRES, A RESORT FOR THE DISCRIMINATING printed on the top in raised blue letters.

"It's not a resort," Greta whispered loudly, "it's a nuthouse."

Amy nodded and started to read.

"Dearest Amy," he wrote. No one had ever called her *dearest* before; her cheeks burned. The letter went on.

I'm sorry about what happened to your house. I know how you feel, which must be hard to believe, since

I've never had a house of my own and never dreamed of having one. I know, anyway. I know many things I have no business knowing. . . .

"He's sure nuts," Greta said.
Amy didn't answer. They went on reading.

When I was eight, like you, I was tall for my age but scrawny, with arms like sticks and knobby elbows and wrists. I was weak and not very brave. We had a local bully (most neighborhoods do) named Benny Trublood, and he took it into his head that he hated bohunks in general, and me in particular (I've never been sure what a bohunk is, but I'm one I guess. Which makes you half one). He'd be waiting for me at the schoolbus stop to beat me up. Usually he hit me in the gut or chest so it wouldn't show, but sometimes he'd get carried away and I'd come home with a bloody nose, black-and-blue shins, and once I think he broke my nose. It's a little crooked to this day, but that might be heredity, mightn't it?

I cried to my mother and father. My mother petted me, but my father would not show sympathy, though he felt it. You could see it in his eyes. He was from the old country and must have seen much worse than anything Benny Trublood could do. "Fight back," my dad told me. I said I was too skinny. "Bide your time," said my father. "You'll fill out . . . your day will come." So I ate and waited for my revenge. Waited for *next time*. My father was right; I gained weight, and a year later I was as big as Benny.

My moment came in the school yard on a nice spring day after a rain. I remember the rain because the school yard pavement was dotted with puddles and the grass was wet. I grabbed Benny Trublood out of a bunch of boys coming out of school, heading for the bus, and punched him with all my might right in the face. That first punch—the first taste of revenge—was wonderful. Down he went, and I went after him, punching, kicking, tearing his hair. The fun stopped as soon as I saw blood smearing his face, staining his nice shirt. I started feeling bad but couldn't stop hitting him.

Mr. Collins, who taught social studies, grabbed me and yanked me off poor Benny, who was blubbering like a baby by then, with blood and snot all over his face. Mr. Collins called me an animal, dragged me back inside to the principal's office. For punishment I had to stay after school every day from then until the end of term, listening through the window to the other boys shouting as they ran up the walk to the bus. I missed one whole spring that way, the spring of 1945. And after a couple of weeks I had to admit that beating up Benny Trublood was not worth the cost. Like Aesop says in the Fable of the Bald Man and the Fly, "You will only injure yourself if you take notice of despicable enemies."

I'm talking about *next time*, Amy. Warning you. But you must know that by now.

"Nutty as a fruitcake," Greta said.

But Amy knew he wasn't. He knew about *next time;* he must know everything. For a second she was terrified, her hand clenched the paper and wrinkled it. Then she realized that he wouldn't bother to warn her, wouldn't call her *dearest,* if he didn't like her, anyway. Then she wanted to hug the paper to her chest, kiss the lines of writing. But she couldn't with Greta sitting right there. He went on.

The best thing would be for you to leave that house.

"No," Greta cried, forgetting that they were keeping the letter secret. They hushed each other and looked at the door. No one came in. Amy said, "I won't leave."

They held hands and went on reading.

But I know you can't choose where you live because you're so young. I can't choose where I live because I'm mad. I have to stay here in an asylum with a fence around it and wire mesh over the windows. Yet I'd hate to leave, it's my home. Which just goes to show you, anyplace can be home—even an orphanage if people are nice to you.

At last he stopped going on about orphanages and asylums and her leaving the Levins and wrote:

If you must stay, I know a way to do it safely. This is the most important part, Amy. The crux, as they say. Make yourself the most ordinary girl on earth; the sort no one notices. Fade into the background; color yourself to fit the wall behind you. It'll be hard at first, but there are ways. For instance, your hair is beautiful. Cut it off. You have a talent for math. Concentrate on art and poetry.

How cruel this sounds, how I hate myself for writing it. But it'll work. And when you think there's nothing left in life, remember the small pleasures. They're all that's real. No one can take them away from you. You know some of them already: hot soup on a cold day, a good movie on TV, ironed cotton . . . I could go on forever, since they are endless. But you'll find your own.

I should stop now; it's getting very late. Miss Crain (the floor nurse) is making her rounds, and she likes us to have our lights out by eleven. Tonight I discovered that Miss Crain, whom I never liked very much before, reads *BC* in the funnies. Now I do like her; seeing her pass and look in on me is a small pleasure I never expected to have. So you see what I mean. But I don't want to make her angry, now that we've just started to be friends after all these years. So I'll stop writing. Please take what I've said to heart. It'd have so much more force if I could see you, tell you these things face-to-face, and other things I don't think I ought to write down. Someday maybe you'll come to see me. You are not allowed to visit me here until you're sixteen; it seems a century. But the time will pass . . . sweetly, I hope. I'll write again. Maybe you'll write to me too.

In the meantime, remember the important part: Beware of *next time*.

Love, your uncle,
Jonathan Kaslov

He's nervous, Moran thought, watching Jeffrey Hall across the desk. Hall's tie knot was sweat-stained, his shirt collar wrinkled. He sat in the patient chair (which wasn't too small for him) with his attaché case in his lap. Moran had seen a case like it at Anthony's on Madison Avenue for three hundred bucks. The jittery silence went on, Moran waited patiently. Mary had once said his patience was patho- logical.

At last Hall took a deep, shaky breath and opened the case. Moran noticed it was leather-lined with compartments in the lid for folders, pencils, and so on. Hall took out a sheet of foolscap with holes running down the sides to put it on the desktop facing Moran. Moran saw computer type, the names Karolinska and Cambridge, and knew he was looking at Ernie Sykes's drunken, mad, middle-of-the-night hypoth- esis from months ago. Sure enough, at the bottom of the page, followed by a question mark, was the phrase, "mental domi- nation."

"You know what that means?" Hall asked.

Moran nodded.

Hall said, "What I'm going to tell you sounds crazy, but bear with me, Doctor. I believe a boy's life depends on it."

Then Hall told his story.

Moran knew a lot of it . . . the names, of course; Amy, Michael, Evvie, Jonathan Kaslov. He knew how Evvie Kas- lov had died and about Amy being locked in the closet. He did not know about the final end of poor Little (the present from the nurse who must be still on three in the next build- ing.) He didn't know about the end of the *Chips* book and the rest of her pitiful treasures. Then Hall told him that *he* knew about the teddy bear from the uncle and the uncle knew because he was telepathic. Hall paused to give Moran a chance to snort, laugh, argue, whatever. Moran was quiet, and Hall went on to tell about the nurse named Ida Barnes. Moran heard old sorrow in Hall's voice that threatened to turn to tears, but Hall got through it without weeping. He finished with the fire and Jonathan Kaslov smacking his head against a stone chimney, then enlisting Hall to get Amy out of the Levin house.

Hall finished talking; the office was quiet. Outside, the phone rang. Evans answered and took care of whatever it was. Moran wanted to tear up the printout, throw the pieces in Hall's face and tell him to get his crazy ass out of the office. But anger would be phony.

He swiveled his chair around and looked out of the window. It had started to rain; fat drops splatted the glass. Across the street was a discount designer store in a small, pretty house; a woman rushed out and crossed the parking lot, holding a newspaper over her head to protect her hairdo.

Suddenly Moran hated Amy Kaslov. She had no right to come into this neat, pretty world, modeled on a TV commercial, and force him to believe something from a George Hamilton movie. Only it wasn't a neat, pretty world. The men drank too much, played golf, and hated themselves. The women drank too much, played golf, talked wallpaper, and hated themselves even more. The kids smoked dope, hated themselves and their parents, and a few killed themselves. It wasn't pretty at all; and mental domination and telepathy weren't any more outlandish (come to think of it) than half the crap he'd heard in this room over the past five years.

The rain got heavier; trees whipped in the wind; the parking lot tarmac smoked. Hall said, "I've got to convince you somehow. We've got to get her out of that house."

"I know," Moran said without turning around.

Paulie came down to dinner for the first time since the fire. He had a black eye from the beating on Sunday; one side of his face was swollen. He sat across from Amy, his black eye uncovered and hideous, staring at her with a little smile on his mouth.

Amy couldn't eat. Jeannie'd grilled lamb chops; the fat was crisp, the inside juicy, but every bite seemed to take forever to chew. Even the raspberries didn't have much taste to her. Paulie ate three chops and chewed the bones, watching Amy every second. Then he ate a whole dish of berries. Joe didn't look at him; he and Paulie said nothing to each other.

Greta and Jeannie tried small talk, but they stopped after a few minutes, and gloom settled over the table. Paulie finished first and left the table without a word. After dinner Amy and Greta watched a grown-up movie that Jeannie wanted to see, about older people falling in love. Amy guessed it was sweet, but she and Greta got bored after half an hour and they went upstairs with the new *McCall's* Jeannie let them take. They pored over it until almost ten, then went to bed.

Amy waited, not sleeping. Joe and Jeannie came up; water ran in the master bathroom, the toilet flushed, then it was quiet. She waited longer until the house had that dead, silent feel of everyone being asleep. Then she got up, turned on the light, and took the letter out of her skirt pocket where she'd left it for safekeeping. She looked around the room, trying to think of someplace to hide it. She even thought of putting it at the bottom of the Kleenex box in the bathroom, but Paulie'd find it, or Jeannie would when she put out a fresh box. No place was safe.

She sat on the bed, read the letter a few times, trying to memorize what her uncle had said and to remember the look of the pages with the letterhead and his handwriting all over it. Then she kissed the paper, tore it into pieces, flushed them down the toilet, and went downstairs.

It was still raining; the carriage lamps threw enough light through the sidelights to see by. She went to the den, got the shears from Jeannie's sewing box and today's leftover newspapers, and took them down the hall to the little washroom under the stairs.

She turned on the light, spread the papers, and looked at herself in the mirror. In his letter her uncle told her to forget math and concentrate on art and poetry. She'd try, but knew she couldn't. Paintings looked like bad photos to her when they looked like anything, and reading poetry was torture. But he'd also told her to cut her hair, and that she could do.

She raised the shears and fitted the blades around a bunch of hair, then shut her eyes and snipped. She opened her eyes, dropped the hair on the papers, and went on cutting. After a few minutes she looked different and started to see the point. Without the whomps of black hair, Paulie might stop noticing her. She'd be like a chair or table that he didn't like but couldn't bother hating. Even Paulie Levin couldn't hate a *chair*. So he'd leave her alone, and *next time* would never come.

Her Uncle Jonathan might be a fruitcake, but he was smarter even than Dr. Moran. She wondered if people called him Jonathan or Jon. Or Mr. Kaslov. She remembered his face clearly; he looked a lot like her father, but she couldn't blame him for that, any more than she could blame Greta for having the same color hair as Paulie.

She'd gotten the front and sides cut and was reaching around to grab hair in the back when Greta opened the washroom door. Amy froze, holding the shears midair. Greta looked at the shears, at the sad, dead-looking curls all over the newspaper. Amy braced herself, afraid Greta'd carry on and wake the whole house. But Greta kept her voice quiet and even.

"I knew you were going to do it the second I read that part. It's a shame. He's nuts."

Amy looked at herself in the mirror. "It's too late now."

"It sure is."

Amy handed Greta the shears. "Cut the back for me? I can't reach."

"Oh, Amy, don't ask me. Daddy'll kill me."

Amy swallowed hard; she hadn't thought about Joe's reaction until now. He liked her hair, he'd be PO'ed for sure.

"I won't tell you helped," she said.

Greta hesitated, then said, "It'd be awful for you to take all the blame alone," and she took the shears and made Amy sit on the toilet seat so she could reach her hair. She cut slowly, carefully; she even tried to straighten out the front where Amy'd chopped it. It was very late when she finished, and Amy stood up and looked in the mirror.

"It's awful," Greta cried.

It was, but that was sort of the point. Besides, not having

all that hair on her neck felt wonderful. She whirled around and let herself hug Greta (she didn't do that very often). "Thanks, Dorothy," she whispered.

Greta turned red, gave Amy one of her warm, sloppy kisses, and they giggled.

Greta took the shears back to the den. Amy rolled up the papers with the hair inside and carried them through the kitchen out to the big garbage can next to the back stairs. She didn't want to leave hair in the house to waft around and get into food. There had been stray hairs everywhere in the house in Bridgeton.

It was very dark out; the rain had slowed to a drizzle. She stuffed the papers into the can and straightened up. Drizzle went through the short hair, cooling her scalp. It was kind of spooky fun being out alone at night. She hadn't done it since that late-night search for Little. The houses were dark, except for porch lights and a faint green square of light in the Chaffe house. It was late. Pretty soon Mr. Chaffe would finish the bottle, or the TV would play "The Star Spangled Banner" and go off the air. Then he'd put the bottle down, stagger to his feet, and prowl through the house, bumping into things, breathing out booze fumes until he got to the kitchen where he'd open the drawer . . .

Suddenly the drizzle turned freezing; Amy shivered, jammed the can cover back on, and ran up the stairs into the safety of the kitchen. But it wasn't safe in here. Greta was at the table. Jeannie stood next to her, wearing the light blue summer robe and the house shoes Greta and Amy'd bought for her birthday. She looked miffed, probably because Amy and Greta were up so late, then she saw Amy. Her face went blank with shock, her mouth turned down at the corners. Amy hadn't thought it was *that* bad, and she raised her hand and felt the front of her hair. It was so short, it almost bristled. Jeannie was finally getting some expression on her face, but it wasn't good. Then Greta—dear Greta—saved the day. She said, "It's kind of short and messy, but it'll be a lot cooler for summer." It was a terrific excuse; Amy would never have had the brains to think of it. Then Greta put her head to the side, pursed her lips, and looked at Amy critically. "I think it's kind of cute," she said. "She looks like Daffy Duck. . . ."

Incredibly, marvelously, Jeannie grinned and choked out, "Daffy Duck . . ." Then she burst out laughing. The girls grinned with her, then laughed to keep her company. It felt so good to laugh after days of gloom they couldn't stop.

The laughter woke Paulie. He lay in the dark, trying to go back to sleep. But his head started pounding again. He still had some of the horse pills, but they fuzzed him out— not like grass—and he didn't want to take one. He gave up, opened his eyes. The laughter was real; he hadn't dreamed it. He looked at his bedside clock; it was after one, and his mother and the girls were downstairs laughing their asses off.

Curiosity drove him out of bed to the door of his room. He opened it and went out onto the landing. They were having a ball down there; he recognized the bitch's voice. He leaned over the stair rail and listened. The laughter started petering out, and his sister, sounding like she was trying to extend the joke, whatever it was, cried "Daffy Duck . . ." and they were off again. Paulie looked behind him at the shut door of the master bedroom. The old man was sleeping through it; he slept like a corpse.

They stopped laughing, and his mother said gaily, "Let's have milk and cookies, so it shouldn't be a total loss." She sounded like she was celebrating. He heard the refrigerator open and shut, then the girls talked a little but he couldn't hear what they said. Then his mother said something about going to Lorna's tomorrow to get it fixed. Lorna was the hairdresser in Westerly Center; he couldn't imagine what Lorna would fix for them. He waited. The girls talked a little more. Their voices were subdued now; they must be sleepy. Then he heard their slippered feet coming through the dining room to the foyer, and he crept back to his room but stayed in the doorway with the door open a crack. The landing light came on, the girls appeared at the top of the stairs, and he caught his breath. The bohunk had cut off all that black hair so it was only a few inches long all over her head. He got the Daffy Duck joke. He watched until they'd gone into their rooms, then he stuck his head out and grinned at the shut master bedroom door.

His father loved her hair. Paulie'd caught him stroking it when she sat next to him watching TV, and sometimes he'd seen his father look at her with that cloud of black around her head like a hellish halo, and the old man'd smile like he'd just seen the first sunshine after an Arctic winter. He'd go crazy when he saw what she'd done to it. But he was sleeping, he wouldn't know until breakfast tomorrow, and Paulie couldn't wait to see the look on ol' Daddum's puss. This was one breakfast he wouldn't miss.

His mother had finished in the kitchen. He heard her come across the foyer, and he pulled his head inside the room and shut the door. He crawled into bed and lay on his back, cupping his aching head in his clasped hands.

The haircut was no big deal. She'd done it herself—neither Greta nor his mother would do it—so she must want it that way. He didn't care what she did with her hair. It'd cheese off his father for a minute, but that'd pass, and Paulie would still be in the same quandary: what to do with Amy.

He sang softly to an old tune. "What to do with Amy . . . what'll I do with Amy . . . ?"

Suddenly he remembered how she'd looked just now in the light from the landing. The haircut made her look older, almost adult. And he'd noticed before—unwillingly—the tiny nubs of breasts under hers and his sister's T-shirts and nightgowns. All at once he got an idea. It was grisly. He told himself she was way too young, then he remembered news stories he'd read about the same thing happening to even younger girls. He sat up in bed, trying to think over the pounding of his head. He wouldn't do it himself; he didn't dare, for one thing. He'd be the goat, and ol' Dad wouldn't try to get him off for this one. He'd kill him. Besides, the thought made him sick. But it wouldn't sicken Len or Bobby.

Bobby already had half a hard for her, and he and Len would do anything if it was fast, fun, and had a little horror to it.

Everyone loved horror, Paulie thought. He lay back down and let his thoughts rove over horror and how much all the nicey-nice folks in this world really loved it. He remembered a *Time* magazine story a few years back, about a girl getting ripped to death by a grizzly out in Yosemite or Yellowstone. Time printed a blow-by-blow because they'd done their research and they knew what people liked. Paulie had read the story avidly, and when he'd gotten to the last part, where the grizzly dragged the girl away from the supposedly safe circle of campers around a fire and she'd screamed, "He's tearing my arm . . . My God . . . I'm dead . . ." Paulie had felt something in his insides tighten and flutter at the same time. It had been thrilling; better than sex. He had wondered how Bobby and the others would react, so he'd shown them the story separately, watching their faces to see how they'd look when they got to the girl's last, despairing cry. Sure enough, Timmy'd blushed and sweat broke out on his face; Bobby got white, tight lines of excitement around his mouth, and the muscles in his jaw had jumped. Len licked his lips and crossed his legs, and Paulie had been sure old Pizza Face Brachman had gotten a rod-on.

They'd do this, okay.

THIRTEEN

THE RAIN STOPPED; the sky cleared and it cooled off. But the small Danbury courtroom must have been shut up for a couple of days, and the air was hot and stale. Levin sat a couple of rows back; the defendant—a seventeen-year-old Shermer had pulled in last week for pushing pot at Bridgeton High— sat stiffly at the front table. He'd been loud and arrogant the first time Levin had seen him; he'd been wearing hand-painted jeans and a dirty T-shirt, and he'd called Levin an asshole for bothering with a little harmless dope when rapists and murderers were on the loose.

By now the full weight of his predicament must have hit the kid, and he was quiet. He wore a suit and tie and had cut his hair.

Like Amy, Levin thought.

Jeannie had told him about the haircut while he was shaving this morning, and he'd cut himself. Blood ran into the cream on his face; he grabbed a washcloth, held it against the cut, and looked at his wife in the mirror.

"Short?" he'd asked.

"Yes."

"Why?"

"I don't know," Jeannie said. She took the washcloth

from him, soaked it in cold water, and held it against his chin. "Maybe she's mad at us, Joe. Maybe it's a sign of grief for the house. I don't know. I don't think she'll tell us if we ask." She took the cloth away and looked at the cut. The blood was clotting. "I'm sorry," she said, "I should have waited until you finished. Don't hit the roof when you see her. I think she feels bad enough about it as it is. It probably seemed like a good idea in the middle of the night like lots of things do."

"She did it in the middle of the night?"

Jeannie nodded and left him alone to finish dressing. He went downstairs, telling himself it was only hair and hair grew back. He got to the kitchen door, took a breath, and pushed it open.

He saw Paulie first.

It was the first time Paulie had joined them for breakfast in weeks; he'd usually take a roll, doughnut or bacon sandwich on the bus with him. And he and Len probably stopped somewhere to chow down before classes started. Yet here he was in his regular place at the kitchen table, grinning up at Levin. For a second Levin thought it was a peace gesture. Then he noticed how tight and mean the kid's grin was. Paulie looked deliberately down the table at Amy, then back at Levin, and Levin could almost hear him chanting,

Nah-nah, nah-nah . . . see what she did . . . nah-nah, nah-nah . . .

Levin looked at Amy. The hair was a mess, but she was such a pretty kid, it almost didn't matter; besides, without all the hair you could see how long and graceful her neck was. She stared down into her bowl of cereal, clutching her spoon. She looked ready to faint. Greta didn't look so great, either.

"See you cut your hair, honey," he said.

She nodded miserably without looking at him. He smiled. "Doesn't look so bad. Maybe a little ragged, but that can be fixed."

Amy gave him a look of love and gratitude and dipped her spoon in her bowl; Greta sighed and started eating, and Jeannie said, from her post at the counter, "We're going to Lorna's to get it fixed."

"Me too," Greta said.

"What about school?" Levin asked. He looked at Paulie. The muscles in his son's jaw jumped as he clenched and unclenched his teeth. The skin around his eye was purple and yellow, his nose and upper lip were still swollen. Between the bruises and expression of thwarted hatred on his face, he looked like a troll. He must have found out about the haircut somehow and come down specially this morning to see his father hit the ceiling. But Jeannie forewarned Levin, and poor Paulie got cheated. Levin almost felt sorry for him.

Jeannie said, "Tests are over. Tomorrow's the last day of school. I don't think they'll miss much."

Paulie scraped his chair back and left the kitchen without a word. . . .

"All rise," called the county clerk.

Judge Bracken came in, and Levin saw the boy's back tense as the judge settled himself and the lawyers went to the bench. This was a hearing to see if the kid would be tried as a juvenile or adult. As a juvenile, he'd get probation or a suspended sentence and maybe a year of community service. He'd go home to his folks, finish high school, maybe go to college. As an adult, he faced fifteen years' hard time, of which he'd serve at least six. He was seventeen, on the borderline, so it was up to Bracken. The kid's mother sat right behind him, wearing a sleeveless ultrasuede dress and twisting a large solitaire diamond around her finger. The father probably waited by the phone in some sleek Fairfield County corporate office to hear whether all the hopes he'd had for his son since the day he was born—that he'd be a lawyer, doctor, senator, or president; that he'd go to Yale, Harvard, Dartmouth—had gone up in smoke.

Suddenly Levin couldn't watch anymore. He bowed his head, looked at his feet. His shoes were dusty. Jeannie usually shined them, but she'd forgotten this morning because of all the tension in the house. They couldn't go on like this. He'd make up with Paulie somehow. It'd be hard, but he'd find a way, and from now on he would only remember the few nice times; the fifth birthday, for instance, and the summer Paulie had gone to Y day camp and made a wood-burned nameplate for Levin's desk. Levin still had it.

The lawyers' voices rose and fell gently as they went through their spiels. Levin was there in case the assistant DA wanted him to elaborate on his deposition, but he didn't. The lawyers finished, the room quieted down, and Levin looked up. Bracken was reading the deposition, the ceiling light shone through his sparse white hair to his pink scalp. A few people shuffled, someone coughed. The kid at the defendant's table did not move; neither did his mother.

Bracken looked up. He had a soft, kindly face and a voice to match, but he was a hard-nosed son of a bitch. Today he ran true to form, and William Dinsmore was bound over for trial as an adult in Danbury Superior Court within thirty days. The boy's shoulders shook, and Levin knew all the kid's seventeen-year-old snot had deserted him, and he was crying. It could have been Paulie sitting there in tears; maybe it should have been. But it was too late now. Hopelessness dragged at him. It was an effort to stand up, leave the building, cross the mobbed parking lot to his car. William Dinsmore was a stupid, greedy snot, but he didn't deserve six years in the slammer. Paulie wasn't stupid or greedy that Levin knew of, just mean. Sick-mean, Levin thought. Prison wouldn't help him, but maybe a doctor could. Moran might recommend someone.

These thoughts occupied him on the drive back to the incredibly ugly headquarters building. It had been molded out of white cement that was streaked brown from gutter runoff and rusting metal window frames. The place must've looked like the cat's ass—the last word in Bauhaus—in 1940.

Baker was waiting for him at the office; it had been a quiet morning, nothing Baker couldn't handle alone. Levin had two personal calls: one from Jeannie, one from Dr. Charles Moran. Levin went into his glass-walled office, took off his jacket, loosened his holster, and called home. He heard laughter in Jeannie's voice. "The hair looks fine," she told him. "Lorna's a genius. We bought a blow dryer, and Greta keeps wetting down their hair so she can blow it dry. They look like Ubangis. . . ."

He laughed with her, said he'd let her know what time he'd be home, then he hung up and called Moran. Moran sounded tense.

"Can you meet with me and Jeffrey Hall tonight at Limekiln? About eight?" he asked.

"Why Limekiln?" Levin asked.

"My building closes down at seven. Can you make it?"

"Is something wrong with Amy's uncle?"

"Can you make it?" Moran repeated.

"Sure . . . but what's—"

Moran hung up before Levin finished the question.

It was dinnertime, but the boys were too stoned to care about eating. They were down in Len Brachman's basement; his folks were up in Maine for the week and they had the place to themselves. They'd already smoked a couple of joints and still had half a bag of good stuff they'd all chipped in for. Paulie was rolling a fresh joint; it was one activity he enjoyed. His fingers felt long and supple; he thought he should be a musician—specifically a violinist—or a surgeon. He finished it, held it out for Bobby to light, then took a long, deep drag. He passed the joint to Len and started telling them what he wanted them to do. Timmy listened for a couple of minutes, then got up and walked across the plaid indoor-outdoor carpeting to the Ping-Pong table. The other two stayed put. Timmy rolled the ball out from under the paddle and bounced it on the tabletop. Paulie kept talking over the click of the ball, and Timmy felt excitement building in the basement.

Paulie finished, it was quiet a moment, then Bobby called, "Whazza matter, Tim, don't you think she's cute?"

Timmy said, "She's just a little kid, for chrissake."

"Yeah," Bobby drawled, "little, young, smooth all over. And cherry. I never busted cherry before, did you, Tim?"

It was a mean question; Timmy'd never gotten laid and Bobby knew it. Bobby had screwed Diane Klausner, Barbara White, Sally Miller, to name a few. Girls went for Bobby; he was seventeen, one of the oldest boys in their class, and Timmy had to admit he was good-looking. He never broke out; his hair never looked greasy. He'd gone from childhood to manhood without the miserable in-between the rest of them were suffering through. Right now he was excited, and his voice had gotten a silky sound to it that made Timmy's skin creep.

Timmy bounced the ball against the green wood table-top; they could do what they wanted to her, but Timmy was out of it. It was a hard decision because they were his best friends . . . asshole buddies they used to call themselves. And he hated getting left out; but he wasn't taking on that little girl again, no matter what. *He*'d been excited that day in the basement, more excited than he'd ever been. When he saw the way she looked at him, he knew she'd never seen one before and he'd almost popped. He felt sorry for her, too, because she was just a little kid and she looked scared out of her wits, but that wasn't going to stop him from looking up her nightie, making her touch him. Then something had happened to her pretty little face; it relaxed, got a dreamy look on it, and turned white, like the skulls that flew out at you in the Chamber of Horrors at Riverview Park; then the Levin basement got cold. *Cold* wasn't the word; the air froze, and he'd known she was going to kill him. But he'd also known somehow that he was second on the list: Paulie was first. If he'd been Paulie Levin that minute, he'd have crapped in his pants. But Paulie didn't seem to feel a thing. Paulie had stone skin and maybe he was right, because nothing happened after all. The cold stopped, and she was just a little girl again. But she wasn't, there was something wrong with her, and Timmy should warn Bobby and the others. Only he'd sound like the prize asswipe of nineteen always, and they'd laugh at him until they pissed themselves.

Paulie was waiting for them to decide.

Bobby said sharply, "She'll talk."

"She won't have anything to tell," Paulie said. He rummaged around in his book bag, pulled out a piece of limp red knit, and held it up. It was one of the ski masks they'd stolen from Kaufman's last winter. Len had kept Old Man Kaufman busy at the counter while the other three ranged through the store ripping stuff off. That time they'd gotten ski masks (Timmy's was blue with Lake Placid 1933 printed on it . . . he still had it somewhere) and some other junk. Notably, as Timmy remembered, some Guinea-green shower curtain hooks that he'd given to his mother. They'd been stoned that day; it seemed to Timmy that they'd been pretty well nonstop stoned for a long time now, and he was getting sick of it.

Bobby took the red ski mask from Paulie and pulled it over his head. His face was hidden; even his eyes were shadowed by the knit. He stood up slowly, stretched out one arm mummylike, and staggered toward Timmy.

"Ooooooh . . . " Bobby groaned, like they used to when they were kids trick-or-treating on Halloween. One Halloween they'd moaned and groaned outside old Mrs. Burns's house until she'd run outside on her porch waving a broom in the crisp autumn air.

"Ooooh . . . hoooo," Bobby moaned. Timmy knew it was just Bobby in a stolen red ski mask, but his heart jumped and he backed up until his butt hit the edge of the Ping-Pong table. "Cut it out," he cried. Bobby kept coming. He was only a foot away, his hand looked huge, and Timmy felt himself pale. Then Bobby laughed and pulled the mask off. "Whattaya say, turd face, you comin' with us?"

"You really going to do that to her?" Timmy asked softly.

"Why the fuck not? Like Paulie says, we'll all get a turn . . . only I go first, right, Paulie?"

Paulie nodded.

"Count me out," Timmy said hoarsely.

"Hey, it's a chance to finally get some—"

"Count me out," Timmy said again. He crossed the basement and climbed the stairs, half hoping, half afraid they'd call him back. But they didn't.

So much for the asshole buddies, he thought.

Behind him, Bobby asked in that silky voice he acquired with dope and sex talk, "Where do we do the heinous deed?" His voice resonated against the painted cinder-block basement walls.

"The old gym," Paulie answered. Timmy opened the door to the Brachmans' empty kitchen as Len drawled, "How do we get her there? Drag her screaming through the grade-school hall?"

Timmy went into the kitchen and closed the door as Paulie said, "I'll get her there."

He ran across the semicircle of Windy Ridge to his house and slammed the door behind him. His mother called, "I kept supper warm, Timmy." He ignored her, ran upstairs, shut himself in his room, and lay down. He was trembling; he tried to relax. He told himself he didn't have to be scared; he was out of Paulie Levin's hellish plot. He was trembling for them, not himself.

He would not join them, but he'd never tell what he knew, no matter what happened down there. And he'd never, as long as he lived, so help him God, think about that little girl again, or mention her name, if he could help it.

Levin drove past neat, pretty houses with lit windows and wished he were home with Jeannie and the girls. The houses got bigger, farther apart, then disappeared, and all he could see from the road were stone pillars guarding long estate driveways. Just south of the town center he turned off on Limekiln Lane. Branches grew across the road, making a leaf tunnel that blocked out the light fading over the hills, and he turned on his headlights.

The wrought iron asylum gates were closed. But the guard was expecting him, and he opened them from inside the gate house. They swung in with a soft electric hum, and Levin drove through and saw the building; ground fog curtained it, lights from the windows hit the mist, making the place glow eerily. Suddenly he wanted to turn around and go home. He'd tell Amy her hair looked great, kiss the girls goodnight, and settle down to watch TV with Jeannie. The impulse was so strong, he slowed up. But curiosity had eaten him alive since Moran's call, he had to find out what they wanted.

He drove up and parked in front; this time no nut wept because he'd blocked the steps. One of the double front doors opened, and a white-uniformed man leaned out and called, "Captain Levin?"

Levin nodded and followed him into the lobby. It was empty except for a gray-haired woman who sat behind the onetime hotel check-in desk, leafing through a copy of *Vogue*. They crossed the lobby, passed the sliding double doors that had been open before and were closed now. He heard the intro music to *Hawaii Five-O* and the sound of people talking loudly over the program like the audience at the kiddie shows he used to take Greta to. A high, sick-sounding giggle pierced the heavy wooden door. Last time he'd been here there'd been people talking and the typewriters clacking and the place had felt more like corporate headquarters in a converted hotel. But tonight, with that hair-raising giggle, the ring of their footsteps on the stone floor, and a feeling of deep silence in the rest of the building, it felt like a madhouse.

They got to Hall's door. The orderly opened it for Levin and closed it behind him, leaving him alone in the anteroom. He crossed it to the office. Hall sat at his desk; Moran stood at the window looking out with his back to the door. The room was lit up, but dark paneling and floor-to-ceiling bookcases made it gloomy, ominous, and his faint case of the jitters turned to black foreboding. Moran turned around and faced him. Both men looked grim, and Levin wanted to say something funny. He tried to remember a good line from a Marx Brothers movie, or *Laugh In*, which occasionally made him laugh until he ached. But he couldn't think of anything except a famous bit of Dante he'd read in high school: "Abandon hope, all you who enter here." That in itself was pretty funny, and he grinned as he walked into the room.

Moran was speechifying the way he had the first time
Levin met him. "Start with neglect, beatings, the virulently
Puritan grandmother scratching a living from dust and rock,"
Moran said. "Add the murdered mother, three days locked in
the dark, the shot-up father and burned-down house. By now
violence is an old acquaintance of Amy's. A friend."

"You've said this before," Levin said.

"This time you must listen to me."

"Maybe I will if you stop crapping around and say something."

"Amy's got to leave your house, Joe."

"Fuck yourself," Levin snarled.

"It's not just the burned-out house," Moran said. "The
house is the last in a long line of things."

"For instance . . ."

"For instance, where's the little teddy bear she brought
back from the hospital, the plush seal you gave her, the book
she's had ever since she can remember?"

"In her room," Levin said shortly.

"No. They're gone. Stolen by your son."

"Bullshit. Paulie's into dope and arson. Why would he
take that kiddy crap?"

"To hurt her."

"Maybe she's wrong about the stuff being gone. Kids
lose things, misplace them. That's it . . . she probably hid
them for safekeeping and forgot where—" Levin said.

"*She* didn't tell me about it."

"Who did?"

Moran and Hall glanced at each other, and suddenly
Levin knew that Moran had heard about the purloined toys
from Hall, who'd heard about it from the nuts uncle who
claimed to read minds; presumably Amy's as well as everyone else's. Levin's temper revved up, and he knew he better
get out of there. He stood up and said, "Amy stays with me,
Moran. That's that."

"No, it isn't." Hall spoke for the first time. "You have a

whole family to consider. Dr. Moran told me how you feel about your son. It's not that rare, you know, but you're the grown-up . . . you're the one who's supposed to understand. Just as you'd expect *your* father to." The words arrested Levin. Hall went on. "Try to see it from his side. He's trapped in his own home with someone he hates and envies. That's terrible."

"It won't kill him," Levin said.

"It might," Hall said.

"What's that supposed to mean?"

Hall and Moran exchanged looks again. Then Hall opened a manila folder on his desk, drew out a sheet of flimsy and handed it to Levin. He recognized the name Cambridge but the rest looked like gibberish, only he knew it wasn't. This was a computer printout; scientific from the look of it . . . maybe medical. Maybe something was wrong with Amy and these two jerks picked this ass-covering way of telling him because they didn't have the balls to come out and say, "Amy's sick . . . Amy's dying." His heart started a sick, heavy thudding. He sat down slowly, staring at the printout, trying to make sense out of the chicken scratches that covered the page. Finally he looked up at Hall. "I don't know what it means. . . ."

Hall started with the chemistry; he said no one was sure what serotonin was or what effect it had. The high levels in her spinal fluid might be coincidental or they might be a hallmark of her . . . He searched for a word and came up with . . . *condition*.

"What condition?" Levin cried.

And Hall told him the rest of it. A couple of seconds into it, all science went out the window, Moran thought, and they entered never-never land. Moran had come to it in bits and pieces. He'd had months to get used to the idea that this child was like no other on earth; but said flat-out like this— in the space of five minutes without the backdrop of a camp fire and night noises in the woods—it sounded like crap on toast. Of course, Levin wouldn't believe it. Levin's face

turned an unhealthy brick color, but Hall kept on and finished without flourish . . . with the fire and how Amy almost
killed Paulie, then didn't because she was afraid Jeannie
would get hurt (information supplied by Moran).

The room was silent; Moran looked away from Levin to
the window. It had gotten pitch-dark since Levin arrived.
The window glass reflected the room with the bookcases and
the three of them sitting frozen like plaster pop-art dummies.
The stillness seemed to go on for a long time, then Levin
said in a voice hoarse with rage, "Now one of you is supposed
to yell 'Gotcha' or 'April fool.' And I say, 'April fool is past
and you—' " He choked to a stop, then got up again and
headed for the door.

"Please listen, Joe," Moran cried.

Levin kept going.

Moran yelled after him, "She's dangerous, Joe. I'm taking her away from you, no matter what you say. . . ."

That stopped Levin cold. He stood with his back turned.
Moran saw his arm move as he reached inside his jacket, and
he turned and faced them with a gun in his hand. It was an
enormous blue thing that gleamed dully in the lamplight.
Moran got dizzy and wondered whether Levin would shoot
him if he leaned over and put his head between his knees to
keep from fainting. Helplessly he glanced at Hall. Against
the dark paneling Hall's face was a white blob topped with
fuzzy light brown hair that looked like it was standing on
end. Maybe he'd faint first.

Levin said softly, "Listen, Doctors, listen good. She's
mine. If you try to take her away from me . . . if you utter one
word of this puke outside this room, I'll kill you. I'm a cop. I
know a million ways to get away with it."

Levin's face was expressionless; his eyes looked like
bluestone chips. Pulling the gun wasn't an idle macho gesture; he'd shoot them and enjoy doing it, Moran thought.
Moran kept his mouth shut and prayed Hall would do the
same. He did. Levin backed toward the door, keeping them
covered. Moran thought he'd stumble or trip on something,
but he moved smoothly and gracefully. It would have been

an impressive exit, but before he got to the door it opened, and a handsome man with a nasty scrape on his forehead walked in. His eyes and hair—except for a gray patch surrounding a small bald spot—were the color of Amy's; he had the same high cheekbones and full lips, and Moran knew this was Jonathan Kaslov, the mad uncle and telepath.

He wanted to shout at Kaslov to get back, but his voice stuck in his throat. Levin turned so the gun pointed at Kaslov. Kaslov ignored it. He smiled shyly and said, "I was watching *Hawaii Five O*, Captain, and suddenly knew you were here. I was sure it wasn't to check health violations, so I thought I'd stop by and add my two cents, as it were. You know they're right, of course. You can't keep her. . . ."

Kaslov's eyes rolled and seemed to flick out of sight under the lids for a second. In a deep, creaking voice that made Moran shiver, he said, "Remember the day in the hospital when it got cold and you gave her water she couldn't ask for?"

Levin gasped, and Moran knew the uncle had hit home. Levin pulled the safety with a sharp click, and Kaslov finally deigned to look down at the gun pointed at his chest. But his eyes went right back to Levin's, and he said mildly, "I'm her only living blood relative, Captain. She'd hate you if you shot me."

Nothing happened for a second. Moran thought Levin was a lot crazier than Kaslov this second—in fact, Kaslov seemed to be the only sane one in the room—and the uncle was taking a terrible chance. But Levin gave a strangled cry, shoved the gun back in his jacket, and ran out of the office.

"I shoulda shot him," Levin muttered. He downed the rest of the Canadian Club and chased it with beer. "Shoulda shot the fucker right in the face."

"What'd you say, Captain?" Nino asked.

"Nothing. Gimme another shot." This was the fifth or sixth; Levin had lost count. He was at Nino's roadhouse getting blotto. Nino looked worried. "Maybe you had enough?"

Levin smacked the shot glass hard on the bar top, and

Nino rushed down the bar to get the Canadian Club bottle. Levin sipped the fresh shot, but his mouth was numb and he couldn't taste anything.

"Cold" and "hospital," the uncle had said. Levin remembered the cold okay; never really forgot it. It was a weird, abysmal feeling that brought with it mindless terror— blind, childish terror that went with your first roller coaster ride or the first time your folks made you sleep alone in the dark.

"Bullshit, horseshit, total, motherfucking, blue mudsucking shit . . ." Levin mumbled. This time Nino didn't ask what he'd said.

Levin had explained the cold to himself back then—he'd been coming down with something . . . that was it. And for the rest . . . He tried to think. The liquor swam in his head and he thought he'd pass out. He wouldn't mind; let Nino and the hired help deal with the remains. But he stayed conscious and his mind cleared a bit. He told himself he'd felt helpless and terrified back then because a few days before he'd found the poor corpse on the kitchen floor and the child in the closet. She was barely alive, and might stay in limbo, never speaking, seeing, or thinking again . . . being fed by a tube and changed like an infant for the rest of her days. So he'd been horrified because he wasn't the hard case he thought he was and he'd let his imagination run away with him. Simple.

He fumbled in his pocket and found his wallet.

"How much?" he asked.

"You know better," Nino said. "Cops don't pay here."

"How much?" Levin asked again. He must have looked really mean, and Nino toted it up in his head. "Twelve bucks," he said.

Levin dragged a twenty out and slapped it on the bar. "Keep the change."

He slid off the bar stool; his legs wobbled. Nino rushed around the bar—the place was empty by now—and took his arm. "Lemme call your wife . . . or one of the other cops to come get you."

"Fuck off."

"You can stay with me," Nino said. "I got a nice guest room. You got your own bath 'n' everything."

"Fuck off."

Levin aimed for the door, but it receded away from him. He grabbed a chair back, wrapped his fist around a slat, and hung on. The door stayed put and he tried again. This time he made it, with Nino right behind him. Nino opened the door for him, and Levin looked down at him. Nino's sallow face was greasy from the long day's work; his mustache looked oiled. He was an ugly little guy with stick-thin arms sticking out of the too wide short sleeves of his white shirt. He looked very worried, and Levin patted his shoulder. " 'S okay, Nino. You can't help me."

He staggered out, missed a step, and grabbed the railing. He made it down the next two steps, straightened up, and walked stiff-backed across the lot. He probably wouldn't have been able to find his car, but there were only three left in the lot; his was the only station wagon. He got in and started the motor. A wave of sickness hit him, and he waited to see if he'd have to throw up. The nausea passed, he eased the car out of the lot to the road and headed home.

He thought he'd get lost, but the homing instinct was strong and he made it to Windy Ridge without one wrong turn only to miss his own driveway and wind up at the end of the development. He turned around, and drove back at three miles an hour. In the Jackson driveway Larry's little ChrisCraft loomed whitely out of the dark on its trailer. By now Larry usually had the boat in the water, moored up in Branford. But Jeannie had told Levin that she'd heard from Nan Chaffe that Larry Jackson had disseminated bladder cancer and the little boat was for sale.

Everything sucks, Levin thought. *The world sucks. . . .*

Thirty-five-year-old men get bladder cancer and die; little girls get locked in closets and come out with something dangerous in their heads . . .

"Can that shit," Levin said out loud.

He found his driveway, turned wide, and felt the wheels

crunch over one of Jeannie's prize yews. He'd never get the car in the garage without scraping the sides, and he left it in the driveway and went inside. He meant to go right to his room and pass out next to his wife, but he stopped at Amy's door, then went inside.

She slept on her back with a square of moonlight right in her face. He knew he'd never get tired of looking at that face. Then he looked around the room for the teddy bear, seal, book, any of the things she called her own. Her schoolbooks were on the little white desk, and a Raggedy Ann doll that belonged to Greta was slumped in the chair next to the bed. The rest of the stuff was gone. He told himself she'd squirreled it away out of sight, but he knew it wasn't true. Amy used to sleep with the teddy bear, the book was kept on the table next to her bed, the seal on the bookcase.

He broke into a sweat, hiccuped and tasted booze and stale pizza. He was tainting the air she breathed and he left her room and went to his own. Jeannie was sound asleep with the air conditioner off, and the windows wide open to the first cool night they'd had in days. He went around to her side of the bed.

"Where's the teddy bear?" he whispered to her. "*They* knew it was gone, why didn't we?" Jeannie didn't stir.

He undressed but didn't bother with pajamas and went to bed in his underwear for the first time in his married life. The room swayed sickeningly, and he thought he'd have to run for the toilet. But he passed out before he got sick and didn't wake up until after the kids had left for school. He didn't see Amy again until it was too late.

FOURTEEN

"You'll get her out of there," Kaslov had pleaded last night.

"Yes," said Moran.

"You have the power."

"Yes."

"She'll be heartbroken. She's just a little girl, she doesn't know why these terrible things have happened to her. She has to be comforted. I should do it." Kaslov had glanced at Hall, and Hall looked away. "But under the circumstances . . ." Kaslov had said.

And Moran had answered, "It's my job too. I'll talk to her."

They shook hands and Kaslov had said, "She won't hurt you, you know. Any more than Joseph Levin will shoot you."

This morning Moran had gone to Martha Dyer's office to fill out forms that would start the process of taking Amy away from the Levins, then left them with the secretary. He wasn't up to facing Dyer yet.

Now he'd come to keep the rest of his promise to talk to Amy. He climbed out of the car and into the parking lot of Westerly Elementary School. The building was long, low, and ugly with aluminum-frame windows in which the kids had hung paintings and construction paper cutouts. Across the road from the school a building crew was busy destroying a little lake. Backhoes crawled over the shore, tearing up trees, stripping the land. Dirt sifted into the water, turning it brown at the banks, but farther out the water was still clear blue. Moran knew that wouldn't last long. There were no town sewers out here, and new cheap houses with inadequate septic systems would poison the water; in a couple of years the little lake would die. He felt a pang for it. They'd ruined this place; they were ruining the whole state. He'd get out; he'd take Mary and the kid to New Hampshire . . . or back to Brooklyn. He grinned at the disparity of choices he'd given himself. He left a window open at the top so the car wouldn't be an oven when he and Amy got into it and walked along a cyclone fence edging the playing field to the school gates. School was almost out, the gates were open, and buses were lined up with motors running, sending clouds of blue smoke into the still, warm air. Women waited in parked cars to take their kids to today's dancing or violin class . . . to orthodontist or shrink appointments.

He took up a post next to the gate.

Kaslov had been right. Amy'd never hurt Moran, but he was going to hurt her in a few minutes and he'd rather cut off his arm. By now he knew Amy Kaslov wanted to be Jeannie Levin someday; to have a husband and kids and a home of her own: to be a super wife and mother, who kept the house spotless and put up jams and jellies and jars of tomatoes in the fall, and baked cookies for Christmas, and kept the weird power that he could still barely conceive of a deep secret until it seemed like a childhood dream.

She had to leave the Levins, but that wasn't the end of her. He and Hall would find a good place for her. She was sweet and pretty, and most people would like her, want to protect her. It was just her lousy luck to wind up in the one house on earth where Paulie Levin lived. They said there was no substitute for blind, dumb luck. It was the only maxim Moran believed.

A gray-uniformed man came out of the school building

and hooked back the doors. A minute later the bell rang and kids started streaming out. Today was the last school day for a lot of the towns around here and the kids were wild. They pushed past each other to get out the door and ran whooping up the walk to the buses. It was a mob, but he knew he could pick Amy's face out of ten thousand screaming kids.

A few minutes later the stream thinned and Greta Levin came through the door, pulled by the hand by another little girl. Greta kept looking back in the doorway. Amy would probably be the next one out, and Moran got ready to intercept her. The girls got to one of the buses, Greta stopped dead, and it looked like she was arguing with the other girl. Then the bus driver leaned out and said something, and Greta reluctantly climbed onto the bus. Gears ground, and the bus pulled away and turned down the drive to the road. Amy had not appeared.

Moran looked back at the school doors. They were empty; so was the walk. The last bus had shut its doors and trundled off down the drive.

When the bell rang, Amy leaped to her feet and joined the crush at the door; it was the last day of school, the best day of the year. No more homework, no more English or history for two months. Greta and Cissy were waiting for her at the front door so they could all ride home together. Amy and Greta lived in the same family, so they couldn't be in the same homeroom. They'd hated the separation, but now it was over and they'd spend all day, every day, together. They'd help Jeannie in the garden, go shopping in town and to the movies with Cissy on Saturday afternoons, and Joe said they'd take weekend trips north to the Berkshires. Amy didn't know what a Berkshire was, but she knew it would be wonderful. Maybe they'd go this Sunday . . . without Paulie. He'd been avoiding them; maybe he'd keep on all summer.

She finally squeezed out the door into the crowded hallway. Someone grabbed her arm and she turned around and saw a girl of about six with thick, blond pigtails that stuck straight out from her head and a line of freckles across her nose. She stared at Amy.

"You Amy Kaslov?"

"Yes." Amy was in a hurry, but the little girl was awful cute with those freckles and that hair that looked like yellow yarn. Amy leaned down to her. "Something wrong? Are you lost?"

The little girl giggled sort of nastily and said, "Your sister Dorothy's in the locker room of the old gym. She says to come quick because something's happened and she needs you." The girl giggled harder and crowed, "The *boys'* locker room." Then she slipped away too quickly for Amy to grab her and got lost in the mob of kids heading for the door.

Amy stood still, trying to think what to do. Kids rushed past, bumping her. She slipped out of the way and stood against the wall.

The little girl had said *Dorothy;* it had to be Greta, Amy didn't know any real Dorothys, and no one else would call themselves her sister. But the whole thing felt wrong and she stood on tiptoe, trying to look over the heads of the crowd to see if Cissy was at the front door. Cissy might know what was going on. But the door was too far away to see who was there. Besides, if Greta was hurt or something, Amy was wasting time.

She knew where the old gym was. Cissy had told her about it one day while Mr. Simms listened, adding corrections and comments. The old gym was dangerous; no one was supposed to go down there. It had been built some years ago (neither Cissy nor her father knew exactly when) and was supposed to be the finest gym wing in the county. Months after it was finished, the floor buckled, and a boy playing basketball fell and was badly hurt.

"They say he'll never walk again," Cissy had said gravely.

The school board sent up to Hartford to get an engineer to come and see what could be done about the place. Nothing, it turned out. The gym architect was a dodo, the foundation was cheap cinder block sunk in a swamp. They could pour enough concrete to build Hoover Dam and it'd still sink. It would only get worse, and someday the roof would cave in and they'd have a bunch of dead kids along with the paralyzed one. There was nothing they could do but close it down and build a new one. So the new gym went up on the other side of the building where the land was ledge, not swamp, and the old gym was slated to be torn down; but by then the town had run out of dough. They tried bond issues, but they were defeated. "We pay enough goddamn taxes," said Mr. Simms. So the old gym stayed where it was, closed off from the rest of the school by a chain across the staircase that led down to it.

Amy got to the staircase. The halls had quieted down; only a few kids passed. They didn't notice her, and she hoped a teacher wouldn't happen by and see her. She unhooked the chain easily, slipped past and rehooked it, then went down the stairs to the gym entryway. This was forbidden territory. It should be dark and spooky down here, especially since there were no windows. But the doors to the gym itself were propped open invitingly (she'd expected them to be shut, maybe locked), and sunlight streamed out into the hall. Amy went into the gym.

Her feet gritted on the dirt on the floor. The windows were filthy, and kids had come down here, even though they weren't supposed to, and scrawled their names and dirty sayings all over the walls. The place was huge, totally silent. She saw the famous buckle where the floor sagged in the middle with boards around it rippling like disturbed water. Paint had chipped off the bleacher benches, exposing light gray wood underneath, and brown drips from leaks in the roof streaked the yellowish tile. A basketball hoop hung at one end, under it was a door marked BOYS. Someone had painted SUCK next to BOYS with an exclamation point after it. It must be meant to be nasty, but Amy didn't understand it. She walked gingerly across the rippling floor to the middle of the gym and called, "Dorothy . . ."

There was no answer. She went to the BOYS door, pushed it open, and called, "Dorothy . . ."

No answer. She went all the way in. It was sunny and dirty here too. Dust particles rode in the streaks of sunlight, sort of like in the house in Bridgeton, and the locker doors were busted open and hung loose on their hinges.

She heard a noise and froze, but it was quiet again. It must have been one of the locker doors swinging in a stray draft. She called a couple more times and was ready to give up when she noticed another door down one aisle of lockers marked WASHROOM. It was crazy for Greta to wind up in a boys' washroom, but you couldn't help where things happened to you.

She went down the aisle and through the last door. It opened to a large room with a tiled floor and walls. On one wall over crusted sinks hung on a long metal frame with a few pieces of mirror left in it. The rest of the mirror lay broken on the floor in mean-looking spikes. Strange porcelain fixtures stood against another wall. They looked like elongated toilets, and she figured they were for boys to use since they peed standing up. She'd seen old Tommy Sloane pee behind the barn once, beating down the grass with a stream of yellow. He didn't know she was there, and she'd sneaked away before he saw her. It had been so embarrassing, she could not look Tommy in the face for days after that.

"Dorothy . . . Greta . . . Dorothy . . ." she called.

There was no answer, and she knew by now there wasn't going to be. Greta was not down here and never had been; the whole thing was a mean joke. Paulie must have bribed or scared the little girl into finding Amy and telling her that lie about Greta. Amy was easy to spot since she was thinner than most of the other girls in homeroom 302, and the only one with black-black hair. She didn't know why he'd done it for a second, then she figured it out.

Greta and Cissy probably waited awhile, then thought she'd taken another bus, and left without her. By now all the buses were gone. Amy would have to walk back.

She didn't mind walking, but she wasn't sure of the way. If she got lost, it would be dark before she got there. Jeannie would be frantic. Frantic women got mad (her mother used to), and tonight's dinner, which should be terrific since it was their first night of freedom, would be miserable . . . courtesy of Paulie.

She could call Jeannie—she'd memorized the number long ago—but she'd loaned Cissy the last of her allowance at lunch today so Cissy could buy soda. Cissy was a spendthrift who'd run out of money every Friday and hit up Amy or Greta. She shouldn't have drunk soda, anyway; it rotted your teeth. Right now Amy was very annoyed at Cissy, but getting annoyed wouldn't help. She had to walk, so she better get started. She'd head for town, ask directions from there, then walk facing the traffic, the way her grandmother had taught her. Amy hoisted her books higher to ease the strain on her shoulders and headed for the door. It opened before she got there, and three masked men came in.

"Captain Levin, please," Moran said.

"Who's calling?"

Levin might not take the call if Moran gave his name. He said, "I'm a physician. I want to talk to him about his ward."

They put him on hold and went to get Levin. Moran was calling because he did not know what else to do. He had waited outside the Westerly School until the gray-uniformed man came back out, unhooked the doors, and shut them. Moran had heard the locks click home, and panic streaked through him. He knew she was still in there, and he'd run up the walk to the door and looked through the glass insert and saw the gray-uniformed man pushing a dust mop down a long hallway. Moran rapped on the glass and the man looked up.

"There's a kid in there," Moran had shouted.

The man turned away and kept mopping. Moran banged on the glass; the man ignored him; Moran kicked the door so hard, he jarred his leg and rattled the door. The man gave

Moran the finger and went back to his mopping. Moran went down the walk and looked up at the building. Afternoon sunlight hit the windows, turning them blank silver. The place looked shut up, empty.

He rushed around the side, looking for another door. There was one leading out to a back parking lot that was empty now except for a panel truck with BLACK OAK MAINTE-NANCE painted on the side. He ran up and tried the door; it was locked. He pounded on it; nothing happened. He went back along the fence to the public lot; his car was the only one left. Across the lake the machines had stopped, and a line of beat-up cars heaved down the track from the site to the road. Everything was shutting down, and Amy was locked in there alone. . . .

The phone connected. Levin's voice said, "This is Captain Levin."

"It's Moran, Joe. Don't hang up on me. Amy's locked in the school."

"What are you talking about?"

"I went to the school to tell her in person that I would not be her doctor anymore. It would seem like a desertion otherwise, and she doesn't need that." This was a lie, but Moran never had minded lying to adults, and riling Levin with the truth wouldn't help Amy. "But she never came out."

"I see," Levin said guardedly. "Where are you?"

"Tuttle's Drugstore in Westerly Center. It was the first public phone I could find. I waited until all the kids were gone. I saw Greta and another kid get on the bus, but no Amy. Now the school's locked. It's probably locked both ways so kids can't hide out until it's empty, then sneak out and vandalize the place and get away. And she's still in there."

"There's five hundred kids in that school, Moran. You missed her."

"I didn't miss her. She's in there."

Levin was silent and Moran lost his temper. "For chrissake, Levin, put a fucking sock on your fucking righteous anger. School's out for the year, there's no chess or drama club meeting, no soccer practice. She's alone in there. They probably turned out the lights . . . God damn you . . . she's locked in the dark, back in that closet—" He stopped, breathing hard into the phone.

Then Levin said quietly, "Go back there, Charlie. I'll meet you."

They weren't men, Amy realized, just tall boys wearing ski masks. She recognized them, anyway: Paulie was the one in the red mask; the other two were the boys from the gauntlet. Bobby wore the green mask with a pine tree on it, and Len (whom Paulie called Pizza Face) had the black one with SKI VERMONT printed on it.

They must be here to help Paulie beat her up so he could get even for the black eye and busted nose he'd gotten on her account. She'd been hit before. It wouldn't be so bad . . . nothing compared to three days in the closet or getting thrown across the room by her father; child's play compared to watching Nana's house burn. And if she didn't carry on, they might get bored with hitting her before she got really hurt.

She decided she wouldn't tell on them. She'd say she'd gotten hurt falling down—that's how Mrs. Chaffe explained the bruises Mr. Chaffe gave her. Paulie might be grateful to her for not ratting on him and he'd start to leave her alone. That'd be worth a beating; everything was for the best, as Tommy Sloane used to say.

She backed away from them; they came forward. Black Mask (Len) circled around behind her and she lost sight of him. She moved to the side. Paulie and Green Mask (Bobby) spread out so she couldn't run around them and get out the door. Then Black Mask grabbed her hard from behind and her books flew out from under her arms and skidded across the filthy floor. She didn't think she'd ever be able to touch them again, which was a shame, since Mrs. Faye had written in Amy's math book, "To Amy Kaslov, my best student of '73, good luck in fifth grade."

Black Mask held her, Green Mask closed in on her, Paulie stayed where he was. She thought Paulie'd get the first punch, but it must be Bobby's turn for some reason. Maybe they'd drawn straws and he'd won. He got very close; she shut her eyes and braced herself. Nothing happened except that he got so close, his dead-grass smelling breath blew in her face. She opened her eyes, ready to shut them in an instant if his fist was coming at her. But he was too close to hit her, so close that she couldn't see anything but his eyes. They were blank, like her father's when he was really plastered and ready to pass out. Except Bobby's were even funnier-looking because the pupils were so teeny. His lips touched her face, slid along her cheek to her ear, and her insides shriveled like they had one night in Bridgeton when she'd gone down to the kitchen to try to find some crumbs in the Saltine box because she was too hungry to sleep. The kitchen had been moonlit and she'd seen the shape of the box clearly on the counter. She crossed the room, grabbed the box, and felt something run over the back of her hand. She'd turned on the light and seen roaches crawling all over the box. One fat brown one ran across her hand and everything in her had shriveled up, like it was doing now.

Bobby plastered his mouth against hers and tried to stick his tongue in her mouth. She gagged; he pulled back. "Aw, honey," he said gently, "it won't be so bad. I know what girls like, believe me. You'll like it after a while. They all do."

Then she realized that they weren't going to beat her up; they were going to do *it* to her. Cissy and Greta had told her about *it*; she sort of knew, anyway. Her mother and father's bed had squeaked when they did *it* at night; the Avon lady had caught her husband doing *it* with his secretary. It was the worst thing they could do to her, short of murdering her. But maybe they'd do that too. The news was full of stories about girls' bodies being found in woods and gullies after *it* was done to them.

Paulie wouldn't join in; he would hate touching her. He must be here for the killing . . . .

She couldn't believe it; and then, as if to convince her, Black Mask-Len reached around the front of her body and unzipped her jeans. She screamed and kicked out, trying to hit Bobby. He danced back, grabbed the cuffs of her jeans, and yanked them off, leaving her with nothing on below the waist except her panties, socks, and one shoe. The other shoe had come off with the jeans. Her face burned, and she thought she'd die from shame. He looked her up and down. "Long legs," he murmured. "I like long legs." He balled the jeans and shoe up and threw them across the room. They sailed lazily past Paulie's head. He watched them land in a heap.

"Please . . . " she cried.

"Please . . . " Paulie mimicked. She couldn't think how he'd gotten so mean. He'd been well fed all his life; Greta told her Joe'd never beaten him before last Sunday. He had a nice house, clean clothes . . . Jeannie was his mother . . .

"I'll tell Joe! You hear me, Paulie Levin," she yelled. "Joe'll kill you."

"You won't tell no one nothing," he yelled back. "You'll be dirt after this. No one who knows will ever touch you. You'll be another dirty bohunk, and Dad won't let Greta come near you. . . . "

"Nooo," she wailed.

"Yesss," he wailed back in the same tone. And he was right; she'd be spoiled when they were done. If Joe found out, he'd try not to look at her, and when he did, it'd be with a cold, distant look, like she used to get from Mrs. Cosmos at the deli in Bridgeton when she asked for another quart of milk on the tab. Paulie yelled, "Greta'll tell Cissy . . . Cissy'll tell the other kids. No one'll talk to you. Everyone knows girls get it 'cause they want it. You want it. . . . "

"Sure she does," Bobby said softly. "She just doesn't know it yet."

Bobby started undoing his pants, and she shook her head violently from side to side. He grabbed her hair, forced her to stop moving. "Don't fight it, sweetie. When it's inevitable, relax and enjoy it. You will too. I promise. Just pretend we're alone. . . . "

"That's right," Paulie yelled wildly. "Pretend we're not here to see the little bohunk with her pants off and her legs spread."

"Ignore them," Bobby whispered hoarsely. "Just think about me. I'm going to give you something nice and hard to hold." He groaned against her cheek; his breath was hot on her skin.

There was no cold, nothing to warn her, but *next time* had come, and Jeannie wasn't here to stop her. She remembered all the things her uncle had told her, but he didn't mean *this*. He didn't mean for her to "relax and enjoy it," then try to feel better by thinking about ironed cotton and bowls of soup. He'd want her to stop them, no matter how.

She looked past Bobby's sweaty face, which was twisted with excitement she didn't understand and didn't want to, and saw the spikes of broken glass under the sinks. One was wide and almost as long as she was tall. Light hit it and made her blink, but she kept looking at it. Suddenly Bobby shivered and jerked his head back, clipping her jaw. She barely felt it. He turned his head and looked at the glass too. Then, with that dragging gait, like her father that time in the prison and Paulie when he pulled himself across the porch back toward the door of the burning kitchen, Green Mask-Bobby shuffled across the tile floor to the spike of broken glass.

"Whattaya doing?" Paulie cried.

Bobby ignored him.

"You okay, Bob?" called Len. Bobby got to the piece of mirror and bent over slowly as if his back hurt. He grabbed the glass and lifted it in both hands, like the sword in a crusader movie. Sharp edges cut his palms and blood ran, but he didn't seem to feel it. Paulie charged at him, yelling, "What the fuck, Whitman, you can't quit now!"

Amy screamed so hard, her eyes bulged. "Hit him!"

Bobby swung the spike and chopped Paulie hard in the

side of the neck. Paulie shrieked and staggered backward.

"Again," Amy screamed.

Bobby raised the sword and brought it down with all his might. It missed Paulie's head and sank deep into his shoulder. Paulie's shriek turned liquid, blood splashed everywhere, a glob hit Bobby in the chest. Paulie staggered away, trying to pull the mask off. But his head hung lopsided; the mask stuck.

"Again!" Amy screamed.

Just then Len ran at Bobby, and Bobby swung the sword again and sliced Len across the neck. The tip broke off and stuck in Len's throat. He screeched, grabbed the chunk of glass, and tried to pull it out. The edges cut his hand, blood slicked the chunk, and his hands slipped on it. It wouldn't budge. Blood pumped over his hands. "Oh, shit," he moaned. "Fucking shit . . . "

Amy kept her eyes on Paulie. In the end he *was* like the girl in the horror movie who ignores all the warning signs and goes up to the haunted attic or down into the basement, even though everyone knows the monster is up there. Amy must be the monster. Paulie got the mask off at last and tried to breathe, but blood bubbled out of the slit in his neck; he was choking on it.

He staggered toward her; she stood her ground. He tried to talk, it came out as a gurgle. Then he fell to his knees, crawled a little way closer to her, and fell forward in the pool of blood. His hands scrabbled around in it and he choked and rattled for another minute, then lay still.

Len was still making noise behind her, but she didn't want to see or hear anymore and clapped her hands over her ears, shut her eyes, and stayed like that for a long time.

When she uncovered her ears and opened her eyes, it was quiet. She didn't remember where she was or how she'd gotten here. She was bare-legged; the floor was covered with someone's blood. She didn't want to get any of it on her. She started across the room, trying to step around the mess, but some wet the bottom of her foot. She looked down. She'd lost a shoe somewhere and was ruining the new pink-flowered socks Jeannie had bought her. She'd find the shoe later, her pants too.

She got to the door and looked back. A tall, almost grown-up boy wearing a green ski mask stood in the middle of the room holding a piece of mirror with the tip broken off. She didn't know what he was doing, but that glass looked dangerous. She'd better get out of there. She opened the door and went into a dusty room lined with lockers. The next thing she knew, she was at a side door that led to the teachers' parking lot. There was a patch of woods around it and a little lake on the other side of the road. If she could get through the woods, she could wash in the lake. She wasn't clear what she had to wash off, but she was sticky with sweat and something else it was better not to think about. She imagined reaching the lake, walking into the cool water. She pushed the door handle. It didn't give. She tried a couple of times, then stood on tiptoe and looked out through the glass inset at the woods and piece of lake she could see through the trees. She banged the handle, pounded on the door. It was no use.

She slid down against the wall until she sat on the floor. It was cold on her thighs and she looked down; her jeans were gone and something stained her sock. Her eyes snapped away and looked at the tops of the trees and the slice of sky she could see through the window. She got terribly sleepy and closed her eyes . . . .

Grandma was walking with her across the pasture toward the house, giving Amy mints that tasted like pine needles. They got to the house (it hadn't burned down after all . . . that was a bad dream). Jeannie and Joe were in the living room having drinks before dinner. Greta was in the kitchen stirring a pot of something that smelled nasty. Amy looked over her shoulder and saw the pot was full of steaming blood. She almost woke up to escape the bad dream. Then she sort of remembered and decided the dream wasn't so bad, she'd stay here, after all. In the next dream she walked into the lake. The bottom sloped, thick black water rose up to her neck, covered her chin. The last time she got locked in, Joe had rescued her. She hoped he wouldn't this time because she didn't want to come back, and she kept going until the black oily water covered her head.

FIFTEEN

"No, Amy, wait . . . " Jonathan cried.

Marty's voice said, "Jonathan . . . Sport . . . Jon . . . "

Jonathan opened his eyes. He was sitting under the maple tree, Marty bent over him. Perkins and his daughter Dorry, who was here for visiting day, stood a few feet away watching. Jonathan looked up at the shreds of blue sky through the maple branches and felt Amy slip all the way under into total blackness. He tried desperately to hang onto her, but she was gone. Marty took his arm. "Want to stand up, Sport?"

Jonathan nodded, Marty heaved him to his feet, and Perkins whined. "We were having a picnic. Dorry brought sandwiches and some coffee and brownies. We were having a nice time. Then his eyes rolled back like they do, and he crawled to the tree like a sick snake. We tried to get him to talk but he sat there staring at nothing, like a nut. . . . " Perkins was close to tears. "It was real nice up to then."

"You want me to take you back, Jon?"

"No, I'm okay, Marty," Jonathan lied. "I just have to go to the can." He turned to Dorry. "Pardon me, Dorry, I'm not used to having ladies around."

Perkins giggled. "That's the God's honest truth.

Couldn't call Irma a lady. She takes her pants off, then pulls her skirt up." He laughed wildly; Dorry blushed purple. From across the lawn Sam Skerry yelled, "C'mon, Marty . . . Billie made a point . . . Billie made a point!" The patient-visitor volleyball game was in full swing. Marty looked at Jonathan. "You sure you're okay?"

"Fine," Jonathan said. Marty nodded at the thermos on the picnic mat. "Don't drink too much of that," he said. "You'll be up all night."

Marty went back to the game. Jonathan started toward the building. "Where're you going?" Perkins asked.

"To the can, like I said. Thanks for the sandwiches, Dorry."

"But you'll be right back?" Perkins whimpered.

"Right back," Jonathan said. He was lying again. He was not coming back.

He hurried across the lawn. Visitors and patients walked together, some with their arms around each other. They were quiet. Visiting day was almost over and everything had been said.

In the lobby more visitors sat on the hard benches built in along the walls. They had come to see the patients who'd lost their nerve at the last minute and would not come down. They spent visiting day cowering upstairs while their folks waited vainly in the lobby with shopping bags full of cakes, cookies, new books, summer shirts. Some of the visitors would cry tonight as they unpacked the bags, and their sadness enveloped Jonathan, weighed him down . . . he waded through it to the desk.

Mrs. Porbichev was on duty reading one of her paperback romances. She looked up brightly. "Can I help you, Jon?"

"I need the phone book for Westerly. I think it's in the Millbridge book." She looked under the counter and pulled out the book and handed it to him. She ought to ask him what he wanted it for; Miss Liddell would. But after three years of widowhood Mrs. Porbichev had found a boyfriend and was too happy to ask questions. He took the phone book to an empty space on the bench and found a middle section of blue pages that listed schools, fire departments, public parks, and so on. But there were several schools in Westerly, all with people's names. It didn't even say which were grade schools.

Jeannie Levin knew the name of the school Amy went to. Calling her would be torture, but he had to do it. He found the Levins' number, memorized it, and took the book back to Mrs. Porbichev. Then he went to the pay phone next to the basement door. He had not used one for years, but there was a plasticized card on the phone with instructions. He followed them, dialed the number, and a tinny voice came on and told him to deposit eighty cents. He searched his pockets wildly and came up with forty cents. He tried to tell the operator that he wasn't going to talk long and couldn't they do it for forty cents, just this once. But the tinny voice repeated, "Eighty cents please . . . that'll be eighty cents for the first three minutes." He hung up and went outside to find Marty, who was still at the volleyball game. Patients and visitors made mixed teams and tried to play together; they were all tired by now, and the game looked like something out of *Alice in Wonderland.* The thought startled him. Suddenly they were *them*—other, mad—and he wasn't one of them.

Marty touched his arm. "Hi, Sport, wanna play?"

"No. I need forty cents."

"What for?"

He lied to Marty again. "To call Amy. Seeing everyone with their relatives made me lonely. I thought I'd call my relative and say hello."

Marty's eyes softened. He dug into his pocket and came up with forty cents.

"I'll pay you back the end of the month," Jonathan said.

Marty laughed. "Forget it. I owe you two hundred thousand in gin losses. Take the forty cents . . . we're even."

Westerly Elementary was officially named General Starr School, Jeannie Levin had told Jonathan on the phone. He'd given her the same story he gave Marty about being lonely and wanting to hear Amy's voice. He told her he needed to know the school's name because someone had asked him, and he was ashamed of not knowing where his only living relative went to school. Jeannie Levin told him to call anytime before nine when the girls went to bed and he could talk to Amy. He thanked her too profusely and hung up feeling colder, crueler . . . saner . . . than he ever had in his life. He knew her son was dead and she didn't, and he didn't tell her because it was in his best interest not to. He hated and admired himself at the same time.

Now he knew which school. Next he had to get out of here and find it. The rejected visitors were still in the lobby. Sun came through the west-facing windows, showing the streaks Mr. McCormack had left when he'd washed them. It was getting late.

Mrs. Porbichev was on the phone, and through the glass staff office window behind her Jonathan saw Marty Vespa's head. He crossed the lobby, trying to keep his shoes from squeaking on the stone floor. He got to the half gate next to the desk. Mrs. Porbichev talked on into the headset with her back to him. He reached over, unbolted the gate, crossed behind her, and went into the office. Marty was at the desk with a sandwich in front of him. "Hi, Sport, did you talk to your niece?"

"She wasn't home yet," Jonathan said.

"Too bad. You can try later. Want half a sandwich? It's deviled ham, which I hate. But Franny makes it 'cause it's cheap."

Jonathan nodded, and Marty handed him the half sandwich. The spread stained the bread pink, but it tasted better than it looked. He glanced through the glass wall; the switchboard was empty. Mrs. Porbichev must've gone to the ladies' room. He said, "I need your help, Marty."

Marty looked wary. "For what, Jonathan?"

"My niece is in trouble. You know about me, Marty. We pretend I'm just like the other loonies, but you know better, don't you?"

Marty didn't answer.

Jonathan said, "You remember Ida Barnes. And that you helped me get my niece out of the closet. No way I could have known she was in there, right, Mart? I pulled my hair out—"

"Don't—" Marty cried.

"I won't. It wouldn't do any good, anyway, because I need much more than a phone call this time. I need your car and all the money you've got."

"You got nerve, Jon. I'll give you that."

"I've got more than nerve. I read minds, whether I want to or not. My niece is in trouble; I have to help her. You're my only chance . . . *her* only chance."

Marty just stared at him.

"Answer me," Jonathan pleaded.

"Eat your sandwich," Marty said gently.

Jonathan stood up and spoke rapidly. "Mart, listen. I'll sock you, steal the car keys and money. You can say you never knew what hit you and that way you're off the hook. I gotta do it. I can't let her go. She's all I got. Besides, it wasn't her fault, any more than it's your fault you're a southpaw and have blue eyes. You can say I just hauled off while you were peacefully eating your sandwich. . . . " The moment was perfect. Marty was staring down miserably at his half of the deviled ham sandwich, and Jonathan hauled off with everything he had and punched Marty on the chin. Planted one on him from the ankle, as the boys used to say in the old neighborhood, trying to talk tough in Connecticut. Jonathan never tried to be tough, but he'd just landed a perfect uppercut— or Marty Vespa had a glass jaw—because his eyes glazed and went dead, and his head fell forward on the desktop with a thunk.

Jonathan almost fainted, then he saw that Marty's breathing was steady, and his color was okay. He eased him gently off the chair onto the floor and dragged him into the office supply closet. He tucked his legs up, took the rubber pad (presumably for someone with hemorrhoids) off the swivel chair, and pillowed poor Marty's head with it. Then Jonathan went through his pockets. He got his wallet, which was stuffed (staff got paid on Friday), his car keys, and the hypo case all the orderlies carried. Jonathan unzipped it. Inside were three disposables filled with Librium or pentothal. Either one'd put Marty out for a while, but Jonathan quaked at the idea of giving the shot. What if the needle broke off? What if he got air in it and killed this man who'd always been so good to him; whom he liked so much. Loved.

Only not like he loved Amy, or none of this would be happening. In fact, he'd never loved anyone, not even his father, the way he loved that little girl. That must be what children did to you. Marty had a kid, so maybe he'd understand. Jonathan lifted the needle out of the case, held it up, and pushed the plunger until a tiny drop of liquid appeared at the tip. Then, before he lost his nerve, he pushed up the sleeve of Marty's white jacket and stuck the needle into Marty's arm exactly as Marty'd done to him a million times and pushed the plunger home. Marty kept on breathing; his color didn't change.

Jonathan grabbed a sheet of paper and scrawled on it, "Sorry, sorry . . . Love, Jonathan Kaslov," and scotch taped it to Marty's jacket.

He looked out through the glass wall. The desk was still unmanned, so Mrs. Porbichev must be doing a full-scale makeup job for her boyfriend. He crossed the lobby, went out the front door and around the building to the employee parking lot.

Marty had a new black Chevy he called Black Beauty. It was the only shiny black car in the lot except for Hall's Cadillac. He went to it, praying that no one would pick this minute to look out a side window, and unlocked the door. It was broiling inside. He'd forgotten how hot closed cars got in the summer. But he was afraid to open the window since reflections on the glass might hide his face.

He pulled out into the back drive, trying to think how he'd get past Mr. Cermak, who guarded the back gate. Mr.

Cermak got chewed out last time Jonathan escaped; he would be on the alert. Jonathan could not sock him. He was never going to hit anyone in the face again. Besides, his knuckles were still sore from the punch he'd given Marty. If Mr. Cermak tried to stop him, he'd just floor it, crash through the barrier, and let them chase him. Marty had said Black Beauty was an eight-cylinder rocket.

But the charter buses that brought the visitors from downstate were pulled up in the drive by the back gate, the bar was raised to accommodate a handsome blue-and-silver bus with the word BLUEBIRD painted on the back of it, and Mr. Cermak and the drivers were shooting crap on a blanket on one side of the line of buses. Mr. Cermak had the dice and didn't even look up as Jonathan squeezed Black Beauty around the far side of the big bus and through the gate to the road.

For the second time in less than a year he was free. Clear road stretched ahead of him, and over the rise, a million more miles of road led anywhere he wanted to go. He rolled down the window, fresh air blew in his face, and he leaned out in a sudden burst of exhilaration and shouted, "Jonathan Kaslov to the rescue!" Then he calmed right down; he didn't know how he was going to rescue her or what he'd do afterward. Come back here somehow, he decided. After all, Limekiln was home.

"He must've missed her," said the janitor. His name, Jackson, was embroidered in red on his gray shirt. Levin looked at Moran, and Moran shook his head. Levin said to Jackson, "Open the door."

"No can do," Jackson said with the joy of petty power lighting his eyes. "Need authorization."

Levin pulled out his badge and ID and held them under the janitor's nose. Mr. Jackson paled and Levin said, "Now open the door." Levin towered over the janitor. He looked mean, and Moran thought the jerk had better move. Jackson stammered, "Y-yes, Cap'n, right away."

He took a ring of keys off his belt, unlocked the school door, and held it open for them. They went past him through a vestibule and into the main hall. "Ammmyy . . . " Levin called. There was no answer.

"See," Jackson said, "no one's here."

Then they heard a far-off bubbling sound, like someone laughing underwater.

"Where's that coming from?" Levin asked.

"Beats me," the janitor whispered. They heard it again . . . a wet, sickly sound that echoed slightly off the metal lockers lining the hall.

"It could be downstairs," the janitor said.

"How do we get down there?" Levin asked.

"Stairway at the end of the hall, to your right. But it's shut up down there."

Levin raced away, and Moran went after him. Then Jackson followed, calling, "It's shut up, I tell you. Place's dangerous . . . no one's supposed to go down there. . . . "

They got to the staircase and looked down into darkness.

"Turn on the lights," Levin said.

"They're disconnected," said Jackson. "It's all shut up, like I said. Whole wing's rotten from the slab up."

"Lemme have that." Levin nodded at the flashlight attached to Jackson's belt next to the key ring. Jackson handed it to him. Levin unhooked the chain and went down the stairs. Moran hesitated a second, then went after him. Jackson stayed where he was. Halfway down, darkness enveloped them, and Levin turned on the flashlight. The narrow beam lit up the dusty asphalt-tile floor and plasterboard walls with holes poked through showing framing and tied-off wires. Straight ahead were shut doors with some chain coiled on the floor next to them.

It was hot and silent. The bubbling sound came from right behind them, and Levin whirled around. The beam hit a huge black figure hulking under the stairs, and Levin gasped and dropped the light. Moran leaped backward and hit a wall; a draft tickled his neck, stray wire poked him, and he came close to screaming. The light stayed on, rocking back and forth dizzyingly, lighting the figure in waves. Moran clamped his mouth shut to keep his teeth from chattering. Levin picked up the flashlight and trained it on the figure. It was just a boy about seventeen or eighteen. His face was ominously blank, tears streaked down his face, mixing with dust and blood. The bubbling sound was his sobbing.

"Bobby?" Levin said. "Bobby Whitman?"

The kid didn't answer; he didn't try to shield his eyes from the light. Levin moved the beam down his body. Blood stuck his shirt to his chest; it streaked his arms and soaked his shoes. Levin whipped the light back to the boy's face.

"Where is she?" he cried.

The kid sobbed.

"Where's Amy?"

"I don't think he can answer you," Moran said.

Levin lowered the light to the shoes again; bloody tracks led away from them and Levin followed them to the doors. He opened one, and let it shut behind him, leaving Moran alone in the dark with the kid.

Moran's eyes adjusted and he went to the kid. He took his arm, which was slick with sweat and crusty with drying blood and led him gently, insistently, around the staircase, up the steps into the light.

Jackson saw them. "Holy shit," he whispered.

Moran eased the boy down to sit on the top step. In one hand the kid clutched a piece of cloth. Moran pried it away from him and held it up.

"A ski mask?" Moran said. "What do you want with a ski mask in June?"

The kid didn't answer. He'd stopped crying, but that was worse in a way. Moran knew hysterical shock when he saw it, and this kid probably wouldn't say a coherent word for a couple of days, maybe longer. Moran went over him while the boy watched with a vaguely interested look on his face.

He was not hurt, except for some deep cuts on his hands, but they weren't enough to account for all the blood.

Moran looked up at the janitor. "Find a phone," he said. "Call Millbridge General . . . they're closest. Tell them we've got a shock victim . . . maybe worse to come."

The janitor took off down the hall. Moran propped the boy up sideways against the railing and rehooked the chain to keep the kid from falling forward. Then he went back down the stairs to find Levin.

He traversed the gym, the locker room, and finally pushed open the door to the boys' washroom, and smelled blood and years' old urine. Levin stood in the middle of the room. "Welcome, Charlie," he said steadily. "Welcome to the chamber of horrors."

The room reeked. Moran imagined the smell coating his tongue, sticking in his hair. Blood pooled on the floor, splattered the wall. He had not seen this much blood since he left the Yale–New Haven ER, and that had been dubbed a MASH unit by those in the know. On a par with Bellevue and King's County. Levin stood over one corpse; another was across the room. Moran looked down and saw Paulie Levin's dead, contorted face. The gaping slit in the neck was raw but drained; the kid had been dead awhile . . . at least an hour. Moran tried to think what could make a slit that wide and deep; even a razor seemed inadequate.

Then he saw the pieces of broken glass on the floor; looked up and saw the almost empty mirror frame over the sinks with a few spikes of silvered glass left in it. A piece of jagged glass would explain the wound in the Levin boy's neck and the cuts on the other kid's palms. He didn't want to know the rest. The silence stretched on. Levin was breathing heavily but evenly; his face was still, his eyes amazingly cold as they stared down at his son's corpse. Moran noticed a limp piece of red cloth in Levin's hand. Levin bent down, forced the boy's milky eyes closed, and draped the cloth over his face. It was another ski mask. This one had snowflakes on it. Levin straightened up and looked at Moran. "I pieced it together, Charlie. Figured it all out. Bobby had a mask, too, didn't he?"

Moran nodded.

"So'd the other one," Levin said, nodding at the body across the room. Its head was covered in black knit. "Look over there," Levin said. He pointed at a scattering of school-books covered with blood. "Look!" Levin commanded. Moran went to them and bent down to see the titles through the mess. There was a book for geography, one for social studies, another for basic math. They were grade-school books; the boys were high-school age.

"They're Amy's," Levin said.

Moran straightened up. A cruel, deadly smile appeared on Levin's face. "Now look over there," he ordered. He pointed at a small pile of blue cloth that lay at the edge of the mess, just outside the lake of blood. "Go on," Levin snarled. "Look."

Moran crossed the floor to it, trying not to think about what he was stepping in. He reached the spot, looked down at the small, pitiful-looking pile of cloth. "Pick it up," Levin said. Moran hesitated. "Go on," Levin ordered. Moran picked it up; there were a few blood spatters on it, but it was mostly clean. He held it in one hand, then both. It was a pair of child's jeans. On the floor under them was one girl's sum-mer shoe. Moran looked at Levin. "Get the picture?" Levin said softly.

Slowly, little by little, Moran did. "Oh, Christ," he whis-pered.

"Yeah," said Levin. "Christ on a bicycle . . . Christ on a Christmas tree. Did they do it, Moran? Did they really do that to her?"

Whatever they did to her, she did back to them in spades, Moran thought. Out loud he said, "I don't know."

"Give me the jeans," Levin said. "And the shoe." Moran handed them over. Levin stuck the shoe in his pocket, held the jeans tenderly against his chest for a moment, then leaned over his son's red-knit-draped face. "You dirty little shit," he whispered. "Fry in hell."

He straightened up. "Take the books, Charlie."

Moran picked up the small pile. Levin looked around the room, and Moran knew he was making sure they left no evidence that she'd been there.

"Let's find her," Levin said.

It didn't take long. She lay curled up in front of a side door with her cheek pressed against the floor. Levin ran to her, dropped the jeans, and sank to his knees next to her.

"Amy, honey . . . it's Joe."

She didn't move. Moran knelt next to Levin and turned her head faceup. Her skin was pale and clammy; her pulse was okay.

"Did they . . . rape her?" Levin whispered.

Moran looked down her body and shook his head. He moved her arms; they were flaccid. He pried at one eyelid; it resisted, then opened, and the pupil contracted quickly. He let the eye shut.

"What is it?" Levin asked.

"Psychogenic coma."

"Like before?"

"I didn't examine her the first time. But this probably isn't as bad. She's not dehydrated and starving."

"How long will it last?"

"Maybe a few minutes, maybe a long time."

"You bastards really cover your asses, don't you?" Levin growled.

Moran looked at him. "No, Levin. We really don't know."

A siren wailed in the distance. They raised their heads in unison.

"We gotta get her out of her," Levin said.

"To a hospital."

Levin glared at him. "No way, Moran. She's going home." He slid his hands under her to lift her.

"She should have an EEG, IV saline—" Moran said.

"No! You make do with whatever you got in your black bag."

"Joe . . . you know what she did down there."

Levin cradled her head against his chest.

"Yeah. She made dirtbag Bobby Whitman slice up the creeps who were going to rape her; same way she once made me give her a glass of water. So here she is, Charlie. Big-time killer. You want to feed her to the cops?"

Moran looked at her. Her hair was cut short, probably to keep cool in the summer; her face was totally relaxed, and she looked about five.

"No," he said, "I don't."

"Then open the door."

Moran tried. "It's locked," he said.

The siren had stopped. Levin said, "See what's going on in the front." Moran went up the main hall, saw the wash of red lights from the ambulance, and went back to Levin. "The ambulance is there. They'll see us if we go out that way."

Levin nodded. "Hold her a second," he said. Moran took Levin's place, letting Amy lean dead weight against him, and Levin faced the door. Moran felt the violence seeping up from downstairs and wanted Levin to pull the .38 and blast the door open. But Levin took a small bunch of picks out of his pocket, pulled one, and slid it into the lock. "Don't use these much anymore," he said as he worked the pick around the lock. "New rules of evidence-gathering and all that." He pushed against the handle. It gave and the door swung open.

Jonathan pulled off the highway at the Westerly exit and stopped in a Shell station to ask directions. The gas jockey was a bent-over man about fifty with a wen on his cheek; he stared at Jonathan's bald patch as he leaned in the window and told Jonathan how to find General Starr School. Jonathan followed the directions, found the school, but by then he was pretty sure she was gone. The drive and school lot were overrun with cop cars; sirens wailed up the road. It was no place for him; he didn't even have a driver's license. He drove past the school toward the town center. She was with Moran and Levin, and they were at Levin's house. He still got nothing from her but blackness. He should hurry, but the roads swarmed with cops, screaming their way to the carnage at General Starr School. It wouldn't do to speed.

He passed a crowded shopping mall with a lit-up Woolworth's in it and decided to stop and buy a hat to cover the bald patch and scraped forehead in case they were looking for him. The store was enormous, full of shoppers who'd stopped on their way home from work. Overhead lights turned people's faces sickly green. He found a bin of baseball caps and looked through them. He didn't have a favorite team, but Perkins loved the Red Sox; he said rooting for the Red Sox had landed him in Limekiln in the first place. Jonathan found a Red Sox cap (he'd make Perkins a present of it when he got back) and started along the aisle to the cashier. On his way he spotted the toy section and turned into it.

The shelves and bins were full of tanks, plastic soldiers, and frighteningly realistic guns. But there were stuffed animals, too, and he found a beige teddy bear with creases sewn into his neck that fit the way he thought her teddy bear had looked. He took it and the hat up to the front. The register lines were long. He got worried about all the time this was taking and decided to leave the bear and cap behind a razorblade display and get back on the road. But as he started to put the bear down it seemed to look at him. He knew it was a crazy man's thought, but Rome wasn't built in a day and he had to be patient with himself. Besides, the bear was cute. He didn't want to go to his niece empty-handed, and the cap was a necessity. He waited out the line and paid, shocked at the amount of money the lady charged him. He tucked the cap's price tag under the brim so it wouldn't dangle in his face and set the teddy bear in the passenger seat of the car. Ten minutes later, finding his way by memory—flying by the seat of his pants, Marty would say—he pulled into Windy Ridge and parked across the road from the Levin house.

He killed the motor and summer evening quiet surrounded him. Setting sun dyed the house fronts pink, and weeds grew up through cracks in Windy Ridge road. Lights were not on yet, the house looked empty, but he knew they

were in there. He crossed the road and went up the walk to
the front door. There was a bell but he hated bells. The
dinner bell at Limekiln made his mouth water, like one of
the famous Russian's dogs; it also made him want to throw
his head back and howl like a wolf. It was better not to ring
the bell and he tried the door.

The knob turned, the door swung in, and for the first
time since he had left his father's fifteen years ago, he entered a private house.

The foyer was cool with a hard, shiny floor of some kind.
A half table sat against one wall with a vase full of fresh
flowers in it. To his right was a neat living room with vacuum
tracks across the carpet; to his left a dining room with the
table set for dinner. The air smelled of lemon oil and roasted
meat, and he tried to forget that it was almost dinnertime at
Limekiln and he hadn't eaten anything since breakfast except half of one of the chicken sandwiches Dorry had
brought and a few bites of Marty's deviled ham.

He swallowed the saliva in his mouth, went to the foot
of the staircase, and looked up. Jeannie Levin was up there;
she knew about her son now, and the feelings that came
down to him out of the shadows at the top of the stairs were
too dreadful to find words for. Even so, they were faded like
old tapestry, and he thought Dr. Moran must have given her
a shot of something. The other little girl was with her mother,
but her sadness was weak and confused compared to what he
got from her mother. Amy was not there.

He turned away and faced a shut door off the foyer, past
the living room. He didn't get much but didn't have to because he heard men's voices. They were in there . . . Amy
must be with them. He raised his hand to knock, thought
better of it, and went into the room, holding the teddy bear
in front of him like a shield.

Levin jerked around when he saw him, but Jonathan had
the feeling he wasn't that surprised at his turning up. You
didn't have to be telepathic to sort of expect things—no matter how unlikely. The doctor said something, but just then

Jonathan saw Amy and didn't hear. He had the same feeling he'd had the only other time he'd seen her: that he'd crossed an immense distance of time and space to stand in this pleasant room with chintz-covered furniture and enthroned TV to get to her.

She lay on a flowered couch with her feet up. Her jeans were back on, her shoes were off, and one sock was stained with dried blood. Her color wasn't so bad, but the blackness he got from her was thick, total, frightening. Her face was relaxed, her mouth a little open. She was pretty, anyway; she'd be pretty when she was an old woman . . . like Lillian Gish. Except Amy didn't look like her; she looked like Michael used to when he was a child and Jonathan watched him sleeping in the youth bed that once belonged to Jonathan. Jonathan felt a lump in his throat and fought it down with all his might. He'd turned up here fresh from the nuthouse, wearing a baseball cap and carrying a teddy bear; if he cried on top of it, the men would gang up and toss him out, and he wouldn't do what he'd come for. Whatever that was. He'd have to figure it out any minute now. "Time to pee pee or get off the pot," Marty would say.

"What are you doing here?" Levin growled.

"I brought her a teddy bear," Jonathan said.

"Get out!"

Jonathan went to the couch. Levin tried to cut him off but wasn't fast enough, and Jonathan leaned over to her.

"Leave her alone," Levin said.

"I won't hurt her," Jonathan said. He knelt down next to the couch. "Amy, it's Uncle Jonathan. I got here." Of course, she didn't answer. Her arm was rolled outward, and he saw red dots on the skin. Dr. Moran had given her shots, and Levin must have talked a blue streak trying to pull her out of it. Jonathan didn't know what *he* could do that they couldn't, but he'd try. He had faith in the small pleasures he'd written about in his once-in-a-lifetime letter. He'd talk about them . . . .

"Amy, school was over today. That means you can sleep

until ten tomorrow if you want and have anything you like for breakfast." He was hungry; he'd be able to talk vividly about food. He said, "You can have crisp bacon, toast dripping butter . . . eggs any way you like them. Scrambled is my favorite. I think the yellow of a scrambled egg is one of the prettiest colors on earth. . . . "

He felt Levin right behind him and knew he was getting ready to grab him by the collar and yank him away from her. Without changing his tone, Jonathan said, "Captain, you'll have to drag me away and I'll fight and rant and scream the house down. I'm a good screamer, one of the best at Limekiln. Your wife and daughter will hear, and they don't need that on top of everything else." He felt Levin recede; he went back to Amy.

"Tonight's Friday. Friday Night at the Movies comes on soon. Maybe they'll show *Shane*. That's my all-time favorite. Remember . . . *Shane?*" He chanted softly, "*Come back, Shane . . . I love you, Shane.* We could watch it together, eat sticky buns during the commercials. God, I love sticky buns, especially licking the syrup off my fingers. The music in it's nice too. You remember . . . " He sang softly, in tune, " 'Put your little foot, put your little foot . . . ' And how about 'Jesu Joy of Man's Desiring?' I know it's hard to believe, but I was sort of with you the first time you heard it. It was on the car radio. You were sitting in the back and it made you feel sad and excited at the same time . . . remember?" He had a lousy voice but good pitch, and he hummed it and thought he felt a thin tear in the blackness around her. He set the teddy bear on her chest and put her hands on the creases in its neck, burying her fingers in the acrylic fur. He had to keep talking.

"It's summer," he said, sliding her fingers over the pink bow around the bear's neck, across its smooth, shiny black eyes. "Daylilies are out up and down the roads. Lakes get still at dusk: you can see trees in them and the fish come up to feed. But the water in the streams is still cold, and you can splash your face with it after a hot walk. And aren't blue-and-white China bowls gorgeous . . . and red gingham? My mother had a red gingham apron I'll never forget. She was your grandmother, by the way. . . . " He could swear the dark was getting gray. They were talking about color; he'd go on with it for a while. "She used to make grape jelly—hold a jar of grape jelly to the light and you see *some* color. Talk about royal purple! And how about the blue of swimming pool water. Fire blue, you could call it. Must be the chlorine that does it. . . . "

The blackness was going; he didn't know if it was the nonsense he was talking or the teddy bear or just her time to wake up. He kept on. "Did you smell the air the other night after the rain? Sort of smelled like mushrooms; almost better than cut grass, though that's pretty terrific too. So's the smell of fresh gas when they pump it into your car. My ma had a clothesline and our clothes smelled of sun. . . . "

Her fingers tightened on the bear's neck, and he got a picture from her of the teddy bear Paulie Levin had destroyed. He babbled, "Sure, that was some terrific teddy bear, Amy. But there's no flies on this little fella. I got him at Woolworth's not fifteen minutes ago. I think he's a dead ringer for the first one. Open your eyes and look at him. Besides, honey, it's getting late . . . time to eat. I'm starving. Bet you are too."

She opened her eyes and looked right at him, then up at his cap.

"Hi," he said.

She tried to wet her lips; her tongue rasped across them. "Get her water," Jonathan said urgently.

Moran said, "Yes, Christ, yes . . . " and ran out of the room. Levin rushed around the sofa and leaned over the arm. "Amy . . . Sweet Pea . . . "

But she didn't take her eyes off Jonathan. "Hi, yourself," she whispered. She looked down at the teddy bear.

"Pretty nice, isn't he?" Jonathan said.

"He's okay. . . . " Her head turned aside and her eyes closed. His heart thudded, but she was still with him. Now he got pictures from her. Not the tiled room, thank God, but kid stuff: a ruffled dress on a mannequin in a store window, a tattered book, and the teddy bear. Then he saw . . . as she saw . . . herself and Greta standing on a bridge over a stream. It wasn't a real place; the scene was painted like the illustration in an old-time children's book, and she and Greta wore long, old-fashioned girls' dresses with smock aprons over them. Suddenly he knew Amy wasn't going to see Greta anymore because he had come here to take her away with him. He must have known since before he left Limekiln but didn't tell himself. Hall said even sane people kept frightening things from themselves; and this was frightening, okay, because he didn't know how to look after himself, never mind a nine-year-old girl. Sweat popped out under the rim of the cap.

Moran came back with a glass of water. "It should be ice," he said, "but I couldn't get the tray out of the freezer. She should just lick some ice. She should be in a hospital, for God's sake. I'm a shrink, I don't remember all this stuff. . . . "

Moran wet the tips of his fingers and stroked Amy's lips; she licked, opened her eyes, and reached for the glass. "Just a little," he said, holding the glass with her. He turned to Jonathan. "Tell her just a little."

But she heard, took a couple of small sips, and let the glass go.

"I think she's okay," Moran said.

"Well enough to go with me?" Jonathan asked. Just saying it brought out more sweat. Levin stared at him an instant, then said softly, "Thank you for helping her, Mr. Kaslov. I'll drive you back now."

Jonathan looked up at him. "And thank you for calling me mister. I can't remember the last time anyone did. But I have a car. It's stolen. I guess that's a problem, though I read they practically never find stolen cars anymore . . . no reflection on the police, Captain. And I have four hundred dollars. Also stolen. It's not much, but it'll get us away from here. I thought we'd head north. Fewer people, and I've heard Northerners are less nosy, so it'll be easier to get lost. And you know she's gotta get lost."

"Get out," Levin said.

Jonathan had done so much talking, he couldn't seem to stop. He said, "I know how worried you'll be. But I'll get a job. I could sell used cars, for example. I bet a telepathic used-car salesman'll make out like a bandit." He smiled. Levin didn't smile back. Jonathan said, "Failing that, I can play gin . . . I'm a whiz at gin."

Levin opened his mouth, but before he could talk, Amy said, "Did you say your mother was my grandmother?"

They all looked at her.

"That's right," Jonathan said.

"Where is she?" Amy asked.

"She died before you were born."

"So I never knew her."

"No. But you look a lot like her."

Amy smiled, the corners of her mouth trembled. "And *your* father?"

"Was your grandpa. He died when you were three, so I guess you don't remember him, either."

"So your children are my cousins."

"I don't have any children."

"What a shame," she said, "but your wife's my aunt."

"I have no wife, either."

"Just me?" she asked.

"Just you."

"Then I guess I'd better go with you—"

"Noooo," Levin cried softly, and Jonathan's heart just about broke for him but he couldn't afford pity now. He'd learned a couple of things since he'd turned sane (if that's what had happened to him) and was learning more every second. Right now he knew that pity pulled your teeth, and he needed teeth because he was going to hurt Levin and all the people in this house and they were already in pain. But he had to do it because if he didn't, Amy would wind up . . . he tried to think then looked sharply at Moran, and knew Amy would wind up on a marble floor in a converted ballroom in East Berlin with a couple of Russian bullets in her head. It made no sense, but he had to keep thinking it, so he

wouldn't get heartbroken for everyone and fall apart before
he got her out of here. In a day or two he'd wake up in some
nice motel near the Canadian border, make sure his niece
was asleep and then he'd cry for poor Joe Levin. Not now.

Jonathan leaned over her. "Put your arms around my
neck."

Levin moved in to pull him away, but Amy grabbed him
around the neck and hung on, and Jonathan picked her up in
his arms with the teddy bear tucked in. He faced Levin.
Levin looked dangerous.

Jonathan spoke gently; he wished Dr. Hall could see
him now.

"You're not going to pull a gun again, Captain, or rip
Amy out of my arms and beat me up. The threats are empty,
it's silly to make them. She's gotta go with me because it's
the only thing she can do. It'll be rough, you'll have to
explain. But you can say she disappeared. Lots of kids do
nowadays. And she's a foster child. No one'll give a flying
fuck. . . . " He looked quickly at Amy. "Sorry, honey." He
went on, "I could talk about how we're blood kin and how
I'm the only one who'll be ready if things go wrong. . . . "
Would he? No way to tell for sure, but it sounded right. He
said, "I don't expect any of that to cut ice with you. But one
thing should. She's done for if she stays here."

Jeannie Levin appeared in the den doorway; none of
them noticed, not even Jonathan. He was too wrapped up in
what he was saying, too amazed at himself for putting so
many words and thoughts in sequence. He said, "It'll go like
this: Every time you look at her you'll see the tiled room.
It'll fade a bit but never go away. And every time she and
Greta argue about who will do the dishes or wear the new
yellow blouse or what TV program to watch, your heart'll
jump so high, you'll think you can chew it. You're a deter-
mined man . . . you'll take it for a while. But soon there won't
be a single peaceful second left in your life, then you'll start
thinking about where you can put her. Someplace nice and
safe. A country club asylum with tennis and a swimming

pool. You'll ask Hall, he'll know a place. But Hall's honorable; he won't dump her on people without telling them why they have to be so careful of this little girl. He'll swear them to secrecy, but how long will it last? I can hear a nurse lady now telling a friend at tea, 'I just heard the strangest thing about the pretty new girl . . . right out of *Amazing Tales.*' Sooner or later someone's going to decide Amy could be a very useful little girl if they can control her. That's when she's done for. Like the German boy." He turned to Moran. "Tell them about the German boy," Jonathan said. Moran reeled and grabbed the mantelpiece because a thought he'd forgotten he had, had been plucked out of his mind and shot back at him. It was like being robbed . . . worse.

"Tell him," Jonathan urged softly.

Moran cleared his throat. "It was . . . he was a boy . . . like . . . who could do . . . who was like Amy."

"And?" Levin asked softly.

"And they gave him to the Russians to study and . . ."

"And?" Levin asked again.

"They shot him," Moran said, and Jeannie Levin cried from the doorway:

"Let her go!"

SIXTEEN

MORAN REALIZED THAT almost an hour had passed. He'd read the short piece in the newspaper so many times, he'd memorized it by now. The amateurish, grainy, newsprint photo that went with it was fixed in his mind. He put the paper down and looked across the room at nothing. He didn't know what—if anything—he should do about it. Maybe nothing. He could spend the rest of the morning tilling the garden, going over patient tapes for Monday, watching cartoons on the tube.

Or he could show it to Levin. If he could find him.

"The more things change, the more they stay the same," someone famous said. Moran didn't know who. It was like the probably billion quotes that sounded profound until you thought about it. For instance, did it mean nothing changed? That all change was only surface? Some bullshit like that, probably. And it *was* bullshit, because nothing stayed the same. Levin had probably moved away from the neat, pretty little house on Windy Ridge years ago. Moran had moved; they'd sold their old house for an outrageous amount of money and bought this almost-mansion in Harwin, a town that claimed it hadn't changed since the Revolution. More bullshit.

He looked again at the picture in the Montpelier paper he'd gotten in this morning's mail. *She'd* changed, but it was her, all right. There was the name—Amy Kastel—and the small white line of the old scar that bisected one thick, perfectly shaped eyebrow—and the whole face, although she wasn't as totally, vividly gorgeous as he'd thought she'd be. She'd looked gorgeous that last day in the Levins' den.

She'd recovered in a couple of minutes, the way kids do. She'd struggled out of her uncle's arms and run to Jeannie. They'd hugged, then Jeannie had told her to go upstairs and change into clean clothes for her trip. (She'd made it sound like a short vacation). But not to wake Greta since Greta didn't feel well, and Jeannie'd given her a pill. It was a lie; Moran had given Greta a shot (a child's dose, calculated by kilograms of body weight) of Librium. Amy probably couldn't wake her if she tried.

Levin kept saying, "I can't let her go, I can't let her go." But Moran had been right in thinking Jeannie Levin had the final say in that house. She had caressed Levin's shoulder, then gone to her purse and pulled out a wad of cash. "The week's household money," she told Jonathan Kaslov. "Take it."

Kaslov reached for it, their fingers touched, and something very strange happened. He pulled his hand back, as if she'd burned him, and said, "You know . . . you knew all along. . . ."

Jeannie shoved the money into his hand and forced his fingers around it. Then she said something like, "I live in an ordinary place with ordinary people. I belong to a bridge club, the PTA, the Garden Club. I help with Meals on Wheels. We tolerate drunkenness, adultery, a little discreet wife beating . . . but nothing ever prepared me . . . "

She never got to finish. Maybe she'd have said that of course she knew about Amy; you couldn't take care of a child, comb her hair, help her dress, feed her, cuddle her, and not know such a thing. Maybe she'd have said that she'd been willing to try, anyway, because she loved the little girl. But now her son was dead, and no matter how she felt about him, she was guilty and scared for herself and Greta . . . most of all for Amy. That's the sort of speech Moran would have made. But just then Amy came back wearing clean slacks and a T-shirt with a butterfly on it. She'd washed her face and looked more beautiful than ever (not like the normally pretty young woman in the news photo). Amy didn't know she was going for good. "Tell Greta I'll call tomorrow" was the last thing she had said to Levin after she hugged him. And as she left the room she'd called over her shoulder to Moran, "Say hi to Miss Evans."

Kaslov got her out to the foyer, and Levin put his hands over his face. Jeannie went with them to the door, but Moran didn't know what her last words to Amy were. Probably, "Be a good girl, brush your teeth," nonsense like that. He'd gone to the den window and watched them cross the road. Kaslov got into the car, Amy started around the front of it, then stopped and turned around. She suddenly looked stricken, as if it had just started to hit her that she was not coming back. But she looked away resolutely and got into the car with her uncle. She was a good, smart, brave little girl, Moran thought with a surge of pride. She knew she couldn't stay. Kaslov started the motor, they drove away, and Levin sobbed out loud. Moran had kept his face turned to the window until he heard Levin cross the room and go out the door . . . .

He should burn the newspaper. But it was May, the temperature was sixty something and Mary'd think he'd gone mad if he started a fire.

Mary had changed like everything else; she'd gone ex-urban on him. Now she used the word *super* a lot and called other women *gals*. And, of course, his kid had changed. He was five ten and shaved every other day; he was in prep school and wanted to go to Harvard. And Sykes had changed: He'd moved to Maine where he said the rotten winters kept his mind clear.

Moran looked at the cold fireplace, then at the long box of matches on the mantel. But he was kidding himself; he'd set his shirt on fire before he'd burn the May 21, 1987, issue of the *Montpelier Press.*

He got up, went to the phone table across the room, and pulled out the phone book for Millbridge, Bridgeton, Westerly, and so on, from the pile under the table. He opened it and looked down the line of *L*'s without much hope. When he'd gotten the mortgage on this place, a bank officer told him that three years was the life of the average mortgage in these parts. People stayed awhile, then moved on, uprooting their kids, ending friendships. No one had old friends anymore. He had not heard from Ernie Sykes for a couple of years, anyway.

The Levins must have moved on like everybody else.

He could try to find him through the state cops. He'd been a captain, fourteen years ago. He must be pretty high up by now; if he had not retired or changed jobs, as well as homes.

But it was still there: J. Levin, 114 Windy Ridge, Westerly. Moran looked at the cover of the phone book. It was this year's. With his heart pounding in his ears, almost drowning out the intermittent clash of the Cuisinart going on and off in the kitchen down the hall, Moran picked up the phone.

He dialed a couple of digits, then put the receiver back on its cradle. It was Saturday morning, Levin must be home, digging in the garden, washing the car, getting set up to watch the afternoon game . . . whatever cops or anybody else did on weekends.

It wasn't a long drive, so he might as well just go there. Besides, if he called, Levin might refuse to see him. The last time he'd talked to Levin, about thirteen years ago, Levin had said, "Look, Charlie, I know you mean well, but every time I hear your voice, it all comes back to me. Especially the fact that I could have saved my son's life and didn't. And when I think of that, I realize all over again how glad I am he's not around. How much nicer our lives are without that *vontz.* A *vontz* is a bedbug, Charlie. And when I think that

... never mind. I've got to forget it or I'll go nuts. Really nuts. If I ever hear from them, or about them, I'll let you know. And you do the same. In the meantime, do me a favor, Charlie. Don't call again."

He still might not want to hear, but Moran had to tell him, anyway. He was like the old rummies in the bar down the street from his mother's house who had gabbed about the troubles in Ireland until you got the feeling the old fools'd die if they couldn't talk about it. For the first time in his life he knew just how they felt. He wondered where most of them were by now. Dead, he supposed. Carr's Bar had been gutted to make way for a cheese shop. A cheese shop in Flatbush! All part of the gentrification of Brooklyn.

He put the phone book away, put on his shell jacket, and folded the paper over a couple of times so it'd fit in the pocket. Then he went down to the kitchen to tell Mary he was leaving for a couple of hours.

Mary was having some women over for afternoon tea, a custom she'd picked up when they'd moved to Harwin and she'd started pretending that she wasn't Mary Reilly from President Street.

They'd broken through the Windy Ridge cul-de-sac, and the road stretched as far as Moran could see. More houses had been put up on smaller pieces of land; the newer houses were bigger and grander than the originals—and uglier. Windy Ridge had become an executive ghetto.

But the Levin house was the way Moran remembered; even the yews at the end of the drive looked the same. Jeannie Levin must keep them trimmed to size.

He rang and waited; the paper rustled in his pocket. Heavy footsteps approached, and Joe Levin opened the door. He knew Moran instantly and looked happy to see him, not wary.

"Charlie, for chrissake." Levin wrung his hand, then held the door wide and waved Moran to come in. He led him across the foyer, which had the same table, same vase with fresh flowers. And the house had the same clean smell that

Moran remembered, with the hint of lemon oil in it and something good to eat cooking or just cooked. Levin led him into the den. They faced each other, examined each other for a moment. Moran knew he'd changed. His hair was thinner, his middle thicker. And the lines around his mouth that Mary used to say made him look sexily dissipated had deepened to form not very attractive folds at the edges of his cheeks.

Levin's hair was just as thick as ever, but the color had changed from the handsome dark blond to a nondescript sandy gray. His face was redder; he probably had to take Inderal or some other antihypertensive. And he was a little heavier, though with a man that big, it didn't show as much as it did on Moran, who'd been almost slight fourteen years ago.

"How about beer or a cup of coffee?" Levin said.

It was eleven in the morning. Moran didn't feel like beer. "Coffee'll be fine," he said.

"Siddown, siddown, Charlie."

Moran took the club chair on one side of the dead fireplace. The newspaper crackled as he sat down. Levin went to get the coffee. Moran pulled the paper out of his pocket and eased himself out of the jacket and hung it neatly over the arm of the chair. He wasn't usually neat. Mary said he was the messiest man in the world; his office was a disgrace. But he didn't feel like himself this morning.

Levin came back a couple of minutes later with the coffee cups and an electric pot. He poured. "You look pretty much the same, Charlie. Little denser in the gut, maybe."

"You look the same, too, Joe."

Levin gave Moran the coffee and offered a piece of nut cake. Moran remembered having it the night he'd come here after Michael Kaslov died. He remembered it had been excellent and he took a piece.

"Jeannie around?" he asked.

"Nope. She's gone shopping with Greta. Greta's married, by the way. Married an executive type from IBM. They moved him here from San Francisco to run their HQ, so he must be pretty good. I try to warm up to him, but it's hard.

They come to dinner every Friday and he wears a three-piece suit. He's the type who'd've had sideburns and gold chains around his neck twenty years ago. But he's good to her; I guess fathers never think son-in-laws're good enough for their little girls."

They were getting close. Any second now Levin would give him an opening, and he got ready to jump in. Then Levin said, "Greta's pregnant. I'm going to be a grandpa."

Moran beamed at him. "Congratulations, Joe. When?"

"September. Greta hasn't changed much; still sweet and cheery, like her mother. . . . "

Odd, Moran thought. He never thought of Jeannie Levin as cheery, but the few times he'd seen her, she didn't have much to be cheerful about (the understatement of his thought made him grin), or maybe Jeannie Levin had changed too.

This room had; chintz had been replaced by the same sort of small-print fabric that Mary had all over the house. Moran hated it; it made his eyes jump.

"How're you doing, Charlie?"

"Fine. Still at Millbridge, though I have another office now, over in Washington. Lots of rich nutsy kids in Litchfield County."

"For sure," Levin said. "Still live in Gloversville?"

"No. Moved to Harwin."

Levin whistled soundlessly. "Hear they got five-acre zoning over there."

"Something like that," Moran said modestly, but he was pleased to see Levin look impressed. Then he realized he had the opening he'd been looking for, and he said, "We also bought a house in Vermont. A vacation place north of Montpelier. We only use it in the summer, rent it out for ski season. But Mary's become the sort who likes to play native, and she subscribes to the Montpelier paper. We get it every Saturday down here. I read it this morning . . . that's why I'm here."

He opened the paper, folded it back to the picture. Levin had gotten very still; his pink cheeks paled.

Moran nodded. "Yeah, Joe. It's about her." He handed Levin the paper. Levin looked at the picture, and Moran wondered if he'd be disappointed, too, at how she looked. They shouldn't be, even though she'd sort of been their fairy princess. They should be glad that she'd run the gauntlet of horror and death and come out on the other side normal and ordinary, just like she wanted to be.

Levin started reading the squib that went with the picture. Moran knew it by heart.

WEDDINGS

Amy Kastel to Donald Armand Steel; Saturday, May 21; First Congregational Church, West Champlain, Vermont, at 3 P.M. Miss Kastel is a graduate of the University of Vermont and teaches mathematics at the junior high school in West Champlain. Mr. Steel is a graduate of the University of Vermont and is the manager of Steel Hardware, the firm founded by his grandfather in 1935. Steel Hardware recently opened a tool-and-die factory in Brattleboro; the firm owns stores in Brattleboro, Montpelier, and Concord, New Hampshire. Miss Kastel plans to go on teaching after her marriage. A reception will be held after the ceremony at the church; with dinner later at the Red Lion Inn, in West Champlain. George King of Montpelier will be best man. Miss Rosemary Kline of Montpelier will be the matron of honor. The bride will be given away by her father, Jonathan Kastel of Kastel Pontiac and Volvo Dealerships, here in Montpelier. The bride's gown was made for her by the Jennifer Bridal Salon in Montpelier. The gown is ecru satin, trimmed with French lace; Miss Kastel will carry a bouquet of white roses. The bridesmaids' gowns are lilac; the groom and ushers will wear evening dress.

Levin looked up at Moran. Moran braced himself, but nothing happened for a moment. Levin said, "She wears glasses."

"Yes. But I recognized her, anyway."

Levin looked down at the picture. His face seemed to swell, his cheeks puffed out, and tears filled his eyes. Moran got ready to cross the distance between them, embrace Levin, and let him literally cry on his shoulder if Levin wanted. Then he realized that Levin was laughing, not crying.

The tears spilled out his eyes, rolled down his puffed-up red cheeks, as he laughed wildly. He rocked back and forth in his chair. His knee hit the coffee table, cups, and the pot rocked precariously. Suddenly Moran started laughing with him. The laughter turned to not so healthy howling, but they couldn't stop. Moran's muscles tensed and started to hurt, and he knew there was an edge of hysteria to the sounds coming out of them. But the release felt wonderful in spite of the burning in his gut, the ache in his ribs. They held their middles. Levin gasped and stopped long enough to say, "A Pontiac dealership . . ."

And they were off again. At last Levin managed to quiet down a little, then Moran did. His eyes still bright with tears, Levin looked at Moran, then down at the coffee table and cups, with coffee spilled in the saucers.

"Fuck this shit," Levin said.

He leaped to his feet, went to a cabinet built in next to the fireplace, opened it, and came back with a bottle of brandy. He poured big dollops into their cups, on top of the cream and sugar. The cream curdled instantly, but Levin didn't seem to care. He held the cups aloft. Moran did the same.

"To Amy and her uncle," Levin said.

They clicked cups and drank. It tasted awful at first but wasn't so bad after a few swallows. They asked each other questions but not about the resolution of the mess in the washroom; they knew how that had turned out. Pictures of the bloodstained room had made it to the network news. Local communities were up in arms. People talked about it when they met on the streets, in shops and restaurants.

It made the local papers for about five days in a row. Then it petered out. Bobby Whitman had been judged incompetent to stand trial, even if he had been indicted, and he'd been put away quietly in some private institution. He'd been in and out of it for years, Moran heard. He'd start to feel sorry for him, then remember why he'd gone down to that room in the first place, and his sympathy would dry up. The case of the two dead boys in the room of that abandoned gym wing was still an open file in some basement or wherever the local cops stored such things. It'd probably never even made it into the computer system installed a few years ago. The pages of testimony from Bobby Whitman, who never admitted remembering how Len Brachman and Paul Levin died, were probably starting to gray with age. In another few years the edges of the paper would begin to crumble a little.

Levin did tell Moran that the black Chevy Amy and Jonathan Kaslov drove away in that day belonged to an orderly at Limekiln. It was found at the bus station in East Hartford. It'd been freshly washed before it was abandoned.

Levin said, "They checked it out because it'd been in the lot for a couple of weeks. No one reported it stolen. Apparently the orderly was ready to eat the cost of the car before he'd set the cops on Kaslov."

"What about the farm?" Moran asked.

"Gone. I paid the taxes for a few years, then stopped. There didn't seem to be much point. The state copped it, and I don't know what happened after that. I asked the lawyer, a nice man named Swain, not to tell me."

Then Levin asked, "What about Hall?"

"Died a few years ago. After a long illness, according to his obit in the *Journal of the American Psychiatric Association*."

By then they were pretty high. Levin looked drunk-sad and raised his cup again. "To Hall," he said. "RIP."

"To Hall."

They drank.

A little later the level in the bottle was down, and Moran

stood up carefully and unfolded his jacket. Levin picked up the newspaper; it was splotched with coffee-brandy stains.

"Can I keep this?" Levin asked.

"Lemme get a copy. I'll send you back the original."

"You won't forget?"

With teary, drunken sincerity Moran said, "I won't for-get."